Praise for *Celestial*

'I loved *Celestial* ... addictively readable: good central mystery, cleverly extended; well-drawn characters, a brisk exciting narration ... taut and tense and absorbing all the way through'   Adam Roberts, author of *The This*

'Fast-paced, exciting and full of mystery, this lunar-based novel explores deep questions regarding religion, meaning, and the nature of reality itself'

Liz Williams, author of *Banner of Souls*

'For a science fiction reader looking for a modern feeling novel, but with a nod to some classic sci fi pondering, *Celestial* is a book that will scratch that itch'   SF Book

'Enter a brilliantly conceived extraterrestial wonderland ... *Celestial* is a visionary escapade redolant of Arthur C. Clarke's *Rendezvous with Rama*'   *The Times*

'A first-contact story with more than just a cold war twist ... all plot threads are pulled together to a satisfying and enlightening conclusion'   SciFiNow

'A refreshing change from the usual macho adventure story, one more about inner than outer space'   *The Guardian*

'A story that is not what you expect, nor one you can you predict'   SFF World

Also by M.D. Lachlan from Gollancz:

Wolfsangel
Fenrir
Lord of Slaughter
Valkyrie's Song
The Night Lies Bleeding

CELESTIAL

M.D. LACHLAN

This edition first published in Great Britain in 2023 by Gollancz

First published in Great Britain in 2022 by Gollancz
an imprint of the Orion Publishing Group Ltd
Carmelite House, 50 Victoria Embankment
London EC4Y 0DZ

An Hachette UK Company

1 3 5 7 9 10 8 6 4 2

A CIP catalogue record for this book is
available from the British Library.

ISBN (Mass Market Paperback) 978 0 575 11526 2

Typeset by Born Group
Printed and bound in Great Britain by Clays Ltd, Elcograf S.p.A.

www.mdlachlan.com
www.gollancz.co.uk

To the brave people of Ukraine

'To live is to be haunted'
Philip K. Dick

Chapter 1

Don Humbucker's office has no name on the door saying 'chief', nothing to mark it out as any different from the other offices of the NASA administrators that are housed in the shining white tower of the Directorate building.

There's a straightforward 808 on the frosted glass, but those numbers alone wouldn't tell you that this is where dreams are smashed. Those 8s have taken on mythic proportions among the astronauts. 'Getting eight-balled' is what the recruits call getting dropped from the programme. As an astronaut, you only get called in to see Humbucker on his turf if he's going to fire you. Otherwise you encounter him in neutral spaces – meeting rooms, test facilities, even the canteen if you don't spot him coming. Humbucker has a habit of popping up when you least expect him, his long, lean, stooping form seeming to cast a permanent shadow before it like something risen from the swamp of legend.

If you do get called to face the 8s, he'll tell you why you're off the programme and he'll tell you straight – you're not physically up to it, not mentally up to it, temperament or brains found lacking. People come out of that

office with all sorts of excuses as to why they got fired – 'budget cuts' is a favourite, but everyone knows that's not strictly true. This is 1977 and, while the aftermath of the war in Vietnam has meant every government department is feeling the squeeze, NASA isn't laying off staff quite yet – far from it, in fact. There's work to be done and they have the money to do it, just about – development on the shuttle, satellite tech, you name it. It's a pretty good time to be a spaceman. Not the best, of course. The days of Armstrong, Aldrin and Collins – when every company in the world was throwing TVs, cars, and whatever else you wanted at you – are over now that no one's going to the Moon any more. Tough to complain about it, though: it's a good living, interesting work and always, always, the prospect of space.

So, when Zigsa – Ziggy to friends – Da Luca hears her name on the Tannoy asking her to 'proceed to 808', her heart thumps at her chest like a cat in a sack. She's a 'mission specialist', not a senior astronaut at all, brought in a year ago and her position has always felt precarious here.

She was invited from Columbia University where she was doing a post-doc in the art and artefacts of Tibetan Buddhism. NASA said it wanted to broaden and deepen its knowledge base, to work in new perspectives and to assess the feasibility of getting a civilian – even a female civilian – into space. That's what they *said*. She can't help feeling – hoping – it's more than a coincidence that her PhD was focussed on what the ancients had to tell us about the Moon. She's been fascinated by the Moon since she was a tiny girl, and the chance to get nearer to it seemed too good to miss. She had no idea the career path of astronaut was even available

2

to US women, particularly from a background in linguistics and history. The job offer felt like fate.

There's been no mention of her work so far, just a lot of training, spinning around, mending things, mind-melting engineering problems that will enable her to survive on a space mission if the shit hits the fan, like it has in the past and doubtless will again.

She sometimes wonders what she's doing there – if they want to put a woman into space there are many others more qualified than she is. Other people wonder, too – what's this weird Asian chick with the Italian surname who doesn't know one end of a rocket engine from another doing coming in and sticking crazy Eastern art on her office walls? Fucking hippy.

Some have asked her to her face why a non-scientist is taking up resources that could be given to someone doing more clearly valuable work. Someone, say, male? Yeah, NASA's like that – plenty of ex-military guys; plenty of guys with inferiority complexes competing with the ex-military guys; plenty of guys period. She can live with it. She has to if she wants to get up there. Space. Man, the very idea. Still, she has wondered if she's wasting her time here – if she'll ever get called as crew. The education brief might have been something to make Congress happy to hand over the dough. Once done, it might be quietly shelved.

She puts down the radio circuit board she was repairing, glances at her communications tutor, Marty Newman. Newman purses his lips. He thinks this is it for her.

'Shit,' she says.

'Hey, Da Luca, you never know.'

There's a brief silence between them, a silence that says, 'you do know'.

Newman breaks it. 'If I don't see you again, look on the bright side. You'll be able to fix your vacuum cleaner if it breaks now.'

She laughs. 'You actually mean that as a consolation, don't you?'

Marty looks puzzled. 'Why wouldn't it be?'

'That's right, dream of a lifetime gone, but I'll save twenty dollars in repair bills. Hey, that's probably nearer forty dollars over a life of domestic drudgery.'

'Every cloud.'

'I've been in lots of clouds recently, Newman. Didn't see any linings at all.'

They hug.

'You're trembling,' he says.

'The thought of missing you, Newman.'

'I doubt it,' he says.

So it was just a dream, a stupid fantasy. Well, she'd once thought she might be some use here. She thought she might make a contribution. Silly me, she thinks. Just good for NASA's image, employ the weird chick, string her along for a bit and then let the guys, the people who matter, get on with the job.

Firings take place immediately and your stuff gets sent to you in the post; contact with others from the base is not encouraged so as to build the idea of an elite and to avoid having too big an effect on morale. She sticks her notes and her angle poise desk lamp into a box, along with the furry Gonk toy her fiancé Andy bought her as a good luck charm and her sister's white khata scarf that she keeps in a drawer. She unpins the mandala her mom gave her from the wall, pausing to look at it. It shows Mount Meru, the centre of

the universe, as an inverted triangle, the sun as a three-legged bird, the Moon as a rabbit next to it. Looks like that rabbit just ran away. She folds the cloth of the mandala and puts it in the box, then makes her way over to Humbucker's block. She wonders if he'll let her take the notes with her. Probably not, but she has a better chance if she carries them with her than if she leaves them to be mailed. She wouldn't be the first to be denied access to their own work.

She doesn't bother to change out of her overalls, just makes her way across the parking lot, past the fly boys' Stingrays, Firebirds, Mustangs and Porsches, their windshields burning in the Florida sun.

As she reaches its perimeter her heart sinks. Pulling up in a long, low Corvette, window down, elbow jutting, is Steve Griffin, just Griffin to most. Griffin is a first-class astronaut and a first-class asshole.

'Hey, no sucky fucky today,' he says as he sees her approach. 'I got things to do.'

She ignores him, walks to go past him.

He steps fully out of the car, slams the door, partly bars her way. 'I used to bomb people like you in Vietnam.' He's smiling at her. If you saw them from across the way, you'd think they were having a pleasant chat but the menace in his voice is unmistakable.

'Bye, Griffin!' she says, stepping round him.

'Fuck you, gook,' he says to her back. 'Fuck you!'

She turns, faces him. 'Can I take the napalm instead?'

Griffin is not a big man – he wouldn't be an astronaut if he was – but he is a hard one. He seems made of something denser than flesh, his muscles taut and lean. He has the look of a useful middleweight boxer. She holds his gaze. He's

not moving, she's not moving. She thinks of her mom. This confrontation would make her tut. Resistance is the cause of all suffering, so says the Buddha.

'Can oi take the napawwwm.' He mocks her New York accent. 'You think you're clever.' His gaze is intense.

'Everyone at NASA thinks they're clever, Griffin, and most of them are right. Do me the favour of a specific insult, not just one you use on everyone you hate.'

He smirks, rolls his head, and for a second, she actually thinks he's limbering up to hit her. Then he glances down into the box.

'Yeah, thought so. eight-balled. No way we was ever putting Charlie in space.'

Charlie. There he goes with the Viet Cong insults again. She feels anger rising in her and has to fight the urge to tip the contents of the box on top of his head.

She concentrates on the lessons her mom gave her. Compassion, hear without judging. Or just tell him to fuck himself, the lesson her dad taught her. She was always nearer to him in temperament, her sister Maria closer to her mom, despite the fact she got the Tibetan name and Maria the Italian. No, she'll go with her mom and her sister for now. She steadies her breathing, regains control.

'You have a great day, Griffin.'

She walks away from him and cuts through the lines of cars. Griffin probably thinks he's won, forced her to walk away. Well, let him. If she gets angry about it, that makes them both losers.

Griffin gives her the shivers. There's something damaged about him – she knows he was shot down over Vietnam and spent some time in a prison camp. She also knows he

escaped and was recaptured. She tells herself to cut him some slack. The guy's a hero, if also a dick. Still, he gets under her skin, and she resents that she hasn't the self-control just to ignore him, let alone treat him with compassion as she's been raised to do.

She goes around a block of portable lavatories that are servicing some sort of construction work going on out front of the building and up to the glass and steel of the Directorate Block, which has a huge Old Glory down one wall, the red NASA logo's wriggly worm letters a good six feet wide next to it.

She approaches the reception desk but Jimmy the guard just looks up from the cigarette he's lighting and waves her through. He's got the same pursed lips as Newman as he eyes the box of her belongings. This is it. The way out.

Habit makes her take all seven flights of stairs, rather than the elevator – she needs all the fitness she can get. Or rather now she doesn't, if she's leaving the programme. She climbs anyway, trying to get rid of the tension she feels inside. She catches her breath at the top. It's nerves, not effort, that tightens her chest as she makes her way down the corridor. It feels as if she's in the anaerobic chamber, the oxygen content depleting, still trying to recite those strings of numbers as vision and reason fade. Her stomach sinks. Was all that for nothing?

She breathes deeply, concentrating on the breath, acknowledging other thoughts, her fear, her disappointment, but letting them slide away. Meditation's second nature to her; her mom had her doing it from the moment she was old enough to sit up straight.

It works until she arrives in front of that door. 808. Facing the 8s. She thinks of the numbers as an infinity loop stood

on their side. Infinity, zero, infinity. Is that what God has on his door? Humbucker may as well be God as far as she's concerned. *Shit. Here goes.*

She can smell the cigar through the door. She swallows, counts to ten, concentrates on her breath again. The smoke irritates her nose and she sneezes. The door glass darkens as a large figure moves quickly toward it and it opens. There's Humbucker: tall, lean, tie tight at the neck, grey suit, big cigar. He's almost dancing on his toes as he surveys her. That's odd. It feels like he's the nervous one.

He nods, says nothing, gestures for her to come in.

He points to a plastic moulded chair in front of his desk. Clearly, he doesn't want anyone getting too comfortable there. If you're firing someone, you want them to leave quickly.

The office is bare and functional: no pictures of family, no sports trophies, no nothing beyond the desk, its chair, a standing ashtray by its side, three squat grey filing cabinets and a TV on a stand in the corner, a big piece of electronica below it – probably one of those new sorts of video recorder, she thinks.

'This is homely,' she says, sitting.

Humbucker lets her attempt at levity hang in the air like a bad fart. He watches her for a while, sucks on his cigar. She finds his gaze uncomfortable and looks briefly down into the box in her lap. When she looks up, she sees him staring into the skew-whiff eyes of the Gonk. She smiles at him, but he does not return it. Ziggy is sure this could be more awkward but can't immediately think how.

He opens a drawer in his desk and takes out a folder, opens it and scans the papers inside.

'You've got a vacation booked.' His voice is a little croaky. She's reminded of the creaking of a coffin lid.

'In a week.'

'What do you want a vacation for?'

'My fiancé wants to go to –'

'You gotta fiancé?'

'Yeah.'

'Yeah, I see that.' He holds up the page in front of him with a slight grimace, as if he's just pulled it out of the trash. 'You close to him?'

'Close enough that he's my fiancé, I guess.'

He nods.

'Yeah. Less than ideal. That sort of thing provides . . . distractions.'

What does 'less than ideal' mean? Ideal for what?

He says nothing for an instant, just sits rubbing his temples.

Then he puts the paper on the desk and taps at it with his knuckle. 'Your undergraduate degree was . . .'

'Language and Linguistics.'

'You speak any other languages?' She doesn't know why he's asking her this – it's all on her résumé in front of him.

'Three Tibetan dialects and I can read Classical Tibetan, obviously, Italian, French, Russian. I fake it in Spanish. It's pretty similar to Italian but with just a different emphasis.' She's aware that she's over-elaborating but she is very nervous.

'Why'd you do Russian?'

'You had to do either Russian, Arabic or Chinese on the course. You had to pick one.'

'But it says you speak Arabic too here.'

9

'I picked two.'

'That must have been time-consuming.'

'I don't watch a lot of TV.'

'OK.' Humbucker is very hard to read. That OK could mean 100 things and Ziggy is convinced 99 of them mean the reverse of OK.

'Then a Master's.'

'In Palaeography. The study of ancient writing.'

'Yeah, that. What was your PhD?'

'Men in the Moon – Lunar geography, ritual practice and religion with reference to Egypt, Iraq and Tibet.'

'A bit of a leap.'

'Not really. Most of it involves decoding ancient writing.'

'How many years on that shit?'

Is he being deliberately difficult? Is this some sort of interview technique or is he just a bully? He has a reputation as a bully, but she thinks this informal way of talking might just be his way of opening up to her. Maybe.

'Five.'

'How'd you get the money for that? Family?'

She laughs.

'I wish.'

'How'd you afford to finance it, then?'

'I worked in a bar to get through.'

'A bar in Tibet?'

'In Brooklyn. My mom still has family in Tibet, so I got put up when I went there.'

'You got a letter through to them?'

'I just turned up. Quite a surprise.'

He snorts, she can't tell if it's in amusement or disdain.

'Mexico, Iraq?'

'The academic community helps you out.'

'Can't have been easy in Tibet. Chinese have an eye on you?'

'Yeah, of course.'

'You didn't get recruited as a spy.'

'No.'

'I was telling you, not asking you. Intelligence gave your life a shake before you were taken on here.' He flicks through the pages in front of him.

'You went to Iraq, too. Who's that guy on the rise there?'

'Saddam.'

'Yeah. He give you any trouble?'

'Not him.' She feels a pang of anxiety in her guts. The guilt never goes away.

He studies his file.

'Oh yeah.' He looks surprised but she can't believe he hasn't read her file already. He must know about her sister. He says nothing for a second, as if weighing whether to explore this avenue any further. Then: 'You lost your sister over there. Tell me about that.'

Is he using her sister's death as a test, to see if she's emotionally stable, to see if she's 'the right stuff'? She feels like punching him in the mouth.

'You OK?'

She swallows.

'She came with me. She helped me out with admin, some research. She was an archaeology postgrad. It was meant to be an adventure. I fixed it so she could come. There was some finishing up to do, just paying people we'd employed, returning a few things. One of us had to stay on for three days. I was feeling homesick, she noticed – she always

noticed even if you tried to hide things – and volunteered to stay. She was killed in a robbery at the office two days after I left.'

He's looking hard at her, looking for what? Weakness? Tears? He won't see any; she cried out of them a long time ago.

'You blame yourself?'

'I blame the dick who shot her.'

The real answer is 'yes', of course, but she's not going to give Humbucker that.

'You were close?'

'Like the same person.' Everybody always said that about them; only close family could ever tell the difference between the two. Even Ziggy sometimes wondered where she ended and her sister began. They talk about twins having a telepathic understanding. It wasn't like that; she couldn't read her sister's thoughts. She didn't have to: she was already thinking them.

Humbucker nods, moves his jaw like he's detected gristle in his teeth.

'You weren't aware of the risks?'

'It didn't seem risky. It's a police state, we were working with Iraqi academics and Saddam was keen on cosying up to the West. The US was doing big business with him. I thought that would protect us.'

He sucks on his cigar. 'We should have paid your fees.'

She keeps a blank face, conceals her surprise. This doesn't sound like a firing.

NASA paying her fees wouldn't have been a good idea. Being on NASA's payroll would have raised a whole bunch of suspicions about espionage.

'Remind me what you concluded.'

He seems almost friendly. This isn't the Humbucker of legend. That Humbucker lives on a sip of vinegar a day and any other sustenance he gets comes from chewing up the dearest dreams of wannabe spacemen.

'There are hints and references throughout Tibetan writing and art, Egyptian tomb hieroglyphs, and in steles recovered from the Temple of the Moon Goddess at Ur to gods – we'd call them aliens – living on the Moon. The precise locations of their dwellings can be traced particularly in mandalas . . .'

He waves his hand, irritated. 'What the fuck is a mandala? I thought he was some terrorist in prison in Africa.'

She holds up the mandala from her box, shows Humbucker its dizzying concentric circles.

'It's a representation of the universe, and an aid to meditation.'

'You meditate?'

'Yeah. It's a Tibetan thing. It helps with my work.'

'How?'

'Just concentration, you know?' She doesn't want to burden Humbucker by telling him about the Twilight Language – too far out for him, she thinks. Some Buddhist writing can't be read conventionally. It requires meditation, insight and sometimes the guidance of a priest, a lama, to understand it. That's the Twilight Language, or the Intentional Language, depending on which translation you prefer. She's always gone for 'Twilight' because it sounds cooler. 'Intentional' is much more correct but, to her, 'Twilight' gets the flavour of thing more accurately. Can she read it? 'Read' is probably the wrong word and 'understand' would be putting it far too strongly, but she can get meaning from it. Explaining that in

an academic paper or to a bone-dry scientist like Humbucker is another thing entirely. Best not even go there.

'And your insight, was?'

'The gods, or the aliens, were living in the Taurus–Littrow crater and the Messier A crater. Investigations of photographs from powerful telescopes and from the limited photography taken by the Apollo missions suggest structures detailed in the mandalas. In particular, a cigar-shaped structure in the Taurus–Littrow crater is worthy of further investigation. It may relate to the 'Thunderbolt Vehicle' in Buddhist writing and art. That's a bit of a weird idea because mostly it has been taken to refer to a stage of enlightenment, where you put your awareness of true reality into practice, but I have concluded that in several special cases it may refer to an actual spaceship. Also references to the Boat of Millions of Years in ancient Egyptian writing.'

He draws on the cigar, exhales with a billowing sigh like a steam train. 'In a sentence.'

'Ancient religious texts indicate there were aliens on the Moon in contact with humans. Present evidence supports at least half of that assertion.'

'That's two sentences.'

Humbucker taps the ash of his cigar into the tall ashtray that stands next to his desk. He takes another manilla file from his drawer, puts it on his desk and pats it with his hand.

'Mandala, insight, Thunderbolt Vehicle. I see why you're having a hard time here. How's that go down with the boys in the jet lab?'

'We tend to stick to discussing football.'

'Yeah. I bet.'

Ziggy shifts in her uncomfortable chair. If this *isn't* a firing, what is it?

Humbucker stubs out his cigar, pushes a button on top of the ashtray. Metal jaws open, the stub falls in and the jaws close again over it.

'OK. I'm gonna ask you and ask you straight. You get one chance at an answer, no changing your mind. At this point, you're in or you're out. I'm about to share some information that will change your entire life. It may end your life. Once shared, there is no return to ordinary street. So, if you want to go to Mexico with Andy, now's the time to say and you can walk through the door. We'll give you a good reference for a university position. Otherwise, you're ours. No discussing this with anyone, not ever.

'This will never be the subject of an academic paper, it won't be the theme of your first novel, nor any pop UFO bullshit book you may care to put out one day. You will never discuss it with me or any other NASA or military employee unless within a certified debugged office like this one and at the direction of myself. It is most secret. If you begin to work on this information, you discuss only the work in hand and share no speculation, information or conversation on this topic. You're going to be a stranger to your loved ones and family in some ways. If you speak about this work, we will know and there will be consequences. Severe consequences. We come first, always. More important than anything.'

'We?'

'NASA. And some arms of the government.'

Ziggy steadies her breathing again. Her heart is pounding. If this is what it sounds like . . . If they really have found something up there . . .

'You mean I'm not actually here for civilian outreach and public relations? There is a real point to me being here?'

He eyes her blankly, like a poker pro watching the flop.

She thinks of Andy. A distance between them is a high price to pay. But if this relates to her work, if there's something that tells her she was right, that aliens really did exist, she has to know.

Humbucker stares at her, unblinking, tiny nods of his head reminding her of one of those thin glass birds that dips its beak into water. She has the idea that any hesitation now will cost her. Would she like to call Andy now? Sure. Will she ask to? No.

'Hit me.'

'Sure?'

Her mouth is dry, her throat tight. 'I'm in.'

Humbucker opens the file on his desk, takes out a piece of paper and slides it across the table. He rolls a biro towards her.

'Sign your life away,' he says. 'That's not an exaggeration. You're about to become a second lieutenant in the USAF.'

'NASA's a civilian agency.'

'Yeah, but this is in close liaison with the military and uses military facilities. We need you in the air force before we go any further.'

'Why?'

'We get to shoot you if you reveal anything at all about this programme.'

'That's not a joke, is it?'

'Do I look like I have a gift for humour?'

Her hand shakes slightly as she signs, the pen scratchy and difficult to get going. Finally, after a bit of scribbling,

her signature is there on the paper. It's a security clearance to Top Secret level.

'Welcome to the service, Lieutenant.'

'You've found something up there?'

Humbucker swallows, drums his fingers on the desk. Is he nervous? He looks nervous.

'Not us,' he says. 'The Soviets. I think they've found your Thunderbolt Vehicle. We've been looking for it for a while, but they've got there first.'

'The Russians are on the Moon?' Ziggy feels a little dizzy.

'Yeah. They keep it secret because of what they're doing up there. We keep it secret so as not to scare the shit out of people. Anyway, the top and bottom is this: we think you were right. We've thought you were right for a while and have been looking into it.'

'You've been working on my paper?'

'It formed part of the Apollo 17 investigations.'

She feels briefly angry that she wasn't told but knows she has no right to that anger. This is the biggest thing in history; who gives a shit how she feels?

She remains quiet, her mind numb. She almost can't think anything at all.

'Watch,' says Humbucker. 'This is from an intercepted communication we got back from the Moon three days ago. The source is a transmitter in the Taurus–Littrow Valley.'

He goes to the recorder, takes up the remote on its cord and presses a button. The screen displays some colour bars and then blinks into a fierce black and white moonscape.

It shows, of all things, the outline of a bulldozer, or something like one, with a bucket scoop against a black sky.

Then the images blur as the camera is moved.

'Investigation of hatch discovered yesterday,' says a voice in Russian. 'Selenic colongitude 20.0 degrees north, 31.0 degrees east, 200 metres direct north of Apollo 17 landing site.'

'That's the Taurus–Littrow Valley,' says Humbucker.

An off-screen voice crackles from the TV. 'It was under the Americans' noses.'

'Long fucking noses, if it was,' says the first voice.

The camera is set down again and the focus adjusted.

The image shows what looks like a flat expanse of rock. Just visible, as if etched upon it, is a rounded rectangle shape.

'This is your hatch?' says a voice.

'What else do you think it is? Have a better look.'

The camera swerves again. A cosmonaut comes into view, wearing a Krechet-94 spacesuit, judging by the white plastic 'hula hoop' around the waist that allows a cosmonaut who falls over to roll and stand again. But it's heavily modified. She notices immediately that the LSS – life support system – pack is huge.

The cosmonaut leans forwards on his hands and knees and brushes the surface. The camera zooms in. An image starts to appear; just a collection of lines on the poor resolution of the camera.

'What's that?' says a voice in Russian.

'I don't know.'

'Focus on it.'

The camera zooms in further. The image is bad at first, but it crystallises for a couple of seconds to show a curve like a bowl, but extended slightly as if to form a wave. She can't tell if it's painted or etched on.

Ziggy swallows. The image resonates with her; she feels its meaning just out of grasp. On carvings in the heart of the

Jokhang temple in Lhasa, in the Moon Goddess's Temple at Ur, in Mexican and Peruvian excavations, she has seen something similar – not the same, often very much more ornate – but that wave line, almost like the bottom of a human lip, is the distillation of something she has seen before.

'Step back from it!' Now it's a female voice, not quite native Russian, she thinks. A bit of an accent.

'OK, I . . .'

'You can't really see at first watch, but he leans on the door to get up,' says Humbucker.

The rounded rectangle pushes forwards, lifts up. Inside, it is light, but that's all Ziggy can see. She swallows.

'My God!'

'Yeah,' says Humbucker.

'We need to discuss this,' says the Russian Mission Control. 'Return to lunar lander and await instruction.'

'There was no point dragging the bigger life support if I'm just going to turn around. This is first contact! I should go in!' The camera comes back a little, showing the cosmonaut on his hands and knees. There is some noise, scraping, and the picture tips and shakes.

'What's that?' says Ziggy.

'We think they're attaching the camera to a tripod, watch,' says Humbucker. The cosmonaut returns into view.

'Major, remain where you are. It is my strong concern that you are not capable of understanding nor even surviving the technologies on this ship. You have done your job. Return.' It's the non-Russian woman's voice.

'Transmission patchy,' says the cosmonaut. 'You have cleared me for entry, right?'

'Not right. Return to lunar lander.'

'Communication dead. Hello, hello.'

'Major, this is not acceptable. You can hear us perfectly well. Return to lunar lander.'

'I can't hear anything. Entering as instructed.'

'Major! Return to lunar lander! You risk damaging important technologies!'

The cosmonaut manoeuvres his bulk through the hatch, the big pack only just fitting. Another cosmonaut comes in to join him, lowering himself through to disappear, the camera left showing nothing more than the barren glare of the lunar surface and the light emanating from the hatch. Humbucker clicks off the TV.

Ziggy sits in stunned silence.

'No communication since. The guy on the orbiter hasn't a clue what happened to them either. First impressions?'

She almost laughs. Little lights swim at the corners of her eyes as if she's got up too quickly after lying down for a long time.

'It's a lot to take in. I can't give a response immediately. It's mind-blowing.'

Humbucker purses his lips, though she doesn't detect disapproval.

'Who was the non-Russian?' she says.

'Yeah. The woman's voice. We think that's Amira Kovacs. She's a Hungarian working for the Soviets. Same field of study as you.'

'I've never heard of her.'

'Well, she's heard of you, according to intelligence. Why do you think she warned the cosmonaut away from the hatch even before it opened?'

'Just general caution.'

'Maybe. But they've got a cosmonaut on the spot, it would be an enormous effort to get him to come back. Why not just let him take a look?'

'It would be speculation.'

'Speculate.'

'The symbol, if it was a symbol, carried some threat she recognised.' Ziggy's speaking intuitively now, allowing herself to run ahead of the facts. She must check that impulse.

'Specifically, what?'

Ziggy thinks: that curve, she's seen it somewhere before. It is very similar to things she's seen in ancient Tibetan writing, if you can call it writing. Puzzles might be a better description, inscriptions in the Twilight Language. Then, in a flash, she sees it. Of course, it was staring her in the face.

'Do you mind?' she says. 'I need some paper.'

He pulls a sheet of paper out of his drawer. She takes it and sketches a shape on it. The same curve that's on the door.

'It's that shape,' she says. 'That. It's not well known in the West, but it is there in the Tibetan Buddhist tradition.'

Humbucker takes the file and turns it towards him. The shape almost resembles an upside-down ice cream cone, but the lower part extends beyond the body of the cone and is formed into a curve unmistakably similar to the one on the hatch.

'What's this?'

'It's a dakini knife,' she says. 'A Kartika, as it's sometimes called.'

'A what?'

'In Tibetan Buddhism there are these spirits known as *dakini* – female spirits that carry knives that slice through all the illusions of the world. This representation of their knives goes back thousands of years.'

'You sure that's what it is?'

'Not sure, but . . .' She hesitates. Can she run this far ahead of the evidence, make these wild links? Yes. That's what reading the Twilight Language is all about, to feel the shape she has drawn on the page calling to the shape she saw in the video, calling to others buried in the depths of temples and tombs.

She'll tell him. She has to. '*Dakini* means "Sky-goer".'

Humbucker sits back down in his chair. He puts his head into his hands, thinks for a second and then looks up and says:

'Could there be one of these knives aboard?'

'It's more a metaphorical thing is my understanding.'

'Hmmm. A knife is a weapon. There's an image of one on that door. If that is an alien weapons store and the Reds get there first, I don't have to explain the implications.'

'It's very likely decayed to nothing, no matter what it is.'

'That door hasn't decayed and it's not a chance we can take. Kovacs thinks there's alien tech there and they seem keen to get a look at it. We know they're planning on sending more people up, and soon.'

Ziggy can hardly take all this in. She sits, steadying her breath.

'We have to get there first,' he says. 'We have to find out what's in there and what the Russians know.'

She's very aware of the movement of blood in her temples, of the tightness of her throat.

'You're on lockdown,' he says. 'You'll be flown to Groom Lake, and you'll stay on that base for a week. After that . . . You go and check this out. In person.'

'Groom Lake. That's Area 51, right, the experimental facility?'

'Yeah. Though you won't be there long.'
She looks at her hands; they're shaking.
'You're sending me to the Moon?'
'Yeah. How are you with a gun?'

Chapter 2

She is allowed one call to Andy, with Humbucker listening in. No point complaining; that's the way it goes. She tells him NASA has seconded her out to Australia for some training for a few weeks. He takes a deep breath.

'How many weeks without you?'

'I dunno. It's kind of a big deal. I'll miss you.'

'A big deal? Are you . . .?' He means to say, 'On your way'. That is, selected. That is, going to the Moon.

'It's just a thing.'

'Everything's just a thing.'

'Yeah. This is one of those. A thing among everything.'

'So no need for . . .'

'What?'

'Er.' Andy's not stupid. He's picked up that their call is being listened to, she's sure.

'Well, you know, undue . . .'

'Undueness?'

'That would be the thing.'

'Undueness is never due, Andy.'

He laughs. There is a silence. Four, five seconds. T minus

four, that sort of silence, counting down to something huge, something important. Is he going to ask her not to go?

He breathes deeply. 'Well, I'll be thinking of you. All the time.'

'And I you.'

'Can you tell me where?'

Humbucker shakes his head.

'No. I'm sorry I can't be more specific.'

'How often can you call?'

'We're in the outback.'

'The outback. That's like, where the snakes live, right?' Andy is a worrier, to an extent. That's why they complement each other. She rushes in. He does the thinking, and somewhere between those two points the right course of action emerges.

'I guess, but people do live there.'

'You be careful, I don't like the idea of you being at such risk.'

'I'm an astronaut, Andy.'

'Yeah, but . . . there aren't any snakes in space.'

'Any we know about,' she says.

They both laugh, nervously, weirdly, a first date laughter, that moment where the ice is broken, a connection is made, you relax and think 'maybe this is going to be OK'. Andy knows something's not right, though – that he hasn't got the full picture. He's clever and he's empathetic. He can read her; she can read him. Secrets are impossible between them. He might not have the detail, but he's worked out this is more important than she says it is.

'I love you, Zig,' he says.

'I love you too. More than anything.'

'How long will you be away?'

'I don't know. A couple of months, I guess.'

'Jeez. Write me.'

Again, Humbucker lids his eyes, shakes his head.

'I can't do that.'

'Well, can you bring me back a kangaroo?'

'Will do.'

She feels tears coming; the phone feels hot under her ear. Humbucker looks at her as if she's the alien species and this is first contact.

'They won't even give us one night together?'

'No. I am so, so sorry, Andy. This is . . .'

There is no need to finish her sentence. He knows how she wants to end her sentence – with the word 'big'. Andy's not an idiot and can hear the sadness in her voice, sense there is more to this than she can tell him. She can never really hide anything from him, which is one of 10,000 reasons their love will endure. It will last. She will return to it, with luck. Maybe with a lot of luck.

'I'll be thinking of you every second,' she says.

'And I you. I love you.'

When she puts down the phone, Humbucker says nothing, just gestures for her to leave the room, glancing at the phone as if he'd like to smash it to atoms just in case there's a chance it holds the remaining scent of a chance of any secrets escaping through it.

Is she being selfish? She would like to put the risk to the back of her mind, but NASA will not allow her that privilege. She has to write a Next of Kin letter before she goes in case the worst happens. On a printed yellow form, in five hundred words or less, she has to say goodbye to

Andy from beyond the grave. The letter will be censored, redacted. She can give no real clue as to what happened to her, though she feels she has to offer him something. What does she say, in that stark office? A desk, a lamp, a chair, yellow light, nothing more. This:

'Andy. Sorry. I know you must have 1000 questions about what has happened and that none of those questions will really ever be answered. I know that what we have between us is something very special. If you are reading this. I am dead. Dramatic, right, and corny but true.

I am sorry beyond words that I will not spend the rest of my life with you, that we can't be companions to each other, best friends, watch our children grow. I am sorry. The officials will have told you how I died.

I missed you every moment we were away and, if I am sliding through the netherworld on my way to my next incarnation, I miss you now and will miss you for a million incarnations. Move on from me but don't forget me. I will be there in the light on the evening water on Siesta Beach, there on the warm breeze and in the lapping of the waves. Look into that light and know that I am there forever, in that dreaming moment.'

She pauses. Will he remember the Moon, the huge red moon over Siesta Beach where they drank wine by the ocean's edge, where the pelicans flapped by, slow and stately, and where a dolphin broke water only fifty yards from the shore, seeming to look at them, say hello, before disappearing again? Of course he will; it's where he asked her to marry him. She wants to write 'moonlight on the water' but knows that any mention of 'moon' will be redacted. Andy is clever, he is empathic. He will get it. He will know where she has been, where she died.

'I am gone but I will find you again, 100, 1000 lifetimes from now. We are meant to be together, that is the way of the universe and nothing, not death, not mystery can prevent that. You are not alone.'

A tear falls down her cheek. The thought of her own death doesn't bother her. She has faith in rebirth, not as a spiritual concept but as a scientific, a mathematical one. In the immensity of time, the vastness of infinity, the precise arrangement of molecules, the impulses, the chemical exchanges that make up her and make up him will come again. It's a mad thought but, in forever, all chances must play out. The thought of Andy alone leaves her distraught. They dealt with that when she accepted the position at NASA, but accepting the possibility of disaster isn't the same as dealing with the reality. In a way, her accepting the position was a chance to test all the brave sentiments of youth against hard reality.

'Better to burn than to rot,' she'd told Andy.

'Better to burn and then rot,' said Andy. 'You can do both, I think.'

'I won't be burning, even if I get this job. I promise to come back and rot with you.'

'That's so romantic,' he'd said. 'I wonder which limb will fall off first.'

That was it, really – her love for Andy was such that she thought nothing could shatter it, like the universe owed her one after Maria. They would grow old together. Writing the letter, she was not so sure. Can she do this to Mom and Dad – have them lose another daughter? Can she do this to Andy, her soul mate – deny him a life lived for love? The letter, finished, seems to speak to her. 'Fold me or crumple me,' it seems to say. 'Send me, or send me away.'

The night is full of reasons to quit. The dangers are enormous. She will be strapped to nearly a million gallons of fuel, fired into space to fly at 25,000 mph in no more than a tin can, delve into what in all likelihood is an alien structure with no guarantee of what they will find, or that their oxygen will last, knowing only that two people have already gone in and not emerged. On top of that, if Kovacs is right, there may be dangerous technologies inside. What was she thinking?

It was too much to ask of Andy, too much to ask of Mom and Dad, she decides.

She crumples the letter, dunks it in the bin, picks up the phone to tell Humbucker she's changed her mind. As the phone rings, she thinks of that cosmonaut at the hatch. 'I'm going in. This is first contact'. She thinks of the Vikings heading west into the grey blue of the Atlantic, their open boats searching for whatever, something, finding Vinland; Marco Polo heading east; Chuck Yeager shoving the thrust forward to break the speed of sound, not knowing if he would disintegrate. Armstrong, Aldrin, Collins. They were all pushed by the same tide: history. And what if the Russians do discover some master weapon or technology in there? What then for Mom, Dad and Andy? Are these her real reasons for agreeing to go, though? Her sister seems to be at her side. 'You just have to know, Zig, same as you always did, curiosity like a heroin habit. You know you're going. You can't fight it.'

'My curiosity got you shot.'

'So take your chances while you've got them. I'd be first on that rocket.'

'Andy, Mom, Dad?'

'Death didn't part us.'

29

It didn't either, not in a fundamental sense. Sometimes, at times of stress or sadness it's almost like her sister has been sleeping within her and that she steps out to counsel or comfort Ziggy. It's a fantasy, Ziggy knows, but a powerful one she's glad she has.

She puts down the phone, writes the letter again, seals it along with her destiny. Then two notes for Mom and Dad, one saying she's going away and another in case she dies. It doesn't say much, just 'all the love in the world' and that she died doing what she loved. She can't face calling them, won't have the strength. In some ways it is so selfish but in another they would want her to be everything she could be. They knew the risks when they gave her their blessing to join NASA. She pulls up the blind, looks up to the silver moon, a sharp crescent of light cut into the veil of the sky. Is that where she'll die? Or is that sliver of light up there the glimmer of a light that will reveal everything she's wondered about for years, a herald of humanity's greatest discovery?

'Coming, ready or not,' she says, as much to herself as to the Moon.

Chapter 3

Nothing really prepares you for this. Not the weeks of training, not the vomit comet weightless airliner flights, not spinning in a centrifuge, nothing. This is space. It's mind-blowing, consuming. From the porthole of the craft, she looks out on a sky awash with stars, comets streaking the vast blackness. She and her companions are themselves a comet, she thinks, searing through the void, a bright slash cut into the velvet of the dark. She has to think like that, she finds. It takes away from the reality that there is a four-inch-thick honeycomb capsule wall between her and, like, everything else. Infinity, the hungry darkness that wants to suck you through any hole or puncture like meat paste from a tube.

So here she is, dozing weightless inside her aluminium bullet aimed at the Moon, the sensations of the launch coming back to her in lurches and drops. She relives that sense of the vastness around her she felt when strapped into her seat for the launch, not just the tons of rocket fuel, the launch pad, the Nevada salt flats stretching out, but wider: the Earth as a ball, the planets, galaxies, the universe expanding out from her seat, waiting for her.

The rocket fires through her sleep like a storm god waking.

As she dreams, she imagines she is being pushed, swept like an ant from a cosmic table. She jolts into consciousness, realises she's strapped in her sleeping bag, weightless. Weightlessness. Wow. That first moment when her chest moved against the straps of her seat and the headset's metalled voice said, 'Earth orbit achieved, begin checks for translunar injection.'

Houston – the mission was controlled from there, even though it was launched from Groom Lake in Nevada – went silent. Everyone was silent.

Dave 'Toog' Myers – mission commander – smiled at her, took out a pen and released it. It hovered in the air as if on invisible strings.

'Welcome to space, Ms Da Luca,' he said.

Toog's short for 'Too Good'. Former top college quarterback who turned his back on a career in football to sign for the air force as a fighting pilot and then as a test pilot. Intelligent, empathic, kind and funny, but with the biggest kill numbers of anyone in the USAF back in 'Nam. Did he get shot down? Of course not. Toog's too good for that. And too lucky. That's something you can't buy, according to the other flyers.

'Let's check the fucking systems and stop being assholes,' said Griffin.

Griffin, yeah, Griffin. *Oh, man, why him?* He's the lunar module pilot – he'll handle the descent. He's the man most qualified for the job – a year up to his neck in swamp water and dead friends in Vietnam as a Marine Corps officer before training as an aviator and duelling with the MiGs over the jungles. They've managed to disguise their mutual loathing

for the two weeks' crash training before launch. It was like a compact between them – they both knew there was no chance of them getting on the mission if their beef was discovered. So it's a little secret, something only they share.

Still, Griffin started to refer to her as 'the cargo' the minute they were in space. In a way, she is. The command module has been adapted and, where there might normally be space for scientific instruments and tools, there is a berth for her.

The remaining member of the crew is Command Module Pilot Danny Perry – another test pilot but of a different mould from the other two. He's quiet, head always in a book and fascinated by engineering problems. He's also a big music fan and, as the command module breaks briefly from the lunar lander to reconfigure for the journey to the Moon, he has Television's 'Marquee Moon' playing on cassette – choppy guitar, urgent, high-pitched vocals – part of a tape of Moon songs he's put together for the journey.

'You mention you like this weird shit during selection?' says Griffin.

'Didn't come up.'

'Thought not. Got any Country?'

'Neil Young?'

'Jesus Christ,' says Griffin, as if someone's pissed in his coffee.

Griffin's attitude to the other astronauts is sarcastic but in a 'just kidding' sort of way, not vindictive. He wouldn't have made selection himself if it was. With her, he allows a sharp edge to jut through, though he draws back from the naked aggression he displays when they're alone. Could she have reported him? Sure, but then they'd have both been dropped from the programme.

In a way, she welcomes his animosity. It takes her mind off the dangers of the mission. It takes her mind off Andy and her parents.

Is she nervous? You bet, and she uses the times that Griffin is busy with work to meditate – mainly on the image of the *dakini* knife. She has to time her sessions to coincide with when Griffin is elsewhere. She can't deal with the level of shit she'll get from him if he catches her hovering full lotus while speeding through space at 4000 mph breathing pure oxygen, like some hippy's dream. Yeah, well, she can sort of see his point, though it won't stop her meditating like she's been doing since she was three years old.

Luckily, Griffin has lots to do, crawling in and out of the lunar lander, so she – a non-technician – gets plenty of time to herself. It's an odd sensation to practise in this way. Flashes of bright blue light register on her closed eyes like TV flickers on the inside of a darkened room. The astronauts say this is because of Cherenkov radiation – cosmic particles interacting with the electro-biology of her eyes. To her, it feels like the universe is saying 'hello'. Free of even the sensation of gravity, her mind breaks away from the aluminium and plastic of the ship's interior, floats past the screens and the switches, the sockets and the signs, and wanders the stars, flies through the deep dark to alight on bright planets, chase comets' tails or pass in wonder through sparkling asteroid fields. She has read all she can on the *dakini* and understands in an intellectual way how the *dakini* is a spirit, an energy, and even sometimes a living woman. Now she seeks to understand it in the Twilight Language, meditating on the image of the *dakini* knife, reciting the Manjushri mantra for the insight and wisdom it brings.

She's seeking to meditate in a conceptual, thinking way and sounding the syllables in her mind. *Om Ah Ra, Pa Tsa Na Dhi* – but that quickly vanishes, and another mantra takes over, unbidden. This is the Green Tara mantra: *Om Tare Tuttare Ture Toha*. This is a protective mantra, against physical as well as mental threats. She has rarely lost control of her meditation like that before, but it doesn't concern her too much. She's nervous, that's all, and has stumbled into a mantra that reflects that. Odder things are happening, anyway.

She sees herself as the goddess Tara, flashing through her twenty-one manifestations, her five colours: green, white, yellow, blue and red. Goddess of compassion, and above all goddess of protection. They're going to need some of that where they're going.

Three days of free-floating in the whirr of the cooling system's fans, the bleeps and clicks of checks and rechecks. Of course, she does have work to do – particularly on monitoring the cooling system. But that's not what she's on the mission for, so she concentrates on the image of the knife and what it means in the Twilight Language. Beyond the image of herself as a goddess, she gets nothing. She feels uncomfortable with that; meditation isn't meant to be an ego boost or even – despite what the hippies would tell you – a trip.

On day two they get some news.

'Soviet launch from Star City. It looks like the Reds ain't far behind you. Pretty much as predicted.'

'A Vostok on our tail?' says Toog.

'Two, by the look of it.'

'I didn't know they had that capability.'

'We neither.'

'Have you agreed non-aggression?'

'We talked with them about that.'

'And?'

'Pretty inconclusive.'

'A conclusion would be nice,' says Toog. 'Good to know, one way or the other. I don't think it would be a good idea to start fighting up here.'

'You make the call while you're up there.'

'The call is, dead Reds,' says Griffin.

Toog shoots him a glance.

'It's up to you if you want to come home, Toog,' says Mission Control, 'you can turn around right now.'

'I'm fine right here,' he says. 'But I'll ask the others.'

No one wants to abort. This is history, this is Columbus coming to the New World, Caesar to Albion, Geshe Wangyal to the West, but so much more than that. The risks are already massive; the presence of the Soviets is just one more thing to factor in.

Ziggy has never felt more Buddhist – her personality, her life, her wishes are irrelevant. She feels swept up, doing the Cosmos's work. The others feel that too, she's sure, though they don't put it that way. To be fair, she also feels pretty Catholic, strange noises from the ship leaving her praying: 'Get me through this safely, God, I'll go to church like for weeks. I'll be a better person, live a better life.'

'Can't let the Reds get their hands on this shit,' says Griffin, who seems convinced they are certainly going to find an alien ship, not just an internally lit garbage disposal container, and that it will be packed with useful technologies.

'Worth dying for,' she says, in agreement, trying to get on his right side.

36

'Dying ain't nothing,' says Griffin. 'There's a whole lot of worse stuff can happen to you than that. Believe me.'

'I believe you,' she says. She tries to offer him compassion but feels him prickle even as she does so. Never mind, keep at it, her mom would say. 'Guy's a dick,' her dad would say.

The gun, of course, she doesn't touch, not that she'd be allowed to. The guns absolutely cannot be loaded until they are outside the lunar lander. An accidental discharge within the spacecraft could be disastrous. But the gun touches her mind. She thinks of it lying there in its crate, in its insulated holster, ready for her. Her weapon is strictly one of self-defence – a modified Colt Cobra .38 with sawn-away trigger guard and extended grip for use with gloves. She didn't have much time to practise with it but that didn't matter – the targets she was aiming at were big and less than five yards away. She isn't going hunting. Getting the shells in alone is a task she's had to practise hard, but the air force considers the revolver more reliable than an automatic, which you could load more easily, in the dusty conditions of the Moon and she isn't likely to use more than the six shots she'll carry with her.

Cobra – she feels its presence hissing in her mind, a snake, ready to bite her. She's never been comfortable around guns, even before one killed her sister.

Do they really think they'll be shooting cosmonauts? 'We want to have that option,' said Humbucker, who had popped up in the second week of her training. Toog and Griffin, who will be coming with her to the TV (Thunderbolt Vehicle) as they've named the alien craft – if it is a craft and not just a hole in the ground or dwelling – she assumes are packing the same guns as her.

She is still undecided if she'll take the weapon, much less use it. It was sort of assumed without question that she'd want to use it to defend herself, but she's not so sure. Shooting a gun at someone else would feel like a sort of suicide – a blowing away of the person she thought she was. A gun took her sister. Does she want to take someone else's sister or brother? Maybe, is the answer to that – if it's them or her. And maybe not. She isn't sure she could kill someone else, even if she was in mortal danger herself.

Also, she thinks that a gun won't help if they do meet the cosmonauts. It introduces immediate distrust into any situation. At least the headsets have been modified so they can broadcast on the Soviet short-wave channel and allow her to talk to the Russians.

There's some grim stuff on this mission, though. She sits toying with an adaptor that will go in the pocket of her suit. It should enable her to use a Soviet LSS if she needs to – the oxygen and lithium hydroxide components at least, the first to breathe, the second to remove the CO_2 created by her breathing. If she does end up using that, it means the cosmonaut won't be.

Toog sees what she's doing.

'It won't come to that,' he says.

'You told the Ruskies that, Toog?' says Griffin.

'They won't attack us,' says Toog. 'They'd be crazy to.'

'Yeah, a mad fucking Russian. Who ever heard of one of them?'

'No aggression,' says Toog.

'Yes, chief,' says Griffin and salutes.

It seems like days, and it seems like hours, and in some ways it seems only seconds since they fired the rockets for the

translunar injection to take them out of Earth orbit before Toog is talking into the headset saying, 'Trajectory looking good for lunar orbit.' The engines fire, with a rumble and a sudden sensation of weight as the craft slows.

She looks out of the porthole, the orientation of the craft not yet right for her to see the Moon. She's half expecting to see the Russian command module hanging in space beside them, but that's long gone – it waited as long as it could and then went back to Earth, according to message interceptions. Anyway, the chances of dropping in at the exact point of a 90-minute orbit where it would be visible are small, though not as small as you'd think, according to Danny.

He starts talking about vectors and tangents, stuff like that, but she can't concentrate. She's too caught up in the nervousness and excitement of arriving at the moon.

There is no sudden rush of gravity, just a faint sensation of weight as the rockets fire and they slow. The craft turns and the surface of the Moon, white and bright, is beneath them. It's incredible, almost overwhelming, and she feels at once elated and vulnerable, flying past in the flimsy structure of her spacecraft, waiting to drop into the arms of its gravity and into orbit.

The radio crackles. 'Looking good, *Salvador*.'

The ship's named after the place Columbus first landed in the New World.

'Good from here too, Control,' says Toog, before reciting a long checklist of instrument readings.

They pass behind the Moon, away from the Earth, and all communications with home go dead. It's silent now; no one speaks, the consciousness of their loneliness weighing upon them. They are on the far side of the Moon from the

Earth, but it's still light. Then they pass out of the sun, too, into the stony dark. Free of the sun's glare, the sky through the porthole blurs with stars – millions upon billions of suns shining in a field of white diamonds so deep and speckled that space is not black, it is white. So many stars, surely so many worlds.

'We're not alone, are we?' she says without thinking.

Toog smiles. 'Maybe. In fourteen billion years, we might be the first, or the last. Or just the end of a series. Or the beginning.'

'You don't think so, do you?'

'No.'

'They've been here, I know,' says Ziggy.

'If everyone wants to take a last piss, we better suit up to descend,' says Griffin.

This is it, then, it's really happening. She gets into the first layers of her A8LB EMU – Extravehicular Mobility Unit – spacesuit for short. There won't be enough room in the lander to get suited up, so they do it in the command module. First, she puts on the Maximum Absorbency Garment – a hi-tech diaper. NASA haven't gotten round to devising a urine collection device for women so she's already 'tactically dehydrated' – that is, she hasn't drunk for four hours, though the diaper can hold enough to see her through an anticipated 24-hour mission. She puts on the soft comfort layer, wriggles into the Liquid Cooling and Ventilation Garment, with its tubes of water that will circulate around her body and stop her from boiling up inside the suit. She snaps on her biobelt and threads all the sensor wires through the pouches and attaches the various pads to herself – the ECG, respiration monitors, temperature gauge. All the time she feels Griffin's eyes on her. She shoots him a look that says

'Is that necessary?' He just leans into her, says, 'I wouldn't even,' through his teeth and goes back to suiting up himself.

Then it's the outer suit, the micrometeoroid layers which can be pressurised. This is much harder than suiting up on Earth, and she finds herself looking at Danny upside down as she wriggles through the back zip. Once she feels her feet in the integrated boots, she pops her head through the neck ring and is ready to start making all the connections between the outer suit and the biobelt and inner layer. Finally, time to zip up the pressure zipper, pulling it up over her back with its long ribbon. Then goes on the Snoopy cap with all its communication gear, and then the intravehicular gloves. She's definitely nervous now, but she tells herself it would be ignoring the reality of her situation if she wasn't.

She offers up a prayer as Toog checks her zips and kit. 'Tara. Protection. Thanks, Lady.'

Then she's crawling into the lunar lander, patting for luck her space overboots and gloves and the bulk of her life support backpack that are stored in there. Life support is highly modified for this mission, which doubles as a sort of test run – a larger and expanded backpack which is detachable in order to facilitate passing through small spaces. Primary life support will be ten hours, followed by an hour's backup. The water bags beneath the main suit are not any larger than on the A7, which only had a primary life support of seven hours. Just have to put up with being thirsty, it appears. They'll take a backup oxygen tank which will last five hours. It's smaller, strapped to the front of the suit. No point taking a bigger one because, though it would be light on the surface of the Moon, the cooling layer she wears next to her skin will only work for sixteen hours.

She plugs in to the lander's life support and then clicks on her bubble helmet. She's done this enough times in training, but a momentary feeling of claustrophobia engulfs her before she calms herself, fights the fear of suffocation and breathes.

Then she finds the Velcro on the floor of the lander with the soles of her flight boots and sticks herself down, pulls out her restraint straps from the bulkhead and clips in. Toog seals the hatch and he and Griffin strap themselves in.

The lunar module is switched to its own power and life support and final checks are done.

'Pressure?' says Griffin.

'0.32 bar,' says Toog.

'Venting to 0.3. Venting.'

He flicks a switch, waits a couple of seconds.

'Pressure?'

'0.29.'

'0.29 confirmed. All good.'

'Probe drogue in place. Capture latch engaged. Access tunnel blocked.' It's Danny's voice from the command module.

'Gyro torquing angles set,' says Toog. There's a whole bunch of other stuff that she should listen to but is too nervous to focus on – pitch and yaw checks, drift checks, computer sequences, pressure readings, radio adjustments, all buzzing through her headset with that cheap transistor radio sound.

'Detach docking clamps,' says Houston.

This is it. Ziggy's stomach tightens; she feels sick.

'Detaching clamps,' says Danny. 'Gas fired. Clamps detached.'

'Confirmed,' says Griffin.

'Fire nitrogen cylinders,' says Houston.

'Nitrogen cylinder fired,' says Griffin.

42

No noise, nothing. Then there is a squeaking, almost a peeling sound as they de-dock and vibrations shake through the structure of the Lunar Lander. She feels the Velcro securing her to the floor tug lightly at her boots.

'Free at last,' says Toog. 'Yaw 2, pitch minus 18, Houston. Everything looking real good. Six minutes to ignition.'

'Reading error, 1407,' says Griffin. He is calm, though intensely concentrated.

Ziggy swallows, crosses herself. One of the benefits of her upbringing was that she was never required to be very consistent about religion.

'Turn on rotational control number 2,' says Houston.

'Firing,' says Griffin.

A slight sensation of movement as the Velcro tugs at her feet.

'Looking good?' says Toog.

'Looking good,' says Danny in the command module.

'Error code gone,' says Griffin.

Six minutes before they'll fire – 50,000 feet above the lunar surface. If the rockets fail, they will be so much debris.

'Yaw right, 20,' says Houston.

'Yawing right. Coming in 83,500 ft. 83,250.'

The seconds seem made of gelatine, soft physical things that you need to push through, things that will not move of their own accord. She hears the feet counting down. 80,000, 70,000, 60,000. Then:

'Go for landing. Commence ignition sequence,' says Houston.

'Commencing ignition,' says Griffin. 'Pressurising propellant tanks. Firing compatibility valve cartridges.' He flicks a switch and there is a dull bang, the structure of the lander vibrating with the charge.

'Propellant tanks at full pressure,' says Toog.

'Firing cartridges to open ambient helium isolation valve.' Another switch flicked, another dull thud.

'Burn looks good,' says Griffin. 'Burning a little more fuel than we need to.'

'Why's that?' says Toog.

'Dead weight on board,' says Griffin. He glances at her. She assumes he's got the radio to Houston shut.

He flicks a switch and the craft shakes. She feels briefly heavier again as the rockets press her feet against the floor, and she leans on her straps to steady herself.

'Descent burn good,' says Houston.

'Sure is,' says Toog. 'Descent engine and oxidiser tanks at optimum pressure. It's a beautiful lunar morning over the Taurus–Littrow Valley!'

'Can you see it yet?' says Ziggy, without thinking.

'You expecting a fucking sign?' says Griffin.

'That's kinda what I'm here for.'

'Keep it civil, Griffin,' says Toog.

She looks over his shoulder through the hatch. The moon rocks are throwing long shadows in the early morning sun, intensely three-dimensional, if such a silly thought makes any sense. The white is whiter and the black blacker than any shade she has ever seen. It looks like a home for the gods. There is no sensation of falling, but the Moon is massive in the viewports, its whiteness overwhelming. Then the craft tilts a little and the Earth flashes into the front window above the curve of the Moon.

Ziggy slows her breathing, concentrates on the here and the now. That doesn't work. The experience is overwhelming. 'Fuck, look at that!' she hears herself say.

'Yup,' says Toog. 'Throttle down, Griffin.'

'Throttle down,' says Griffin. 'Not so easy as the simulator. 12000 feet, throttle looking good.'

'What the fuck is that?' says Ziggy.

'What?'

'A white streak just went over us.'

'A what?' says Griffin.

Across the window another streak, high above them.

'Just land it, Griffin, you'll be briefed on this on the surface,' says Toog.

'Reds already? Is that them up there?' says Griffin.

'Yeah, Reds.'

'Why weren't we told they were so close?' says Ziggy.

'It's the military, not a fucking democracy,' says Griffin.

'How's the speed?' crackles Houston.

'10,000 feet. eleven forward, thirty degrees,' says Griffin.

'Looks good.'

'Soviet command module sighted,' says Danny on the headset. Ziggy swallows, breathes in, concentrates on lowering her heart rate.

'5000 feet. ten forward, beautiful,' says Griffin.

'Soviets closing,' says Danny. 'There are two of them. Very close. Well, hello boys, what do *you* want?'

'4000 feet. Easy, easy. 3000. 2000, very nice,' says Griffin. 'Burn beautiful right now, burn beautiful.'

'Soviets matching perilune orbit,' says Danny. 'You boys trying to dock, you should know I'm not that kind of girl.'

'700 feet. Down at four,' says Griffin.

'Holy shit!' It's Danny's voice crackling over the radio now. 'Houston. Lead Soviet vessel seems to possess armament. From here it looks like an auto cannon like they had on the Salyut 3 space station.'

'Get out of there, *Salvador*,' says Houston.

'I can't leave the guys on the Moon.'

'If you stay, you'll be leaving them anyway. Get out of there. It's diplomacy here on Earth that'll get them a lift home.' That sounds like Humbucker's voice.

'I'm not leaving them! I . . . Oh shit. What was that?'

'Is the cabin intact?'

'I think it is, I think—' The radio falls to white noise.

'*Salvador*! *Salvador*!' says Houston.

'250 feet, six forward. Landing imminent,' says Griffin.

'Have they killed Danny?' says Ziggy.

'Can't think about that now,' says Toog.

'100 feet. Five forward. Drifting left a little,' says Griffin.

Ziggy has gone cold. If the command module is destroyed, they have a few days' air and no way home.

'50 feet. Stable. 20feet. And down. Contact light.'

A soft thump and she has the sensation of gravity again, though much reduced from what it is on Earth.

There is silence for an instant.

Then Toog says, '*Salvador*, respond please.'

The radio crackles. Nothing. Ziggy knows there's no contact with Houston because their message has to be relayed through the lander until they can set up their own antenna.

More crackling. Toog turns the dial through the frequencies, trying to pick up anything they can.

Then a voice in Russian.

'What's he say?' says Griffin.

Ziggy thinks she's going to be sick. 'Target destroyed,' she says. She excludes the 'nice shooting' she heard in the background. That wasn't in a Russian, or a male, voice. Amira Kovacs? Maybe.

46

Toog crosses himself.

'Jesus Christ, Danny,' he says.

Griffin stands slumped forward. She doesn't know what to say, so she says nothing.

'What now?' says Griffin.

'Give me a minute,' says Toog.

It's a long minute. Ziggy's mind is blank; it's all too much for her. She stands looking out at the lunar surface, white against black, in what should be the most incredible moment of her life, but she is shaking, mouth dry. Is this where she's going to die? Breathe, breathe, accept, focus on the breath. Fuck that!

When her mind does kick into gear again, she thinks of her mom, her dad, Andy. My God, she had been selfish to take this mission. Her parents can't lose another daughter.

'We need to prepare for disembarkation,' she hears herself say, 'now.'

'You speak?' says Griffin. 'Because this to me seems way outside your remit, lady. This is a military decision. By military, I mean man's military, not the typing and blow job section.'

Ziggy ignores the provocation. 'Our best way of staying alive might be to find something the Soviets want behind that hatch. We find out as much as we can, make ourselves priceless. Then they'll want to bring us back.'

'The alternative's to sit here, conserve oxygen and wait for either a relief mission or the politicians to sort it out for us,' says Toog. 'I'd guess that incident up there is going down like cold sick in Washington right now. That's an act of war right there. But they must have planned for it. I don't get it.'

'Are we going back to World War Three?' says Ziggy.

'Nope. We ain't going back,' says Griffin.

Toog waves his hand in dismissal. 'We've got to concern ourselves only with what's facing us here and what we can affect. The guns would be mounted to the lunar orbiters. They're much sturdier structures than the landers and it would be virtually impossible to shoot at us accurately from orbit. So the chances of them arming a lunar lander are minimal. Landing can be hit-and-miss. Even if they do land near us, they'll have sidearms at best. We need to stay alive and hope they find a political solution.'

'It took ten years for the politicians to do jack shit in Vietnam,' says Griffin. 'Get real, Toog. Da Luca, we ain't getting out of here. Let's wait till they land, shoot the fuck out of them and then die or wait to die.'

'That doesn't fit with mission objectives,' says Da Luca. 'We examine, understand and retrieve any technologies that we can. That's the deal.'

She leaves out the other bit – they are to destroy anything they find rather than let it fall into Communist hands. She's not sure she could do that.

'Mission objectives? Well, we can get right on with them if you call your boyfriend to give us a lift home.' His contempt is palpable, like a sensation of something frying, burning. It's a powerful feeling, so powerful Ziggy has to take an instant to refocus. 'Waste some Reds is the only achievable objective here.'

'I disagree. We need to enter that hatch, where at least their numerical advantage will count for less. We need to find what we can, make ourselves valuable to the Russians for our knowledge, and if that doesn't work, maybe kidnap a cosmonaut,' says Ziggy. 'That's our only ride home. We

have to assume we will succeed in this and follow the mission objectives accordingly.'

'The Reds won't give a shit about one cosmonaut,' says Griffin. 'Do you know anything about them? I can tell you, the recruiting poster for the Russian military reads "necessary qualities: expendability".'

'Kovacs isn't expendable,' says Ziggy. 'If she's here, directing this, she's calling the shots – you heard. She is the whole knowledge base on this mission and in understanding what this structure is and how it can be used. They can't afford to lose her. We need to find her and ransom our way out of here. That's our ride home. Maybe to the USSR, but the government can deal with that when we get there.'

'Our ride home's currently scattering itself around the Moon in an orbital ring,' says Griffin. 'This is a kill mission now, no more. We stop them getting out of here with whatever's in there, if anything. If we have to, we smash it to shit.'

Toog thinks for a moment.

'Remember the training. Stay calm. We can survive outside the craft for maybe twenty-four hours. Prepare auxiliary LSS and get ready for EVA. We'll set up the antenna first and talk to Houston.'

'What happens if the Reds get here in the meantime?' says Griffin.

Toog nods. 'See to the weapons. We'll follow Da Luca's plan and access that hatch. I want to get home and if I do, I'm coming back with something to justify the cost of my ticket here.'

Chapter 4

Ziggy is sweating inside her suit as she exits the lander. She tastes the salt on her lips. This isn't heat – the suit regulates that perfectly. It's stress. Thoughts of home come into her mind: Andy, her mom, her dad. Will she ever see them again? No, she can't allow herself that distraction. Focus on the here and now, each step of the exit ladder, each breath. Focus on the breath, in out, in out. That's loud enough in the suit.

Carefully down the ladder, placing each foot slowly and methodically. At the bottom, she stops to find her balance in the reduced gravity. Griffin follows her down, closes the hatch against dust.

At least all she can see is the gold of his sun visor in the glare of the Moon's surface; she doesn't have to see him scowling at her.

Toog – who has been outside for some time setting up the communications dish – asks her if she's OK.

'Yeah.'

'Good. Mission Control are on it. No chance of rescue from home, but they're going to get us a ride out of here with the Russians if they can make the diplomacy work.'

Toog is calm and certain but Ziggy senses that is a front. His voice sounds fragile to her; it's hard to put her finger on how. Maybe the effect of the short-wave. Maybe not. She has an acute sense of people here, beyond any normal empathy. There's a feeling coming from Toog as he speaks, tottering, shaking. She sees a tree bending in a high wind, a black sky. Wow, where did those images come from? She steadies herself, dismisses the vision. She needs to concentrate.

'If not?' she says.

'Your plan's a good one. Party forwards, after me,' says Toog.

'We're not taking the Rover?' says Griffin.

'We're near enough not to need to.'

Each astronaut carries a spare LSS tied to their front, so De Luca feels incredibly bulky. Still, the load isn't heavy, though she's carrying enough to make her knees buckle if she tried it on Earth.

They move across the lunar surface in long hops, not too fast so as to conserve oxygen and to guard against falls. Around them the silicate in the surface of the Moon glitters; distant mountains rise in layers, casting deep shadows against bright white.

Her footsteps leave orange prints in the surface when she turns to see them. If the mission had gone to plan, these would have reassured her – she could find her way back to the lander using them. Now, they just remind her that there's no point in going back. That lander will never dock with anything.

They follow a direction decided in the module based on the landmarks around them – a boulder that lines up with the humped ridge of a mountain of the Taurus Massif.

They pass the Soviet lander from the previous mission, lonely on its field of white, footprints arcing from it to lead the way to the hatch. The journey is not far, maybe five hundred metres, and Toog leads them to the hatch without any problems.

'This is it,' he says.

'Yeah.'

Ziggy sinks to her knees to inspect the hatch, the sensation of slow falling very strange to her.

Up close there is no doubt – that is a *dakini* symbol on the door – the knife of all illusions, the skinning blade that reveals the within. A thrill goes through her. What's in here? Sky-goers? Gods, aliens or at least their remains? Can she touch it? Strictly, she shouldn't, but the cosmonaut touched it before, didn't he? Yeah, and then the hatch opened. Bad idea, best leave the 'first through the door bit' to the military guys.

She presses 'record' on her arm unit.

'Symbol on door seems etched in,' she says. 'It's smoothly done, manufactured looking. I'm fairly sure it's the *dakini* knife as first speculated. In which case, as least one earthly religion is alien influenced. Wow. That's, er, notable.' She feels slightly useless making a recording that it's very likely no one will hear but, even if the next person to listen to that tape takes it from her dead body, it's worthwhile.

'Da Luca.'

'Yeah, Griffin.'

'I loaded it for you.'

He passes her a revolver. She puts it on to the specially adapted holster at her belt. It still makes her shiver.

'You don't use that unless you get a specific instruction,' says Griffin.

'Understood.'

'Good. Let me see the hatch.'

She steps aside. 'I go first.'

'There could be a Russian in there,' says Griffin.

'I'll do it,' says Toog. 'No weapons.'

'That wise, Chief?' says Griffin.

'Don't know, but it's an order,' says Toog.

Toog takes a photo of the hatch door.

'Optimistic,' says Griffin, meaning he doubts anyone will ever see it.

Toog kneels, puts his hand to the hatch. It moves away, up on a hinge and then to one side, silent, of course.

'Oh my God!' says Ziggy, as she sees what's within.

It's a tight tunnel – tight in an EVA suit anyway, stretching away in a long curve down. It's not steep but it's lined top, sides and bottom with a tangle of translucent pink tubes that glow faintly. Each tube is about the width of a garden hosepipe, but they are twisted in on themselves and apparently so deeply layered that no gap appears between them.

Toog takes another photo.

'Better get in, if that's the plan,' says Griffin. 'Commies won't be far behind.'

'OK,' says Toog. He attaches a thin rope to his leg.

'I'll give two tugs, repeated for a total of three times, that's six tugs, for OK to continue if we lose radio,' he says. 'Rapid tugs means pull like fuck.'

'Got it,' says Griffin. 'Send the spare LSS down after you?'

'Yeah.'

Toog goes in head first, crawling. The LSS takes some manoeuvring through the tight hatch, but he gets through with little drama, then he wriggles down.

'Seems to be some sort of liquid in these tubes,' says Toog as he goes.

'Liquid on the fucking Moon!' says Ziggy. She has lost control for a second, she's so surprised. There's a lifetime's work for someone right there.

'Looks like it. I can see occasional bubbles. No sign of fragility, though I'm checking by pressing as I go. There is enough light here for me to dispense with the torch. Proceeding with caution.' Silence for a little while.

Ziggy's mind is racing. These lights are powered by a source that must have lasted millennia. That technology alone would make the entire trip a success. No human-produced battery could last that long. If the lights are powered by the astronauts' movements in some way, that would make them incredibly efficient in transforming physical energy into electricity, or in using that electricity. Again, another huge step forward. She makes those observations on her tape while Toog is still quiet. And then: 'Well, ain't that something?'

'What?'

'A large chamber. It's probably big enough for about ten people. Also lined in the pink tubing. No apparent exit.'

'Shall we come down and look?'

'Yeah.'

'You next,' says Griffin.

Ziggy steadies her breathing, crawls within. It's immediately very dark, so she slides her sun visor up. That's better; the passage is lit by a pink glow. She crawls on, pushing her spare LSS canisters in front of her. She looks down at the tangle of glowing tubes as she goes. They're not made of any material she recognises. They look slightly rough, more plant-derived than plastic but, unable to even feel them, let

alone investigate them closely. The only thing that makes her think the tubes might have a liquid within is that she is sure she sees the occasional bubble, or something floating within – a flash of colour, the edge of some strange shape. That could be the effect of stress, she thinks, or of cosmic particles interacting with whatever's in the tubes, or her eyes, or any one of one hundred fascinating things. This thrill of discovery, or the edge of discovery, almost makes her forget her predicament. To show all this, to relate all this, to open the eyes of humanity! What a privilege to do that.

No time to stop and observe further. Down she goes, emerging about ten feet above the floor of an almost spherical chamber, where Toog takes her spare LSS, before helping to lower her down, her weight nothing to him in the low *g*. Griffin isn't far behind, his feet emerging first, his LSS canisters dragged behind him, falling in with him in a slow-motion tumble.

'You OK, Griffin?'

'Yeah, just wanted to be facing the commies if they come in behind us.'

'They shouldn't be landed yet,' says Toog.

'Standard caution,' says Griffin.

'Sure thing. With that in mind, you gonna stand sentry, Griff?'

'Pleasure.'

'If it's Kovacs, don't kill her,' says Ziggy.

'And how am I going to know if it's the super-important Kovacs if she's shooting at me?'

'She won't be. She'll be behind the military guys.'

'You heard, Griff,' says Toog.

'Got it. I'll do my fucking best.'

Griffin fixes his eyes on the entrance shaft, hand on the gun on his belt.

'What do you think, Professor?' says Toog.

She looks around the chamber. The floor and walls seem to have a slight give in them, though it's hard to tell through the layers of her spacesuit. There! She sees it – a bubble, passing through the pink liquid.

'Is this all there is to it?' says Toog. 'No sign of the cosmonauts who came down here before us?'

'They could have left,' says Griffin.

'Not without their lander,' says Toog. 'Hmmm. This is uncomfortably like a stomach for my liking.'

'Maybe,' says Ziggy, 'though a stomach would have a way out. But we should get out of here at the first sign of anything corrosive.'

'Get out to what?' says Griffin.

Ziggy gets on to her hands and knees to examine the tubes more closely.

'There are certainly tiny bubbles in here,' she says.

'Great,' says Griffin, 'we got lemonade.'

She ignores him, pushes gently at the tubes where they rise in front of her. The pipes part and a hole opens – more than a hole, another small passageway, like a pipe, lined by the faintly luminous, tangling tubes, heading away from her.

She stands up, pushing on the tubes as she does so. Another hollow opens, only the diameter of her palm. She makes a voice recording to note that.

'That's crazy,' says Toog.

Ziggy tentatively puts her hand into the hole she's made and tests its walls. It moves, actually moves position on the wall, as if it were no more than something stuck to the wall,

not sunk into it. She pushes it over to the other tunnel. They combine, making one larger tunnel heading down.

'Mad shit,' says Toog.

'Can we risk going any further?' says Ziggy. 'If these tunnels can open, they can close.'

'Presumably we can open them again,' says Toog. He shoves at the wall. The tangle of tubes yields and another hole appears, a lit tunnel the width of his arm going down.

'This is nuts,' says Griffin.

'Never seen anything like this,' says Toog. 'Any ideas on this, Prof?'

'Only on the practicalities,' says Ziggy. 'We've nothing to go back to, so our only hope is to go on. That's fraught with danger, but I don't see any option than to make a tunnel big enough to walk down if we can and to continue exploring. But there is one question. Why don't the holes appear when we touch the pipes with our feet? I mean, they do when we use our hands, right?'

She pokes at the wall with her toe, almost losing her balance in the low gravity. Nothing happens; the wall remains intact.

'I don't know,' says Toog.

Ziggy has an idea that she keeps to herself. When she pushed at the wall with her hand, she was seeking a way out. When she pushes with her foot, most often she is requiring grip. Does the structure respond to her intentions? She has no time to check that now, as Griffin reminds them.

'We go back, we die sitting in the lander. If we stay here, it takes one grenade and we're done.'

'Are you *agreeing* with me, Griffin?' says Ziggy.

'Who says they brought grenades?' says Toog.

'They'll have come dressed for the party, believe me,' says Griffin.

'Can a grenade explode in zero oxygen?' says Ziggy.

'Wanna sit here and find out?' says Griffin.

'Can it?'

'It contains its own oxidising agent, like the bullets', says Toog. 'It can. So let's press on.'

'Better to die doing something than doing nothing,' says Griffin.

'Yup,' says Toog. 'Let's at least see if we can make this comfortable.'

He pushes at the walls and they give, creating hand-span tunnels down. The others join in and pull the holes across until they have a tunnel wide and tall enough to stand up in.

Toog goes first into the tunnel. Ziggy follows and Griffin brings up the rear.

The tunnel keeps dropping as the astronauts walk down, the colour of the bubble tubes changing from pink to violet, to deep red back through purple, to blue and green. She thinks of the tales of the Vikings, walking the rainbow bridge to Valhalla.

In these tubes shapes float like those strange whorls that appear in the eye when you look at a white sky, though some of them take more geometric shapes: angled lines intersecting, like letters – she sees a T, she's sure, then an X, an arrow, one like a spiky Greek *psi* – Ψ. The others see them, too, looking up in wonder as they float above their heads, or swirl beneath their feet.

'What's this all mean?' says Griffin.

'Don't know.'

'Thought you were the linguist. These are some sort of symbols, right?'

'Who knows?' Ziggy doesn't want to leap to conclusions, largely because it's out of her field of strict expertise, but the symbols in the tubes look like runes, the old Viking system of writing. Or is that just because she had Vikings on her mind and she's reading that into what she's seeing? Human writing, here? No. That idea should be dismissed. Any similarity to earthly systems of representation is a coincidence. And it's a stretch too far to say these shapes are symbols at all. They could be something else entirely. Certainly not runes. But this needs so much investigation, speculation, minds other than her own to address the problem. She thinks of Andy, complaining about having to go to maths conferences. Ziggy was always jealous of his trips away. She could get a lifetime of conferences out of this. She finds herself laughing a little, as she would if she made that joke to Andy and, in that, feels both closer to him and aware of the immense distance between them. Runes, though! She makes a tape note of what she's seen.

Stress is doing weird things to her. She thinks of those Norsemen, loading into their open boats with their families, animals and slaves, riding west into the waves on no more than a promise of new land. Yeah, gotta feel some kinship with that. How did that go? Drowned, dead of disease or butchered by the locals.

'Anything up front, Toog?'

'Nothing, Griffin, just more tunnel.'

They keep going on, down and down, half an eye behind them for what might be following. Air supply down to eleven hours now. They press on until the tunnel bulges out into a wider space. Here the colour of the pipes is different, a sort of stony, cement grey, though there is still a light source from somewhere, wavering like candlelight.

Ziggy touches the wall and is surprised to see a bloom of colour around her hand, a deep ochre. She puts her other hand next to the one already on the wall and the colour spreads further, like paint in water. When she removes her hand, the print of it remains, a pale outline on the earthy colour.

'Da Luca?' says Toog.

'Can you hear something?' says Ziggy.

'No.'

'A whistle?'

'Feedback in your audio loop?' says Toog.

'Maybe. More tuneful than you'd expect from that. Like a boiling kettle but up and down.'

'Nothing here,' says Toog. 'Griff?'

'Negative.'

But there it is: a high, piping sound playing something like a tune, meandering, strange, but a tune nevertheless.

Ziggy wipes her hand across the wall, experimenting to see what effect it might have. Every time she pauses, the print of her hand stays on the wall.

'What do you think?' says Toog.

'Maybe leave it,' says Ziggy. 'I shouldn't have touched it. We can't come blundering in here changing everything, this whole thing needs scientific investigation. Man, we are on the verge of such discoveries. We've got to get back. This is so important.'

'We'll do our best,' says Toog.

Toog stands back from the wall, snaps as she records a note.

'Looks like Lascaux,' he says.

'The fuck is that?' says Griffin.

'Cave paintings in the south of France.'

'No bison here,' says Griffin.

'No, but the effect is similar to the hand painting in there.'

'Or the same as a kindergarten art display,' says Griffin.

'It says the same thing,' says Ziggy.

'What?'

'I was here. It's a statement of . . .' She doesn't bother finishing. She was going to say 'a statement of individuality. Of personhood'. But that's a stupid point to make in this situation. She doesn't know why it came into her head.

'What?' says Griffin.

'Never mind.'

They walk on, the walls dropping back to the blank stony colour.

When they stop to rest, Toog puts a finger to the wall and draws the figure of a horse. It's almost magical to watch, as a darker, charcoal colour emerges under his fingers to shade the mane.

'Look at that,' he says.

'How did you change the colours?' says Ziggy.

'I don't know. I was just thinking of those cave paintings and that's what emerged.'

'Weird,' says Griffin. 'Hey!'

Beyond Toog, from down the passage a swinging white light sweeps the walls.

Griffin comes to crouch beside Toog.

'What's that?' he says.

'I don't know,' says Toog.

Ziggy peers through the weak light. Something is moving down the passage, accompanied by that bobbing light.

Toog gestures for her to lie flat, which she does. Griffin frees his weapon from his holster.

'Detach spare air,' says Toog. 'If this is the Reds, we don't want a bullet hitting a cylinder.'

Ziggy unclips the smaller oxygen cylinder from her chest.

At first, she sees what looks like a floating sphere of silver, then a metal glint beneath it, then a dark form cut out against the light – arms, legs, unmistakably human.

'Reds!' says Toog.

From the gloom, two cosmonauts appear, one with a flashlight in his hand. Both men are armed, carrying stubby guns.

'Da Luca, Soviet wavelength, tell them we want to collaborate to get out of here,' says Toog.

Ziggy quickly adjusts the dial on her chest and says in Russian, 'American astronauts are in this structure. We want to talk.'

Immediately the men raise their guns. A red flash up ahead, a feeling like she's been pushed in the back and all the air is driven from her lungs.

She sees the red flash of Griffin's pistol muzzle as he shoots over Toog's shoulder, though it's all like something from a dream, no sound. A sphere of gunsmoke hangs above him, a perfect ball.

She fumbles with her pistol, hands shaking, breath frantic. Another flash, another white sphere puffs out. She can't get the flap on the holster open. She feels sick, her heart pounds. The thick gloves make it impossible for her to get a grip on the flap and tear away the Velcro.

Griffin comes to her side, hand on her shoulder. He is speaking but she can't hear him. Why can't she hear him?

'I can't hear. I can't hear!' she says.

Griffin reaches forward to the dial of her receiver on her chest, clicks it right.

'Dumb bitch.' She hears that. She still had the radio tuned to the Soviet wavelength.

Toog gets up, gun before him as he ducks down the passage.

'Room clear,' says Toog.

'Enemy neutralised?' says Griffin. His pistol is glowing red at the muzzle, like it's been left in a fire.

'Two dead,' says Toog.

'What happened to talking?' she says, getting to her feet.

'Pieces of shit shot at us,' says Griffin. 'All OK?'

'I felt something,' says Ziggy. 'They might have hit my pack.'

Toog examines her.

'They did,' he says. 'There's a hole. The good news is you're still breathing.'

'The bad news?'

'We'll have to see. Do you notice any effects?'

'No.'

'We'll monitor the situation,' says Toog. 'My gun is very hot, even through my glove. Yours, Griff?'

'No atmosphere to dissipate the heat. I suggest we lay them on the floor for a while so they can cool, or we'll have a misfire on our hands.'

They do that. The pink tubes on the floor bubble around the guns, little stick figures of cowboys running through the liquid away from the weapons. Cowboys? Cowboys? Really? Yeah, that's what they are, unmistakably, wide hats and lassos, pistols jabbing upwards as if shooting in celebration. What can you make of that? Ziggy isn't aware of herself or any of the others showing signs of CO_2 narcosis brought on by too much oxygen, but that has to be a consideration.

'That's something,' says Griffin. 'Yee ha!' So he can see them, too.

'Sure is,' says Toog. 'What does that mean, Da Luca?' He photographs the figures in the tube.

She thinks: are the stick figures a response to the gun? You'd think so. Strange ideas rise in her. Cowboys. Do alien civilisations have cowboys? What if the rest of the universe was one big Texas? It could be worse, she thinks. At least the chili con carne would be good. Ziggy feels odd, light-headed, not quite in control of her thoughts. Maybe she is starting to suffer from narcosis; the pure oxygen has reduced her desire to breathe. But she is breathing and her gauges indicate no problem. She's scared, desperate, and such frivolous thoughts seem madly out of place but also irresistible. Her thoughts are like little stick figures, running off of their own accord.

But cowboys! The astronauts' expectations must be influencing what's in the tubes, or at least their thoughts. Which means the tubes are operating by some sort of telepathy. That would be truly remarkable. She tries to go for Occam's razor, to come up with the simplest explanation. The cowboy figures were already in the tunnel and have nothing to do with the shooting that just took place. That means whoever, or whatever, built this place knew about cowboys and included them in its iconography. So human, then, and recent. But it can't be. No nation has the technology to get a structure like this up to the Moon. She records her thoughts, such as they are.

'I don't know,' she says.

'Glad you came,' says Griffin.

'You got any ideas?'

'I just did my job, lady. You do yours.'

They pick up the guns and walk down the tunnel warily. Here the tubes of the walls glow a faint green. Corpses of two cosmonauts lie in front of her. Away to her left, a glowing green tunnel curves up.

'Two LSS to hijack if we need them,' says Griffin, bending to one of the bodies. 'They're undamaged.' He struggles for an instant to turn off the oxygen valves on a pack. 'And look, in case you were worried they got treated too rough,' he says. He rolls one of the men over to reveal a stubby little shotgun beneath him. Only one purpose for that, a close up man killer.

'How did they get in here so quickly?' says Toog. 'Unless they're the original two who found this place. But they'd be long out of air.'

'Beats me,' says Griffin. 'Unless they dropped right on top of an entrance we don't know about.'

'Griffin,' says Ziggy. She's so shocked, she finds it hard to speak.

'What?' His tone is impatient.

'Look at his face.'

'I tend not to look at the faces of guys I kill, it makes for better sleep.'

'Look!'

He does. She can hear his breathing now on the short-wave. 'Fuck.'

'What?' says Toog.

'His face.'

'Shit,' says Toog.

It's unmistakable: the face in the bubble helmet's is almost the image of her own. But it is not her own. It is her sister's, eyes open. She swallows, looks into her sister's eyes. *Maria, I left you. I'm so sorry.*

'The fuck is this?' says Griffin. 'These are fucking gooks.'

He's shaking the body of the dead cosmonaut, as if he's trying to get it to come round, or to confess, even.

Ziggy goes to the other cosmonaut. The face in the helmet, too, is her sister's. She tries to remember her training, checks the pressure on her suit. It's fine: 3.5 psi. No oxygen problems.

She wants to embrace the body, to hug it close, but it's too odd. Two Marias? This is too strange.

'What?' says Toog.

'That guy ran my camp in 'Nam,' says Griffin, gesturing to the corpse. 'He put me through—'

'That's not what I'm seeing, Griffin,' says Toog.

'What are you seeing?' says Griffin.

'Just a dead Caucasian. Probably literally, given he's Russian. What are you seeing, Da Luca?' says Toog.

'It's hard to say, it's . . .'

She doesn't want to say it's her sister. She can't digest what that means right now.

'What?'

'*Ziggy, you left me.*' Is the voice in her head or on the radio? She can't be sure.

'I . . . Ah!'

The cosmonaut near to Ziggy grabs out at her leg. She shouts, falls a slow-motion tumble, her bulk unwieldy in the low *g*. Griffin levels his gun again but the tangled tubes of the chamber floor are now tendrils, reaching up to ensnare and engulf the bodies of the cosmonauts, pulling them down into a mass of what now seems more like an organism's tentacles, than a technology. Toog stamps the arm away from her leg before the cosmonaut can pull her down with him.

In a blink, the bodies of the cosmonauts are gone.

Griffin points the gun around, as if looking for something to shoot. Ziggy feels a wave of empathy for him sweep over her. He's trying to make sense of what he's just seen, responding to an unconventional threat in a conventional way, trying to kill his way to logic, to understanding. The empathetic feeling is so intense, it almost makes her gasp. Pain, anger seem to sit in him, a fire in his chest. The experience fills her with compassion so giddying that she cries out.

'Oh!'

No one says anything. Ziggy feels absorbed with the incidentals – the movement of the tendrils, the sparkle of the bubbles within them, Griffin's burning emotions. She tastes acid in her mouth when she looks at him; hears, or rather imagines, jangling, crashing instruments – cymbals, violins, drums; feels overwhelmed by a livid crimson that seeps from him – not seen but felt, if such a thing is possible. She cannot quite come to focus on what she needs to; her mind feels like a shopping trolley with a broken wheel, pulling everywhere but where she wants it to go. Did that happen? Did the tunnel just eat the cosmonauts?

'This is odd,' says Toog.

'Nice line in understatement,' says Griffin.

'Don't worry about it,' says Toog. 'Stress, fear, the whole strangeness of this first contact stuff. It's bound to have some unwanted psychological effects. We need to be calm and consider what we've seen.'

Ziggy steadies her breathing. Toog's right. It's hard to imagine a more stressful situation right now, and stress plays weird tricks on the mind.

'The tunnel!' says Griffin. She looks the way he has pointed. The tunnel they came in by has sealed and, when she looks

back, the ceiling ahead flops down to meet the floor. Their spare oxygen is back where they left it. They are in a glowing emerald orb of tendrils with no apparent exit. Then the light fades and goes out.

Ziggy breathes, hard, feels her own fear, that of her companions. The fear is like something solid in the dark, something you could touch. *Maria, I'm so sorry. So sorry.*

'Save batteries,' says Toog, evenly. 'I'll use my flashlight, no one else use theirs.'

He clicks on his light, sharp and bright against the flat dark.

'I'm going to find the O_2,' says Griffin.

He puts his hand to the wall, pulls tunnels together. But this tunnel glows blue and curves down. It's very clearly not the one they came in through. Toog tries the same thing, parting the fibres, creating tunnels. None of them lead back to the discarded canisters.

There is a silence.

Ziggy waits for someone to speak, but these are military men, and they say nothing until they have something to say, which is a while.

'Status report,' says Toog. 'I'm physically OK, about nine hours' O_2 left. You, Griffin?'

'OK. Same for air.'

'Da Luca?'

'OK. nine hours' air.'

'How are we mentally?'

'I saw the face of my torturer on those cosmonauts,' says Griffin.

'Da Luca?'

She may as well say what she saw. The mission commander needs all the information he can get.

68

'I saw my sister.'

'What?' says Griffin.

'Her sister,' says Toog. 'OK. Anything else?'

'I'm getting some strange feelings,' says Ziggy.

'What feelings?' says Toog.

'Strong empathy, sort of overwhelming, really. A sort of synaesthesia. I'm experiencing people like music, or colours.'

'You never had this before?'

'Not like this. It's like a drug experience. Or meditation, but much stronger. Almost like telepathy.' She is recording the conversation.

'See if you can guess what I'm thinking, you fucking hippy,' says Griffin.

'Fear,' says Ziggy. 'But a complicated sort of fear. It's not fear of death. There's a sense you're welcoming this. It's like you feel you deserve it.' She doesn't know where that came from.

'Am I going to meet a tall, dark stranger?' says Griffin.

'If we get back, then one day, I guess.'

'That's a "no", then,' says Griffin.

'Let's check your LSS again,' says Toog. 'You might be suffering from oxygen toxicity. You got any visual effects? Myopia?'

'No.'

He examines her pack. 'Looks OK. How's your heart rate?'

'Elevated, but it'd be a surprise if it wasn't.'

'Damn right.'

Again, silence as Toog thinks.

'There is no plan,' he says. 'We can't look to escape from here, there's nowhere to escape to. As far as I can see, this

entire structure is non-navigable. Even if we can open more tunnels, we have no idea where we're going.'

'We're comprehensively multi-fucked,' says Griffin.

'Yeah. But we have to behave like we're not. There's nothing to be gained by sitting here, probably nothing to be gained by moving. But probably isn't definitely, so we move, if we can. Anyone got any ideas why we might be seeing different things?'

'Beyond oxygen toxicity, which shouldn't be affecting us, then no,' says Griffin.

'No,' says Ziggy.

'OK,' says Toog. 'We'll put that in the "weird shit" box.'

'Not much room left in that box on this mission,' says Ziggy.

'It was full with just you in it,' says Griffin.

Toog puts his hand on Griffin's shoulder. A gesture of 'halt'.

'Griffin,' says Toog. 'I have to address this hostility. If it had emerged during preparation, you would never have made the mission. I need you to can it, Griff. Properly. It's a luxury we can't afford.'

'I'm trying,' says Griffin.

'I'm not asking you to try,' says Toog. 'I'm asking you to succeed.'

'Yeah. I'm going to say this because the mission commander needs to know. It's worse than it was. I mean, I never liked . . . Look. You don't have to like everyone you work with. But I am getting strong feelings of animosity.'

'Towards Da Luca?'

'Yeah.'

'Do you think you can handle them?'

70

'I'll let you know if I can't.'

'Do you need me to take your gun, Griff?'

'Nah. I'm safe. I'm OK.'

Ziggy looks at Griffin. She has a sense of him, very strong, almost as if he's boiling inside. That violent red he sparks in her mind, that music like someone kicking a string quartet down the stairs. These sensations unsettle her. They're not totally new to her – she has a sense of them with people she meets in her day-to-day life – but here they're amplified, not easily dismissed. Yet there's something else in Griffin – a restraining force. He's a soldier, she's on his team. Maybe that's it.

'OK. Let's see if we can open a tunnel,' says Toog.

'Down, up or sideways?' says Griffin.

'I think our best hope now is contact with the Soviets. We only get off this rock in a Soviet ship,' says Toog. 'So up.'

'We just had contact with the Soviets,' says Griffin.

'Bad first date,' says Toog. 'Let's see how the next one goes. We need this Kovacs, if she's here she might even have an idea about what's happening here or how to navigate this place.'

He goes to the tangled pipes of the wall and pushes in his hand. A hollow space appears running perpendicular to the wall. He makes another space next to it, pulls them together, another and another, until they have a tunnel. It doesn't head up but proceeds on the level for about fifty yards in front of them.

'This is weird,' says Griffin.

'Observation confirmed,' says Toog.

They go on along it, coming to an intersection, a kind of T-junction, one tunnel heading down, the other up. The up tunnel is lit in a faint amber light.

'Up,' says Toog.

They walk along, the tunnel folding in behind them as they go, collapsing like a windsock into dead air.

Ziggy prays, to the goddess, to God, eventually to her sister. 'Maria,' she says. 'Help me here.'

The tangle of pipes that surround them seethe and stream with symbols, or at least with things that appear to be symbols, floating dark glyphs in the amber liquid. Some seem familiar, crosses, T's, C's and V's, but others are wholly unfamiliar to her. What they mean, she doesn't know. She should look; they might offer a clue to navigating the ship.

'Hold on,' she says.

'What?' says Toog.

'I need to look at these symbols, to see if there's anything we can learn from them.'

'What the fuck?' says Griffin. 'This is a survival mission at best, probably just a kill mission. We've got no time to be gazing at the scenery.'

'You got something better to do, Griff?' says Toog.

Griffin says nothing.

'If Da Luca can find something that gives us an advantage, I'd say it's worth letting her take a look,' says Toog.

Ziggy bends to examine the symbols more closely.

At first, they seem to be incomprehensible squiggles, little curly and crossed lines swirling in the pipework. Then she notices a pattern: the symbols group in fives. This is a key number in the Twilight Language, one of the central classifications of reality. Is that a coincidence? Very likely, but it gives her an idea.

She puts her entire focus on the symbols, lets the world around her fade away, trying to get a sense of them. Ten

minutes, twenty, go by. After half an hour she is starting to get a sense of them as they pass. Male, Female, Union, Water, Fire. Earth, space, mind, no mind, all mind. Flesh, breath, soil, growth, spirit. The symbols swim before her eyes: crosses, stars, curlicues, moons. Flesh, breath, spirit, seed, flower. The ellipse she sees floating in the tube is the seed, the many-limbed crosses are flowers, then more seeds. Or are the seeds eyes? They have the feeling of eyes, almost the look; seeds dropping from a flower that watches from the wall. Realisation. She has the sensation that the images are something to do with realisation, of enlightenment. Of what? She thinks of the mind, knowing itself, the universe, knowing itself. That is all we are – the universe regarding itself. Did her mom tell her that? Was it some lama wisdom or just something from a cheesy hippy book? She can't remember.

'I'm hoping to run out of oxygen in a minute,' says Griffin, 'just to kill the boredom.'

'Da Luca, how much longer?'

'How long have I been?'

'An hour.'

'I'll . . .'

The symbols swim in her mind, a blow of seeds from a great tree, the tree beneath which the Buddha sat, the cross on which Christ became a god, where Odin hung for nine days for wisdom, where the apple struck Newton. Was that the same branch from which Adam ate, the apple that hangs below the ten sephiroth of God and emanates into the world as Malkuth, creation? She thinks of other trees: ones from a kid's story book, bright and big lined; the big tree in the courtyard at Columbia University . . . She scents pine, sees a jagged symbol dangling before her and recognises it as a

Little Tree car air freshener. She feels that sensation of being in an overheating car on a hot day, waiting for her dad to finish in a shop, sticky plastic seats, the smell of the pine air freshener, a sickly-sweet song on the radio. She wants to get out.

'Open.' She doesn't think the word as much as feel it resonate within her, like a temple gong.

The tubes of the floor peel away from each other, a glowing silver light fills the chamber, and a corridor opens in front of them, dipping down and away from them.

Ziggy feels words rising inside her, like an overwhelming truth that needs to be spoken.

'We need to go down there,' she says. 'She's down there.'

'Who?' says Toog.

'Kovacs,' she says, and surprises herself as she hears the name.

Chapter 5

Down, down, down, bouncing along in the low gravity through the strange, collapsing passageway. The floor is sloped, so they have a muted sense of progress, half tumbling forward but, as the ceiling falls in behind them, the little bubble of space that they inhabit is always the same silver cocoon, its walls swimming with symbols. The space unpeels, opens as they move, falls in behind them so they cannot be sure if they are making progress at all.

'Are we going anywhere?' says Griffin.

'We have to believe that we are,' says Toog.

'This way feels right,' says Ziggy.

'Oh, the feels,' says Griffin. 'Right behind you then, Lieutenant.'

His sarcasm feels acidic, sharp. More feels, she thinks.

'There's something happening here,' says Ziggy. 'Emotions seem amplified. I have a strong sense that we should keep going. I have a sense that Kovacs is down here.'

'A sense?' says Toog.

'It's difficult to explain. There are so many contradictions. It's like a conscious autopilot, like when you go to the same place

at the same time every day and then one day, you're meant to go someplace else, but you forget and go there automatically? It's like that, only stronger. It feels there's a trail here.'

This is a bad explanation, she feels. It's more like a hunch, but a really powerful one. She's certain that if they keep walking, they'll find Kovacs.

'I know what you mean by the amplified emotions,' says Toog. 'I've been thinking a lot about my childhood, like to a point where it's distracting me.'

'My emotions are just how they were,' says Griffin.

'You seem more hostile,' says Ziggy.

'You'll fucking know when I get more hostile, gook!'

'Griffin!' says Toog. 'Act like a fucking soldier!' It's the first time she's ever heard Toog swear, and the sensation that comes from him is not quite rage. Anger, yes, but wobbly anger. A desperation to him. The sensation fades. 'Forward, stay still, go back. We're Americans. Forward,' says Toog.

They press on, Ziggy making taped notes as she goes. She first realises something is wrong after an hour. Her temperature is elevated, she's sure. Toog looks again at her pack.

'It's hard to tell,' he says. 'I can't conduct a proper examination in this suit, but I think you might be leaking coolant.'

'Right. Which means . . .'

'We gotta patch it. Sit down. Open your valve and vent some O_2. That'll cool you down.'

'Won't that waste oxygen?'

'No other good option right now.'

She unscrews the valve on the arm of her suit, imagines the hiss of warm air escaping. A brief moment of breathlessness as the LSS compensates for the sudden drop in pressure and she screws the valve back up again.

Toog gets to work on the pack. She concentrates on her breathing, controlling her heart rate. It feels like having surgery while awake. If he slips, hampered by his gloves, by his big suit and visor, or if he just makes things worse, causes the flow of escaping cooling water to strengthen, she is dead. She'll cook in her own body heat.

Still, if you're going to have someone do this, you'd choose Toog.

'Yeah, you're lucky,' says Toog. 'The bullet's nicked a coolant line, but it's a minor one and I can seal it, I think.' He takes a roll of tape from his utility pouch, cuts off a length with some big-handled scissors.

There's no way to top up the coolant, unfortunately. You'd need access to the undersuit to do that and, in a vacuum, that would be impossible.

'It won't be a perfect fix. You're going to have to void oxygen once in a while.'

'If we kill any more Reds, we better scavenge their air before they get swamped by this floor,' says Griffin.

Ziggy winces at his words, but there's no getting round it: Griffin's reality is now hers. It's looking like a kill or be killed situation – she'll use oxygen at a faster rate if she's having to purge her suit to cool down. They need to find some cosmonauts and kill them.

The symbols swirl in the tangle of pipes above her, seeds that are eyes, eyes that are seeds. 'The cosmos is watching,' they seem to say. Maybe you just put your money where your mouth is – you believe in Heaven, sit down and wait to get there, you believe in reincarnation, sit down and wait for the next life, you believe in nothing, sit down and wait for nothing to come for you, obliterating everything into

non-being, making your life – bad or good, miserable or happy – irrelevant, as if it had never existed. Why fight to survive, to avoid the dark, because when the dark comes you won't know that there was ever light? She's sure that atheism makes its way back to Buddhism eventually, though no religion provides consolation now. She wants to live, to see Andy again, to bathe in all the variety and richness of experience that life has to offer. Can you do that when you have blood on your hands? 'It was him or me,' you'll say, and wonder by what right you decided it was him and not you.

Or perhaps the solidity of belief in Heaven, in the next life, in eternal non-being, will console you as you think you simply sent your enemy to a better, or different, place, or to no place, where the thirty years between you killing him and him dying are irrelevant, unmeaning. These are strange thoughts, far different from anything she's ever thought before. The symbols bubble and seethe. She is dizzy. Griffin's anger sweeps over her, Toog's quiet nervousness, then she tumbles in on herself. It's like being drunk, stoned, something else entirely, like her head is a radio set that's been tuned to one channel and now someone has knocked the dial so it wobbles between stations, picking up three or four at the same time, their waves intersecting, colliding and phasing. Her sister stands before her under a high tower, a grey sky. 'She should have died hereafter.' She hears herself say Macbeth's words inwardly, and it seems not a statement of moral collapse or resignation but just a fundamental truth. Nothing matters and only nothing. Time takes us and leaves no trace.

'Maria,' she says. Maria. Why is her sister's name on her lips? Ziggy didn't steep herself in blood, try to overthrow

kingdoms. She just went home a few days early and her sister died when she should have been there to protect her – take her place, even. She thinks of the stars around her, billions deep in years, an abyss of billions of years before them. In such a frame, our lives are not even blinks. So in fifty, sixty years, maybe in a few hours, she will join her sister in the deep dark and the distance between them will be gone forever. This comes to her not as a series of thoughts but as a deep conviction, a welling sensation she feels tightening her chest, drying her mouth. She needs her sister back, like she needs to breathe. There is only us, us against the dark and we will always lose, always, but we can protect a moment, a moment only, by wrapping it in love.

'What?' says Griffin. 'Who the fuck is Maria?'

Jesus, did Ziggy say that aloud?

'All good for now,' says Toog, patting her LSS. 'Let's go.'

'I'm experiencing some strong emotional effects,' says Ziggy.

'Like what?'

'Religious feelings, memories of my dead sister. Sadness.'

'Yeah,' says Toog.

'You?'

'Some of that. Griffin?'

'Clear as a bell.' The words seem to shake the walls. He's lying, she knows, but that knowledge isn't of the dry intellectual sort. It's a feeling, as close, sick and heavy as a hangover.

'How's that anger?'

'Manageable,' he says. 'Just anger, good, clean all-American anger. No miserable shit.'

'Just you and me, then,' says Toog to Ziggy.

'What are you feeling?'

79

'I think the details are unimportant,' says Toog. 'Some weird grief about people I've killed.'

'You don't normally get that?'

Toog laughs. 'I don't know. Maybe a little but, no, not like this.'

'Fuck that shit,' says Griffin.

'You saw dead Viet Cong in those spacesuits,' says Ziggy.

'Not dead,' says Griffin.

'Then what?'

'If those motherfuckers were dead, I'd be dancing a jig right here.'

'So who were they?'

'It don't matter.'

'Tell her,' says Toog. 'That's an order, Griffin.'

Griffin walks up to Ziggy, pushes the visor of his helmet against hers.

'Horror,' he says. 'The living embodiments of horror. I never killed those guys I saw in the suits, but I wish to fuck I had. And slowly. Happy now?'

Ziggy trembles. She feels as if she could be pulled into Griffin, as if inside him was all space and his anger had opened a little window into that vacuum through which she might be pulled.

'The walls are closing,' says Toog.

They are, too, folding in slowly behind them.

'Keep going,' he says. 'I want no conflict, no dispute. We're down to twelve hours' oxygen, a lot less for Da Luca. Communication will be reduced to essentials. Follow.'

He walks on – the strange, loping, comic moon walk – and the wall unfolds like a blooming flower, peeling back and away as they pass.

Ziggy wonders about the technology here. What's the point in this odd, collapsing, folding tunnel arrangement? Does it allow for more to be crammed into the space? Is it designed for some unguessable, alien reason? It responds to their interventions, both physical and mental, it seems.

But physical is mental, isn't it? The intention to open a hole in the wall precedes the opening of the hole. Their intention to move forward precedes them moving forward.

Toog's light bounces before her. 'The walls are getting tighter,' she says.

The ceiling's dropping, too. It's coming to the point where Toog almost needs to stoop to proceed.

'Fuck,' says Griffin.

Ziggy vents her suit. The heat inside is becoming unpleasant. A welcome rush of cold oxygen filters in. It won't be cold for long, but it's temporary relief.

They have stopped moving. The walls seem to breathe but only in, never out, moving incrementally closer.

'Open a corridor,' says Ziggy.

She puts her hands to the wall to try to pull apart the tubes as she has done before, but they won't budge. The chamber contracts; she stumbles as she is pushed into Griffin. He's too concerned even to shout at her.

'Shove at the walls,' says Toog.

She knows in her heart it's useless, but she does. There is some give – the tubes have an elasticity – but there's no parting them. Symbols collect around her hands as she pushes, letters and glyphs swarming in.

They're on top of each other now, the walls contracting the chamber to the size of a four-man elevator, but there are three of them in bulky spacesuits.

She feels the fear of the other two screaming alongside her own, a harmony of terror.

'Ideas?' says Toog, controlling his voice.

'I'm turning off my O$_2$,' says Griffin. 'Not waiting to be crushed by this shit.'

'Don't do that,' says Toog. 'That's an order.'

The tubes light up about her, tendrils licking at her visor, obscuring all vision beyond them. She tries to push them off, but her arms are trapped. Symbols float in front of her eyes – sycamore seeds, little helicopter blades spinning by in a liquid light, an eight-spoked wheel turning, a snake eating its tail, spirals, a pillar of a house that is not a pillar but a man who is a god, a beetle crawling.

The tubes are tight about her, constricting her breathing.

'Nuzhna pomoshch. Nulevoy signal. Prikhodi nam na pomoshch.'

The tendrils must have turned her radio to the Russian frequency. But these Russians are themselves asking for help; calling for someone to zero in on their signal and come to their help.

'Prikhodi nam na pomoshch.' Signal received. Where are you? It's a different voice.

Are the Russians close?

'Ya ne znayu.' I don't know.

Her legs are bound together, her arms are by her side. She is mummified, living, unable to move, but her suit's LSS is providing oxygen. Breathing is hard but, after a minute, an hour, who knows, the tendrils are no tighter but nor do they let her go. How long will it take her to die? If she can't vent the suit, then not long. An hour, she guesses.

'Can anyone move?' It's Toog's voice. But she heard the Russians on their frequency. What's happening?

'Negative.' It's Griffin.

'Me neither,' she says.

Tinny screams from her earpiece and the tendrils grip once more, this time much tighter, driving all breath from her body. She cannot breathe in again. Her vision swims, little lights emerging at the periphery of her sight. Such a waste. All that love she could have shared. All the knowledge she could have brought back. She could have spent a lifetime solving the puzzle of this place. All gone now. Those thoughts dissolve, tumble away, and in their place another solidifies.

'I'm sorry,' says Ziggy. 'Maria, I'm sorry.'

Her sister is there, in front of her, as the green lady, Jetsun Dölma, the lady born of tears, she who hears the cries of the tormented, lady of the night lotus that opens its blossoms to the Moon; her sister is Green Tara and Blue and Gold and she is Yeshe Tsogyal, the wisdom lake queen who extends her hand to give her the *kartika* – the *dakini* knife.

'I cannot take it,' she says, 'I cannot take it.'

'What is this? What is this?' Griffin's voice saws in her headphones.

Her sister holds out the knife to her and Ziggy's hand is somehow free. Is it her hand or is it her mind that takes the blade? She touches its handle and the tendrils contract, snap away, as if severed. She is propelled up and out of their embrace, squeezed up to find herself standing in a pool of silver liquid, like mercury, two astronaut shapes enclosed in fibrous tubes of light standing next to her. The knife is gone, so she pulls at the tendrils, tears at them and they come away, revealing first Griffin, who fights to free himself once

83

his arms are loose and then sinks panting to his knees, and after Toog, who wobbles forward, sits and stares about him.

Ziggy is sweating. She vents the suit, feels the rush of cold oxygen, but she knows this coolness won't last long. Her suit is thick with insulation and there's no way for the heat to escape. Already her visor is slightly misted and there's nothing she can do to clear it.

From behind the misty glass, she can see she is in a vast space lit by a soft green light. The floor is no longer constructed from the fibrous tubes but is one long pool of silver that comes up to cover her ankles. If the chamber itself has walls, then she cannot see them; it's as if she is standing in the silver pool beneath a vast, starless night. Ascending like a staircase about 200 meters in front of her are three huge discs of a shimmering liquid silver that float above the floor at a height of six, twenty and maybe forty feet, stretching out as far as she can see. It's as if someone has cut off the surfaces of moonlit lakes and left them hanging supportless in the void.

Ziggy can't let herself become absorbed in her wonder.

She looks at her short-wave on her arm. It's turned to the American frequency. So how did she hear the Russians? The dial must have been knocked back again. 'You OK, Griffin?' She is panting, trembling. She struggles to control her breath.

'I'm fine, you look after yourself.'

Ziggy breathes deeply. 'Toog?'

'Yeah.'

'Take a minute,' says Ziggy.

'What is this we're standing in?' says Toog.

'I don't know,' says Ziggy. 'It doesn't look dissimilar to the stuff filling some of the tubes.'

'No symbols,' says Toog.

'Corrosive?' says Griffin.

Toog lifts a shoe and looks at it.

'Who knows? I think we need to get out of it, if we can.'

'How? Where do we go?' says Griffin.

She looks around her. It's as if they are under an immense night sky on an edgeless plain. There are no obvious ways out at all.

'Let's inspect these floating structures,' says Toog.

She is hot now, and the venting of the suit is less and less effective for a shorter and shorter time. She can feel the sweat soaking her Snoopy cap, running down her torso. If the cap gets too wet, some of the communications might short or, worse, the moisture might start to interfere with her breathing. Better not think of that. Better just get on with getting on.

They make their way through the silver pool towards the other floating sheens of silver.

'So how did you get out?' says Griffin to Ziggy.

'I don't know. I started to hallucinate in there and the next thing I knew, I was free.'

'I hallucinated, too,' says Toog. 'You, Griff?'

'Yeah.'

'What did you see?'

'Stuff,' says Griffin.

''Nam?'

'Yeah. Same guys as I saw on the faces of the astronauts. What about you?'

'Religious stuff.'

'Which religion?' says Ziggy.

'Christian. I'm not a Christian but I was raised that way.

Christ was coming to help me. I didn't want his help. It felt just like a different sort of death he was offering me. What did you see?'

'My sister. She helped me cut myself out, I think.'

'Right,' says Toog.

'What does that even mean?' says Griffin.

'She passed me a knife and I cut myself out.'

'A hallucinated knife that cut real fibres?' says Griffin.

'Yeah, I guess. I can't make sense of it.'

'It's just claustrophobia, stress and knowing we haven't got long,' says Griffin. 'I don't know why we're even discussing it.'

'It's a phenomenon we've encountered since we've been in the ship,' says Toog. 'We have to mention everything. We have to have all the information and maybe eventually a pattern will appear, or something we can make sense of.'

They walk over to the hanging lakes. Everything now is a maths problem, but one with too many variables to solve, at least according to Toog and Griffin. Increased effort equals reduced time of movement, but also increased oxygen consumption and body heat. Is it better to move quickly for a shorter time or slowly for a longer time? Is there some optimum rate of progress where she can balance staying cool with the need to move and get out of this place if they can? None of the astronauts can be sure. It's something they haven't tested for.

She vents the suit as she goes but is still very uncomfortable when they stop beneath the vast extent of the silver liquids. There, she vents the suit for a long time. The escaping jet is visible, heavy with the moisture of her sweat.

'Now what?'

There is no exit in sight, not even a wall. The chamber they're in is enormous.

The three lakes rise like a giant's staircase in front of them, the lowest at just above head height. It doesn't appear to cast any shade or to lower the light beneath it in any way. In fact, it's impossible to tell where the light source is.

'Wow!' says Toog.

'Impressive shit,' says Griffin.

They're right. What civilisation had the ability to construct these? And to what purpose?

She checks her oxygen level. Venting at this rate, it's probably good for another three hours. Wow. The reality of her situation strikes her. There is next to no likelihood she will ever see home again.

She sits with that thought, letting the sadness filter through her mind; there's no point fighting it. Tears tickle her cheeks. Mom, Dad, Andy. I'll never see you again. All I want is to see you again. I don't want to be the light on the fucking water over Siesta Beach, I want to be there with you, Andy, your hand in mine, breathing, living, together. She stills her breathing, regains a measure of calm. The surface of the lake that floats above her splashes, as if an invisible fish has just leaped downwards and flown back up within it.

'Did you see that?' she says.

'What?' says Toog.

Again, just above her head, the silver liquid splashes.

'What is that?' says Toog.

'Reds!' says Griffin.

By the time she has turned her helmet-restricted view in her bulky suit, he has his gun out and is firing silently at what, she can't see.

She searches around. Back the way she came, one cosmonaut is hacking tubes of light from the smothered form of

a colleague; another is advancing towards them through the silver liquid, pausing to steady himself to fire, then scurrying forward again in ungainly bounds to stop and fire again. The flash of his gun is red against the darkness of the cavern. The splashes were bullets!

She fumbles for her radio, switches to the Soviet wavelength. 'No use in hostilities! Stop firing! We need to talk!' she says in Russian.

'Fuck you!' comes a reply as the man keeps firing, his gun puffing out perfect balls of smoke, but another voice says, 'Melnyk, stop firing, that's an order!'

The order comes too late because Griffin has hit the shooter. She hears the impact over the mic as a sharp exhalation of breath. The cosmonaut drops his gun, clutches his side and falls to one knee.

'Griffin, stop firing!' she says, but she's still on the Soviet frequency. She clicks her radio over but it's too late. There is a soundless flash, much bigger and yellower than the flash from the gun and, when it passes, both the cosmonaut in the fibres and the one who was helping him are flat down in the silver liquid, one of them with a huge, burned hole where his life support used to be.

'Griffin, stop shooting!' she says.

Luckily, Griffin has to reload and Toog puts a hand on his arm. 'Enough, Griff!'

She bounds over to where the nearest cosmonaut has fallen. His gun is gone, disappeared into the liquid, and he holds his side, doubled up in agony. She clicks her dial over.

'Let me see!' she says.

He moves his hand to reveal a small hole in his suit that he's been attempting to block with his finger. That will need

patching as soon as possible, but it's not immediately life-threatening. The suits are under low pressure, and while a leak is serious, it's not unfixable. There's no way of inspecting any wound, so she'll just do what she can. She takes out an adhesive patch from her pocket, unpeels it and slaps it over the hole in his suit.

'Why did you attack us?' she says. 'Why did you attack us?

'You attacked us!' he says, his voice straining. 'You destroyed our ship!'

Chapter 6

Toog has had an idea about how they might get fluid into Ziggy's suit, using a running Soviet cooling system to attach to the heat exchanger in her suit via a Soviet pipe and thereby pump water in. You leave the circuit open until it fills and then seal it when you see a spurt of water.

He tries to scavenge cooling fluid from the dead cosmonauts' suits but it's hopeless. Griff's bullet hit an oxygen tank and the resulting explosion put enough shrapnel through both cosmonauts to result in the destruction of their cooling systems and the explosion of their tanks. Nothing useful has survived.

While Toog and Griffin inspect the wreckage, Ziggy questions the one surviving cosmonaut. Is he in pain? Does he think he's bleeding? Can he stand? Was Kovacs with him?

'No go here,' says Toog.

'Da Luca, Toog, turn to the US channel,' says Griffin.

Ziggy does.

'What's wrong with taking the cooling fluid from the live one we got?' says Griffin.

'Everything,' says Ziggy. 'Morality, decency, respect for life.'

'OK, Buddha,' says Griffin. 'Try a different question. What's to stop us taking it from this guy?'

'Same answer,' says Ziggy.

'For fuck's sake, this is him or us,' says Griffin. 'You'll see it differently when you start to cook.'

Ziggy says nothing. Griffin's right, in a way. She wants to get back. But what if the price of her slim chance of survival is murder? Could she really be said to have survived, if she somehow managed to return but with a death on her conscience? But could she cook inside her suit as an act of moral will? She's not a monk or nun, to immolate themselves on a point of principle. One thing's for sure. These ethical dilemmas are a lot easier when you're sat on your ass in a seminar.

The remaining cosmonaut is in pain but – after a short wait – it seems there isn't a catastrophic bleed, nor anything to worry too much about in the immediate future. The bullet may have grazed him, or struck something inside. Or it may not.

Once the practicalities are dealt with, they can think a little wider.

'So what's the deal here?' says Toog. 'Ask him what he's here for.'

Ziggy does, but first she asks him his name.

'Melnyk,' he says. 'We're here to find out what happened to our colleagues and to establish the nature of this place, take any weaponry there might be before it falls into capitalist hands.' He speaks in English, so Ziggy tells Toog and Griffin they can turn to the Soviet channel.

'You think we attacked you?' says Ziggy.

'You destroyed one of our orbiters and have attacked us in here. We had no choice but to retaliate.'

'Retaliate?' says Griff, who has clearly tuned to the Soviet frequency. 'You attacked our only orbiter – you spread it into an orbital ring.'

'You have three ships here,' says Melnyk. 'And you fired on us!'

'Horse shit,' says Griffin.

'How many ships do you have?' says Ziggy.

'We have one now, after you destroyed one.'

'We destroyed jack shit,' says Griffin.

'I saw,' says Melnyk. 'And you have repeatedly attacked us since we have been here.'

'Your guys came shooting at us,' says Griffin. 'What d'you expect was going to happen?'

Toog, who has also been listening, it seems, cuts in: 'Where are your colleagues now?'

'I don't know. The corridors here are strange. We got separated. You've killed two of us right there.'

'You started shooting,' says Toog.

'You have attacked and harassed us since we got here. Like your friend said, what do you expect? I'm sorry about your dead friends but, if you come shooting at us, you will get a response.'

'You killed Americans?' says Ziggy.

'Three.'

She hears someone grunt over the radio, an expression of disbelief. Maybe Griffin, maybe not.

'And what happened to their bodies?'

'They were absorbed by the floor. Eaten, almost.'

Ziggy turns to the bodies of the two cosmonauts Griffin killed. Their bodies are still there.

'We had a similar experience,' she says. 'Two cosmonauts

attacked us. We killed them; their bodies were reabsorbed. But that's not happening here, is it?'

'No,' says Melnyk. 'When did this happen?'

'Two or three hours ago,' says Toog.

'We haven't lost anyone until right now. I was with the whole crew just an hour ago.'

'Weird shit,' says Griffin. 'So, who did we kill?'

'Not my friends,' said Melnyk.

'At least you killed something, Griffin, there's always that,' says Ziggy, immediately regretting her sharpness. She is feeling her hostility to Griffin rise. She needs to watch that. It's bad for the mission and bad generally – cosmically, for want of a better word. She's been brought up to believe that meeting aggression with aggression is not the way. Well, half of her has.

'Feels like a good day to me, then,' says Griffin.

'This is very odd,' says Toog. 'So what is your role here, Melnyk?'

'I'm a cosmonaut, a flyer and an engineer.'

'Do you have any idea about the nature of this ship?'

'None at all.'

Ziggy goes to inspect the bodies. Their helmets have protected their faces from the worst of the blast and they are intact. They are just men. No sisters.

'Griffin, come over here,' she says.

'You don't give me orders,' says Griffin.

'I do,' says Toog. 'Do as she asks.'

Griffin walks over.

'What do you see? Tell me about their faces.'

Griffin examines the dead men.

'Nothing weird,' he says. 'Just ugly Reds.'

'Neither Griffin nor I are suffering any hallucinations here,' she says. 'And the bodies are not being absorbed. What do you make of that?'

'Real Reds,' says Toog.

'Yeah,' she says. 'Sorry, Melnyk.'

'Too late for that,' says Melnyk.

Ziggy thinks. They have been suffering hallucinations. Melnyk seems to believe it was his command module that was destroyed, not theirs, so it's possible that Danny's death was a hallucination. It offers some hope. Or not. Even if it is a hallucination, they need to break it to be able to contact Danny again.

'Where is Kovacs?' she asks.

'I don't know who that is,' says Melnyk. 'I told you. We were parted.'

'You do. She wasn't killed by the explosion?'

He says nothing.

Ziggy is stifling hot and vents her suit again, not even daring to look at her gauge to check how much she's got left.

'We need to work on present assumptions until we can be sure otherwise,' says Toog. 'But establishing a way out and returning to at least the Soviet lander seems a good idea. There'll be more air there.'

'Two more spaces on one lander anyway, now,' says Griffin. 'One to go and all three of us have a berth home.'

'Do you know how to rendezvous with the rest of your party?' says Toog to Melnyk.

'No.'

'What the fuck is that?' says Griffin.

His gun is aimed behind Ziggy. She turns to see the silver liquid breached by a mass of fibres, glowing blue in

two separate mounds, six feet apart, each about a foot in diameter. They are rising slowly from the liquid to reveal the shape of cosmonauts, the bulky LSS of the Sokol suits behind them.

'Hold fire, Griffin,' says Toog.

Melnyk runs across the liquid, the silver rising in slow-motion splashes as he does.

'Help me get them out!' he says. 'Help me!'

Ziggy comes to his side and starts stripping away the fibres. They come away easily, melting to nothing as she pulls at them. Melnyk does the same and two cosmonauts fall limp into the silver liquid. Ziggy pulls hers up into a sitting position to stop his pack being contaminated by the liquid.

'My God!' says Melnyk, in Russian. 'My God!'

'What?' says Ziggy.

'Look at them, look at them!'

Ziggy does. The cosmonaut's eyes are rolling; he appears to be fighting for consciousness. There's nothing she can do to help him. In his suit, he may as well be behind a locked door.

Melnyk comes to her side.

'No!' he says. 'No!'

'What?'

'That is Komarov!' he says. 'That is Mishutin! Over there!'

'I don't understand,' says Ziggy.

'These are the men who are dead,' he says, 'These are the ones you just killed!'

Ziggy looks over to where the bodies lie. They are still there.

Komarov blinks, coughs, his eyes steady. He speaks, his lips move, but there is nothing on her radio.

'Can you hear him?'

'No!'

'What are you talking about in Russian?' says Griffin.

'These cosmonauts are the ones you killed,' says Ziggy.

Griffin comes over, looks into Komarov's face. Komarov tries to speak but nothing comes through on the radio.

Griffin bends, removes the pistol from the holster at Komarov's side. As he holds it, it dissolves and becomes just a splash of the mercury-like liquid that falls slowly to the pool at their feet.

"What is this, Da Luca?"

'I have no idea.'

'Having ideas is your job, ain't it?'

Melnyk reaches to Komarov's suit, fiddles with the radio dial but nothing comes through. Mishutin stands up.

He walks towards the floating planes of silver. As he approaches, the silver liquid they are all standing in seems to deepen, coming up to Ziggy's boots first, then her knees, then up to her waist. The liquid is deepening fast.

'Nothing to be done,' says Toog. 'Don't waste effort struggling.'

He's right. There is nowhere to go and nothing to be done. She steadies her breathing, becomes very aware of the bulk of the suit as it floats in the liquid. Behind either Toog or Griffin – she can't tell which – the planes of silver still hover, but they are closer to the liquid than they were. The lowest one is just inches above the silver surface now, and there is Mishutin standing on it. She strains, tries to look up. Still no visible ceiling.

'Floating,' says Toog. 'You, Griff?'

'Yeah.'

'Da Luca?'

'Same.'

She can hear her colleagues on the short-wave but can't see them. She paddles around to see two American spacesuits beside her, two cosmonauts, too. That leaves them a cosmonaut short – Mishutin, who walked to the planes, or whatever looked like him. She has a gut feeling that the cosmonauts who were seemingly reincarnated are not real, that they are hallucinations, or some other class of manifestation of this place. Chimeras – maybe that's the best way to describe them.

She concentrates on her breath, says the Green Tara mantra for *'om tare tuttare ture soha'*. One of its functions is protection from floods, though here she'd prefer a boat of some sort. She only gets a few repetitions through before her radio sounds in her ear.

'There's a cosmonaut on the silver plane,' says Toog. 'Let's get onto it. It may lead to a way out.'

They splash and half-swim towards the plane, the mantra in her mind the whole time. Even though she has experience in a water tank for training, this is something else entirely. For a start, she feels actually buoyant – not neutrally buoyant like in the tank. In her air-filled suit, she's bobbing on top of the liquid and feels she would find it hard to sink even if she tried. In the tank at NASA, you are weighted and floated to be completely neutrally buoyant – if you push down, you'll go down. If you do nothing, you'll stay where you are.

Then there's the way the liquid splashes around them. As they paddle forwards, clumsy in their suits, they raise plumes of silver that fall much more slowly than they would on earth. Ziggy is very hot now but is loath to vent her suit.

She doesn't know what the pressure might be in the silver liquid and whether the oxygen would even come out – it's only at four bars of pressure. Worse, the liquid might foul the vent; she knows nothing about its consistency.

They swim over to the first plane where the cosmonaut is standing, and she puts her hands on it. It's firm, not liquid, and she pulls herself up relatively easily in the low *g*. The others do the same. The liquid level is approaching that of the plane now.

She checks her suit as best she can for any signs the liquid has damaged it. It appears fine, but Toog insists on an inspection for the whole team.

'Fine,' he says. 'At least it's not corrosive.'

'Hey, the day's brightening up,' says Griffin.

'You OK, Melnyk?' says Ziggy.

'I think so.' He still holds his side where the bullet smacked him, but he clearly isn't losing much blood or he wouldn't be talking.

She checks his suit. 'It looks fine to me,' she says.

'How you doing for heat, Da Luca?' says Toog.

'OK, though it's depleting my O_2.'

Griffin comes past her, clicks her radio over to the US band.

'If you need more oxygen let me know. This Red here's got plenty.'

'That won't be necessary,' she says.

'Yeah, it will,' says Griffin. She clicks her radio back to the Soviet wavelength.

A cosmonaut – she really can't tell which one it is, though it's not Melnyk – walks along the plane, away from them.

'Follow him,' says a voice in Russian; Melnyk, she thinks.

'What's he say?' says Griffin.

'Follow him.'

'All communication in English now,' says Toog. 'But do as he says.'

They follow him down the plane. The second plane is just above them, like a ceiling, shimmering with watery light. They've been walking for five minutes when the liquid begins to splash over their boots. She vents the suit, feels the cold oxygen swim over her.

'I say we turn back,' says Griffin. 'We're gonna get squashed up into this ceiling.'

The cosmonaut in front of them keeps walking.

'He may be leading us out,' says Melnyk.

'Or nowhere,' says Griffin.

'What do you think he is?' says Ziggy.

'What do you mean?' says Toog.

'Well, he's not a cosmonaut, is he? Or at least, he's not the cosmonaut he appears to be – Griffin killed that guy.'

'So what is he?' says Melnyk.

'I don't know. But he's not caused us any harm so far. He could be a group hallucination, in which case you'd have to question what is causing it and marvel at how consistent the hallucinations are among members. He could be an alien life form, in which case he may or may not be associated with whatever this structure is. He could be a mechanical product of this structure. Or an externally introduced mechanical element.'

'So what do we do?'

'I think we follow him. There's at least a chance he's doing something. The liquid level's rising slowly. If it gets to our waists, we'll turn back.'

'Seems good,' says Toog.

'Apart from the other guy is still standing right at the edge of the pool,' says Griffin.

She looks back. Another cosmonaut has emerged onto the plane and appears to be watching them.

'I say we follow,' says Melnyk.

'Follow,' says Toog.

They splash down the plane for a long way. She looks above her head. Dark shapes move in the silver of the ceiling. She starts, almost clutches her hand to her chest as a shark suddenly looms out of the silver, or more like a line drawing of a shark, its teeth looming at her before it wheels away again.

'Anyone else seeing anything in the ceiling?' she says.

'Gravestones,' says Toog.

'Skull for me,' says Griffin.

Not too hard to read that one – images of death. It feels almost like they're in a funfair or carnival sideshow, images flashed at them to increase a sense of dread.

'What do you see, Melnyk?' she says.

'You,' he says.

'Me?'

'Astronauts with guns.'

'That seems very specific,' says Ziggy.

'At least it's not the real thing,' says Melnyk. 'I've seen enough of them on this mission.'

The plane goes on and on, no walls, no doorways.

The liquid is at her thighs before Toog says they should turn back.

She wonders what for. She looks at her air supply meter. Two and a half hours' now, but it won't last that if she has to keep venting. Wow. The reality of her situation leaves her

mind numb. She's going to die, isn't she, like soon? Human life, human sanity, exists on the uncertainty of the moment of death. Most people don't know, even as they enter their final second, that their time is up. She does: she has a gauge, a measure of the breath available to her. All that she can be sure of is that her existence in this life will be shorter than what's indicated on the dial.

The cosmonaut they were following stops and turns to face them.

'What?' says Griffin, as the wave strikes.

Ziggy is lifted up, smashed into the ceiling. She can't tell what's up or down; her visor is submerged in the bright, silver liquid, her body shoved into a tumble. She can see nothing, though it is not dark, just that blank silver light.

'Hello! Hello!'

She feels her helmet knock on the ceiling, puts her hands above her head to feel where it is. The liquid pressure feels immense, squeezing her suit, shoving her hard. The ceiling has the properties of a membrane; she feels it stretch, push back and then snap away as if she has burst through the surface of a party balloon.

The liquid drains from her visor. The light is bright. Next to her, the cosmonaut stands but he is melting, as if he were a candle, the suit sloughing away to reveal nothing within. He just dissolves, collapses in on himself.

She looks around her. Even through her suit, she can hear the noise. Traffic. Horns honking. She looks away from the cosmonaut to see where she is. She is in a street, the street where her office was in Baghdad. It's a market day and trucks queue full of livestock, vegetables, clothes, while people are setting up stalls. A man drops a cabbage, and it falls slowly

to the ground. Kids chase a football in cartoony big bounds down the street, the ball itself bouncing extravagantly high, falling as if through an invisible jelly.

No one seems to pay her any attention in her spacesuit. The sun is bright and there is a gun in her hand.

Chapter 7

She walks across the road to the TV shop below the office. She takes the stairs up. Her suit is bulky, but she doesn't feel heavy in the low gravity.

She opens the frosted glass door to the office. Her sister, Maria, looks up from behind her typewriter. Fear creases her face, though; she takes out the sheets of paper she's working on, puts them down on the desk. Very like Maria. If she's going to lose the typewriter, it won't be with whatever she's typing in it.

'What do you want?' says Maria in Arabic.

'Mare, it's me,' she tries to say. But that's not what she hears. 'You owe,' she replies, in Arabic.

'If it's money, there's some in the drawer.'

'Maria. It's Ziggy. Maria.' But again, the words don't match. 'You owe,' she says again. She holds out her hand to Maria. There is a gun in her hand.

'If you lay one finger on me, I'll jump through this window, and you can do your explaining to the police. This is an important project. The governor himself invited us here! I am a friend of the governor's, and he is a friend

of Saddam's!' She speaks her last sentence while getting up to take a heavy Sellotape dispenser from the desk. She holds it up threateningly.

'Maria! It's Ziggy! Maria!'

Do not squeeze the trigger, Ziggy, do not squeeze the trigger. She feels her grip tighten on the gun. She is trembling. 'No, no,' she says. She sees the flash of the pistol, flame at the barrel.

Her sister clutches her chest, says 'Ziggy!' and dies.

Ziggy is shaking. She should have been there to stop it. She was there to cause it. She was the killer; she fired the gun. This must be some sort of narcosis. But that thought itself does not feel narcotic. That is to say, it's a clear, contained thought that feels like it's the product of reason, not one of those woozy, half-self-aware, sniggering, sneaking thoughts you get after a blast on a joint.

She breathes hot air from her roasting suit. She vents to feel the coolness of the new oxygen on her skin, breathes deeply. She didn't kill her sister – she was in New York when Maria died. But the gun is in her hand.

The bright sun streams through the blinds. Her sister's body lies in front of her, folded over forwards on her knees, as if in devotion or prayer.

Her sister is folded like a lotus; Ziggy's thoughts feel folded like a lotus, turning in on themselves. She struggles for clarity, but she can feel her mind fogging, thoughts becoming unwieldy, encumbered.

She breathes. Breathe. She hears her mother's voice, helping with the meditation. Breathe. Breathe.

Maria is in front of her, her body slumped. A bloom of blood seeps through her white shirt at the back. It is a lotus,

white kissed with red, creamy petals in a loosening bud. The lotus. The lotus. The lotus. It's all the lotus.

She reaches out to her sister, to touch the blood flower and, as she does, the office dissolves, melts into silver; walls, desk, the typewriter, the windows and blinds liquify, fall and swirl away through the wound lotus on her sister's back until there is nothing left, and her sister's body falls in on itself to disappear through the bloom of its own blood.

'You OK, Da Luca?' says Toog.

He is bending over her; she can just about see him. The inside of her visor has misted with breath.

She tries to speak. Toog takes the gun from her hand.

'Did you shoot this?'

'I think so.'

'What at?'

She just grunts, can't tell him.

'You saw some weird shit,' he says. 'Same as me, I guess.'

'Yeah.'

'She's cooking in her suit. We're going to have to vent a lot of O_2.'

Toog opens the vent on the front of her suit, and she feels the cool air coming in. He leaves it open for a long time and the visor clears slightly. She looks around her. Toog, Griffin and Melnyk are there. There's no sign of the resurrected cosmonaut they followed, nor the one who was behind. There is a greenish light. They are at the bottom of some sort of pearlescent sphere, its radius about three times her height. It seems to be submerged in some liquid, as shapes and symbols float by its exterior – letters, runes, hieroglyphs, flashes of what appear to be strange scripts, squiggles and crossed lines.

'You're down to maybe an hour's oxygen,' says Toog, 'given the need for venting.'

'US frequency,' says Griffin.

Toog clicks over his radio, does the same for Ziggy.

'We have the adaptors,' says Griffin. 'Seems to me we've got a ready supply of O_2 right here with this Russki.'

'Don't do that,' says Ziggy. 'What happened?'

'We were engulfed by the liquid,' says Toog. 'I think we were pushed through another membrane. It appeared to make this sphere.'

'Any more strange effects?'

'Hallucinations again,' says Toog.

'Yeah,' says Griffin. That's a first, Griffin admitting to any mental effects at all here.

'Bad stuff?'

'Yeah.'

Melnyk gestures to them. He's clearly uncomfortable being left out of the conversation.

'I'm going to kill him and take his oxygen,' says Griffin.

'He's our hostage,' says Ziggy. 'He's the way out.'

'No way out for you without oxygen,' says Griffin.

'No way out for you without Melnyk,' says Ziggy. 'You suddenly decided you like me, Griffin?'

'I like any American better than any Red.'

'For the minute we need any expertise Melnyk can offer us because I can't see a way out for any of us right now,' says Toog. 'Return to Soviet frequency.'

They click their radios.

'Hello,' says Toog.

'Do I live or die?' says Melnyk, who is no fool and has guessed what the conversation was about.

'Live,' says Toog. 'We need you as a hostage.'

'That's a relief. Have you thought about what we are going to do here?'

'Not yet. Let's do that now.'

A deep noise sounds, an undersea clang, like metal on metal. The sphere shakes and turns and everyone loses their footing and ends up beside Ziggy sitting down.

Another deep noise, this time like a boom.

'I'm scared,' says Ziggy.

'Keep that shit to yourself,' says Griffin.

The symbols outside the sphere now have a drift; they fall from top to bottom. The sphere is not steady any more, but vibrates. It seems to be travelling upwards – either that or it's stationary and the symbols are flowing past them.

'What do we do?' says Melnyk.

'I don't know,' says Toog. 'It appears we're in some sort of liquid again. If we try to get out of this bubble, we don't know what we'll end up in.'

'How did we get into it?' says Griffin.

'I don't know. We were rising up in that liquid and pushed through the floor above us, I think. Maybe it made some sort of integument around us.'

'Why would it do that?'

'Perhaps it's part of the ship's immune system,' says Melnyk.

'What?' says Griffin.

'Everything we've seen about this ship suggests it has some organic qualities. We are foreign bodies, invaders. This may be its way of dealing with us. It wraps us up in skin, waits until we die and then dissolves us.'

'Thanks for the comforting thought,' says Ziggy.

'It's not a matter of if we're going, but just when and how,' says Griffin.

'Got that, Griffin,' says Ziggy.

'Enough,' says Toog. 'Let's concentrate on working out what we know. What did you see when the liquid engulfed us?'

'I had a strong hallucination,' says Melnyk.

'What?'

The cosmonaut breathes out, audibly.

'My neighbour in Mariupol was taken by the KGB, when I was a child. His wife tried to stop them and they knocked her down, she hit her head. They left her there in the street. I saw all that. I saw it again before I arrived in here.'

'From what point of view?' says Ziggy.

'What do you mean?'

'Were you seeing it with your own eyes, or someone else's?'

'I was the KGB man,' says Melnyk. 'I saw myself hit her.'

'What's the point of this?' says Griffin.

'We need to establish what's the nature of this place,' says Melnyk. 'Are you an idiot?'

'We'll see who's the idiot when I put a bullet through your visor and harvest your tanks for oxygen,' says Griffin.

'Guys, this isn't helpful,' says Toog. 'I had a similar thing. I was back in Vietnam but this time I was flying a MiG. I got shot down.'

'Do you feel guilty about what you did in the war, Toog?' says Ziggy.

'You should, you were fighting an imperialist war,' says Melnyk.

'Not that I know, or knew,' says Toog. 'The other guy up there was trying to kill me. I had to kill him first. There wasn't a lot of deeper thinking attached to that.'

'How did the scene fade, Toog?' says Ziggy.

'It didn't fade, it collapsed,' says Toog. 'I ejected and the whole thing just melted in front of me.'

'You didn't see anything religious?'

'Not this time. Like I said, I'm not a religious guy,' says Toog.

'Unusual for an American,' says Melnyk.

'Less so than you'd think,' says Toog. 'I'm a scientist.'

'Gotta feel like praying now,' says Griffin.

'No,' says Toog.

Ziggy feels like praying but can't afford the time. The way into this place might also be the way out. Or it might not, but what else has she got?

'How did your scene end, Melnyk?' asks Ziggy.

'My neighbour had a rose at her neck. Not a rose. I don't have the word in English. A design, six petals in a circle. It's a folk symbol, I don't know what it means. In my hallucination, I went to her and looked at that. The whole scene collapsed in on it. Like bathwater down a plughole. Swoosh.'

Griffin slumps inside his suit.

There is a pause and then he says: 'That was exactly like what I saw. Back in the jungle, we were looking for gooks. We came across a village. I entered a house, a hut, really. A kid came running out and I shot him. I didn't think much of it at the time. He was ten or so. Probably hung up some of the claymores that killed my friends. That's what I saw. From his view.'

'And how did you get out?'

'Heap of shit,' says Griffin.

No one says anything; they give him time.

'In the house was a sort of carving, a kind of goddess with lots of arms. In the hallucination, it got up and led me out of the door. Then everything melted and I was here. I walked past myself in the doorway.'

'We're seeing ghosts,' says Melnyk.

'In Toog and Griffin's case, they're being ghosts,' says Ziggy. 'Why not us?'

'What did you see?' Toog asks Ziggy.

'I saw my sister's death. Though in the hallucination, I was responsible for it. I shot her.'

'All we can say,' says Melnyk, 'is that this is a gateway to the unconscious. Or that's how it seems. Again, that might be part of the ship's defence mechanism.'

That might be true, but it kind of assumes that the ship has a defence mechanism. This might be something else entirely, thinks Ziggy, though the men seem fixed on the idea that this is planned as a hostile environment.

'You seem sure it's a ship, not a city, not a house, not anything else,' says Toog.

'Our adviser was very sure that's what it was,' says Melnyk.

'And your adviser is?'

'We know about Amira Kovacs,' says Ziggy.

'Your mission leader?' says Toog.

'C'mon,' says Melnyk, 'it's traditional to at least tie me to a chair and beat me about a bit before giving up that sort of information. We can't cut corners here.'

'What did she expect to find here?'

'She? I don't recall a *she* aboard. Maybe a cat snuck in at take-off.'

'We're all going to die,' says Ziggy. 'Whatever you tell us will go nowhere. If what you tell us enables us to survive,

which is unlikely, then you are at least alive to deal with whatever the consequences are. I believe we may have suffered a hallucination that our orbiter was destroyed. Until we can break that hallucination, we can't contact it. It may as well be destroyed. Together, Kovacs and I might work out what to do. Or, if you've been told anything, you need to tell us now. We're your ticket out of here, too.'

Ziggy breathes, her suit very hot. Air is running low; she can't afford to keep venting and must just endure as long as she can.

Melnyk whistles into the radio.

'Look, I give you this. Our party is six strong. Me, three other pilots, one marine, one specialist.'

'You have marines here?'

'A marine.'

'In space?'

'Space marines, yes. Cool, eh?' says Melnyk, with a little laugh. 'We don't know what we'd be facing here.'

'What did you think was here?'

'Weapons?' says Griffin.

'No. No one was clear. Just something fundamental, that's all.'

'Fundamental to what?' says Ziggy.

'Us. Life. Something to do with the start of life on Earth.'

'We're on the Moon,' says Griffin.

'Don't ask me,' says Melnyk. 'That side of the mission isn't my concern.'

'And what's your concern?' says Griffin.

'Flying. Engineering. Equipment repair and operation.'

'So how about my suit?' says Ziggy. 'The cooling's compromised and I'm having to vent oxygen.'

'I saw,' says Melnyk.

'Is there anything I can do?'

'No. Not in this environment.'

'Should I wait for the temperature to build or vent little and often?'

'I don't think it makes much difference,' says Melnyk.

The sphere shudders and then is still. Outside, the symbols have gone.

A spot of white light is visible at the top of the sphere, just off centre. It has the quality of sun behind clouds.

Toog stands, presses his visor to the wall of the sphere.

'I don't think we're in liquid any more,' he says.

'Should we try to get out?'

'I don't want to die inside a fucking bowling ball,' says Griffin.

'Where would you prefer to die?' says Melnyk.

'Earth,' says Griffin, 'but as that's not an option, killing a commie would be second favourite.'

'I'll try the wall,' says Toog.

He tries to part the material, like they did in the tunnels they first encountered, but it doesn't yield.

He takes out a knife from his utility pocket and scores it along the surface of the sphere. Nothing. Not even a mark.

'Say "open sesame",' says Melnyk.

'Glad you find it so funny,' says Griffin.

'I'm Ukrainian. We expect worse than this,' says Melnyk.

'Yeah, well, I got a feeling you won't be disappointed,' says Griffin.

Toog pushes at the wall, scores it again without effect. He won't allow Griffin to shoot at it. Half an hour goes by. The gauge on Ziggy's arm is entering the red zone and she needs to let out the hot air again.

Griffin comes over to her, clicks her radio to the US channel, does the same for Toog.

'We're getting to the point of no choice here,' he says. 'The Red has air, he has batteries. We need both those things if we're going to survive any longer here. It's time to kill him.'

Toog exhales.

'How much air, Da Luca?'

'thirty minutes.'

'Yeah, it's that time.'

'I'm going to shoot him in the face,' says Griffin. 'That way we won't run the risk of damaging anything valuable.'

'No,' says Ziggy.

'No?'

She's been thinking about this ever since they captured Melnyk. She can't put her own survival above that of the mission. We all go to extinction in the end, whether to nothingness or, through many lives, to Nirvana. Either that or it's Heaven. She hopes it is Heaven, or something like it. She has seen herself as a goddess flying, she has seen the *dakini*, seen her sister. Perhaps they are more than hallucinations and there is more than the world we see. Whatever, the end is the same. Also, she's in the military now. Laying down your life for the team comes with the job.

'No. You have your hostage. It's a pyramid of needs, isn't it? Both you two could fly a lander, both you two have military and engineering experience. I'm the luxury here. Griffin was right from the start, I don't know why he's changed his mind. I'm the cargo. I was mission critical when we had a way to return. Now the mission is only about getting the most people back alive. It should be me who's sacrificed.

You know my thoughts on this place. If you get back, make sure NASA gets to hear them.'

'Recap.'

'This is some sort of consciousness enhancer. It's giving form to our fears, but I don't think it's inherently hostile.'

'What is it then?' says Toog.

'Us, I think. It is whatever we are. It's a shame. I think if I was here longer, I might open some sort of dialogue with it, or if we'd found Kovacs maybe we could have done that with her expertise. But that's just an "if only".'

'This don't sit well with me,' says Griffin.

'To be honest, Griffin, I think it should be you,' says Ziggy. 'You're the paranoid, hate-filled macho man, so who knows how much of this shit is on you? I realise, however, that you wouldn't sacrifice yourself in this way, and that overpowering you isn't an option, so it has to be me.'

She feels a wave of anger coming off Griffin like a rocket blast.

'Maybe you should die,' he says. 'How much of the shit is on you?'

'I'm not going to end this in confrontation,' says Ziggy.

'You just did,' says Griffin. Hot shame comes over her. Of course, she allowed her anger and frustration to get the better of her. Why end in acrimony? She's blaming Griffin for things he can't help, the experiences he's been through, the torture he's endured. She wants to say 'sorry' but the words won't seem to come. How much further has she to travel down the road of compassion, to follow the example of the Buddha? A lot longer than she's got in this lifetime, it appears.

Toog leans on the wall of the sphere.

'It's a brutal calculation,' he says. 'But the conclusion is inescapable. Killing Melnyk will be a risk, discharge of firearms again, a fight, too many variables. And Ziggy is right. Melnyk has hostage value. I suspect we may only be prolonging the inevitable anyway. There's no immediately obvious way out of here. This could be where it ends for us. You really OK with this, Da Luca?'

'OK would be putting it strongly,' she says. 'I can't see another way, though.'

'How about we kill this guy, then fight the Russians when we find them?' says Griffin.

'Too much uncertainty,' says Ziggy. 'We, you, could avoid a fight with Melnyk as a hostage.' She desperately wants to tell Griffin to save her but there is no point, in the short term or philosophically. They will all die here, it's just a matter of when.

She feels uncertainty coming from Toog, real, dreadful, deep uncertainty. He is thinking of shooting Griffin, for sure. *Kill him, she thinks. Kill him.* The thought is as horrible as it is unpreventable. She cannot master herself; she wants to live and wants Griffin to die. Could she shoot him?

Griffin takes his gun off his belt.

'You are not to shoot Melnyk, that's an order,' says Toog.

'Wasn't thinking of it,' says Griffin. Ziggy catches his meaning and Toog does, too. Any reassessment of mission priorities that involves Griffin getting a bullet to the face isn't going to fly. The barbarity of her own desire to kill him sickens her. Her own sacrifice is the only moral path.

'It's me,' she says. 'It should be me.'

A silence and then:

'Goodbye, Da Luca. You're a hero,' says Toog.

Ziggy doesn't feel like that; she feels like a failure for dying so poorly, raging, not composed and calm. She feels a failure for even coming. She has done something remarkable, seen remarkable things and maybe even offered an insight that, if NASA ever get to hear it, could prepare the way for future missions, but it's not her who will pay the cost. That will be left to Andy, to her mom and her dad. Another daughter gone.

'I'm just going to meditate now,' says Ziggy. 'So I'll be turning the radio off.'

'Whatever you need to do,' says Toog.

She clicks off the radio, vents the suit of the precious oxygen to cool it.

Then she breathes, concentrating on her breath, reciting her Shakyamuni mantra, to dispense with all the harmful actions she has done through 800,000 aeons, to dispel the thoughts she had towards Griffin. *Om Muni Muni Maha Muniye Soha*. She sees the Buddha in front of her, his face radiating light upon her, which she reflects on the whole world. This is unlike any meditation she has done before. Here, on the Moon, it seems she is capable of going further, faster than she has ever managed.

She falls into her breath, a dizzying, rapturous loss of personality. No I, no centre, no outside, no inside. The word 'she' no longer works. 'We', 'everything' – something like that is better but still not close. The universe looks at itself and holds itself instantaneously and completely in thought. Lattices of energy sparkle and are known totally, from the tiniest structures of the atom to vast suns blazing over infinities of space, all boxes within boxes, lattices within lattices, the space between the points of energy as present in her universe mind as the points themselves.

There is no time, or there was none. Time none. None. Experiences like this cannot be examined while they are being lived. Only afterwards, and in glimpses, might they return.

Breath tightens. Constriction is there.

In the sphere, the spacemen stagger and sway, and this is known by the universe too. The sphere is shrinking in on them. Griffin saws at its skin with his knife but it will not relent. This is a different material from the fronds of light they cut away to enter the silver lake. That is noted in the meditation – which is a thing of itself, beyond Ziggy and her personality.

The universal attention, wide and inclusive, contracts now to the surface of the Moon. It sees a ship, embedded in the lunar rock and soil like a seed on stony ground. It is a power source; more than that, it is an information source, a structure built in something beyond the observable and the physical.

Other things are known, too. Toog is bending over a body, 'her' body: The word 'her' seems funny to the watching attention; it sparks the feeling you might have looking back at a photograph from ten or twenty years ago, observing the hairstyle and saying to yourself, 'What was I thinking?' There is an association between the attention, whatever it is that comprehends Toog's concern and Griffin's anger and Melnyk's resignation and the woman who lies dying in the spacesuit, but it's an association marked as much by difference as it is by similarity.

'She's very low on air,' says Toog.

'Might be better to shoot her than let her choke it out,' says Griffin. He is still stabbing at the wall of the sphere.

'No shooting,' says Toog.

'I could do with a drink,' says Melnyk. 'And a cigarette. Trust me to die where I can't have either. I bet they even get a little vodka before they shoot them in the gulags.'

'I'm going to shoot this bubble in a minute if it keeps closing in,' says Griffin.

The attention sees that the bubble does contract. The four bodies within it are now almost on top of each other.

The attention is the bubble. It feels its elastic skin, its need to contract. It is not a pleasant feeling; it's nervous, unsettled. The attention puts it aside, not quite releasing it but backgrounding it, as the stars, the planets, the lives of teeming billions of things throughout the universe are backgrounded. There is a feeling that something is separate and that needs to be united, widely and specifically.

In a cavern, in the ship, are four lattices of energy that speak and breathe and argue, and one of those lattices needs to come to the four other lattices in the bubble. The cavern is not like the rest of the ship; its wall is glittery with minerals, deep red and blue and green. There is a structure in those minerals and one of the breathing lattices is open to their influence, subtly rearranging under its sway.

A tunnel opens in the cavern, and the attention is aware that it itself has commanded it to open.

The bubble contracts again. The attention is widening now, changing. Jupiter squats in space within the attention, a giant marble, wonderful and terrible. Saturn's rings glitter in sunlight and a child throws a baseball to its father, calling 'Crazy Horse hits 'em with the screwball!'

In the bubble, Ziggy's air gauge reads empty.

The attention widens again, sees beings in the ship, fast-moving lattices of energy who configure one place and then

another and are in the ship and on a moon vast spaces away and who travel space like light beams, eternally still as galaxies turn and whirl, galaxies who are part of the attention itself. The beings have been here, are not here, and want to be here. Or rather their desire is here, in the walls of this ship; it exists itself as an energy. This makes sense only in the moment of its thinking, like logic from a dream.

The universe beholds itself. The attention diffuses. In Gainesville, Florida, a math grad looks at a picture of funny-looking girl in a spacesuit. She carries the helmet under her arm. He looks at her, she looks at him and they are the universe beholding itself. Even that point of view melts and it only seems right to say that the universe beholds. And that's it. The attention falls through the young man's love, is frozen in that moment and then it holds everything, everywhere, simultaneously within itself. All the bubbles of the universe rise, petrolled soap skins floating against a bright sun, deep ocean burps of gas, foam on surf, a sphere of energy, a universe, boiling up through nothing, reality perched on a membrane. All bubbles must burst. All burst.

'She's dead!' says a voice.

The bubble bursts.

'Shit!' says another.

'Don't shoot, don't shoot, this is stupid!'

A flash of yellow, perceived, not seen. Red first, then yellow. Time is slow. Smoke drifts.

'Hold it! Hold it!' A woman's voice.

Pulled, thumped, turned, twisted, Ziggy breathes again. Faces are all around her, visored, helmeted, cosmonauts and astronauts. A woman bends over her.

She sucks in air, cold and beautiful, puts her hand to her

face, feels the rough surface of the glove against her nose and she realises, she's not wearing a helmet.

'Zigsa Da Luca!' says the woman – she hears her voice buzzing in the earpiece of her Snoopy cap. 'You called us here. How did you do that?'

She looks up, her vision swims, she coughs, and gasps. When she finally manages to focus, she sees the label on the suit of the cosmonaut: 'Kovacs', it says.

So, according to Toog, this is what happened.

Ziggy stopped breathing in the bubble. No drama, no thrashing, she just stopped breathing. The bubble contracted one last time, until the astronauts were squeezed together tight, and then it suddenly expanded and burst.

Then it was chaos: the Russians were on them. As he talks, it's as if his words cast a spell. She can see what he's describing as if she had witnessed it herself or, rather, she sees more than he is describing. He gives her the bare bones and his words flare and pop in her imagination. 'I don't know who fired first, but someone did. We closed and there was fighting until Kovacs called a halt. I did too. We need to help each other here.'

She sees the flash of a gun, a plume of flame, sees sparks dropping red from the end of the pistol, gunsmoke hanging in wisps; tinny shouts and screams; men bounding towards each other to grapple, falling in the slo-mo of the weak gravity.

She feels fear like acid in her throat, anger thumping a blood roar at her temples; she feels she is going to be sick, just with the intensity of emotion, the horrible potential for

the loss of human life. That, in particular, feels repugnant to her here. She feels the miracle of existence; that matter – the same stuff that comprises her suit, her boots, her gloves – should wake to regard itself.

She must communicate these feelings to Toog and the others – for the mission, yes, but also because she feels the burning need to share them.

'This is wonderful,' she says, but doesn't know why she said it.

'She is delirious,' says Kovacs. 'Give her a minute.' Her voice sounds in Ziggy's earpiece. Kovacs still has her helmet on.

'You saved me.'

'Melnyk saved you. He told me you were out of air.'

She sees that scene, too, as if outside herself and observing.

Kovacs reaches for Ziggy's helmet. Griffin goes to stop her, but Toog holds him back. She twists off the helmet and immediately starts compression on Ziggy's chest, calling for the men to help her. There is a desperation to Kovacs in these moments, beyond the natural concern for another human life. Something precious is threatened, something personally valuable to her.

Ziggy hears Toog's account and is simultaneously watching Kovacs resuscitate her from outside but also looking up at her, consciousness blinking, coughing, spluttering back.

'There's air,' says Toog. 'There's air!'

Ziggy is turned, put face down into the recovery position. She draws in breath in shock. There is no visible support, no floor. It's as if she is floating a hundred feet or more above a churning silver river, but she can feel the floor hard and cold on her face.

'How the fuck did you know to do that?' says Griffin.

'Secondary muzzle flash,' says Kovacs. 'Every time you've shot at us or we at you, the muzzles have flashed predominantly red. That's because only the oxidising agent in the powder was burning. The muzzles stayed red for a long time because there was nothing for the heat to dissipate into. It had to warm the whole gun, then your gloves, your suit, for it to go away. There was also a noticeable white flash when I fired, between the cylinder and the barrel, primary muzzle flash. You wouldn't see that in an atmosphere because the heat would dissipate so quickly. Here there was no white flash from anyone's gun, just a big yellow flame, sparks following the shot. I also noticed a quick cooling of my gun, the red glow fading instantly. I wouldn't have absolutely concluded that meant we were in an oxygen-rich atmosphere, certainly not enough to be able to breathe, but, since our friend here's situation was hardly likely to get worse if I removed her helmet, that is what I did.'

'What's your job?' says Griffin.

'Same as hers,' says Kovacs.

'So how the fuck do you know so much about ballistics? Who's ever heard of all that shit?'

'I paid attention in training,' says Kovacs. 'How come you know so little?'

'We never even discussed how guns behave in space,' said Toog.

'Not very thorough,' says Kovacs.

'You were pretty thorough when your gun brought down our orbiter,' says Griffin.

Kovacs looks genuinely surprised. 'Our ship carries no armaments,' she says.

'So what did we hear? Where did our orbiter go?'

'I don't know. We've seen a lot of strange things on this mission. But I expected that we would.'

'Why?' says Toog.

Kovacs smiles. 'That's classified for the minute, I'm afraid.'

'Bullshit!' says Griffin. 'You killed our friend and stranded us here.'

'You're an idiot!' One of two other cosmonauts who was with Kovacs squares up to Griffin.

'Leave it, Lenov! So where are the rest of Melnyk's team?' says Kovacs. 'Where are they?'

'Dead,' says Melnyk.

'Who killed them?'

'This man here.'

'You came out shooting, Melnky,' says Griffin.

'Because every time we encountered an American, he started shooting at us!'

'We have not been aggressive,' says Toog.

'And yet two of our team are dead. Yours is intact. I'd hate to see you if you were aggressive,' says Kovacs.

'Wouldn't you just,' says Griffin. 'You got payback for blowing our command module out of the sky.'

'We didn't do that.'

'Yes, you did.'

'So why did I rescue your friend here? That would demonstrate a very un-Soviet lack of consistency. This is a peaceful mission.'

'So why did you bring guns here?' says Griffin.

'Soviet missions have always been armed. We don't land in the sea; we land in Siberia.'

'What the fuck difference does that make?' says Griffin.

'The bears might get to you before the helicopter does,' says Melnyk.

'And you chose to take them with you on the EVA, rather than save weight and leave them in the landers?'

'Yes. And it seems we were right to do so, given your attacks. Which brings us to the question of why you have guns.'

'Because you have,' says Griffin. 'And we're the good guys.'

Kovacs snorts. 'I think you might find a large section of humanity disagreeing with you.'

'I don't give a fuck about a large section of humanity.'

'There, you've passed the "is he American?" test,' says Kovacs.

'Damn right!' says Griffin.

'Not so much a nationality as a diagnosis,' says Kovacs.

'Shall we stop wasting time and come up with a plan?' says Toog. 'I think it's fairly imperative we work together here.'

'Absolutely,' says Kovacs. 'We have no way out of here otherwise.'

Ziggy breathes deeply, coughs, sits up, looks around her in awe.

She is in a large dark space that flickers with a watery light. There is no apparent floor – that is to say, she is sitting on something that supports her, but it is as if it's made of an entirely invisible glass. Beneath her, maybe 100 feet, flows a churning silver river. Above her a ceiling, more a sky, slowly turns from red to blue to green to yellow and back again. There is a flicker at her feet and shooting snakes of light race beneath her: some sort of symbols. When she turns to look more closely, they are gone.

Kovacs smiles. 'Interesting, isn't it? Did you see what the shape was?'

'No.'

'It was a representation of an atom, as far as I could see. You know, as in the popular imagination – a little solar system.'

'What makes you sure it wasn't a solar system?' says Griffin.

'It could have been,' says Kovacs, 'but it felt like an atom.'

'Felt like one?' says Griffin.

'Atomy,' says Kovacs. 'You know, it had the air of an atom.'

'Jesus, more of the feels! Are we going to put up with these kooks, Toog?' says Griffin.

Toog ignores him.

'We've seen a lot of scientific and mathematical symbols since we've been here,' says Toog.

'A veritable hotchpotch,' says Kovacs.

'You didn't learn your English in the USA, then,' says Toog.

'No. Cambridge University, England.'

'But human symbols would indicate that this structure is of human origin,' says Toog.

'Yes,' says Kovacs, and says no more.

Ziggy looks at Kovacs. She's a tall woman – 5'8" or so, she guesses – though taller in her spacesuit. She can't see her face clearly – the flickering light reflects off her visor – but she has a sense of her: that amplified, synaesthetic feeling she gets when she looks at Griffin. It's like looking into a computer, she thinks. There is a buzzing within her, an enormous energy, a scurrying intelligence, a brain like a termite mound, working, always working.

She withdraws her attention, steps it back.

Kovacs asks Melnyk to help with removing her own helmet and he twists it off. She kneels to Ziggy. She has an inquisitive, pointy, intense face that reminds Ziggy of that of a curious fox.

'What are you experiencing?' she says in Russian.

'I don't know.'

'Telepathy?'

'What is she saying?' says Griffin in Ziggy's earpiece. She ignores him.

'Feelings akin to it. Probably not. Like a narcotic or hallucinogenic experience.'

'Have you had many of those?' Kovacs puts her hand to Ziggy's shoulder, tips her head like a cat trying to work out the source of a squeak.

'My freshman year at university was 1967. I've had two.'

'Only two. You don't use hallucinogens to help read the Twilight Language?'

'I don't think they would help. You know about the Twilight Language?'

'Of course. That's why we're here.'

'You read it using LSD?'

'A little. Just to open me to suggestion. It's how I found you here. On reflection, that seems very likely.'

'You're on acid?'

'Just a bit,' says Kovacs. 'It's a help to insight and no danger to the mission.'

Kovacs explains that she and her cosmonauts had found themselves in a cavern full of glittering mineral deposits. No one on their team had any geological expertise but they thought they were some sort of quartz, a twinkling purple. They'd come in through the tunnel tubes, which sealed behind them. They were inspecting the rock when another tunnel opened, and they heard cries of distress on the Soviet wavelength.

They went down the tunnel and saw an orb emerge on a spurt of silver liquid, like a ping-pong ball on a waterspout. The liquid fell away and left the orb apparently hovering. They were afraid to go towards the orb because it appeared to be floating above a long drop. They were debating what to do

when the orb popped or vanished, depositing the astronauts and cosmonaut on an invisible floor. That's when the shooting started, and Kovacs noticed there might be oxygen present.

'You may as well save oxygen and remove your own helmets,' says Kovacs.

'No guarantee this is going to last,' says Toog.

'How quick can you put the helmet back on?'

'I'd guess not as quick as twelve seconds, which is roughly how long it takes you to black out in a vacuum.'

Kovacs snorts. 'So you Americans do some preparation after all.'

Ziggy feels no real conviction behind what Kovacs says. This antagonism is some sort of posture, or pretence, she thinks. These thoughts come to her very powerfully. Emotions are amplified, brighter, more tangible, almost as if she could pick them up, examine them for texture and feel.

Kovacs turns to her and a strange feeling washes from her, warm and positive, almost like maternal love.

'We'll remain in suit for the meantime,' says Toog. 'If we encounter low O_2 or noxious environments, at least we'll be able to get to you quickly to help.'

'I have a feeling we'll be all right,' says Kovacs.

'Well, whoopie do. Thank God for your feelings,' says Griffin.

'Thank him for meeting us, too,' says Kovacs. 'You stand a chance of getting out of here with my expertise combining with that of Ms Da Luca. We'll co-operate for her sake,' she says. 'She is the only one of you we can't do without.'

Chapter 8

They walk like gods on nothing. It's a strange sensation, looking down at the planes of silver from high above. 'How are we all feeling?' asks Toog.

'Healthy, elated, actually,' says Ziggy.

'As those who have just avoided suffocation are wont to do,' says Kovacs.

She smiles at Ziggy and a wave of images sweeps through Ziggy's mind. Home, Christmas, her dad shovelling snow; Andy on the little scooter they had when they first moved to Florida, fetching her ice cream from the store; Maria coming in from the prom, glowing with the heat of her first kiss.

Kovacs is present in all these scenes, and it is violating, like a stranger rifling through your personal possessions.

'Get out of my head,' says Ziggy.

'Woah!' says Kovacs, out loud. 'You brought the shutters down quickly.' Then, whispering, 'I heard you. In my head. I was just seeing if it was a two-way street. This is why you are important. The rest of them are dead heads. You are in tune here.'

'Da Luca?' says Toog, who has picked up something is amiss.

'Nothing, Toog,' she says. No, she should tell them. 'There seems to be some evidence of telepathy between me and Kovacs.'

'This place is a wonderland,' says Kovacs.

Toog looks nonplussed, like he doesn't know what to make of that.

'Only between you two?'

'It appears so,' says Ziggy.

'OK,' he says. 'Keep me informed,' his voice buzzing in the radio of her Snoopy cap.

'We'll go on instinct. It seems right to follow the flow of the stream of these symbols on the floor,' says Kovacs.

She has a total confidence to her. Ziggy finds this a little unnerving; she feels like a sorcerer's apprentice in the presence of the grand wizard.

'Does that feel good to you, Da Luca?' she says. 'It feels good to me.'

'I think so.'

There is almost a magnetic sense here. If she were to close her eyes and turn around, open them again, she wouldn't feel comfortable if she was not facing in the direction of the symbols' flow. They walk on and Kovacs keeps close by, her radio presumably shut off and inaudible to the others, who have not yet removed their helmets.

'Your man Griffin. Do you think he's dangerous?'

'More to you than me.'

'Really? Can't you feel his hostility to you?'

'Yes, but he's a professional and a soldier. He'll do his job.'

'I wouldn't be so sure. What do you get from him? The feeling?'

She talks as if this heightened emotional sensitivity were entirely normal, as normal as discussing your general impression of someone.

'Hostility. Simmering aggression. Even as I was running out of air, I felt it. He has this anger and then another anger on top that's angry at you for not sharing his anger. Even if that anger's with yourself.'

'Yes. Watch that.'

'I am watching it. What's your speculation about the nature of this place?'

Kovacs purses her lips. 'I don't know. It certainly seems to work as some sort of emotional amplifier.'

'My thoughts too. Which would be why were attacked by cosmonauts and you by astronauts. Have you genuinely killed astronauts?'

'Three.'

'They were nothing to do with us. And we've killed cosmonauts.'

'For real, if what Melnyk tells me is true.'

'We were defending ourselves.'

'Maybe you were,' she says. 'The evidence suggests that there are here very strong hallucinations or even simulacra, which may be hallucinations given physical form by some method.'

'Yes. Maybe. All the cosmonauts we encountered instantly attacked.'

'Yeah, and all the capitalists we encountered did the same.'

'So it's easy to see why it went so wrong when we encountered the real thing.'

They are moving above a different scene now. The silver planes have given way to clouds of steam. When they part,

she can see they are billowing from three great dark chimneys that rise from the floor below.

The clouds do not rise above the level of the invisible floor.

The walls, sky, horizon or whatever it is around them flash red and green in great sheets like lightning. Ziggy is still very hot, but she is at least losing some heat through her head, her hands where she's taken off her gloves, and her respiration – the chamber they are in is cool enough to fog her breath. She'll be uncomfortable but she won't die. Toog gestures to her to turn her mic back on. She does.

'Do you think that's the ship's power source?' he says. 'I mean, chimneys suggest power generation, don't they?'

'She doesn't know,' says Griffin.

'I don't know,' says Ziggy.

'Same answer as always,' says Griffin.

'It's been a long-lasting source of power if it is,' says Melnyk. 'The whole of human history.'

'You don't know that,' says Kovacs. 'It could have come here much more recently.'

'Or much longer ago,' says Melnyk.

'Leave that side of things to me, Commander,' says Kovacs.

'I don't think it's a power source,' says Ziggy.

'Why not?'

'It, I don't know. It has the feel of a representation. You know, like it doesn't do anything at all.'

Griffin exhales heavily in exasperation.

'It's not quite that,' says Kovacs.

'No, not quite,' says Ziggy. 'Then what?'

'I don't know,' says Kovacs.

'Hey, you two should get along just swell,' says Griffin.

They walk on. There is a frustrating lack of anything

resembling a wall, a door, a hatch, anything at all. When they stop to rest, Toog removes his helmet.

'Why you doing that?' says Griffin.

'Itch at the back of my head,' says Toog. 'It's been there too long.' He uncomfortably lifts up his arm to scratch behind his ear.

'I think, if we're going to sleep anywhere, if we can,' says Toog, 'this might be a good place to do it. There's an atmosphere, we can give the LSS a rest.'

'I don't need to sleep yet,' says Griffin.

'No. But this might be our only opportunity. We don't want to have to sleep in an environment where we might have to use up valuable oxygen.'

'Let's press on,' says Kovacs. 'I suggest we all remove helmets to save air until it appears that we are going to transition from this area to another.'

There's a pause until Toog says 'OK'. The whole group take off their helmets. Heads are scratched, rubbed, and the rustle of it fills everyone's earpieces.

Toog insists on a drill. Each member of the party must try to put on his own helmet as quickly as possible. That doesn't go well. The arms reach high enough to engage the helmet and twist it on its neck ring in an ungainly way – basically throwing off the helmet and catching it again as it slowly falls, but not high enough to exert enough downward pressure to re-engage it. For that, they need someone else.

In that case, it's a fairly quick action, no more than a couple of seconds.

'Fairly clear then,' says Toog. 'If we hit a vacuum or anything like it, we each need an assigned member we go to first.'

'Gotta be mission commander,' says Griffin. 'We get the helmet back on Toog. You're boiling out in the vacuum, you use your twelve seconds or whatever God grants you to get the helmet on Toog. He takes it from there.'

'I am mission commander,' says Kovacs.

'Not my mission,' says Griffin.

Kovacs snorts. 'We need to establish a command structure,' she says.

'We established one at NASA, thanks,' says Griffin.

'This is an unhelpful attitude,' says Melnyk. 'We will stick to teams. I will reattach my mission commander's helmet. You reattach yours.'

Griffin jabs a finger at Kovacs. 'And that's your mission commander?'

'Yes,' says Melnyk.

'I'd say my chances of getting a helmet put back on are better than yours,' he says.

They practise the drills, to familiarise themselves with each other's kits, and it becomes apparent that, in twelve seconds, the best person to help is the one next to you, not the commander at all. For this reason, they adopt a strict order of march, each carrying another person's helmet. Griffin carries Toog's, Toog carries hers. She carries Griffin's. They practise, Griffin reattaching Toog's helmet while she reattaches Griffin's. There's no point reattaching hers. The attempt doesn't really work. She interferes with Griffin's attempts to work on Toog's helmet and he gives her a snappy 'get the fuck off.' So they decide there will be an order of reattachment: Toog first, if near enough and convenient; Griffin second; no point putting hers back on at all without any air. The idea is that, if Toog gets his helmet back on

quickly enough, he can reattach Griffin's at relative leisure – that is, up to about a minute. Animal tests have shown good recovery from vacuum exposure at around that time.

'You OK with this, Da Luca?' says Toog.

'No good if I'm not. Better practise on the Soviet helmets and have them do ours.'

'Yeah.'

They do – not much difference, really: a push down, a turn, a click. The Soviets, too, are happier sticking to their own squad – four of them, Kovacs, Melnyk, Lenov and Shirokov.

They press on another hour. Below them steam billows and now the ceiling or sky or whatever it is, is marked with strange shapes. She sees a grainy view of a rooftop, sees something flash and move, the shadow of some sort of great mechanical arm revolving about a circle; the sky boils with fire and black smoke; spoked wheels turn. Beneath their feet, on the floor, a whirl of symbols flutter and mass like starlings. Some she doesn't recognise; some she thinks are alchemical symbols. Others are just glimpsed.

'What do you think of this?' says Kovacs.

'She doesn't know,' says Griffin.

'It's not religious imagery,' says Ziggy, ignoring the provocation, 'unless that's the dharmachakra, the Buddhist wheel.'

'I know what the dharmachakra is,' says Kovacs. 'It doesn't look Eastern in its design. It's very spare, it looks more like something from industry.'

'Whatever it is, it's very suggestive of human iconography,' says Ziggy.

'It would appear so,' says Kovacs.

'So are we in the home of the ancients?'

Kovacs says nothing.

'What's the power source for these images; have they been playing for aeons?' says Ziggy.

'They may not have been playing for that long. I think there's a chance they appeared here for our benefit.'

'Why do you think that?'

'The weird simulacra we killed, they took on a personal appearance, didn't they?'

'Yes.'

'So why shouldn't all this?'

'You think this iconography may be a reflection of us, not the whatever built this structure?'

'Congratulations. You may have a gold star,' says Kovacs.

Beneath their feet, on the invisible surface, a twinkling golden star, about the size of a dinner plate, slides into view, hovers and shoots away.

Ziggy actually laughs.

'You're right,' she says.

She thinks about the implications of that. The ship, whatever it is, is being influenced by them and, if the growing feelings of empathy and awareness are anything to go by, is influencing them.

When she ran out of oxygen, she envisaged herself calling for help and Kovacs came, a tunnel opened. Which means there may be a way to move throughout this ship without doing all the footslogging.

She explains briefly to the others.

'Click your ruby slippers and say, "There's no place like home"?' says Griffin.

'I didn't think that would be your taste in films, Griffin,' says Ziggy.

'I preferred the book,' says Melnyk. 'The slippers are silver in that.'

Kovacs gives Melnyk a quizzical look.

'What?' Melnyk says. 'I've only read about the film. It was seen as decadent back home. It is decadent, isn't it?'

Kovacs continues to fix her eyes on Melnyk.

'I mean,' says Melnyk, 'who would want to back go to the oppression of Kansas? Ellie would want to go back to the Soviet Union, where farm life is collectivised.'

'Ellie?' says Griffin. 'Surely Dorothy.'

'He's read the Soviet version,' says Kovacs.

'Hey, Griffin, who knew you were such an Oz fan?'

'I admired the quality of the colour printing technology,' says Griffin.

This causes a laugh. Griffin doesn't look quite comfortable with that.

'This isn't getting us to a doorway,' he says.

Symbols on the surface swirl and coalesce, divide, shimmer and turn.

When the movement stops, only one is left. It's made of three broad black lines, about eight feet long and five wide, viewed from where they are.

'That's a *pi* sign,' says Toog.

'It's a gateway,' say Kovacs and Ziggy, almost simultaneously.

'Whatever it is, it's . . .' They never hear Griffin finish his sentence. He taps the bottom of the symbol with his foot and disappears through the floor. He doesn't fall nearly as quickly as he would on Earth, but still too quickly for anyone to react to catch him. It's as if the invisible structure keeping Griffin on the same level as the others disappears, and he tumbles into the billowing clouds of steam below.

Ziggy looks down but all that is beneath her are the clouds – no sign of Griffin at all.

'Griffin, Griffin,' says Toog, holding the mouthpiece of his radio. 'Come in, come in. Can you hear me?'

Nothing, just a static buzz in her earpiece.

Toog gets on his hands and kneels, feels forward to the edge of the symbol to see if he can find the space into which Griffin fell. As soon as he touches the edge of the symbol, he gives a cry, grasps in front of him, but it's too late. The floor has gone and he disappears into the clouds.

'Shit,' says Melnyk.

'Griffin, Toog!' says Ziggy. 'Come in. Answer, please answer.'

More static. Griffin and Toog are gone.

Chapter 9

'That is a gateway!' says Kovacs, pointing at the symbol on the floor.

'We don't know that,' says Melnyk.

'Why not? That's exactly what it looks like.'

'They could have fallen a very long way,' says Melnyk. 'Even in this weak gravity.'

'Da Luca. What is your impression?' says Kovacs.

Ziggy looks hard at the symbol. It is like a temple gateway glyph. Very like one.

She approaches it.

'I have a warm feeling,' she says.

'So does the fish when it sees the worm on the hook,' says Melnyk.

'It feels friendly,' says Ziggy. It does, too. She thinks of picket fences, of ivy-covered gates to secret gardens, Heaven, even.

'I think we need to be careful,' says Melnyk.

'This is no time for an excess of caution,' says Kovacs. 'It feels friendly to me, too. I think this is how this place works. You call a portal when you need one. Here, help me suit up.'

She passes Ziggy her helmet, opens the oxygen valve on her LSS. Ziggy secures the helmet on Kovacs' head.

'You can hear me?' says Kovacs.

'Yes.'

'I'll try to send a message. Luckily we sent a few canaries ahead of us.'

She walks to the edge of the symbol, touches it and floats through the floor, arms crossed.

'What do we do now?' says Lenov. He's a ratty-looking man with a wispy moustache, a nervous feeling seeping off him. She can't say she blames him.

'Wait,' says Ziggy. She is ridiculously nervous, her stomach tight with anxiety.

'Know any songs?' says Melnyk. 'Or did you bring a pack of cards?'

'You wouldn't like my singing,' says Ziggy.

'I like Western music,' says Melnyk.

'Careful, Melnyk,' says Shirokov. He must be the marine; he's built like a bull, with a taut, sinewy face.

'You wouldn't like it the way I do it,' says Ziggy.

Melnyk laughs and begins to sing.

'And if the band breaks up years and years too soon,
And if there's no fool upon the hill,
And if your head blows up with dark exploding tunes . . .'

Ziggy interrupts. 'That's not how it goes. That's nothing like how it goes.'

'It's how it goes in my head,' says Melnyk.

'If we ever get back, we can write and tell Pink Floyd you improved it,' says Ziggy.

'I thought that was the Beatles,' says Melnyk.

'No.'

'"Brain Damage" was by the Beatles; those are the right words. I'd put money on it.'

'You'd lose it.'

He smiles at her.

'Do you think we're going to be OK?'

'We've got air. That's the bottom of the pyramid of needs ticked off.'

'And we've got conversation and jokes,' he says. 'So that's the top.'

'Yeah, just need the layers in between filled in now. Food, water and stuff.'

'Details,' says Melnyk. 'Details.'

She's glad of this stupid talk; it takes her mind off what's happening to the others, what might happen to her.

She feels dizzy, as if she's stood up too quickly. Kovacs is trying to contact her, she thinks, not on the radio but through thought.

'Yes,' she says. 'What have you found?'

'Come and see.'

'How's the atmosphere?'

'A regular party. Fine. Both Americans breathing.'

Ziggy shivers. This is weird stuff.

'Your boss says to proceed,' says Ziggy.

'I didn't hear her,' says Melnyk.

'I did,' says Ziggy. 'I'll go first if you don't believe me.'

The cosmonauts help each other into their helmets as Ziggy walks over to the symbol, helmet tucked under her arm.

She touches it and gives a start as the support of the floor underneath her gives way and she floats down. It's as if an invisible hand has given her a shove in the middle of the back and, as she slowly falls, she is propelled forwards.

She looks down through the clouds and is breathless. Below her flow rivers of what looks like lava, but in ordered, regular channels, more like you'd see when steel is poured into a mould than you'd expect in a volcanic eruption. She feels heat on her face from the flow and instinctively crosses herself with her free hand and she descends. The fall is long – five or six seconds – and she is travelling quickly by the time she lands.

She has time to see where she's going. It's a thin strip of what appears to be a loading bay or a quay of some sort between the lava field and a flat, black expanse of water.

She lands easily and, when she looks at her feet, she sees there is another of the gateway symbols on the dock floor. And it is a dock, too, because in front of her are the unmistakable forms of three moored sailing ships – not constructed from wood, rope and canvas, as she might expect, but almost as if from light, the quality of which reminds her of what you might see from a light box for viewing slides. But the ships are not uniform and the material from which they're made is not stable. It flickers with symbols and flashes of shadow.

Kovacs has her helmet off again.

'Where's Griffin and Toog?'

'On the ship,' she says. 'Were you impressed by your landing? I think we must have been doing close to ten metres a second by the time we landed. You'd expect a thirty odd kilometre an hour jolt to shake you a bit, wouldn't you? But you and I landed like cats.'

She puts her helmet at her feet as Melnyk floats in beside her. The ships are very curious structures. There is very little detail to them. They are just blocky shapes of a dull light, pulsing with symbols – crosses, crowns, sunbursts and even things that look like coins.

'What do you make of those?'

'It looks like an art installation,' says Ziggy.

'What's its message?'

'Pretty Soviet of you,' says Ziggy. 'Does art need a message?' It seems strange to want to discuss something so irrelevant to their situation, but she has a powerful urge to do so.

'If art doesn't impart a message, what does it do?'

'Call to light the impossibility of messages. Confuse things.'

'Then that's not art, it's just the stuff of existence put in a gallery.'

'That's art,' says Ziggy.

'For decadent simpletons, maybe,' says Kovacs. 'But why do I feel I want to discuss this? You're right. It's a very odd thing to think about right now.'

You're right? Ziggy was thinking about how odd it was to be having a freshman conversation about art, given the other pressing concerns they are facing, but she *said* nothing about it.

Ziggy looks again at the ships. The quality of light shifts from green to blue, through red. Or not exactly shifts. It suggests those colours without ever really drifting into them.

'Why are we discussing this?' says Ziggy. 'This is a conversation for a wet Wednesday in a common room, not when we're in peril of our lives.'

'A good point,' says Kovacs. 'But it feels like that's what I need to do. What do you think this place is?'

'Strange, I think it's strange. Or, if you want the academic response, I haven't enough evidence to make a judgement yet.'

'I think it might be a museum,' says Kovacs.

Lenov lands in the circle, with a loud shout in Russian. She doesn't get the word, but she guesses it might be idiomatic for 'shit'. Shirokov comes down behind him, landing more quietly.

'A museum for who? And why?'

'I don't know. But why do we have museums on Earth? This seems to be of human construction, we have to assume that. Why not a museum? Humans make museums, don't they?'

'Yeah, but this one doesn't seem ideally positioned to get a lot of footfall,' says Ziggy.

Kovacs smiles and says: 'I take your point. If you put together a museum, you must have some idea of who you expect to attend. So either there were regular space flights between here and who knows where, or a colony here. It's one of those.'

'Or we're the intended audience,' says Ziggy.

That explanation came from nowhere, but it feels correct, in the way that the direction they went across the invisible floor felt correct, just intuitively.

'This whole thing built just for you? American exceptionalist thinking,' says Kovacs. 'You don't understand your insignificance in the scheme of things.'

Ziggy doesn't say anything. She's pretty sure she had a fairly good glimpse into her significance in the scheme of things when she was suffocating to death in the bubble. You can't say you're insignificant in the universe because you are the universe. She knows that's like something you find on a fridge magnet, but it feels very true.

'Why the weird ways of getting about?' says Ziggy. 'If it's a museum.'

'Fun?' says Kovacs.

'So you've got a cosmic Disneyland here,' says Ziggy.

'Or All-Union Exhibition of People's Economic Achievements,' says Melnyk.

'Glory to rabbit breeders, seamstresses and young nationalists!' says Lenov.

'The rabbit breeding pavilion there is really very good,' says Shirokov.

'I'll stick with Mickey Mouse,' says Ziggy.

'You can't eat mice,' says Melnyk. 'That mouse is a perfect capitalist symbol. Good for nothing but you buy it anyway. Give me the useful rabbit any day. Fur, food, companionship, and they even live in collectives. The hard-working rabbit is the symbol of the communist future.'

'I assumed you guys only spoke like that when the state was listening,' says Ziggy.

'The state is always listening,' says Melnyk, Lenov and Shirokov, almost in unison.

'You might want to come up and see this.' Griffin has emerged from one of the ships.

Ziggy and the others move towards him, but Griffin puts up a hand.

'Americans only,' he says.

'Fuck that,' says Kovacs.

'You want to come on this ship, you come through me,' says Griffin.

'If that's the way you want it,' says Kovacs. 'I seem to recall you're out of bullets.'

Griffin takes a knife from his utility belt.

'It's OK,' says Ziggy. 'You look at the other ships. I'll report back honestly on whatever's in there. We're in this together, aren't we?'

144

Kovacs looks into Ziggy's eyes for a long moment. Ziggy imagines a searchlight beaming through the cavities of her skull, flashing left and right to try to discover the truth of her intentions. She actually sees the searchlight, high on a tower, swinging its cone of light in broad swoops.

'Don't shut me out,' says Kovacs. The voice is in her head.

Ziggy doesn't reply, keeps her mind blank, meditative. It's an instinct to do that, almost a reflex, a hand moving away from a flame or flying up to shield a blow.

Kovacs looks away. 'OK. I believe you. Melnyk, you two, follow me to the second ship.'

Was Kovacs trying to read Ziggy's mind, she wonders. That's how it felt. It also felt possible for Ziggy to return the compliment. There was a sense of an opening before Ziggy, a strong intuition that, if she just allowed herself to open, too, she might step into Kovacs' consciousness. Kovacs has asked her if she'd experienced telepathy before. Perhaps the structure has sparked that, along with the widening consciousness she has felt since being in space. It would be correct and pertinent to the mission to do an experiment with herself and Kovacs, and the other crew members. It's one thing to think you're experiencing telepathy. It's another to be demonstrably able to perform it. Something holds her back, though. Kovacs frightens her slightly. Even though she has only glimpsed it, her consciousness feels like a strange and dangerous place.

Ziggy goes up what appears to be a gangplank into the ship. Its surface shifts and shadows, as if a film is playing on it. She sees what she thinks are tall buildings growing up, a horse falling, a tree felled. The images might be none of those things either. They are shapes, blocks of dark and light

that come and go like figures cut by trees in the headlights of a car moving through a deep night.

Inside, the ship is a blank space, the walls made of a faintly glowing white substance that bleaches out perspective and depth.

'Up here,' says Griffin.

She climbs up a ladder to an upper deck. This place is similarly unadorned, the walls emitting a harsh red light.

'Look', says Toog, who is within. He is bent over a long grey coffin-like structure that rises from the ship as if part of it, no seam or join. It emits light from its top, making Toog look like a kid making a scary face with a flashlight at Halloween. 'What do you make of this?'

In the long case of light lies what very much appears to be a gun – some sort of rifle. It bears the same relation to a real rifle that the ships bear to a real ship. It's simply a long cylinder, in a neutral grey material that could be metal, could be plastic or something else, widening into a stock. There is no trigger and no apparent mechanism for loading, no sights. It flickers with images, too: abstract blocks, sudden explosions, even a target at one point, four concentric rings. It's a rifle. Everything about it seems to say so.

'Alien weaponry,' says Griffin. He has awe in his voice, like a miser describing a fabled hoard. 'Mission success!'

'Seems likely,' says Toog. 'What do you think, Da Luca?'

She examines the gun without touching. She wants to say it feels like a gun, in her head. It's like a coiled snake to her, full of latent power and deadliness; she can almost hear the rattle of a snake's tail as she looks at it.

All she does say is: 'It's a gun. It looks like a gun.'

'We knew that,' says Griffin.

'Thought that,' says Toog, correcting him. 'What makes you sure?'

'I've seen it before,' she says. 'There's a stele, beneath the Pyramid of the Moon in Mexico.

'It shows someone shooting it?'

'No. It's an image for "war". Or was thought to be. It's been called the "War Bone" and people have remarked on its similarity to a gun, and that shape is its exact line, I'm sure.'

Griffin lets out a snort. 'So your certainty that it's a gun comes from having seen something like it that wasn't a gun but a symbol.'

Five seconds ago, Griffin was certain it was a weapon. Now she is of that opinion, he's open-minded all of a sudden. She lets it go; no point in confrontation. Look where that got her last time. The shame of her hostility to Griffin is still with her. She wished him dead, genuinely. That is a bad, bad thought, no matter what the circumstance.

'It's a gun,' says Ziggy. She can sense its purpose, feel it. It's an unmistakable shape – the guillotine blade, the noose, the human skull: it carries that resonance, that feeling. Death.

'Whatever it is, we can't let the Russians have it,' says Toog.

'Damn right,' says Griffin.

'There's no way of hiding it,' says Ziggy.

'I'm just gonna carry it,' says Griffin. 'If the Reds want it, they'll have to take it.'

'Jesus,' says Ziggy.

'Don't fit with your liberal attitude?' says Griffin.

'It don't fit with getting out of here alive,' says Ziggy. 'We should be concentrating on co-operation, not confrontation. And besides, you don't even know it's safe to touch that.'

'Spare me the peace protest slogans,' says Griffin. 'This here's the real world.'

Ziggy looks around her, at the interior of this box of light, thinks of the structure she's in with its engulfing bubbles, its folding passageways, its strange simulacra, and begins to laugh.

'What's funny?' says Griffin.

'Nothing,' she says. 'Nothing at all.'

Ziggy tries arguing that they should leave the gun, or whatever it is. Toog accepts there's a risk in picking it up but, as it appears to be the first piece of portable alien technology they've encountered, he says they have to take it with them. In the unlikely event they do get back to Earth, it will be invaluable.

'So who's going to lift it?' says Ziggy.

Griffin just reaches down into the case and takes out the gun.

'Jesus!' They all say it at the same moment. The gun is no longer a long featureless sweep but an M16 rifle.

Griffin stares down at it. Then he detaches the magazine, looks inside.

'Full clip,' he says. 'And . . .'

He almost can't speak.

'What is it, Griff?'

'This is my gun. The one I had in the infantry in 'Nam. It's got my daughter's name on it.'

He holds it forward. There it is, on the metal just above the magazine: 'Chrissie'.

'Give it to someone else,' says Ziggy. 'We need to see what happens to it.'

Griffin is kind of stunned. He holds out the rifle to her.

She takes it. It blurs, almost like it's losing focus, writhes in her hands, and it reverts to what it was, a long, bone-white gunnish form.

Ziggy passes it on to Toog. In his hands it blurs and transforms again into a long hunting rifle. 'I had this back home,' says Toog.

'What the fuck?' says Griffin.

'It's changing according to our experience,' says Ziggy. 'It's influenced by our experience of guns.'

'And yours is?'

'Just the training at NASA for this mission. I never touched one before that. Guns haven't really featured in my life, or my imagination.'

'I used to hunt as a kid,' says Toog. 'This was my dad's old gun. He gave it to me when he got a new one and always said he regretted it.'

'Does it fire?' says Griffin.

'Do we really want to discover that?' says Ziggy.

'Give it back to me,' says Griffin. 'An M16's the most use if it comes to a fight with the Reds.'

Toog, looking stunned, passes the gun back to Griffin, where it mutates again into the M16, blurring the edges of the hunting gun as if seen through a clouded glass before sharpening into the more aggressive lines of the combat rifle.

Ziggy thinks. This whole structure has seemed to respond to the astronauts within it. At the moment it's responding to accidental thoughts: the buried stuff of the subconscious, fears and trauma. Will it respond to a conscious intervention? And how should they try to influence it? Do they want an exit? She still has no air. Could she create air by thinking

about it? She needs time to decide exactly how and what she might try as an experiment.

She hears Kovacs calling from outside the ship. 'Let's go,' says Griffin. He pats the M16. They walk down the gang-plank, Griffin first.

'You've found something,' says Kovacs, eyeing the gun.

'Yeah,' says Griffin.

'You found an American military carbine on the Moon.'

'That's what it looks like,' says Griffin.

Kovacs frowns.

'You have been here before?' she says.

'Not me,' says Griffin.

'The US. If that's the case and you have information pertinent to our survival, you need to share it with us now.'

'We haven't been here before,' says Ziggy. 'Not that any of us know. If there have been other missions, no one has told us.'

'It would seem that there have been,' says Kovacs.

Ziggy is about to speak when Toog interjects.

'We can discuss the gun later,' he says. 'It's even stranger than it looks.'

'Well, I can top that,' says Kovacs. 'Melnyk, come down. It's unbelievable.'

Melnyk walks down the gangplank of the second ship, followed by the other two cosmonauts.

Something is moving behind Melnyk, though, a little flash of movement at about the level of his knees. When he reaches the dock, he steps aside. Behind him, tongue lolling, is a little dog. It's a dachshund by the look of it, long, low and dark.

'How about this?' says Melnyk. 'Her name is Lyuba!'

None of the astronauts say anything for an instant. The dog walks around the dock, looking up at them, wagging its tail.

'Well,' says Melnyk. 'This is not what we expected from an extraterrestrial life form.'

'I'll say,' says Toog.

'Mother of God!' says Griffin, staring at the little dog in wonder.

'This is my Lyuba. She was my dog when I was small. It's incredible, isn't it?'

The dog comes and sits on Melnyk's spacesuit boot.

'It's clearly not a real dachshund,' says Ziggy.

'Or it's some life form imitating a dachshund,' says Toog.

'What makes you think it's a life form?' says Kovacs.

'It doesn't feel like a life form, or rather it has some of that resonance, but not all of it,' says Ziggy. She can't explain that statement. To her, it's the difference between looking at a convincing waxwork and a real person. It's obvious that it isn't real.

'Here we go again with the feels and the resonance,' says Griffin.

'Touch it,' says Kovacs.

'You touch it,' says Griffin.

Melnyk laughs. 'There's no problem with that. Look!' He scoops up the little dog into his arms. 'Say hello, Lyuba!' he says, waving the little dog's paw for it.

'Give it to Da Luca,' says Kovacs.

Melnyk extends his arms, dangling the little dog before him. She takes it, feels it briefly writhe in her arms and then twist more sharply and strongly than she imagined it might be able to. The dog's outline blurs, out of focus. When the

focus sharpens, it's no longer a dog. She is looking into the flat face of the big white Persian cat her mother keeps – Shiwa. The cat mewls, uncomfortable at being held, and she drops it to the floor.

'Would you look at that,' says Griffin.

'Same as the gun,' says Ziggy.

'Don't share information with the enemy,' says Griffin.

'Are we the enemy?' says Kovacs. 'I'm a scientist. I'm not anybody's enemy. What of the gun?'

Ziggy glances at Toog, to see if it's OK to speak. He shrugs.

'It's a thing of mutable form. It appeared different to that and changed to its present form when Griffin picked it up.'

'It'll still blow your brains out,' says Griffin. 'Full clip, all functional.'

'I hope it won't come to that,' says Kovacs. 'But it seems that the dog or cat is similar. It didn't appear in its present form either. It was sort of a dog-shaped thing.'

'Was it moving?'

'No. I touched it and it became Lyuba.' says Melnyk. 'You touch it and it becomes a cat. Let's just hope no one here has an emotional bond to a brown bear.'

'I got my favourite dog, you got your favourite gun, Griffin,' says Kovacs.

'I wouldn't call it a favourite,' says Griffin. 'It did the job and I was glad of it.'

Kovacs scratches her head.

'It's fairly clear we are projecting our own reality on to these base forms,' she says. 'If this is a museum, it's a museum of us.'

'Is it?' says Griffin.

'You have a better suggestion?'

'Keep the speculation to a minimum and keep accumulating evidence,' says Toog.

'Agreed,' says Kovacs. 'Let's explore the third ship.'

'We should try it together,' says Toog.

'Suits me,' says Kovacs.

They walk on to the third quay. The ship here is not quite like the others. The first ship is no more than the shape of a hull. The second has a risen tower at the back. The third is more like a hull, too, but sleeker, more knife-like. It appears more modern.

Griffin goes up the gangplank first, gun poking in front of him.

'Always the guns with Americans,' says Kovacs. 'What makes you think you will need that?'

'Just for security,' says Griffin.

'Security might be better achieved by a positive attitude and a friendly demeanour.'

'That going to deliver thirteen rounds a second?' says Griffin.

'I'm being serious,' says Kovacs. 'We've seen how the ship responds to at least part of our interior lives. Open and friendly attitudes might actually influence what we encounter.'

'Or get us killed,' says Griffin. 'But if it's open and friendly you believe in, why don't you take the lead and put your money where your mouth is?'

'Gladly,' says Kovacs.

'Second thoughts, I'll stay where I am,' says Griffin.

He goes up the gangplank, which shifts and moves with squiggling symbols. Ziggy thinks she recognises some – a star, an anchor, a crown, maybe. Naval stuff, or at least the navy of the popular imagination.

'Get away!' It's an unfamiliar voice, in Russian.

'Stay where you are! Stay right where you are!' she hears Griffin shout.

'No shooting!' shouts Kovacs.

'You heard, Griff, no shooting!' says Toog.

Kovacs and Toog run onto the ship, long moony hops carrying them forward. Ziggy follows.

The room is dimly lit, flickering with a watery light from glowing walls streaked with wavy shadows.

In a corner, pistol drawn, arm shaking, sits a cosmonaut in his tattered flight suit, his spacesuit beside him, his helmet nowhere to be seen. He is gaunt and drawn, with a straggly grey beard

'Don't shoot, don't shoot!' he says in Russian. 'I can tell you where to find food. There's treasure here. Treasure if you want it!'

'Major Antonov?' says Kovacs.

'Get away from me,' says the cosmonaut.

'We're here to get you out,' says Kovacs.

The cosmonaut shoves himself back against the wall, as though he might push through it. If he did, Ziggy would not be surprised in this strange place.

'You're here to kill me,' says the cosmonaut. 'Fucking KGB!'

'We are not the KGB!'

'Prove it!'

He jabs the pistol towards Kovacs as if it's a magic charm and she is a monster he can ward off with it.

'You want me to provide credentials showing I'm not in the KGB. A "not in the KGB" certificate, perhaps? Be serious, Antonov. Why would we spend all this money coming up

here to get you if our only aim was to kill you? As far as we knew, you were dead. Out of oxygen days ago.'

'You've already tried!' says Antonov, as Ziggy guesses he must be since Kovacs seems so certain. 'I see your agents everywhere.'

'We're American, we're not the KGB,' says Ziggy.

'I've seen you too, hunting!' he says.

'We're hunting no one,' says Ziggy. Again, that weird, intense feeling of empathy washes over her. It's like she can feel his fear inside her, a cringing, beaten sensation. But this was once a brave man. He came into the ship against orders; he dared to do something most people would not even dream of doing – entering what he believed to be an alien ship with only limited oxygen, no sure return home. And yet the feeling emanating from him is one of a frightened child in the dark.

'Tell him to drop the gun or I'm going to put his brains all over the wall,' says Griffin. 'And speak English, God damn you!'

'Please, drop the gun,' says Ziggy. 'My friend here doesn't understand what we are saying and is afraid you might hurt us. We've seen strange astronauts, too. Ones who attacked us and who melt into the floor when they die.'

'That happened to you, too?'

Antonov puts the gun slowly down. 'Approach me and I can grab it again,' he says.

'We're not going to approach you,' says Ziggy, first in English and then in Russian.

Antonov sits for a while.

'Yes.'

'You survived?'

155

'I did, yes, and I found great treasures. I can take you. There's food there. Plenty of it. Don't hurt me.'

'Where is Lyamin?'

'He was taken. He is gone and hurt. I'll take you to food. Forest food. No cheese. I would love a piece of cheese, love one.'

Antonov's mind has clearly gone, thinks Ziggy.

'We aren't here to hurt you,' says Ziggy. 'We think the hostile forces here are some sort of creation of this structure, not real at all.'

'You're a foreigner. Are you? How do I know you're real?'

'We are cosmonauts of Closed Military Townlet Number One,' says Kovacs.

'And you have brought Americans,' says Antonov. 'I don't know you're real. Are you real? Real cosmonauts wouldn't be with Americans. I have seen Americans here before. I don't know if they were real. One tried to kill me. He died and went away.'

'What's he saying?' says Griffin.

'He doesn't know if we're real,' says Ziggy.

'I can give him a burst on the M16 if it'll convince him,' says Griffin.

'Your hostility is becoming really boring,' says Lenov.

'I can make it exciting in a second,' says Griffin. Ever since he picked up the gun he has seemed more edgy, not less. Ziggy had thought it might give him some security, but apparently not.

'Calm down,' says Kovacs. 'Have you any idea what this place might be?'

'I only have ideas,' says Antonov. 'I think it is real.'

'Is it a museum?' says Ziggy. 'Are we visitors in a museum?'

Antonov seems to find this very funny; he giggles out a stream of sighs and whoops, seemingly having difficulty catching his breath.

'Visitors,' says Antonov, still highly amused. 'Visitors!'

'Do you want to try making more sense?' says Kovacs.

Antonov steadies himself, regains control.

'Not visitors,' he says. 'Not visitors! Exhibits!'

Chapter 10

There is a conference, outside the ship, on Antonov.

His account of landing and entering the structure is somewhat confused.

He and Lyamin entered the ship to find the same malleable tunnels that Ziggy discovered. However, they quickly found their way to a large hall.

'It was like a cathedral,' says Antonov. 'Huge, the roof supported by enormous pillars, but more like a cave than a man-made construction. At the centre of it, unsupported, hanging in space, was a gigantic red star. I had never seen anything like it. It was the symbol of the Communist party, of the Red Army. We didn't know what to make of it. But then the symbol changed and became a cross, and then a Star of David, a flower, a yin-yang thing, a crescent, many different religious symbols, and then, strangest of all, it became an American flag. A huge, rippling American flag.

'I swear, as I sit here. The implications were so vast. We had expected to encounter alien structures, but to encounter something so recent. I mean, when was the American flag first designed?' So Antonov does speak English!

'How many stars did it have?' says Griffin.

'I don't know. Lots. Like you see on your spacecraft.'

'1960 at latest, then,' says Griffin. '1912 if it only had forty-eight stars. I don't suppose you counted.'

'No,' says Antonov. He wipes his face with his hand, scratches at his hair. 'And after the flag came the astronauts. Four of them. They attacked us and we defended ourselves. Lyamin sustained a blow to his visor with a pick. It penetrated but didn't touch him. I shot all of the astronauts. We tried to scavenge what we could of their oxygen, but we had no adaptors. We had no patch we could make stick to the visor; it was all so coated in moon dust and nothing to clean it with. I watched as Lyamin's oxygen ebbed away from him. And then we realised – he could breathe. This place has an atmosphere.'

'What happened to the astronauts?' said Ziggy.

'They were absorbed into the floor. Everything. The whole kit, even their picks, just disappeared.'

'That tallies with our experience.'

'We pressed on. But Lyamin was suffering. I don't know if the shock of the attack had disordered his thinking, or the idea of his suit being damaged so he couldn't return to the orbiter. I mean, the best he could hope for was to wait for a rescue mission. Who knew how long that might take, or if it would be launched at all? He began to say that I had made a bad decision coming in here. I shouldn't have led him in. I had been reckless and it was him who was paying the price. I said I should return to the surface, contact the orbiter and Star City and ask them for solutions. There might be a way of using something in the lander to repair the helmet. He said that, if he let me go, I would desert him.'

'You could still find your way out at this point?' says Ziggy.

'Yes, easily. The tunnel to the entrance was still open.'

'So what happened?'

'He turned his gun on me and told me to remove my helmet. It was my mistake that had got us in here, I should be the one to wait for rescue.'

'And you did?'

'I removed the helmet and gave it to him. He went back up the tunnel. I haven't seen him since, though I have heard him.'

'How?'

'I hear his voice, on the radio. He is asking for help.'

'I'm surprised the battery has lasted this long,' says Toog.

'It hasn't. My battery is dead. I still hear his voice.'

'You moved from your initial location?'

'Yes. Too many astronauts. Too many KGB calling my name. This place is full of nightmares. It doesn't want us here.'

'How did they call your name? Over the short-wave?' says Ziggy.

'Yes. Again I think so. It sounded like it. But it might have been in my head.'

Kovacs laughs. 'It must have been. This would be some place to be able to produce a radio transmitter, learn Russian and guess your name.'

Ziggy glances down at the floor. Letters are forming in its dark, opaque surface. Roman numerals.

Kovacs appears not to have noticed.

'They attacked you?'

'At first, but when I ran out of bullets and became too weak to resist, they just watched me. The cathedral hall was full of them, row upon row of spacesuited men looking up at

that shifting symbol, saying nothing, doing nothing. It was eerie. I couldn't stand it; I was afraid and I had to move. That's when I came to this shore.'

He looks desperate. His eyes have a haunted quality to them and he looks around as if something might emerge from the shadows to bite him. Ziggy notices a letter drift across the floor, almost like an image on a screen. It is a Roman A. She watches as another comes alongside it. An E; at least it looks like an E.

'How did you get here?' says Kovacs. 'How did you move from one space to another?'

'I don't know. I wandered along the length of the flag room and then I was in a corridor like a grotto, a cave with shining mineral deposits. I didn't notice the transition. In the cave there was something, a being. I had the idea of it watching me.'

'What nature of being?'

'Female is all I could say. It seemed female and it was watching. I think it was a rusalka. My grandmother spoke of it. A man-killing spirit.'

'That's just a tale invoked by women to stop their men beating them,' says Lenov.

On the floor, the letters are clumping into twos or fours. Ziggy is too preoccupied with them to draw the others' attention, though no one seems to have noticed them. She starts as she sees her own name form: Zigsa. Spontaneously, she crosses herself.

'What did it look like?'

'It didn't exactly look like anything. I just had the idea of a presence, like an energy field. You know, if you approach a strong static electricity reservoir, you can feel the hairs standing up on your arms? It was a feeling akin to that.'

'You saw nothing?'

'I felt an energy. A watching female energy and it felt at home here. I imagined it. Maybe I saw it. I don't think I saw it. I imagined it as like the rusalka.'

'What exactly is a "rusalka"?' says Griffin.

'A female water spirit,' says Kovacs. 'They give me the creeps.'

Antonov goes on: 'A small pale girl with long arms and green hair. But I don't know I saw that, only that I thought I saw it and then thought I imagined it. It wasn't scared. It wasn't friendly but it wasn't hostile either, but it filled me with dread.'

'How so?'

'It felt vast. Like, you know, if you stand at the bottom of a huge building and look up, the universe seems to sway, you feel tiny. It was like that.'

Ziggy looks down at the floor.

The words are quite clear now: 'Love you Zigsa'.

She feels dizzy.

'Have you seen this?' she says.

'What?' says Toog. The letters disperse, float away.

'It said it loved me. There was a message on the floor here and it said it loved me.' She steadies herself. It's almost as if she can feel her sister beside her.

'Someone does,' says Griffin.

'Fuck yourself, Griffin.' The anger comes over her hard, out of proportion to Griffin's stupid provocation.

'There's nothing there,' says Griffin. 'You are losing your shit, lady.'

'I'm losing nothing,'

As she says the words, it's like something jolts inside her mind, comes loose. She feels like she wants to sit down.

'I have seen writing,' says Antonov.

'What did it say?' says Kovacs.

'It said the spirits of the dead are here,' he says.

'Which language did it use?' says Kovacs.

'Russian.'

'My sister,' says Ziggy. 'It feels like she is here.'

'How the fuck you weren't picked up by the shrinks before you got up here, I'll never know,' says Griffin. 'You know what, forget helping you. If I had my way, I'd leave you stuck right here.'

'Here is where I belong,' says Ziggy. 'Here is . . .' She doesn't know where these words are coming from, nor what she means by them. It's as if she's in a dream, watching the words being said rather than saying them.

'Good,' says Griffin. 'Good. We should've cut you loose hours ago. You and the space beatnik here will make a good pair,' he says, pointing to Lenov.

'I don't think,' says Toog, 'that . . .' He doesn't finish his sentence. He looks down and waggles his leg. Then he pulls at it.

'I'm stuck in the floor,' he says. He wobbles, tries to stay upright, but his legs are fixed as if by concrete. 'Don't come near me!' he says. 'This could be dangerous. You can't, uh . . .'

His feet sink to the knees. He cries out.

'What?' says Griffin.

'The pressure. It's crushing my calves. It's . . .' He sinks some more, going down faster than you would think the Moon's weak gravity would pull him, up to the waist.

The shock jolts Ziggy out of her reverie. 'We have to pull him out!' she says, and starts towards him, but Griffin bars her way.

'Commander said keep back,' he says.

'He's in danger!'

'Yup, and there's only one of him! You go, there could be two!'

She turns to Antonov. 'What's happening? Do you know what's happening here?'

'He's one of them!' says Antonov.

'What?'

'He's being reabsorbed. Like the others who were here when I came!'

'Fuck this,' says Melnyk. He strides towards Toog, takes him under the arms and pulls hard.

Toog shrieks, high, almost girlish, unlike anything she would have expected from him. His torso falls through – Melnyk pulling back his hands to avoid having them trapped under Toog's armpits – and then only his head is sticking out. His face is contorted in agony, but he no longer screams.

'I can't pull his head! I'll break his neck!' says Melnyk.

'Stay there,' Toog manages to mouth. And then he's gone.

Melnyk drops to his knees and taps at the floor.

'It's solid,' he says. 'Not soft at all.'

Ziggy drops to her knees and touches the floor. Melnyk's right. The floor is hard as teak.

'You Americans are cowards,' says Melnyk. He squares up to Griffin. 'You let your friend die.'

'The commander gave an order to stay back,' says Griffin. 'His assessment, his call.'

Griffin is boiling inside; she can sense it. It's an acidic, stinging feeling, bright as brass in the sun. It comes with sounds of hissing and an intense, close heat. She has never felt such sensations before. It isn't telepathy, she's sure,

but it's a vivid empathy. She is trying to get control of her thoughts, to steady her mind after the jolt it received from feeling her sister so close.

Melnyk radiates dismay, his anger like a needle jabbing into her heart. It's painful, sorrowful, sharp. She senses what is between the men, too: a space, a void, bounded by two growing sparks in each man's breast. The air is charged with static from those sparks and she senses their desire to unite, each longing to leap across to its mate, to burn and crack the provoking air between them.

'Easy to hide behind an order,' says Melnyk.

'That what you were doing when you shot my buddy out of orbit?'

'I shot no one,' says Melnyk.

Ziggy interposes herself between the two men.

'We don't know Toog is dead!' she says. 'This place has weird transitions between its spaces. He could have just been transported somewhere else.'

'He was being crushed!' says Melnyk. 'Let's get out of here, I don't want to be next.'

'Antonov, is there a deck under this? He could be there,' says Griffin.

'This is the lowest point of the boat,' says Antonov.

'I'm going to look,' says Ziggy.

She goes outside the ship, over the glowing gangplank, down on to the quay. The cat follows her, slinking around her feet.

She crouches at the side of the ship but can't see anything below the waterline.

'Griffin! Griffin!' she shouts.

Griffin comes loping out to stand beside her.

'One of us needs to go under the ship to find Toog,' she says.

Griffin looks about him. 'You want me to go?'

'You have air.'

'I need to watch these Reds,' he says. 'I don't trust what they'd do to you if I go. They could get this weapon and then we're both done for.'

'Be realistic, Griffin, that's not going to happen.'

'You think?' Again, that acidic, fizzing feeling comes off him. The fix for this – literally the thing to fix upon – is action. To regain her mind she needs to be doing, not thinking.

'Give me your oxygen, then, someone needs to look for Toog.'

'You'll cook.'

'I'll be under for no more than a couple of minutes. Come on, hurry up, we're wasting time.'

'How are you going to sink with a suit full of air?'

'Let the air out.'

She unclips the O_2 canister from his pack and he puts it into hers. He pushes her helmet onto her head while she clicks on her overgloves and her suit pressurises.

'Here!' Kovacs is next to her. She passes a thin line under her arms.

'How long is that?'

'Long enough. We need to be able to pull you out if anything goes wrong.'

Ziggy jumps into the water, falling slowly to bob on the surface.

She vents oxygen from her suit, reducing the internal pressure momentarily. Already she's hot and the draught of cool air is welcome. The suit sinks a little. This is useless; it's like

166

trying to sink a balloon. She'll have to hold her breath. She hyperventilates for a while, sucking in huge gulps of oxygen, and then turns off the O_2 and lets everything out of her suit. It sinks, trailing bubbles from the void valve as it does.

The water is murky and a patina of steam has formed on the lower part of her helmet, but she can just about see, her vision helped by the lights of the boat hulls. These flicker with symbols, anchors, mermaids, treasure chests.

She looks around her. There's no sign of a seabed, just darkness beneath, no sign of Toog. She falls under the boat's hull, down until the rope tightens and holds her.

She steadies herself by holding on to it, looking around for any clues to what became of Toog.

There is what appears to be a hole in the hull – a breach. This gives her a brief stab of panic – surely the ship should be sinking if its hull isn't intact, but it shows no sign of movement.

She opens her oxygen valve and the suit inflates, pushing her up against the hull. It's good to let go of her breath and breathe in the cool oxygen. She pulls herself along the hull to the hole. It's a ragged tear; she has no idea what might have caused it. As she approaches, the skin of the ship loses its shine, the symbols cease to pulse. The lights of the neighbouring ships are still enough to see by.

There is something about this breach that needs investigating, she has a strong sense of that. She must look into the hole. She reaches out to touch the edge of the ship. Something is stuck in the tear. It's white, about the length of her index finger. She pulls it free and sees that it's a shark's tooth. She steadies herself against the hull. As she does so, it bobs very slightly, Toog's battered

head rolls into view, the rope tightens, and she is pulled hard along the hull up and out of the water as the shark smashes into her.

She's ragged like a doll in the grip of a dog and then let go. The rope tightens again and she shoots out of the water, flying high above the quay with the force of the pull. She lands on her back, coughing and spluttering; terrible pain in her ribs.

Every one of her companions has pulled on the rope to get her free and now they rush to her, sitting her up, taking off her helmet.

'Are you OK?'

She looks out between the boats where a giant dorsal fin breaks the surface before plunging back down.

'It got your LSS!' says Lenov. 'My God, it's battered it!'

Ziggy is gasping, her chest convulsing.

'No Toog?' says Kovacs.

'His head rolled out of a hole in the hull, it was like . . .'

'*Jaws*?' says Melnyk.

'Yes.' She is sick, just salty water. Toog is dead? Or seems to be. The similarity to the movie scene makes her wonder, though. Is he? She saw his head! It felt real.

'Is that an American film?' says Shirokov.

'Yes,' says Melnyk.

'You've seen it?' The marine bristles.

'It carries a good message,' says Melnyk. 'It shows how the profit motive of capitalism overcomes basic human decency and endangers a whole town. "We need our summer dollars, now!" It's perfectly OK to watch it. I think it has a revolutionary spirit.'

'Have you ever seen an American film that doesn't?' says Lenov.

'No. I think it's safer that way,' says Melnyk.

'*Invasion of the Body Snatchers*?'

'Yes. Capitalism satirising its own fears and contradictions,' says Melnyk. 'An attack on McCarthyism.'

'I thought it was part of the Red Scare,' says Lenov.

'No. Because then I wouldn't have been able to watch it,' says Melnyk.

'You are very clever,' says Lenov.

'The gulags are full of clever people,' says Shirokov.

Kovacs is checking Ziggy over, inspecting her kit.

'Your pack looks like you've been hit by a car,' she says. 'Do you think you're injured?'

'I don't think so.'

'Is Toog dead?' said Griffin.

'I saw his head.'

'I wouldn't take that as any sort of proof,' says Kovacs. 'We've seen a lot of strange things here.'

'No more undersea adventures,' says Griffin.

'Yeah,' says Ziggy, 'Then what next?'

She wants to keep talking, keep thinking, keep going forward. Her mind, unoccupied, has produced spectres.

'I think we take Antonov up on his offer of an island of food and treasure,' says Kovacs. 'I'm pretty hungry.'

They make their way back into the ship, where Antonov is still cowering.

He says that it's possible to travel in the ship, but they'll have to get up on to the helm. He says there is an elevator at the back of the room.

'I got caught by it,' he says.

'How?'

'I stood on it. You can come down again. You just have to remember the spot.'

He points to an area of floor that looks no different from any of the rest of it.

'You go,' says Griffin.

'I don't go up there,' says Antonov.

'Why not?'

'I don't like it up there.' He sounds like a petulant child and looks a little like one, too, crossing his arms and turning away his face. Ziggy guesses he won't be much use to them anyway in his condition. It's unethical, though, to leave him – inhuman.

'I'll go,' says Griffin.

'I will,' says Kovacs.

They eye each other; again that sensation of bubbling and boiling within Griffin.

Kovacs smiles. 'Why don't we go together?' she says.

'Suits me,' says Griffin.

'You can all go,' says Antonov.

'How will we steer the ship?' says Ziggy.

'It pretty much steers itself. I wouldn't have gone, but I was starving. I needed food and water. What could I do?'

'Takes you where?' says Ziggy.

'To the forest,' says Antonov. 'That's where the food is.'

'What sort of food?'

'Food you can eat,' says Antonov. 'But no cheese. Come down and tell me when we get there and I will show you.' He sits and turns to the wall.

'You'll tell us now, Major,' says Kovacs, but Antonov is resolute, turned away.

She goes to the spot on the floor that Antonov indicated. Griffin follows her, stands beside her.

'How does this work, then?' says Griffin.

Kovacs shrugs. It's as if her shrug has summoned a

bubble from the floor. A red translucent membrane floats up above them, engulfing them in a sphere. It floats to the ceiling, apparently carrying Kovacs and Griffin with it. When it reaches the ceiling, it bobbles slightly and then floats through it. It doesn't become insubstantial; it's more like a pill breaking through a membrane of foil above it, a membrane that reseals as the sphere passes through.

'Wouldn't an elevator be easier?' says Melnyk. 'Or stairs?'

'To us, maybe,' says Ziggy. 'Maybe this looks easy to whatever built this place.'

Her side still hurts from where the shark slammed into her. She's always had a thing about sharks. That was the image of death that she saw in the floating lake while Toog and Griffin saw skulls and gravestones. Or did the suggestion of the shark lead to the shark in the water? Or was it a real shark? Of all the explanations, she doubts the last most.

'You still think it was built?' says Melnyk.

'Yes. What do you think?'

'I think it's organic. Or there's a large organic component. An organic system would be much better at producing oxygen over millions of years.'

'You're sure it's been here for millions of years?'

'No. Just . . .' He struggles to finish the sentence. 'mind-boggling.' He coughs, clears his throat. 'I want to go home,' he says.

She feels the sadness around him, like a cold current pulling her in. She could give in to it if she wanted, fall in, be swept away. The sensation is that strong.

'We better try the elevator,' says Ziggy.

She and Melnyk go to the spot on the floor.

'How do we make this work?' says Ziggy.

'There's no place like home,' says Melnyk, deliberately. 'No. Hmmm. It worked in the book. Ahhh!'

A sphere engulfs them in its crimson light and ascends towards the ceiling. Ziggy thinks it's like being trapped in a bubble of blood. It floats them up to the ceiling, which gives way with an elastic 'pop'.

The bubble continues to transport them up to the deck. She sees Griffin and Kovacs looking forwards, out over the sea, and she sees something else, extraordinary. There are five helmetless astronauts standing alongside them on the deck. They are all Toog: sandy blond hair, strong American jaw, white American teeth. Each carries a carbine across his chest and stands proudly, as if on parade.

Another pop; the bubble bursts and the ship lurches, Ziggy fighting to retain her balance. Where there was the bare outline of a ship, a ship reduced to its most essential elements of line and proportion, there is something else entirely.

Ziggy is thrown together with the others on the deck, before righting herself, clinging to a rail. Around her, the water is no longer black, no longer silver; it's dirty brown and the ship she is on is much smaller than the bare structure she left behind on the deck below.

She is in front of a cabin, above which is a small cockpit housing what are clearly two linked machine guns. The boat is a drab olive, fifty feet long, and she is standing along with the other astronauts and the five Toogs on the open section at the back.

'We're on a fucking PCF,' says Griffin. 'This is my PCF, from the first part of the war.'

'What's a PCF?' says Melnyk.

'Patrol Craft Fast. It's a standard US Army riverboat,' he

says. 'This is what took me up the Mekong Delta. We hit a mine. I . . .'

He doesn't need to say; she can feel the grief, the fear coming off him. Bad things happened to him on a boat like this.

'What about these guys?' she says.

'I don't know,' says Kovacs. 'It's a strange phenomenon.'

'Fucking word,' says Griffin. 'None of them respond. None of them say anything.'

'Do you think any of them might actually be Toog?' says Ziggy.

She looks at one of the Toogs, very closely, examining him an inch from his face. He doesn't show any signs of recognition.

'Some of this is clear, at least,' says Kovacs.

'What, exactly?' says Griffin.

'We are being provided with an experience here based at least in part on our own mental make-up. We expected hostility from each other, and we faced astronauts and cosmonauts who were hostile. We were presented with the form of a gun, the form of a ship, and we have shaped them to fit our preconceptions and our experience. When Ziggy dived beneath the ship, a memorable scene from a movie that scared her came back into her mind. In this case, Griffin, it appears to be you who has set the tone or the scene. I have no idea why that might be.'

Ziggy has an idea.

'The strength of the imprint in the mind,' she says. 'For me, boats are just once a year or less when we visit Staten Island. I don't know how they are for you. Griffin here has a strong emotional bond with this sort of boat, very strong

173

– a bond of fear, regret, maybe even affection. None of our associations with "boat" come anywhere near to that. Hence he sets what we see.'

The door to the deckhouse opens. Antonov steps out. 'I was downstairs,' he says. 'And now I'm here. I didn't want to be here. The whole shape of the ship has changed.'

'Has it done this before?' says Ziggy.

'When I sailed it, when I went to the forest, yes. It changed.'

'You didn't think to mention this before?'

'I thought you'd think I was mad.'

'Too late,' says Griffin. 'What did it change into?'

'It became the *Ismail*.'

'Really?' says Kovacs.

'What is the *Ismail*?' says Griffin.

'A torpedo boat,' says Melnyk. 'It was the one that sailed alongside the *Potemkin*. They took it over. One of the acts that inspired the revolution.'

'Which revolution?' says Griffin.

'Please,' says Melnyk. 'Which fucking revolution do you think?'

'The whole world's on about revolution now, how the fuck should I know?'

'Russian,' says Kovacs, absently. 'Can you sail this thing, Griffin?'

'Yes.'

'And you know how to get to where we can get food and water?' says Kovacs to Antonov.

'Yes. It's obvious once you set off. But I warn you, there are things there that are difficult to see.'

'Do we go?'

'We need to eat and drink eventually,' says Ziggy. 'That

will allow us to stay here indefinitely, find an exit and wait for rescue.'

'Ain't you the optimist,' says Griffin.

'Our only aim for the moment has to be survival,' says Kovacs. 'Drive the ship.'

'Do we take these with us?' says Melnyk, gesturing to the five Toogs.

'I don't see any alternative,' says Griffin.

Ziggy looks at the astronauts. They remind her of shop dummies, staring straight ahead, expressionless, their hands clasped to their carbines.

'Would you gentlemen like to get off the ship?' says Melnyk.

One by one, the five strange astronauts go on to the gangplank and walk down on to the dock. The cat – her cat – watches them.

Melnyk shrugs. Griffin shakes his head. 'I'll start the engines,' he says.

The boat grumbles into life. It's quieter than Ziggy expected, the engines just a heavy, low thrum.

'What happens if we lose sight of land?' says Ziggy.

'The lights will come on,' says Antonov. 'You wait, the lights will come on.'

The boat motors out away from the quay. Ziggy goes to the prow to see what is ahead. Around the boat, maybe two or three hundred yards, the water is a dirty brown and now the sky transforms from black to a hazy blue but only in a patch, as if someone has begun painting it but ran out before they finished.

'Was this the ship you travelled in last time?' says Ziggy.

'No. It was much smaller. And there was a helmsman.'

'What sort?'

'The Greek sort. I think it was Charon, the rower of the dead. He had the cloak, the cowl, the whole lot. It seems almost comical, but it was terrifying.'

'He normally doesn't bring you back the other way,' says Ziggy.

'No.'

'How did you get back?'

'With difficulty,' says Antonov. 'I stole the boat. But such nightmares. When I arrived back at the quay, I slept and the ship was transformed again. I haven't had the courage to go back but I expect I would have had to – I have to eat.'

'What is there to eat there?'

'It's a forest. Whatever you can find in a forest.'

'I grew up in Queens,' says Ziggy. 'Foraging wasn't a big thing.'

Antonov scratches, sucks his teeth.

'There are fruit trees there. There are animals to trap and lava flows. You can cook on them – I did.'

'There's a volcano?'

'Apparently. There are roads of fire, anyway, they are useful. There's everything you need there.'

'So why did you return?'

'It is a place of nightmares,' says Antonov.

'What sort of nightmares?'

He waves his hand in dismissal. 'Nothing can prepare you for them. We have no choice but to go there if we don't want to starve. By telling you I will only worry you. They are survivable. I am proof of that.'

They sail out into the retreating darkness.

After an hour, they can no longer see the quay behind them, but they press on.

After another hour, Griffin calls her up.

'There are no landmarks. No compass. We could be going round in circles.'

'Antonov!' she calls down. 'Where are these lights?'

As she says it, a row of flickering lights float before them over the brown water. There are nine of them, evenly spaced, and it's impossible to be sure of their size or their distance.

'Those are the lights,' says Antonov. 'Those are the lights, aim for them!'

'What are they?' says Ziggy.

'Who knows now?' says Antonov. 'Last time they were beach fires. But everything changes here. Everything changes.'

Griffin turns the boat towards the lights and the patch of sky, the patch of brown water beneath them, follows the boat.

She can't tell if they are making progress – after an hour the lights seem no nearer. It's warm, though, under the bright sky and, though it might be dangerous, she has Melnyk help her out of her heavy, sweaty suit. She pitches the diaper overboard and pisses from the back of the boat. This seems to set off a chain reaction. All the cosmonauts climb out of their own suits and discard their diapers. Griffin has her hold course while he does the same.

They all sit in their undersuits, like tatty androids, wires poking out of sleeves, of legs, of the chest. She enjoys the relief. The suit wasn't heavy in the low g, but it was uncomfortable. She'll need help to get it back on again when she needs it but – in this moment of downtime – it seems right to be as comfortable as possible.

The effect of the passage of the boat fascinates her. It rises higher and falls much more slowly than it would on Earth,

with the result that they make more of a plume than a wake, throwing a long cascade of water up into the air.

'Over there!' shouts Griffin.

She comes to the prow of the boat. Now she can see the nine lights are indeed flickering bonfires. In their light, a line of spiky columns rises behind them – as if in a parade at attention.

They glide closer and she can see the fires are on a wide beach of black sand. They are smaller than she had assumed, each about the size of a campfire rather than the bonfires she'd imagined them to be from a distance. Behind the black sand are row upon row of upright columns in the same pearly grey as the ship was before it transformed. Each sprouts stalks at regular intervals along its trunk. And, yes, trunk is an apt description. The shape is clearly suggestive of that of a tree.

Griffin throttles back and the shallow-hulled boat does what it was designed for and grounds smoothly on the shore. Griffin throws out an anchor and they disembark. Ziggy insists they don't leave the spacesuits on the boat. They can't afford to become separated from them and, if it means they have to carry them, so be it.

She puts her suit on to her shoulder and takes a long bound down onto the sand. Somehow, falling is even stranger out of the suit than it was in it. She lands with an unaccustomed lightness that nearly throws her off balance on the sand.

When she catches her balance, she sees the colour of the trees shift, blur, flicker and she is looking no longer at row upon regular row but on a jungle out of a dream: tall trees rising to a thick canopy, vines dropping down, the call of birds from within.

Kovacs glances at Ziggy.

'Whose forest is this?' she says.

'It wasn't like this before,' says Antonov.

'How was it?'

'Russian,' he says. 'A good Russian forest. I don't know the words. Different trees. *Doob. Sosna.*'

Oak and pine, if Ziggy's vocabulary is still up to scratch.

'There was a river in there,' says Antonov. 'About half a day in. I'm scared, though. Try to move quietly.'

'Will do,' says Griffin. 'But whatever's in there should be scared of me. This is my terrain.'

I'm going to be in there, thinks Ziggy. And I'm scared of you.

Kovacs shoots her a look of complicity. Ziggy shudders. It's as if she has thrown the thought to Kovacs and Kovacs has caught it and thrown it back to her. The understanding goes beyond a mere glance. Kovacs feels what she feels; she feels what Kovacs feels. Griffin is a liability, a danger, and this forest has been generated from Griffin's thoughts, from his nightmares, maybe. How much else of the dangers they have faced have come from him? The immediately hostile cosmonaut simulacra? Maybe even the roaming bands of murderous astronauts. Toog was trapped just after Griffin shouted that they should leave Ziggy 'stuck' on the Moon. Is that pushing it too far?

They assemble on the broad shore. Ziggy approaches one of the fires. It gives off a good heat and has the aroma of scented wood, but the logs at its centre are like the trees were before they changed – more like a minimalist take on logs than the real things, short cylinders with stubby projections from their trunks. She can't really discern their colour in the fire but it's not the familiar dark of wood, more like the neutral grey she

saw in the ship before it transformed, or on Griffin's combat rifle when it lay long and featureless in its box.

A wave of homesickness sweeps over her as she looks into the fire. She remembers her family holidays, all pouring into the blue interior of her family's Ford Falcon, setting off for Goosewing Beach in Massachusetts. Her dad's friend had a house there, more a hut really, but they'd spend long days on the shore, cook on a Primus and light fires on the beach at night to watch the sun go down. Maria was beside her then, and she'd put her arm around her and watch the sun make a road of gold on the evening sea.

Other kids bickered or fought. Never with her and Maria. They were best friends, who'd come into the world together and should have . . . Oh God, Maria. I should have been there, I really should. She catches herself. Always, since Maria died, she has carried a feeling of guilt, but here it's amplified, corrosive. Maria wouldn't want her to feel like that.

'Hey, look at the dog!'

'Oh my God, it's Oscar!' says Ziggy.

The cat from the ship has transformed. He's now a big, friendly, vaunting boxer dog, shaking sand from his jowls at the water's edge. He bounces up to her, thrusts his body into her leg, and she bends to pat him.

'This is the dog that used to play on the beach when I was a kid. He belonged to the guy who ran the ice cream stall. 'Oscar. My God. Oscar!' She takes the wet leather of his collar in her fingers, turns it to show the tag. There it is: 'Oscar. Don't worry 'bout me, I'll find my way home,' it says.

Something else has happened, too, utterly odd. The muted light is not muted around Oscar. It's as if he is in Technicolor and the rest of the world is in dirty sepia. The beach beneath

his feet is bright with little pebbles, russet, red and grey. The sand is not black but that muddy brown she remembers as a kid. 'Why can't we go to a more sandy beach?' she'd asked her dad.

'Not so many people out here where it's rocky,' he'd said.

'Yeah, for a good reason.'

That conversation comes back from her adolescence. As a younger kid she'd loved the beach, learned to surf there, been enchanted by the unreliable weather, its sunlit showers dropping like rains of bright pennies, the rainbows over the headland, dark clouds lit at the edges like cinders in a fire.

Oscar carries that light with him now. He reminds her of one of those gaudy transfer stickers that used to come with breakfast cereal, the sort you rubbed with a coin to get them to stick to a scene. It's as if someone has taken one of those and rubbed it on to the dreary photograph that is the rest of reality.

As she strokes his wet fur she finds tears in her eyes. She can put one hand on the past, those bright days on the beach, but she cannot step into it, to lever a Frisbee from the dog's slobbery mouth, send it skimming down the shoreline to Maria. She sees her sister now in her imagination, a skinny brown thing leaping high to catch the disc, the dog bounding in a four-paw vertical take-off beside her to try to get it before she threw it back.

The memory is vivid, almost tangible. It's like her mind is a projector, casting the image onto the screen of the black beach, bringing it to a vivid colour.

'Where's this food?' says Griffin.

'Further in,' says Antonov. 'Can you trap game?'

'No need,' says Griffin. 'I think I can just about hit a goose with an M16.'

'The game is bigger than that,' says Antonov. 'And save the M16. You might need it.'

'What for?'

'I don't know. This place is full of surprises.'

'What sort of surprises?'

'Your nightmares come true here,' says Melnyk.

'Oh great,' says Melnyk, 'Can't wait to discover what's in all our heads.'

'Are you being sarcastic?' says Griffin.

'I am being ironic,' says Melnyk.

'Same thing,' says Griffin.

'Yes, that's why they bothered to have separate words for them,' says Melnyk. 'Now I am being sarcastic.'

That wild feeling rises in Griffin again. It's almost as if Ziggy can hear it, like the baying of hounds, the howl of a storm, the hiss of a big cat.

'Griffin, keep calm.'

'I give the fucking orders now. And if I order you to lose your shit and shoot this smart-ass commie, that's what you'll do.'

'No it isn't,' says Ziggy.

'Then I'll shoot you first.'

'And what will that achieve?'

'I don't know, but I'm willing to find out.'

He levels the gun at her. She can see sweat on his lip, a feeling of abandonment radiating from him, a tremor, a rupturing, the verge of an explosion.

Kovacs takes out her gun and points it at Griffin's head, a distance of no more than three feet.

'I'll tell you straight, Griffin, you are a liability to this mission,' she says. 'In three seconds, or if you kill Da Luca, I will shoot you and all the treasures of this place will be the sole property of the Soviet Union. Your only option is to put down the gun.'

Griffin's hands shake.

'One,' says Kovacs.

'I'm trying,' says Griffin. 'I want to put down the gun. I don't want the fucking commies to—'

'Two!'

Ziggy looks directly at Griffin.

'I'm an American soldier,' she says.

She sees a burning American flag, she sees burning villages, she sees Griffin saluting in the sun – a passing out parade, his proudest moment.

'Three.'

'No!' says Ziggy as Griffin lowers his gun. He collapses to his haunches, makes a sound that Ziggy might take for a sob.

'You need to surrender your gun, Griffin,' says Ziggy.

Oscar the dog loses shape, shrinks and is the featureless form of a small four-legged animal again, the beach only black, no window of colour around the animal.

'I will fucking . . .' says Griffin. 'Oh my God! Look!'

He points back out to sea, and they turn to see the boat they came on is no longer there.

It's entirely vanished; whether drifted away or simply dissolved into the sea, she doesn't know.

She feels panic well up in her, though she doesn't quite know why. There is no retracing of steps now, just pressing on and hoping for the best.

'Did it do that before?' she asks Antonov.

'No! At least it was there when I went into the trees and there when I came back. I don't know what it did in the meantime.'

'It makes no difference,' says Ziggy. 'We can't stand here, there's no gain I can see in going back, we have to go on, particularly if there's a chance of food and water here. We need to maintain hope. We don't know what technologies might be on this ship or museum or whatever you want to call it. We might be able to manipulate them. We might be able to get out or make contact with Earth. We need to remain hopeful.'

Griffin is still hunched on the beach, looking at his gun, as if it will act as an oracle, tell him what to do.

'Griffin, are you with us?'

'I . . .'

'Do you want to sit down on your ass now and give up, Griffin?'

'No.'

'Then let's accept the facts as they are and decide what we're going to do about them. As far as I can see, Antonov has managed to get food in this forest, weird as it is. He's found water. Hierarchy of needs determines they're first on the list, as air seems taken care of for the minute. I say we press on into the trees.'

Griffin grunts.

'In our case, that's an order,' says Kovacs. 'We don't need a debate.'

'OK, let's go.'

'Me first,' says Griffin. 'This is my sort of terrain. Behind me, no talking.'

They step into the jungle. Ziggy has never been in a place quite like this before and it's a surprise to her that there is no even footing. Dead logs, spiny plants, and tree trunks make for an assault course.

'This is Griffin's creation. If he weren't here, the going would be easier.'

It's Kovacs' voice but not on the radio, or even spoken out loud. It's in her head. The voice is shifting in tone and volume, as if coming in and out of tune on a radio but the words are clear enough.

Ziggy replies. 'We should try to manipulate it. If Griffin's associations can determine the form of the forest, so can ours.'

Her head aches, swims, as if she has stood up too quickly.

'So you have opened yourself up,' says Kovacs.

'Yes.'

The words come with a wave of emotion attached, a certain excitement from Kovacs, the 'yes' kind of tumbling from Ziggy, like a tambourine dropped downstairs, if that noise was a feeling. It's the sound, she knows, of her own shock and confusion.

'Can the others hear?' says Ziggy.

'I have been experimenting and it seems not. This place is allowing us to communicate like this. This place is . . .'

Images come in to Ziggy's mind. A birthday present, a snowball fight before big imposing tower blocks, a horse pulling a sled on snow. Surprise, a feeling of awe and excitement, accompanies them. They come from Kovacs and it feels – as much as Ziggy can tell – that they are spontaneous. Perhaps they are not even thoughts, just associations, chains of images that attach themselves to Kovacs' thoughts, stretching away into the darkness of her deepest memories.

'Yes,' says Ziggy. It's not excitement that registers in her mind, but nervousness. She sees a big old door in an old house, a key in its lock. She wants to turn the key but dare not. Is it a dream or an image from a film or a story? She doesn't know, but it's no door she ever recalls seeing in reality.

Her head aches.

'This is hard,' she says to herself.

'I don't find it so,' says Kovacs. 'Tell me, what do you really think this place is?'

There's a sensation of intrusion now, of someone going through her things, almost of burglary. She withdraws her mind, snaps back.

Kovacs is gone.

Kovacs comes to her side, puts her hand on her arm, but Ziggy walks away from her, pushes on.

They go into the trees for about 100 yards. The terrain is very hard and Griffin says several times how much easier things would be if he had a machete. Or does he say it? He has told everyone to be silent. Is she hearing his thoughts?

Presently, the stubborn vegetation of the forest's edge gives way as the canopy above becomes thicker. It darkens the ground beneath, so nothing grows and the way is much easier, though gloomy.

'Do you have an idea on a direction?' whispers Griffin to Antonov.

'No,' he says. 'This is different.'

'We'll have to find some sort of landmark,' says Griffin. 'Otherwise, we'll be going round in circles.'

They press on through the trees. Ziggy's spacesuit is not too much of an encumbrance here, draped across her shoulders. It's not heavy but it is bulky. She manages to wear it

like a hunter might carry a big animal pelt and trap a sleeve under one arm, a leg under another, so it doesn't fall off. They move quietly through the forest, or as quietly as they can with their big, bouncing strides.

It's hot, despite the lack of sun, and she finds herself sweating.

Finally, they hear something ahead. Running water!

'Steady,' says Griffin, gesturing for the others to stay where they are. He takes his suit off his shoulders but keeps the carbine.

He creeps forward, pausing for long minutes behind trees as he does so.

Finally, he crawls forward, carbine always ready in front of him.

Ziggy watches as he disappears over the lip of what must be a bank. After about a quarter of an hour, he returns.

'OK,' he says. 'There's water and it looks like it's safe to approach it. Let's go.'

They file through the trees. When she gets nearer she can see a stream cutting a bank through the jungle. The water falls in slow motion; even over a little waterfall there isn't much in the way of white water or disturbance. It's oddly tranquil.

'This is water?' says Ziggy.

'It's similar to the other stream I drank from,' says Antonov.

'Anyone want to try?' says Griffin.

'I will,' says Ziggy.

She feels a flash of concern from Kovacs, who says, 'I'm not sure that's wise.'

'Someone has to,' says Ziggy.

'You are the most useful on this trip,' says Kovacs. 'If it's poisonous, we can't afford to lose you.'

'Why am I useful?'

'You are in tune with the ship. You can understand the Twilight Language. The ship is sympathetic to you. Can't you feel that?'

'That's only half the truth,' says Ziggy. The realisation has struck her like a thunderbolt. It's as if Kovacs had clouds across her mind and suddenly they have parted, allowing a glimpse of the truth in golden rays.

'What is your purpose?' says Ziggy.

'Survival,' says Kovacs, and the clouds come back again.

'You know more about this place than you are revealing,' says Ziggy.

'I don't think anyone *knows* anything. But I have the sense you are central to the whole purpose of me being here. The Twilight Language has revealed this to me. You are without doubt crucial here.'

'There I was thinking the guy with years of jungle combat experience was the most useful in a jungle,' says Griffin. 'You learn something every day.'

Kovacs gives him a hard look. 'This is your jungle,' she says. Or rather, doesn't. Ziggy hears her but her lips don't move, and Griffin says nothing.

Ziggy feels the strong need to break from Kovacs. Her presence is magnetic, or perhaps not. Perhaps more like a whirlpool or a deep current. She feels that if she gets too close to her, she could be lost.

'I'll try the water,' says Ziggy.

She lowers herself down the bank and dips in a finger. The water is cold, though the current is not strong, given that the stream is on a reasonably steep gradient.

'Wait ten minutes,' says Kovacs. Ziggy does. She suffers no adverse effects, so she dips in her finger again and licks

it. Another ten minutes and she is fine. She scoops water up into her hand and takes a drink.

'It's water,' she says. 'I feel OK.'

Kovacs insists the Russians wait at least another twenty minutes. They do, and then everyone goes down to drink.

'Now we just need the food,' says Melnyk.

There is a noise from the trees, a cry.

'What was that?'

Another noise, a dull boom. Griffin flinches.

'Shit,' says Melnyk.

Griffin levels the rifle at the trees.

'Any ideas?' says Melnyk.

'That bang was a fucking claymore,' says Griffin. 'It's an anti-personnel trap.'

'Here?' says Antonov. 'Why would . . .?'

He never finishes his sentence as a black mass leaps from the trees to take him straight off his feet. The shock sends Ziggy tumbling down the bank into the water.

Chaos, shouting. Screaming. Some of it is in a language Ziggy doesn't understand, but some she most definitely does. 'Make Love, Not War!' 'Hey, Hey, Lbj, how many kids did you kill today?' 'We won't fight another rich man's war!'

When Ziggy regains her feet she sees a huge spider, the size of a horse, squatting on Antonov's chest, its jaws wrapped around his head. All along its body, human heads protrude, some Eastern-looking, three or four long-haired, bearded, with headbands. All of them are shrieking. Also sticking out of its back are two placards, like protestors use – one bearing the peace circle, the other saying 'Stop the War'.

Griffin levels the carbine and puts a burst of four shots into the spider. It turns to face him, withdraws its mandibles

and pounces, knocking him off his feet. He tumbles down the bank in an exaggerated, slow-motion fall, turning and twisting to try to regain his balance.

The gravity is so weak that he manages to get his feet underneath him before he hits the stream and lands upright, gun trained on the spider. It leaps for him again, but he gives it the full clip at close range. The spider disintegrates, blown to pieces, its great black body falling apart under the assault of the bullets, legs, signs, heads tumbling free to fall, as if through water, to the forest floor.

Kovacs runs to Antonov. He is flat on his back, twitching, his limbs in spasm. Ziggy goes to him. He gives a final convulsion, a groan and lies still. Kovacs takes his pulse, starts pummelling his chest in an effort to resuscitate him.

Antonov coughs, says, 'I'd like cheese,' and then closes his eyes.

'Do the breaths, Da Luca!' she says, but as Ziggy bends to breathe into Antonov's mouth, he begins to fade, almost to deflate, to crumble in on himself. Ziggy and Kovacs step back to watch as Antonov is absorbed into the forest floor.

'He was one of them,' says Melnyk.

'Who's "them"?' says Kovacs.

'The creations of this place. The dummies.'

Griffin is looking at his gun. 'This thing has reloaded,' he says. 'The belt's full!'

It now has a belt, too, where it was just a conventional magazine before.

'Shit,' says Kovacs and sits down. 'This has some far-reaching implications.'

Ziggy looks down to where Griffin is. The peace sign placard crumbles and is sucked into the floor.

Ziggy swallows. Antonov was entirely convincing. When she faced the other simulacra, she had no sense of them as human, no window into their thoughts and feelings. Antonov was different. He felt real. Kovacs is right. There are far-reaching implications. The only person here who she knows for sure isn't a creation of this machine is herself. She feels the same disquiet in Kovacs, but tinged with something else. A hostility, distrust.

'What was that thing?' she says.

'Someone's nightmare,' says Kovacs. 'And I don't think we need to look far to see whose.'

Griffin comes up the bank in a couple of big bounds. He stands above her.

'Are you saying I brought that thing on us?'

Kovacs says nothing, just stands up. 'We need a moment to calm down and take all this in,' she says. 'I propose ten minutes of silence.'

'This is hippy bullshit,' says Griffin.

'I suggest you think of that spider and see what good that attitude does you here,' she says.

Griffin shrugs. 'Nothing to say it came from me.'

Kovacs says nothing, just sits. Ziggy does too.

Ziggy can feel Kovacs' mind working and shifting, like you might be aware of the workings of a theatre by seeing a sudden ruffle or bulge in a stage curtain. She can't tell what she is thinking exactly, but she has the sense of deep activity taking place.

Finally, Kovacs speaks.

'I want to propose an experiment,' she says. 'We take control of this situation. Da Luca, what associations do you have with woods?'

'None, beyond Kissena Park,' she says. 'I grew up in Queens.'

Kovacs taps a tree.

'I suspect you'll have some associations gleaned from books and films, but no lived experience of the deep woods. Melnyk, you?'

'I'm a seaside boy, never went much to the woods. Cold and bears. They're my main associations.'

'Lenov, Shirokov?'

'Cold and bears,' they both say.

'Don't dwell on the bears. All right, this is what I propose. We Soviets are going to think deeply of our experiences of woods.'

'Why not us?' says Griffin.

'We're in your woods now,' says Kovacs. 'And I can't say that I like them much.'

Griffin snorts.

'You think I'm controlling what goes on here?'

'Controlling is the wrong word. Creating is better. But I think *we* could control things. It's clear that this place is feeding off our expectations and our fears. Your associations with woods, or jungle, are the strongest and they are full of fear. We need to see if we can take that over.'

Griffin shrugs. 'Always find a way to blame the American.'

'This is not blame,' says Kovacs. 'I don't think you can help what's happening here. Melnyk, Lenov, Shirokov, sit with me.'

They sit together and they link hands, looking almost as if they're about to start a séance.

'Imagine the woods near your home, or that you think of when you think of woods,' she says. 'I will, too. Listen to my voice. We'll try to use a hypnotic state.'

'So where did you learn to do that?' says Griffin.

Kovacs says nothing but Ziggy guesses. She's used it to read the Twilight Language, to understand the clues that led her to the Moon.

Kovacs begins softly, talking the others through a progressive relaxation, their toes, feet, calves up to the thighs, belly, so on. She leads them by counting down, down, into a hypnotic state. Studying the faces of the Russians, Ziggy can't tell if this is working or not. Griffin reacts as she would expect, just going off a little way to examine his gun, to check its operation. Kovacs talks in Russian, telling her squad to remember walks in the woods as a child, to smell the leaves of the forest, to hear the twigs crunching underfoot.

The dog approaches again, grey and featureless, and then it's Oscar, the beach boxer, and then a black dog she doesn't recognise. It's large, with pointed ears and a great lolling tongue. It seems friendly enough and comes to her side. She pats it and it wags its tail.

Kovacs' voice drones on, talking of oaks full of leaves in the summer, of bountiful mushrooms, of nuts and game birds.

There is a noise like thunder, far off. The canopy of the trees shakes in a stiff wind. Faces take shape in the bushes – Eastern faces like her own. Bodies are visible beneath them. One is a soldier and he carries an AK-47.

She goes to stand, to run, but the trees sway and the faces become indistinct and then they are flowers, big white blooms. She looks up and the dark canopy of the trees parts; the sky becomes visible, an evening red. All around, the trees are transforming. They are no longer tropical giants but wide oaks, pines and firs. The air cools; grass sprouts at her feet and a wide-trunked tropical tree transforms to a slim silver birch at her side.

The forest is still deep and quite dark, but it is undeniably no longer a tropical jungle. Kovacs stands up.

'That bodes well,' she says.

'Shit,' says Griffin, looking about him.

'Let's see about food,' says Kovacs.

'If Antonov was a creation of whatever this place is,' says Ziggy, 'might he be lying, or at least wrong about there being food?'

'Let's see,' says Kovacs. She bends to a tree where large white mushrooms sprout at the base.

'These are edible,' she says. 'My mother would collect them back in Transylvania.'

'You're from Transylvania?' says Griffin.

'Yes. We're not all vampires,' she says. 'No more than all Americans are cowboys.'

'So some of you are vampires?' says Griffin.

'No more than one in three,' says Kovacs, making a kind of biting gesture.

'Mushrooms and vampires,' says Griffin. 'I signed up for a space mission, not a fucking fairy tale.'

'Look on it as preferable to a return to the Mekong Delta,' says Kovacs.

She breaks off a mushroom and takes a tiny bite.

'It seems OK,' she says. 'We'll collect them and eat them later, provided I suffer no reaction. There should be nuts here, too. I tried to imagine nuts.'

'What if they just crumble in our bellies like the dummies crumble?' says Melnyk.

'Then at least we've had the comfort of eating,' says Kovacs. She turns to Griffin.

'Try not to think about your experiences in Vietnam,' she says. 'Try to think pleasant thoughts.'

He laughs. 'I always do. I can bury things; I wouldn't be standing here if I couldn't. NASA would have had me out.'

'I wonder,' says Kovacs. 'I suggest everyone drinks, replenishes the water supply on their drinking reservoirs and then we'll be on our way.'

The temperate forest is easier on them than the tropical one. It's pleasantly cold, which makes the burden of movement less arduous, less sweaty as they bound through the trees. When you have the hang of it, the weak gravity allows quick travel loping steps propelling you on at speed. They harvest pine nuts from cones and pick wild garlic and more mushrooms, big russet ones that look like the back of clamshells. This does a little to ward off hunger, but it's clear they can't live like this for long. They will have to capture an animal or something soon, and they do see good-sized birds flapping in the trees – pigeons, maybe. They would make a meal if they could be caught, thinks Ziggy, provided they're not just illusions that will crumble to nothing before they can be cooked.

Dusk falls, a silver sky visible through the trees, a sharp crescent moon caught in the topmost branches. Can you see the Moon from the Moon, wonders Ziggy? Here, it seems that you can.

As the shadows deepen, Kovacs calls a halt.

'We have to assume that, tomorrow, the sun will come up,' she says. 'In which case we should sleep.'

It's getting colder, but Griffin wastes no time in putting together a fire, lighting it by using the battery and some wire stripped from Ziggy's defunct cooling system to conjure a spark.

'What do you think this place is?' says Ziggy.

'I'm sticking with cosmic Disneyland,' says Melnyk. 'It's

a place where your dreams come true. And, unfortunately, your nightmares, too.'

'I don't have any hippy/gook/giant spiders with signs in their backs in my nightmares,' says Griffin. 'How 'bout you?'

'I don't know, maybe,' says Melnyk. 'I don't remember my nightmares. Maybe here I'll find out what they are.'

'We should avoid that,' says Kovacs. 'Let's try to relax, think good thoughts. Think of things that would make us happy.'

Griffin snorts. 'Great. I'll look forward to visiting my brother in Houston and seeing the Astros play next week, shall I? Gee, I can't wait to see Niekro throw his knuckleball.'

'Why not?' says Kovacs. 'False hope is always preferable to true despair.'

'Difficult to have hope if you call it false hope,' says Melnyk.

'Let's be realistic,' says Kovacs. 'At the moment, the best we can hope for is to survive here. The task of getting home may be beyond us for now, but not all our hopes may be false. Both of our governments cannot risk there being something here that the other could use against them. There will be future expeditions, bigger ones. We may be found.'

'Thank you, Mother, for chasing the monsters of doubt away. Now may I sleep?' says Melnyk.

'No bother.'

'We need to set a watch,' says Griffin.

Ziggy senses what Kovacs is thinking: 'Yes, Griffin, we need to watch you.'

It's agreed, however, that they will each sit a two-hour watch throughout the night, timed through the watches built into their suits.

Griffin says he's not sleepy, so will sit up. He does a brief scout of the area but is satisfied there is nothing else around.

Ziggy uses her suit as a pillow in front of the fire. The dog is back, the black, sharp-eared version. Kovacs nods. 'This is good. He was a neighbour's dog when I was growing up. This is our reality, not Griffin's more hostile one.'

Ziggy is exhausted and, though she is still jangling inside from the attack of the spider, she falls asleep quickly. Almost as quickly, it seems, Kovacs is shaking her awake.

'Look!' she whispers. 'Look!'

There is a gigantic face, eyes of fire, mouth of fire, leering at them through the trees. It has the aspect of a giant Halloween lantern, but it seems to move in a series of tilting, staccato hops through the darkness.

Melnyk is blinking himself awake but Griffin is still asleep, and she goes to wake him but Kovacs says 'No'. She hears a voice in her mind: 'He will only make things worse. We'll wake him if necessary.'

The flaming face comes nearer and, in its own light, Ziggy can now see that it's not a lantern at all but a hut made of sticks and daub, two bright windows and an open door flickering with firelight. It's not floating, as she thought, but conveyed on two enormous chicken legs, each as thick as a tree trunk.

'Baba Yaga!' whispers Melnyk.

'What?' says Ziggy. She vaguely remembers something about that from a fairy tale.

'The witch of the woods!' he whispers. 'You asked for a Slavic wood and, by Lenin's dick, you've got one!'

The hut turns one way and another, tilts and twists. To Ziggy, it appears almost as if it's sniffing the air.

The hut stops, momentarily. Then it runs towards them, quick bounds in the weak gravity. It stops again, tilts. It runs

backwards a little way. Then forwards again. Finally, it sinks down on the chicken legs until it is two or three feet off the forest floor. A set of steps flops out from the doorway, leading up to the hut.

'What shall we do?' says Melnyk.

'Go in,' says Kovacs to Melnyk.

'Do you think that's a good idea?' says Ziggy.

'Isn't the thing to do with your fears to confront them?' says Kovacs.

'Go on, then,' says Melnyk. His face is white in the hut's firelight.

'They're not my fears,' says Kovacs. 'This is something from your culture, your unconscious, your tribal memory: maybe. That's Russian folklore. I'm Hungarian.'

'Jung would be proud of us,' says Lenov.

'Jung isn't here,' says Melnyk, 'and I feel quite sure that, if he were, he would advise against going into that hut.'

Griffin stirs at the fireside.

'If he wakes up, the shooting will start,' says Kovacs. 'How did he make astronaut selection?'

'He's a hell of a pilot,' says Ziggy, 'and whatever's coming out here is emerging from deep down. I think he was picked for his cool ability to handle fires in the cabin, not to confront his inner demons in a hellscape. This place. You know what it does. It's an amplifier for . . .' She can't quite think of the word. 'Everything,' she says. It's the closest she can come.

'A shame,' says Kovacs. 'If I ever get back, I'm going to recommend feeding large doses of LSD to cosmonaut candidates. We need to weed out people like that.'

'Yeah, do that in the States and you'll have a queue of hippies around the block,' says Ziggy.

'Not once word gets out what I'm putting the LSD subjects through,' says Kovacs, her eyes on the hut. 'They'll run like mice.'

The hut sits immobile, the lights burning at its windows and open door suggestive of an angry face.

'We don't have to go in there at all,' says Melnyk.

'No, but I have the strong feeling we should,' says Kovacs.

'We're at a place of safety, as far as we know. The safety of the inside of that hut is unknown. Logically, it's no sort of swap,' says Melnyk.

'This is not logic, it's intuition,' says Kovacs.

'You can't make decisions on that.'

Kovacs looks at Ziggy. 'What do you think?'

Ziggy looks towards the hut. An excited feeling overtakes her. Not quite a child's Christmas morning, but not far off. There's something in there she needs to see, she feels sure.

'There's a strong attraction to going in,' she says. 'But there's no guarantee this structure isn't influencing my thoughts in order to deceive me.'

'To what end?' says Kovacs.

'I don't know. To eliminate me, to get rid of me.'

'Damn right,' says Griffin, sitting upright and making Ziggy start. 'Since we've been here, we've been attacked, deceived, nearly killed. We must assume all contact is hostile until it proves straight A that it's not.'

'The voice of the American century,' says Kovacs.

'Thank you, quite a compliment,' says Griffin.

Ziggy feels something rising in her – a feeling of childish wanting, a desire for comfort, for holding, for home. The fires in the eyes of the hut no longer look angry. They look inviting, cosy.

She hears herself speak. 'There are sweets in there,' she says.

'What?' says Griffin.

'In that hut, there are sweets and all good things to eat.'

Kovacs puts her hand on Ziggy's shoulder.

'Is the hut communicating that to you?'

'Yes. It doesn't seem hostile.'

Melnyk laughs. 'Let's see – witch's hut promises to be full of candy. How does that one normally end? You are really feeling this?'

'Yes, aren't you?'

'I feel a little odd,' says Melnyk, 'but nothing completely out of the ordinary. Maybe a bit drunk. Two glasses of vodka drunk, not properly, just a little, I don't know, looser than normal.'

'Griffin?' She doesn't need to ask there, really. She can feel the rage coming off him like a dry heat.

'I'm fine. I'm always fine.'

Ziggy really does feel an overwhelming desire to see what is inside the hut. She can gain enough distance on her thoughts to know that idea is perhaps something that's being kindled in her by an outside agency, but it doesn't really feel like that. It has the sense of a genuine and heartfelt need, something that almost short-circuit her rational decision-making process.

It's like that feeling where you think 'I shouldn't have another potato chip', and then you just have another three without thinking about it, maybe more after that, but magnified.

'We need to explore every aspect of this structure,' she says. 'We can't afford to miss something that would allow us to get out of here or provide food. I'll go and look.'

'I'd strongly advise against that,' says Melnyk, but Ziggy is already walking towards the hut.

She can feel the heat of its fires from even ten paces away. Close up, she can see it's constructed of a weave of tiny feathers that stick out at all angles.

What is in that hut? The question burns in her mind. She really needs to find out. That is an unreasonable curiosity, she can see. She has a sense of abandon, of damning the consequences.

She puts her foot on the bottom step. It is made of a weave of tiny bones.

This fascinates her, and she bends to look at them. They do appear to be small chicken bones, like you might have left over from a drumstick. She goes to the second step. Now she can see into the hut. A cloaked figure is sitting in front of a raging fire, its back to her. It shows no sign of discomfort, despite the heat.

She feels sure this kind lady, because it's obviously a lady, will welcome her in. The second step is under both her feet. She looks down. It's made of bigger bones. She guesses they might belong to something like a small dog or a cat.

She ascends the third step. This is made, she sees, of larger bones. She can't be sure, but she'd say they were human.

'Good to put them to use,' she thinks. She is struck simultaneously by the ridiculousness of that thought and by its correctness. It's the right thing to think, the best thing to think.

She steps into the hut. The interior bursts with rainbow lights. They circle and dance around her. Music starts up. It's a song she knows, unbelievably – Abba's 'Dancing Queen'.

She looks around her. The room is large. The woman by the fire is still turned away from her, but she has two hi-fi turntables next to her and is playing a disc.

All around her, astronauts have appeared, fully kitted in EVA spacesuits. They are dancing with each other, in each other's arms, swaying to the music, bopping and up and down in big, moony strides.

She has a strong urge to join in. She's very aware her thoughts are disordered, but she can't seem to get them in order again. She wants to dance, very much.

She taps an astronaut on the shoulder. 'Can I dance?' she says.

'Sorry, I'm with someone else,' he says. She sees the face inside the helmet bubble. She almost jumps. It's her fiancé, Andy.

He turns his partner in his arms and, as she rocks back in his arms, she sees he's dancing with her sister.

Maria has blood dripping from her mouth.

'He always loved me most,' she says. 'You were the consolation prize.'

Ziggy reels.

'Andy, is that so?' she says.

"Fraid so,' he says. 'Dem's da facts! But it's OK because we can be together here.'

'Aren't you waiting for me back on Earth?' says Ziggy.

'No need,' says Andy. 'I followed Maria up here to Heaven.'

'You're not dead, are you?' says Ziggy.

'If I was dead, could I jive like this?' says Andy. He allows Maria to spin away from him to the extent of his arm before pulling her back into him in an extravagant twist.

'Were you together?' says Ziggy. 'Was there something I didn't know going on.'

'Only together in mind,' says Andy. 'Yours, largely. We are a dance troupe, Maria and me.'

'What are you called?'

'The Deep Suspicions,' he says. 'We'll dance for anyone who is willing to dig us up. We are dancing for you!'

'No!' says Ziggy.

She rushes over to the fireplace, where the cloaked figure is playing the discs, and she wrenches the arm back off the player. There is a squeal from invisible speakers and all the astronauts stop dancing, freezing like musical statues.

'What is this place?' says Ziggy. She tries to pull at the shoulder of the seated figure, but she won't turn around.

'Who are you? What is this place?'

She tries to come around the front of the figure, but she can't. It's too near the fire and too hot.

'Bird legs and lizard brain,' chants the figure. 'Feelings that we can't explain.

'I sit here in the House of Doubt. Fire within and fire without!'

'What's that mean?' says Ziggy. 'What's that mean?'

'Sister so similar, fiancé so fine. What's yours is hers, what's hers is thine,' says the seated figure.

She feels a tap on the shoulder.

It's an astronaut who bows towards her. She sees the face of her sister's boyfriend, Tariq. 'Would you like to dance?' he says. 'I know you would. I always felt close to you. I'd hoped you would call me when she died.'

'That's horrible,' says Ziggy. 'Horrible. I thought you loved her.'

'Loving her means loving you,' he says. 'You're the same. You're exactly the same.'

Her head is pounding. All this is too much. She sways and staggers as if drunk. The figure at the turntable puts

another record on. It's Lesley Gore's 'It's My Party'. The cartoony, bratty vocals resonate in her bones, buzzing her skull, blurring her vision.

'Da Luca, you don't get to plot against me in there, I'm coming in,' says Griffin.

'No!' says Ziggy.

'Guilty is the thought, as much as the deed. The face is a flower, the heart is a weed,' says the figure at the fire.

Griffin steps into the hut, a look of appalled wonder on his face.

'Who the fuck is in here?' says Griffin. 'I killed all of you, all of you! I can easily kill you again.'

'No, Griffin, no.' A gun is not what is needed. Expressions float through her mind, aphorisms, sayings. One of them contains the key to what is needed. You don't get a boy to do a man's job. You don't cast a clout till May is out. You don't bring a knife to a gun fight. No, it's the other way around. You don't use a gun when you need a knife, Griffin. She starts to snigger, as if stoned. You don't cut a cake with an M16. She imagines it, so strongly she can almost see it, the bullets smashing into the cake. It's a wedding cake, her wedding cake, three big white tiers of the sort she thought she'd have with Andy. She doesn't need a gun. She needs a knife.

The astronauts turn to her. They have guns, AK-47s and they have Asian faces, full of fear, full of hate. 'Yankee go home! Yankee go home!' they're chanting.

Griffin shoulders his M16. 'Fuckers are everywhere!' he shouts.

The image of the *dakini* knife is there in front of her, its curve flashing in the firelight.

'Oh,' says the figure, her back still turned. 'You've got one of those!'

The *dakini* knife is in Ziggy's hand; she raises it high.

'These thoughts,' she hears herself say, 'are expected. They are usual, known. I don't fear them or recognise their reality. All illusion gone,' she says. 'The veil is cut, the truth is plain.'

She slashes down with the knife and the astronauts split, as if themselves cut, their insides opening to the firelight, insides of cake, layers and layers of cake crashing to the floor.

The fire flares, the figure stands. 'You are welcome to my hut,' she says and turns to face Ziggy, her hands at her side, her face invisible beneath her hood. A flash of firelight, and then the harsh glare is gone. The fire burns low at the hearth, and the room is empty apart from her, Griffin and the cowled figure at its turntable.

'The place was full of gooks!' says Griffin.

'No it wasn't, Griffin.' She looks down at her hand. The knife is gone.

'I swear to God, it was full of them!'

'No, Griffin,' she says. 'You are. You are full of gooks. And if we're going to get out of here in one piece, you need to get them to leave.'

Kovacs comes into the hut.

'What happened here?' she says. 'And who is that?' She points to the cowled figure.

'I don't know, but I think I've started to see how we might get out,' says Ziggy.

'How?'

'We need to . . . to face ourselves. To heal.'

'Ah, what fucking hippy bullshit,' says Griffin as a beating, thumping wind rises over the forest. Ziggy goes to the door of the hut.

Above them is the dragonfly eye of a helicopter, guns blazing. Lenov and Shirokov just stand looking at it and are blown to pieces, demolished by cannon fire, folding in on themselves in plumes of blood as the huge shells strike. Melnyk comes diving into the hut and shells shake the walls and roof. Melnyk's final jump into the hut was so strong in the weak gravity that he hits the back wall near to the line of the rafters and slides down the wall. The helicopter roars past, the downdraught shaking the reeds of the roof.

'Griffin is a danger to us!' She hears Kovacs' voice in her head. 'We have to get rid of him, cut him loose at least.'

'No,' says Ziggy. 'I know this place.' Those words surprise her. 'We are compassionate or we are nothing! We need to help him. Run!'

The hut rises up, sways and tips and explodes into movement, the helicopter chasing it through the trees.

Chapter 11

The hut bounds through the forest, leaping above the level of the trees as the helicopter pursues them, slamming round after round through the walls, through the roof, sending up plumes of splinters as they strike.

Ziggy lies flat, as do the others. They have no choice if they don't want to be slammed into the walls by the violent jerks of the hut's jumps and turns. Still, they bounce off the floor, tossed up violently before falling slowly, only to be tossed up again. Only the cloaked figure is unmoved.

As the hut turns and dances, through the open window, she sees glimpses of the helicopter, guns blazing away.

'It's a Huey! It's friendly fire!' shouts Griffin. 'It thinks this is a gook's hut.'

'Great!' shouts Melnyk. 'It makes it so much easier dying knowing it was all a big mistake!'

'Griffin! Relax. Breathe in. Think of something that makes you happy!'

'Fuck you!'

Clearly the meditative approach isn't going to work here. 'Well, shoot back at it, then!'

Griffin tries to get his gun pointed in the right direction but it's impossible; they are being thrown around like beans in a rattle.

This is an illusion, thinks Ziggy. She tries to conjure up again the image of the *dakini* knife, but she can't concentrate enough to do it. She's too busy trying to avoid being thrown through the hut's door.

A flash, and something impossibly fast goes through one wall of the hut and out of the other, leaving a trail of sparks and smoke behind it.

'Rockets!' shouts Griffin. 'They're using rockets!'

Ziggy is thrown violently to the back of the hut, where she falls in front of the cloaked figure. The figure hands her, of all things, a single record. The hut bucks and Ziggy is thrown up into the air. She has the strong sense the figure wants her to play this record.

Anchoring her feet under the turntable, she steadies herself, pulls the record from its sleeve. It's like trying to work a turntable while on a bucking bronco, but she manages to get the disc on to the turntable and the arm onto the disc. It holds its place well as music begins again. A guitar like a machine gun begins and a raw voice calls out, 'Demolair, demolair, da da da da.' She thinks it's Spanish; yes, it is Spanish, not demolair but *demoler* – demolish.

The hut swivels; the world through the door as the singer rasps about tearing down a train station, and the hut leaps skywards. The astronauts scream as the hut turns upside down, pitching them towards the ceiling. On Earth, they would break their necks, but here they float down towards the rafters quite gently before being pushed hard against the roof as the hut goes into a violent spin, sticking them to the ceiling in a centrifugal whirl.

A great sound, a crunch, and a rotor blade comes winging through the hut. She sees the stricken helicopter belching smoke beneath her, astronauts at its controls flailing their arms as the machine twists and turns.

The chiming, ringing, opening bars of 'Ticket to Ride' blare out; the hut lurches upright, Ziggy sees the world at the open door swivel, and then they are away, hopping through the jungle in huge, springy bounds.

Its passengers are thrown into the air and sink slowly down. Ziggy is reminded of one of those water-filled games where children try to get little plastic hoops onto tiny pegs, the hoops shooting up and then slowly sinking through the liquid, though here, she and her companions are the hoops.

She braces herself as best she can by clinging to a roof rafter, but it's a bumpy, sick-making ride.

Trees bob into view, then sky, then trees once more as the hut careers through the forest. Once or twice she sees something flash like a little meteor past the windows and, only when it's joined by a line of three more does she realise it's tracer fire.

'I am going to throw him out of the door right now, before one of us is killed,' says Kovacs, her voice in Ziggy's mind.

'What happens if something dangerous comes from my mind. Or from yours? Do we get rid of us?'

'Nothing dangerous has come from us.'

'How do you know? I got bitten by a shark!'

'You and no one else.'

The light outside becomes dimmer, though it can't be nearer sunset yet. And then:

A last lurch and the hut abruptly stops, settles down on its legs.

Ziggy lies on the floor. Her head is spinning.

'Oh, man!' says Griffin.

He is grasping the front windows of the hut, looking out. Ziggy sits up, steadies herself and goes to the door of the hut to look out.

Above them, towering seemingly miles into the sky, is an enormous grey featureless representation of a tree, a giant version of what they first saw on the shoreline. It is at the centre of a huge field of the pipes they saw when they first came in; the entire floor is made of a tangled lattice of tubes, each the size of a garden hosepipe. They stretch as far as the eye can see, under a red sky, though the shadow of the tree casts the hut into a gloom and a carpet of feathers extends fifty or so metres from the tree's huge trunk.

The tree blinks, blurs, shifts and changes.

'Better hope people have good associations with giant trees,' says Melnyk.

The tree seems to flicker, as if it's on an unreliable TV screen, and then it settles into view.

It's an enormous, broad thing with a wrinkled bark trunk stretching up to a vast crown of green. It flickers again and apples appear on its branches, flickers once more and it's a tuberous thing with many intertwined trunks, then it blurs and shakes once more and is the single-trunked tree with the crown of green.

Kovacs steps out of the hut, tries the ground with her foot.

'Solid,' she says.

She walks out of the hut and gazes up.

Ziggy and the others join her. Ziggy bends down to look at the pipes. They stream with symbols of every conceivable sort – heraldic beasts, Stone Age stick figures, a Volkswagen motif, a Coca-Cola bottle, letters, mathematical symbols, Chinese ideographs, Cyrillic script, alchemical glyphs, every

conceivable form of human sign. She remembers her vision just after they had killed the first two cosmonauts: a great tree shaking seeds of light, seeds that were eyes. Is this it, this enormous tree, the source of all the symbols?

'What is that?' says Griffin.

'Not a jungle tree,' says Kovacs, 'which is a relief, as we're not going to have any giant freedom fighters popping out of your subconscious to attack us. Well, let's hope not.'

'Freedom fighters?' says Griffin.

'Let it go, Griffin,' says Ziggy. 'What is this?'

The pipes darken and stain, as if with ink. They and the symbols are now gone and they stand on a huge field of ash and cold cinders.

Something stirs at the base of the tree, an enormous, shiny black coil of muscle rising from the cinders to slither around the tree's vast roots.

'Oh no,' says Melnyk. 'That's . . .'

'Yggdrasil,' says Ziggy. She's done enough comparative ancient religion to recognise it.

'What?' says Griffin.

'The Norse World Tree,' says Ziggy. 'And that, at the bottom, is a serpent that gnaws at its root.'

'We have Scandinavians here?' says Kovacs.

'I'm Ukrainian. My mother was from Kyiv,' says Melnyk.

'So what?' says Griffin.

'Viking blood,' says Melnyk. 'Kyiv is an old Viking outpost. Or so she said. I had a book of the Norse stories when I was a kid.'

'It seems you took them to heart,' says Kovacs.

'Either that or Jung was right,' says Melnyk. 'The collective unconscious, coming back to bite you on the ass.'

'You'll be lucky if that son of a bitch stops at your ass,' says Griffin.

The massive serpent slithers over the tree again, its shiny black coils rattling against the bark. Its body is enormous, wide as a subway train.

'I saw it briefly as the Bodhi tree,' says Ziggy. She has her eyes fixed on the huge snake, in case it comes towards them.

'And what might that be?' says Griffin, with an air of strained patience.

'The tree under which the Buddha sat to receive enlightenment.'

'Did it have a fuck load of apples?' says Griffin.

'It was a fig.'

'I saw it with a load of apples,' says Griffin.

'Are you a Christian, Griffin?' says Kovacs.

'Yes I am.'

'It's possibly a vision of the tree in the Garden of Eden.'

'Or just one in my backyard,' says Griffin.

Kovacs weighs this for a moment.

'Yes. But the other two images we have seen, and the one it has settled on, are trees that feature heavily in myth.'

'The Bible ain't no myth,' says Griffin.

'Yes it is,' says Kovacs. 'It seems that earlier things of this nature we've encountered project fairly straightforwardly. The dog is a dog, not a holy dog, the gun is a gun, not a holy gun, not Shiva's bow or anything, or Odin's spear or something, the trees were ordinary trees when they took form. Each took a form peculiar to us. This, however, has more attached to it.'

The snake's body twists once more around the tree. Ziggy can't see its head; doesn't want to see its head.

Ziggy tries to remember the myth of the tree Yggdrasil. As far as she can recall, it was a connection between the underworld, middle earth where humans live, and Heaven. Wasn't there a cosmic squirrel that ran up and down it? Thank God, that seems absent.

'What do we do?' says Griffin.

'For a bit, we think,' says Kovacs. 'We could do with going back to collect our spacesuits.'

'Where is that?' says Melnyk.

They let his question hang. They are probably miles from where their journey in the hut began and have become completely disorientated. There's no way of saying which way they came from.

'Can we try to go back in the hut?' says Ziggy. 'We could see if we could influence it in some way.'

'How?'

'Choice of records?' says Melnyk. '"Get Back" by the Beatles. Ask the witch or whatever it is if they have that.' As if on cue, the marching beat of 'Get Back' begins. The hut gets up, swivels as if looking around for something.

'No! No!' says Ziggy, running towards it, but it's too late. The hut lowers towards them, almost like a bow, but it takes a hop, another, and then bounds away.

'Great,' says Melnyk. 'We move from fucked to utterly fucked.'

'We've been utterly fucked for a while,' says Griffin, 'just you haven't noticed.'

They sit for a while, momentarily defeated by their situation until Kovacs speaks.

'What does anyone know about Yggdrasil?'

'Snake at the bottom, squirrel in the middle, eagles at the top,' says Melnyk. 'The gods visit daily.'

'It connects the worlds, upper and lower,' says Ziggy.

'Which means . . . Whoa!' says Kovacs.

Above the tree, there is a flash of white light. At first Ziggy can't tell what it is, it's so far away, but then she recognises it. It's a rocket firing. The shape she can just make out on the higher branches is of a spacecraft. It's white, flashing red in the sun with a great mantis-eye cockpit, a lattice body behind it. It hovers near the top of the tree, then settles on a broad branch.

'Can you see that?' says Ziggy.

'It's an aircraft,' says Kovacs.

'That isn't an aircraft,' says Ziggy. 'It's a spacecraft.'

'What makes you sure?'

'It's from *Space 1999*, the TV series! Moonbase Alpha, all that. It's an Eagle. It shuttles between the Earth and the Moon! That could be our way out!'

Kovacs shakes her head. 'That is from a TV show?'

'Yes. It's popular in the States.'

'If Catherine Schell's going to be in that, I think we better try to flag it down,' says Griffin.

'We need to stay here and watch,' says Kovacs.

So they do. Dusk falls and the Eagle takes off, a blast of rocket fire bronzing the top of the tree, so much that Ziggy is surprised it doesn't catch fire. That's odd. From what she remembers of the TV show, the Eagles didn't have much of a rocket blast. Everyone watching, though, is experienced with rockets. They expect the engines to show a blast, and so they do, she thinks. Also, the shape of the cockpit area isn't quite right: the windows smaller than she remembers. Is the memory of the TV show blending with what she knows about space capsule design: windows have

to be relatively small – or rather, always have been on the Apollo craft.

Ziggy hears a voice in her head. 'We can't trust Griffin.' It's Kovacs, she's sure.

'Please say anything you have to say out loud,' says Ziggy in her mind. Then, herself out loud: 'The mental effects of this place are starting to make me feel a bit sick.'

'What mental effects?' says Melnyk.

Ziggy laughs, gestures all around her. 'I'm still not a hundred per cent convinced we're not going to find ourselves back in the orbiter, having gone through some O_2 psychosis or something.'

'That'd be good,' says Melnyk. 'If we come out of it.'

'It raises the question of whose hallucination this is, if that's true,' says Kovacs 'Are you in mine, or I in yours?'

'Back in Philosophy 101,' says Ziggy.

'You ever get further than that?' says Kovacs.

'No. I'm kind of wishing I had.'

Ziggy is half speaking the truth when she says she is feeling sick. Kovacs' speaking in her mind – this telepathy or whatever it is – does make her feel slightly nauseous, in a way you might get when you've eaten a bit too much of something sweet. It hovers on that feeling between enjoyment and nausea; one too many cinnamon rolls, or maybe not. Maybe you could eat another. It's that sort of feeling.

It's kind of welcome in one way; it stops her feeling hungry, though her stomach rumbles. As they sit and rest looking up at the tree, she decides to meditate. Buddha thought trees good spots to meditate, so how can she disagree? That said, Buddha didn't have a large serpent periodically writhing up from the tree's roots. Although he did have the demons. As soon as she has the thought, she tries to pull it back in

again. The last thing she wants is the demon Mara, Lord of Death, popping out of her subconscious.

She quiets her mind but finds herself somewhat in the 'don't think of a pink elephant' problem, in that her efforts not to think about Mara in fact constitute thinking about him. Last Lord of the desire world. King of fear. He who controls through fear, who ties the soul with knots of fear, he who uses desire, fulfilment and regret to bind us to the cycle of eternal rebirth.

In her meditation, she feels her mind running, monkey mind, forever busy. You can't tell this mind to be quiet. You must let it run itself into tiredness. She thinks of Kovacs.

There's something about the cosmonaut she finds slightly disquieting. She thinks it's her certainty, the way she seems so driven. Ziggy's pretty driven herself – no one gets to be an astronaut who isn't – but Kovacs has shown no fear, nor even much hesitation. Ziggy supposes she should admire her.

And Melnyk – what does she really know about him? Nothing. He seems something of a joker, quite laid-back considering the circumstances. She feels she can trust him, but she would feel she could trust almost anyone in this situation. The odds are so stacked against them that only idiots wouldn't work together.

Griffin – is he an idiot?

She lets the thoughts pass through her mind like so many fireworks, brilliant and engaging for an instant and then gone.

She tries to remember how she called the *dakini* knife to her, the killer of illusion. Then she casts effort aside, does not try. The image of the *dakini* knife floats before her eyes; she accepts it, watches it.

Immediately it takes on a vivid appearance, her imagination more powerful than she has ever experienced at home. The knife's blade is curved, like a chef's blade she once saw – she doesn't know its name, cooking isn't really her thing. It glimmers like the surface of the Hudson under the city lights, a deep golden lustre. It doesn't have a conventional handle, but its grip rises out of the convex inner curve of the blade in an elaborate series of stages, almost like it could be a softer, more rounded pagoda.

To slice through all illusion – that is the knife's purpose; to allow us to see what is and what is not.

She moves the image in her mind to where Griffin is sitting, cradling his gun. Should she drop the knife on him, slice away all his illusions? She doesn't quite know if Griffin will be free of illusion if she cuts him, or if she will be free of illusions about him.

She allows the image of the knife to float down on top of Griffin. If he notices anything, he doesn't say, but as the knife falls she feels a great pressure in her head, her vision swims and Griffin's body seems to split. Out of him come thousands of tiny soldiers, all fighting each other, tiny planes trailing fire, or spitting it, little boats floating across a beach, hammering shells out of the guns at their prows. So much, so Griffin. Vietnam had a huge impact on him, as you'd expect considering what he suffered. And now, as she looks closer, she can see some of the little soldiers are wrestling or something. She squints, adjusts her vision and then allows her mind to quiet. The soldiers are not wrestling. Groups of them are dragging other soldiers across the ground. They are laying out stakes; they are tying the other soldiers to them. A firing squad? No. The positions are too unconventional.

The soldiers who are tied are stretched between poles, are splayed out like skins. No need to go to all that trouble just to shoot someone. No, this is worse. The soldiers who have brought the victims to be splayed between poles are walking away. This is a slow death, if it is a death at all, a chance to make the enemy pay. She allows her mind to move closer. It's Griffin between those poles, it's Griffin when she looks to a man being shoved into a tiny box, Griffin kneeling on the floor with a gun to his head, Griffin being beaten, Griffin being smothered and drowned. She has learned precisely nothing about Griffin in terms of new information, but a wave of compassion has come over her, the like of which she has never felt. Of course he is like he is. How couldn't he be?

She moves on to Melnyk. The knife hovers above him in her vision and then falls. She sees model aeroplanes, space-ships, sees him running with a Sputnik he's constructed out of tinfoil and coat hangers, sees a woman sick in a chair, sees twelve princesses dancing, a firebird rising, Baba Yaga's hut stalking. He suffered a death when he was young. After that, a part of his mind could not move on, she senses. A large part of him, internally, is still the same age as he was when the woman in the chair left him, the woman with the stories of armless maidens, the Sea King and the apples of youth.

She feels the wings of the firebird as it sweeps by her and knows that he, Melnyk, is the firebird that must always fly forwards, never rest, in case the flames consume him. He is running always from that terrible moment when he found that woman lifeless in the chair, always immersing himself in something – work, flying, space – so he never catches a glimpse of himself on the day he feels his life stopped.

She goes on to Kovacs. She is wary here, not quite knowing what she will find. The great knife rises and falls on Kovacs. Nothing. Kovacs is still there, sitting on the cinders.

'We are magicians,' says Kovacs. The words jolt Ziggy out of her meditation.

'What do you mean?'

'We shape the world by a word. We do magic.'

'Not much use if you can't control it,' says Melnyk.

'Who's to say you can't?' says Kovacs. 'We've already created a forest, what else might we do if we put our minds to it?'

'Fly,' says Melnyk. 'I've always wanted to fly. Like, by flapping my arms or some shit. We could get to the top of the tree.'

Griffin shoots him a dirty look.

Melnyk smiles and laughs. 'What can I tell you? I'm a big kid.'

'War would have knocked that out of you,' says Griffin.

'And that would have been a good thing?' says Kovacs.

'Fuck you,' says Griffin, who is at least consistent.

Kovacs thinks for a moment.

'Try then,' she says. 'Try to fly.'

'What, like "flap, flap"?'

'If you like.'

'Great to think I could be stuck here with you folks forever,' says Griffin.

'The feeling's mutual,' says Kovacs. 'Fly, Melnyk.'

'I can't. That's impossible.'

'Have you seen *Dumbo*?'

'Yes, it's a parable about the enslaving nature of capitalism and the emancipatory potential of revolution as embodied by a flying elephant and a mouse.'

Kovacs bends and picks up a feather. 'Here you go then,' she says. 'Fly.'

Melnyk takes the feather.

'The shit I'm seeing,' says Griffin.

Melnyk flaps his arms up and down. 'Nope,' he says.

'Try again, believe you can.'

Melnyk scrunches up his eyes, tenses himself and says, 'I can fly'.

He gives a big jump off the floor but only succeeds in jumping up to about head height before floating down again.

Kovacs smiles. 'Mustn't have been a magic feather, then,' she says. And then they all burst out laughing.

There is something hysterical to the laughter, though, an edge to it. The joke was OK, but it doesn't warrant the kind of hilarity that ensues here. Even Griffin laughs. An effect of this strange place, or just a release of tension? No way home, no ship, no suits, no nothing, really. Dead friends, and the strong possibility you will join them. Laughter is a better response than the alternative.

'You were kidding, right?' says Melnyk.

'I don't know,' says Kovacs. 'I mean, we have seen how we can influence certain structures here – the gun, the trees. I wondered how far that influence went. It would have been good to fly to those ships up there.'

At her words, another Eagle comes to dock on the top branches, its rockets flaring, its great mantis head lighting up in their glow. It really is not quite how Ziggy remembers the Eagles from *Space 1999*. The back end seems duller in colour; she is sure the original was white. It is an Eagle, though, unmistakably.

'Do you think they could get us home?' says Melnyk.

'They're models in a TV show,' says Griffin.

'Baba Yaga's hut was something from a fairy tale and yet it transported us,' says Ziggy. 'I can't see many other alternatives.'

Griffin looks around him. 'Guess you're right,' he says. 'But flight's out of the question. So how do we get up there?'

'Climb,' says Kovacs

'It's a very long way.'

'But not impossible. There are branches to rest on and I weigh all of twenty pounds here, you not much more. The bark looks like it offers a good grip. I think we can get up there.'

The black coils of the snake emerge and wind around the base of the tree.

'You think he's gonna have something to say about that?' says Griffin.

'He is a problem,' says Kovacs, 'but not insurmountable.'

'I have a different idea,' says Ziggy. 'Give me your gun, Griffin.'

'No one's taking my gun,' says Griffin. 'If you're going to shoot the snake, don't. Let me.'

'I'm not going to shoot the snake; I'm going to see if I can attract the attention of the Eagles.'

'Maybe we've already got their attention.'

'And maybe not. If I can turn it into a flare gun, we could call them down.'

Griffin weighs this. 'I'll turn it into a flare gun,' he says. 'That way I can turn it straight back again if needs be.'

He looks down at the M16. 'Can't believe I'm doing this,' he says. He looks at the gun hard, mutters. Nothing happens. He strokes the gun. He says, 'Be a flare!' Still nothing happens.

'There's a problem here,' he says. 'I've never seen a flare rifle. Plenty of pistols, never a rifle. I don't know what to make here.'

'Shall I try?' says Ziggy.

'I ain't letting go of the gun,' says Griffin.

'We need to try.'

'And I need to keep the gun. I'm all that's stood between you and being eaten by that weird spider, hippy, gook thing. I'm the best shot, the most experienced. I keep the fucking gun.'

'So it seems we're stuck,' says Kovacs. 'Still, this seems a great spot to starve to death.'

'I say we take our risks with the snake,' says Griffin. 'I'll go first if you like. If it emerges, I'll just blow it to shit.'

'The American answer to everything,' says Kovacs.

'It's a good one. It works,' says Griffin.

'How'd that go for you in Vietnam?' says Kovacs.

'Would've gone better if we'd seen the job through,' says Griffin.

Kovacs snorts. 'How does everyone else feel?' she says.

'We're assuming the snake is hostile,' says Ziggy.

'As snakes tend to be,' says Griffin.

'It might just ignore us. If we can make the tree, we can climb quickly, I'm sure, and be out of its way. It's only come up to the level of the roots so far. It may not be able to climb the tree, or rise that far up it.'

'Or it may,' says Kovacs.

'Yeah, or it may,' says Ziggy.

'Let's do this, then,' says Griffin. 'One at a time or all together?'

'I'm not convinced,' says Kovacs.

'Looks like it's one at a time, then,' says Griffin.

'I'll come with you, Griffin,' says Ziggy.

The words just seem to come out of her mouth. It just feels like the right thing to do.

'Are you sure?' says Kovacs.

'Any decision's better than none,' says Ziggy.

'The flare gun sounded like a good decision to me.'

Ziggy shrugs. 'Pain plus resistance equals suffering,' she says.

'Massive snake plus massive fangs equals death,' says Melnyk.

'There is that,' she says. Ziggy thinks Griffin's probably right anyway. The rifle is a base type of a long gun. A flare gun is a short gun. Maybe it can't be changed. Though she'd like to try, were Griffin less obstinate.

'We'll all go,' says Kovacs. 'If the snake grabs one of us, it may leave the rest. One in four seems like good odds on this trip.'

They approach the enormous tree. Its trunk must be the width of a city block, and its roots plunge like gigantic fingers into the black earth around them. As they get nearer, they can see there are some hollows under the roots where the snake might emerge, dark on dark, black holes in a black soil.

Griffin puts his gun to his shoulder and advances slowly, his moon steps light.

The others follow. As they get nearer, they can see that the bark on the roots of the tree is gnawed away, showing white fibre beneath.

Griffin signals for them to move around, Ziggy guesses to find where the roots aren't gnawed. That might indicate an area the snake doesn't go.

It's a long way under the branches. Above them now are other shapes: birds, which drop feathers and worse from the branches. She only sees them as dark cut-outs against the sky, shadows against the stars.

They reach the roots without disturbing the snake. Ziggy looks up. Are they really going to climb that? It's like Everest: even the lowest branches at the height of a skyscraper.

Griffin gestures with his eyes for them to start climbing. Ziggy puts her hand on the root and levers herself up. It's a trade-off between stealth and speed and she errs on the side of stealth, lifting herself easily up to the main trunk of the tree.

The bark is firm, thank God, and provides a good grip, lots of fractures and splits to jam the fingers and toes into. It's an easy climb, she weighs nothing.

The snake takes Melnyk with a great whack of its coils, knocking him sideways onto the ground. It has come from nowhere. She can't see its head, but its coils run over the roots in even, muscular pulses, the shiny black scales pouring over the roots in a liquid flow.

'Fuck you!' shouts Griffin, and fires. A flare strikes the creature on the flank and as soon as it appeared, the snake is gone. Griffin's gun has made its transformation: the base of the tree is bathed in phosphorescent light, the birds above spooked into shrieks.

'You OK, Melnyk?'

'Fine!' He's up and running at the tree, climbing as quick as he can. All four of them tear at the bark, climbing, flying up the tree like squirrels, so little do they weigh.

The snake comes again, this time corkscrewing around the trunk. She sees a glimpse of its broad head, as wide as a truck. Thank God it hasn't struck with its teeth yet.

She clambers up the bark, slips, regains her grip and climbs again. The snake writhes around the base of the tree, not coming straight for them but circuiting the trunk, winding around, up and up and up.

Griffin has the flare gun on a strap on his wrist and he fires again, whitening the night.

This time, the snake doesn't pause but keeps coming. The base of the tree looks like a whirring cog with the movement of its body.

They keep climbing, shooting up the bark faster than Ziggy ever thought was possible, but it's not fast enough: the snake is gaining on them. Even if it doesn't bite, its coils will just throw them from the trunk. She finds herself, ridiculously, doing maths as she climbs. How high is she? two hundred metres. One sixth of two hundred metres? Like falling thirty-three on Earth. Easily enough to kill her.

'Go!' screams Kovacs, as unnecessary a command as was ever issued. Ziggy keeps climbing, keeps pushing up. The snake is circling the tree only five metres below her, its massive body ready to pitch her off. Then three metres. She keeps going. Even in the weak gravity, she's beginning to tire at this pace.

Something is shooting towards her, not up the tree but down it. A flash of red fur; a flick of a bushy tail.

'Stop!' says a voice. 'Stop in the name of the lords of the higher realms. You are reminded that your domain is the lower part of the tree. You may not climb so high, serpent!'

Chapter 12

The coils stop writhing. The serpent retreats, slithering back the way it came.

Next to Ziggy on the tree is an extraordinary figure. It is about her size and has a man's face. In fact, it may be a man in a suit, or it may be a very strange creature of another sort entirely. It is, as far as she can see, a giant squirrel. No, it is a man in a suit – she can see a zip at the front.

'Who in the name of God are you?' says Ziggy.

'Antonov!' says Kovacs. Ziggy realises that this man's chubby, strange face is very similar to the much thinner, careworn man they met in the ship.

'Major Antonov!' says Melnyk.

'Ratatosk,' he says. 'My name is Ratatosk.'

'Do you think this is another creation of this place?' says Melnyk to the group.

'Undoubtedly,' says Kovacs. 'It has mixed our associations with trees with our desire to find the major. This is a corporeal illusion.'

'I am no such thing,' says the squirrel. 'In the name of God, or rather the gods, I am a messenger.'

The man hangs easily from the tree, long talons on the suit's paws gripping the bark securely.

'And what message did you deliver to that snake?' says Kovacs. She is less secure on the huge trunk, gripping nervously.

'Do one,' he says. 'There are firm rules about how high that snake can go for prey. Roots only.'

'My grandmother used to tell me stories of this creature!' says Melnyk.

'There you go,' says Kovacs. 'This has come from you. I had no idea you were so keen on fairy tales, Melnyk.'

'We had no TV when I was growing up,' he says. 'This is the squirrel that lives on the World Tree! But he looks like Antonov!'

'My fame is great,' says the squirrel. 'Come, climb with me and I will let you feast on a nut hoard the like of which you have never seen. You are my guests!'

'Up there?' says Ziggy.

'Yes.'

'What are those ships?' says Kovacs. 'The Eagles. Will they get us out of here?'

'Come to the first branch,' says Ratatosk. 'Climb, and I will assess your worth. If you are worthy, I will take you to the Eagles. They fly to other worlds.'

'To Earth?' says Melnyk.

'Wherever you want to go,' says Ratatosk.

'Can you make this squirrel speak English?' says Griffin, but no one replies.

The squirrel turns to climb and they follow him up to his nest, if that is what you'd call it, on the first of the tree's mighty branches. This one stretches out across the cinders for a hundred yards or more and is as wide, and nearly as level, as a tennis court.

The nest has armchairs, a fridge, a big TV and a bath. There are also twenty or so barrels upright, forming a kind of fence between the living area and the rest of the branch.

'Welcome to my drey. Care for a nut?' says the squirrel.

'Yes,' says Ziggy.

'Help yourselves, they're in the barrels.'

Ziggy goes to a barrel, removes its lid and takes out what appears to be a peeled chestnut. She bites it. It is a chestnut.

'Help yourselves,' says the squirrel. 'Beer's in the fridge.' He speaks in English.

Griffin opens the fridge and takes out a Colt 45. If this is an experience influenced by their expectations, Ziggy wonders, does even Griffin's choice of beers relate to guns?

'In the dull and commonplace occurrences of day-to-day living, one thing stands out as a completely unique experience: Colt 45 Malt Liquor,' says Griffin. He starts to laugh. 'Man, this could be an ad for it,' he says. 'Stuck up a tree on the Moon in a squirrel man's apartment – that's commonplace, man, that's dull.'

The others laugh, too.

The squirrel grins nervously, not quite getting the joke.

Ziggy tries to include him. 'So what's your role here?' she says. 'What do you do in this tree.'

'I'm a squirrel,' says the squirrel. 'I don't really have a role beyond that.'

'I see,' says Ziggy.

'Joking!' says the squirrel. 'I'm kind of middle management. I carry messages from up there to down there. Logistics, I suppose you'd call the role.'

'And what are the messages?'

'About the nature of this place,' says the squirrel.

228

'And what is that nature?'

'I don't know, I never read the messages. There's no point in philosophy when you've got nuts to harvest.'

'Who do you deliver them to?' says Melnyk, who is also drinking a beer.

'The snake. He may not know he's a snake. He might think he's something else.'

'Like what?' says Kovacs.

'Me, you, a human, a squirrel, a sack of nuts. Who knows what goes on in a snake's mind?'

'A snake,' says Melnyk.

'Depends what you're calling a snake,' says the squirrel. 'You know, if he believes himself to be a tree, or part of this tree, is he still a snake?'

'He is what we believe him to be,' says Griffin.

'Then he's a snake, for now. But if you believe him to be a vacuum cleaner or a fire hose, does he still know what goes on in a snake's mind? Does a former snake know what goes on in a snake's mind, or does he only know it from the point of view of himself, now a vacuum cleaner?'

'Good beer, considering it may not actually exist,' says Melnyk, clearly trying to change the subject.

'Don't drink too much of that,' says Kovacs. 'We need to keep climbing. I have to say, the top branches don't seem like the most convenient docking area for those spaceships. They're not easy to reach.'

'That would be the point,' says the squirrel.

'What do you mean?'

'In my time here, I have come to the opinion that this whole place is set up as some sort of test. Everything here just seems to be unnecessarily difficult. Only the pure of mind go on.'

'So how come you're here?' says Griffin. 'Are you pure of mind?'

'I'm very focused on foraging nuts,' says the squirrel. 'I got as far as this tree and just naturally felt at home. I forage nuts. I eat nuts. I store nuts. I eat more nuts. Then I forage some more. It's a great life and I feel privileged to live it.'

'You weren't always here?' says Kovacs.

The squirrel looks puzzled. 'I don't think so,' he says. 'I was a major in the Red Army, a cosmonaut,' he says. 'You should know, I saw you at Star City. But to be honest, I don't really care what I was because I'm sorted for nuts so everything else seems a bit by-the-by. I'm staying here.' And then he says, in careful, slow English. 'I'd be nuts not to!' and bursts out laughing.

Ziggy defocuses her thoughts, tries to read the squirrel's mind. She sees the journey here by rocket, the landing, the opening of the hatch, squeezing through those strange tunnels and finally arriving here. His mind feels jittery, not balanced. She sees him coming to the tree, finding the squirrel suit. Home, support, the end of quests. All these emotions come from him. Something else, too. Shame.

She sees Kovacs looking at him. She must know, mustn't she? This really is Antonov. The sensations that come from him are different from those that came from the man they saw in the boat – they're stronger, much clearer. With that man, reading his mind was like listening to an echo. With this one, it's like listening to someone speaking clearly right next to you. Mind you, this man is obsessed with nuts, the other one with cheese. And then she realises why the first Antonov was so keen on cheese. Ben Gunn. *Treasure Island* by Robert Louis Stevenson – she'd done that in high school

and loved the character of the castaway. Ben Gunn was desperate for cheese. She, or one of her companions, had just filled in that detail to the space castaway.

'What is this tree?' says Kovacs.

'I think,' says the squirrel. 'I think, it's a tree. A big one.'

'Is it always like this? Does it ever change?'

'It's always changing,' says the squirrel. 'Spring, summer, autumn, winter. A tree is change. But there again, so is everything else. I hope that's helpful.'

'If this squirrel is a manifestation of anyone here's subconscious, I pity you,' says Griffin. 'I think I'd rather have gooks.'

The squirrel twitches. 'Where are you from?' he says.

'From Earth.'

'Everyone must call their home planet Earth, or variations on it,' says the squirrel. 'Be more specific, please.'

'The nearest planet to you. Everyone? There are others here?'

'Two others. Two like you,' says the squirrel. 'Lyamin and Too Good. Lost men looking to be found. Are you lost men, too?'

'Men and women,' says Ziggy. 'You saw Toog?'

'I saw a man dressed like you. He said he had only just arrived. He called his home Earth.'

'And where did they go?'

'Up,' he says. 'Up.'

'Toog might be alive!' says Ziggy.

'We need to be careful,' says Kovacs. 'Any of this information might just be products of our own minds being fed back to us.'

'You might be products of my mind,' says the squirrel. 'Thought of that? I have. There was quite a lot of confusing stuff here until I became a squirrel and focused on nuts.'

Ziggy glances at Kovacs. She must have tried to read the squirrel's mind and, if she did, she'd have discovered what Ziggy discovered. This is a man, not a hallucination made flesh.

'You should come with us,' says Ziggy. 'We're looking for a way home.'

'So was I,' says the squirrel. 'And then I thought, the quickest way to get home is to set up home here. I found the armchair and a few other things and life became very tolerable. The Eagles supply me with beer.'

Why would Antonov have had the same hallucination as Melnyk? Did his grandmother read him Norse fairy tales too? Or . . .

'Where was Antonov from?' says Ziggy.

'Ukraine,' says Kovacs.

Home of the Viking Rus. Is this some sort of collective unconscious thing coming to the fore like Melnyk said?

Ziggy is convinced they can't leave the squirrel, Antonov, on the tree. They have to persuade him to come with them when they get to the top. He's clearly suffered some very strange episode, but he's a man and he belongs on Earth, if they can get him there.

When they have rested a while, they climb again. Ziggy can't look down, though the climbing is easy enough. Even if she were to slip, she thinks, she would easily catch herself before she picked up speed. Falling here is not like falling on Earth; you would get a lot of time to regain your grip on the tree.

They rest along the way. The squirrel has brought nuts with it, which it produces from a bag it wears about its waist, not from cheek pouches, thank God.

They sip on the last of their water supplies and gaze up through the branches, into vast stars. The spaceships come and go, lighting up the leaves, though never burning them. Closer up, Ziggy can see that it's as she thought – the ships are not like the Eagles of *Space 1999* after all, or rather they are an imperfect copy of them. The rear of the ships, which was a white lattice arrangement on the TV Eagles, is here made of scaffolding, like you might see on the side of a building. The cockpit at the front is more mantis head-shaped than the snake head of the original and has smaller windows.

They climb and climb. Ziggy's hands become raw, despite her light weight. The squirrel has no such problems. He clings easily to the tree with his long claws.

They go up a day, two days, and sleep on the branches. The squirrel has happily placed supplies of various sorts at different levels, and there is even a washbasin and a supply of water in big plastic containers. When Ziggy does summon the courage to look down, she feels sick. They are so far up, so far.

Another day's climbing and her hands begin to crack. One more and she must rest. The squirrel has some sheets on a high branch, and he strips them to allow her to wrap pieces around her hands.

At last, they get up to the higher branches and, finally, one that bears the marks of rocket engines.

'Here?' she says.

'Here,' says the squirrel.

Ziggy leans back against a tree.

'Will you come with us, Antonov?'

'Why would I?'

'To resume your life on Earth.'

'I wouldn't be sure this creature ever had one,' says Kovacs.

'He did,' says Ziggy. 'I can see inside his mind – can't you?'

'Yes,' says Kovacs. 'But I saw inside the mind of Antonov too.'

'I feel something from him,' says Melnyk. 'I feel sure this is a real man. You should return to Earth, Major.'

'Why would I go with you?' says the squirrel.

'To see friends, family.'

'What's the nut situation like down there?' says the squirrel.

'There are plenty of them,' says Ziggy.

A fire on the horizon, red against black.

'It seems a long way to go when I could just stay here and have all I need,' says the squirrel. As the words come from his mouth, they sound hollow to Ziggy. The squirrel does not have all he needs, she's sure.

'What more do you want?' she asks.

'Nothing I can have. Anyway, here we are,' says the squirrel. 'I hope they've brought me some of those nice American beers.'

Ziggy thinks. Why would a Russian project American beer? Unless he was a real Russian, with real likes, passions and dislikes. Maybe he got some American beer in the Ukraine. Maybe just a bottle of it and, to him, it meant luxury. That's why he dreamt it into existence here.

The fire on the horizon gets bigger. She hears a rumble. It hasn't occurred to her until now that she's likely to be standing directly underneath a powerful rocket blast.

'Should we take cover?' says Ziggy.

'We'll be fine here,' says the squirrel.

Out of the dark, she sees the gunmetal steel of the ship emerging. It moves swiftly, its mantis eyes taking shape from the blur of its body.

'Here it comes,' says Griffin.

The ship fires its retro-thrusters, slowing as it comes into the tree, great footpads extending to take its weight. Close up, it's a dog's dinner: scaffolding poles, planks, twine binding it together.

'This safe to travel in?' asks Griffin.

'Oh yes,' says the squirrel. 'It brings my beer.'

The ship swivels about as if acknowledging their presence, then drops to a branch below them to settle. Quickly, they scramble down.

A hatch on the side opens, though no one comes out.

'Go in!' says the squirrel. 'You can help carry my order out!'

Ziggy walks onto the ship. She is in a broad cargo bay. It has crates of various canned foods, beer and potato chips. There is also a large inflatable swimming pool folded in a branded box and a garden umbrella.

'Aha!' says the squirrel. 'Everything I need for when it rains!'

'Is anyone piloting this thing?' says Kovacs.

'Look up front,' says the squirrel.

Ziggy walks down the cargo bay to a bulkhead marked in red. She puts her hand to a circular panel on the door and it slides back.

Within is a cabin area, sloping, uncomfortable-looking modern seats, and a drinks bar of moulded blue plastic set into a wall. She's tempted to pour herself a wine but that can wait. Melnyk clearly can't, however.

'Cigarettes!' he says.

There are packets lying on the bar, along with a book of matches.

'Belomorkanal!' he says, and lights up.

There is another bulkhead marked out in red, built into a wall with a hexagonal lattice pattern. She has watched *Space 1999*, more to see what they got wrong or right about space travel than for any interest in the drama, but she hasn't been aware of taking in this much detail.

Here on the Moon, it seems, there is a whole area of her brain that has lain dormant, full of the plans of science-fiction TV's ships, of weird discos, of images of her sister.

'I better go in first.' Griffin is at her side now.

'No,' she says. 'Me.'

She touches the circle on the door and it slides back. Two chairs face a console of flat lights. The whole interior, left and right, is panelled with lights like these, which she thinks must be switches if she recalls the show correctly.

A figure is sitting in one of the chairs. She can see that he – his hands look male – has some sort of asymmetric tunic on, one arm green, the other purple.

'Hello,' she says.

'Oh my God!' says Andy, standing up from the seat. 'They told me you were dead!'

He goes to embrace her, and she finds herself accepting him, hugging him. He feels exactly how Andy feels to hug – a little angular, not presenting comfortable curves and cushions of flesh at all. It's a little like hugging a lamp post, she'd told him.

'Tall and skinny!' she'd said.

'And bright!' he'd said.

There's no reticence to him; he squeezes her tight, just like he does at home.

She steps back from him. Even though she knows he's a simulacrum, an invention of her back brain given life by this strange place, she's overwhelmed with love.

'I can't take this,' she says.

He takes both her hands. 'Why didn't you tell me you were coming here?' he says.

'I had to work out how to follow you.'

'You're not Andy,' she says. She has tears in her eyes now. 'I wish you were, but you're not.'

'I am. I have followed you.'

'How?'

'When they told me you were dead, I went to the ocean. I swam and I swam, and I didn't turn back and eventually I swam down to the bottom of the ocean and fell through the seabed to find you here. That's where you are, at the bottom of the sea.'

'You're telling me you killed yourself?' says Ziggy.

'I found a way back to you. And for that, I had to go through the gates of death. But here I am.'

Ziggy feels like crying properly now, but she holds on to her tears. At times on this trip it has occurred to her that she is in some sort of afterlife. Had the lunar lander spread itself as litter across the Taurus–Littrow crater? Was this the place between incarnations? The Bardo – the place between death and rebirth, as near as Buddhism has to a Hell?

At first, in the Bardo, people experience reality very clearly. But then, as time there progresses, hallucinations occur, based on the soul's past life. These – according to Buddhist teaching – could be terrifying, linked to your past karma in weird and distorted ways. Is that not what Griffin has been seeing with the Viet Cong?

Wasn't that what she was seeing with Andy and the strange disco playing the song that was on when they met?

For some more worthy souls, the Bardo can provide a time of great opportunity, the ability to secure an advantageous

rebirth. For others, they come face to face with the damage they've done. She thinks of finding herself in that office in Baghdad, pointing the gun at her sister.

Oh my God. If she is dead herself. If Andy is dead. Then what?

Then nothing. Should she secure a good rebirth? How to do that? And what for? In what way will she still be herself when reborn? Maybe she should stay here with Andy.

Kovacs comes into the cabin.

'Who's this?' she says.

'My fiancé.'

Kovacs laughs. 'Nice of you to come all this way,' she says.

'I missed Ziggy,' he says.

'Sure you did,' said Kovacs. She takes out her pistol and shoots Andy between the eyes, the bang deafening in the enclosed space.

Andy crumples to the floor, a bloom of blood at his forehead.

'What did you do that for?' screams Ziggy.

'Too many distractions,' says Kovacs.

Ziggy runs to Andy's body, but he is already fading, absorbing into the cabin floor.

'He wasn't real,' says Kovacs. 'See, he vanishes, just like the others.'

'Are you real?' says Ziggy. She's glad she no longer has her own pistol because she has a great temptation to use it.

'I'm real.'

'So why can't I get inside your head? I feel you crawling around in mine like a burglar searching for loot. Why can't I get inside yours like I can everyone else we came with? You're just like one of the zombies here, like him!'

'I'm real,' she says. 'Ask Melnyk. I came with him.'

'You could be Melnyk's creation, his hallucination, or he could be a hallucination, too, or—' says Ziggy.

'No,' says Kovacs. 'If you want to see inside my mind, I'll let you. But I have learned, in my studies of the Twilight Language and my meditation, to remain focused on the here and now. This is why no aspects of my inner mind have come crawling out of the walls here. I remain in control. Maybe, if I do open myself up, then some of the things in my subconscious will come out. Do we want that?'

'I don't know – should I be afraid? What will come out?'

'I don't know. That's why they call it the subconscious. It's *sub*conscious. If I knew what was in it, I would be conscious of it and therefore it wouldn't be *sub*conscious.' Her tone is patronising.

'Do you know what I think?' says Ziggy, 'I think . . .'

Kovacs holds up her hand. 'You ask a question and don't wait for the answer. I do know what you think. You think we are dead. You think this is the Buddhist Bardo, the clearing house for souls. All that pushing through membranes. Trying to be born somewhere? Weird, don't you think? Or rather, you do think it's weird. I know.'

'And you?'

'No. I don't think we're dead. This is what I expected. I have seen the writing you have seen and I have explored it in that Twilight way. I have meditated, I have starved myself, I have used hallucinogens, I have done old-fashioned comparative research, and my conclusion is that this is truly the Thunderbolt Vehicle. Its nature is beyond what I expected, but I think it's intimately connected to life on Eearth.'

'How?'

'I don't know. But I do know the gods, or rather the goddesses, travel in this thing. That is what I found in my explorations.'

'And you'd like to be one of them?' The words come without thought, surprising even Ziggy.

For the first time, Ziggy feels a strong emotion coming from Kovacs. It's like the purr of a cat, like the warmth of a fire on a cold day, a soft bed after hard labour.

'Wouldn't you?'

'No. I want to get home.'

'All is changed, changed utterly. A terrible beauty is born,' says Kovacs.

'You'd use this to impose communism on the world?'

Kovacs laughs. 'I'd have to see how I felt afterwards. You can't think as a god until you are one.'

'I thought you socialists didn't believe in gods.'

'Who said I was a socialist? Anyway, socialism is a scientific ideology. I'm sure that if they were presented with the evidence, they'd change their tune.'

'So the Soviet Union will get nothing out of this?'

'Nothing they'd like,' says Kovacs.

'And NASA? America?'

'That would be up to you. To us. Are you with me?'

She doesn't get chance to answer because Griffin comes in, sits at one of the pilot seats.

'This shit is NASA designed,' he says. 'This is laid out like a cross between a lander and a fighter plane. I can fly this! I can fly this fucking ship!'

Ziggy ignores him.

'I ask again,' says Kovacs. 'Wouldn't you like to be a goddess?'

'I wouldn't even know what that might mean.'

'In the old sense of an enlightened being? When you reach enlightenment, aren't you then a goddess?'

'I'm not enlightened, so I wouldn't know.'

'On the way here, did you meditate?'

'Yes.'

'And you saw yourself as a goddess?'

'Yes.'

'I did, too. I think that's what's happening to us here. This is a trial, of a sort, but the only people who can destroy us or make us fail are ourselves. This is a challenging environment, but it's not a hostile one. We are the hostile elements and if we can deal with ourselves . . .'

Ziggy laughs.

'We become gods . . .' says Griffin, who is examining the Eagle's console.

'Not you,' says Kovacs. 'Us, women. We are the ones who are destined to be the *dakini*, sky-goers. Why do you think we, women, are evolving telepathy? Why do you think the manifestations of our minds – or rather Da Luca's – have been so benign?

'You men have given us soldiers and hostile astronauts and cosmonauts, constricting walls, terrifying, helicopter-eating huts. You, Ziggy, have given us a discotheque, a friend and a lover, maybe even this ship. My studies tell me that it's only the female mind that is flexible enough, imaginative enough, peaceful enough to transform into being a sky-goer. This is the next stage of evolution and we don't need men. We will have ceased to be human.'

'Burn your fucking bras, see if I care,' says Griffin. 'I'm going to concentrate on getting us back to Earth in this

thing. If I can enter Earth orbit, we can work out if it can stand re-entry. If not, we get someone to come up and get us. So fuck trying to ascend to Heaven. Though we can crucify you, if you like.'

Ziggy thinks. The Stele at the Temple of the Moon at Ur would support this idea of the Thunderbolt Vehicle being both a physical thing and a means to enlightenment, Buddhahood, Godhead, even. It showed a woman floating into Heaven, sprouting wings. Underneath it, after a monumental effort of translation, were the co-ordinates of the Taurus–Littrow valley. But that's not a lot to base a whole hypothesis on. Well, it wouldn't be for conventional academia. It is to someone practised in the Twilight Language. She should have spent more time meditating on that image.

Obviously, Kovacs' ideas seem preposterous, but everything she's seen since she got through the hatch to enter this place has been preposterous. Telepathy? Thoughts made flesh. That was certainly near to having magical powers, if not quite being a god.

'It doesn't matter.' She hears herself say the words, almost has to guess what she means herself. 'We should go back to Earth on this if we can, or at least make the effort.'

'I agree with you for once,' says Griffin.

'You don't want to see what this place has to offer us?' says Kovacs.

'I think I'm going to find out if I like it or not. We're going where we're going,' says Ziggy. 'If you're right, then we're not in command of things here anyway, if it truly is some sort of trial. If not, maybe we get home, maybe we don't. We have to try to get back anyway.'

'Shouldn't you be resigned to your fate? Not very Buddhist,' says Kovacs.

'I'm a Buddhist, not Buddha,' says Ziggy.

Antonov the squirrel pokes his head around the door. 'I've unloaded and I'm off back to the tree now,' he says.

'Come with us,' says Ziggy.

'I have the good life here,' he says.

Ziggy stares at him, tries to see his thoughts. She feels for the root of the recklessness that brought him into this structure in the first place, that leaves him unwilling to return to Earth. There is a jumble in there; he's almost certainly gone a little mad. She sees an empty apartment in a grey block under a heavy Soviet sky. The place is disordered, not like what you'd expect from an astronaut. There is a picture on the side of the table: Antonov and a young woman. The young woman steps from the picture. She is in her mid-twenties, round cheeks, a little buck-toothed, quick, intelligent eyes. She is a squirrel in human form. She died: Antonov holds her in a web of grief. What is her name? Galina.

He doesn't care for himself or anyone else now, and will never move on from her. So much pain from so many people here? Not so unusual, she thinks, that's just the human condition.

'Do you want her?' she asks him with her thoughts.

'More than anything,' he says.

'She will be like her. Not her.'

'Bring her.'

'I don't know her so well. Think of her.'

He does, so vividly that Ziggy almost takes a step backwards, as if the young woman had reached out to touch her.

'What are you doing?'

It's Kovacs' voice in her head.

'Trying,' Ziggy says. 'And not trying.'

'This is a waste of effort.'

'Not trying,' Ziggy says again.

The young woman appears in her mind as if she stands in front of her. She feels Antonov's love, his grief, radiating from him. It's a source of creative energy, of great power. The young woman will be there. She will be there. He hears her voice projecting from Antonov's mind, her laugh, And, finally, she is there.

There is a call from down in the cargo bay, a woman's voice in Russian.

Antonov opens the door.

Emerging from behind a pallet of beer is the young woman. She, too, is in a squirrel costume, long taloned gloves and boots, hair tied back in a ponytail, like a squirrel's tail from a fairy tale.

'Anyone got a nut?' she says, in Russian.

'Galina?' says Antonov.

'Maksim?' says the woman.

They run into each other's arms and embrace.

'It's been so long, so long!' says Antonov.

'My darling!' says the squirrel woman. Tears are pouring down her face as she squeezes Antonov.

'You did that?' says Kovacs.

'I think so,' says Ziggy. She feels very tired. The effort of pulling Galina into existence, of channelling Antonov's thoughts, has drained her.

'How?'

'I have a sense of this place,' she says. 'It reflects what you bring to it. Antonov brings love. I just, I don't know, encouraged him to express that.'

'You *are* a goddess!' says Antonov. 'A sorceress. You have magical powers.'

'Well done,' says Kovacs. Her words are warm but there is something behind them. Suspicion? Jealousy?

'I think I can fly this if you're ready to go,' says Griffin. The squirrels are still hugging.

'Time to decide,' says Kovacs. 'Come with us or get back in your tree.'

'We'll go back to the tree!' says Antonov. 'Come on, Galina. I need to show you this paradise! Take a crate of beer.'

They both pick up crates of beer and go out of the ship on to the branch.

'Give us a few minutes to get clear!' says Antonov.

Ziggy sits in the co-pilots chair and wonders if they can really fly this thing home. She'd assumed that any creation of the Thunderbolt Vehicle would only last while they were within it. If it endures outside, then they truly are on to something. If it doesn't, they're dead.

'Haven't I seen you somewhere before?' says Griffin.

'Yes, Griffin, we came here together.'

'Oh yeah.'

She can't tell if that was a joke or not. She would try to read his thoughts to discover if it was, but she is exhausted from calling Galina into existence and, besides, Griffin's head is not a very good place to be. If they do get home, she's going to write one hell of a debrief and will have words to say about NASA's psychological screening processes. An ability to tough stuff out, to be decisive under great pressure, doesn't necessarily mean you're a stable individual and a good team player. She needs to let them know that.

After about quarter of an hour, Griffin decides it's time to go.

Griffin stamps at a few switches and reads a checklist out loud; various things need priming, purging, opening and closing.

Finally, he slides forward what looks like a throttle stick and a vibration shakes the body of the craft.

'Time to strap in,' says Griffin.

The Russians clip themselves in to some sideways-facing seats. These can only have been something from a TV programme, thinks Ziggy. They're impractical for space travel, with its rocket-powered acceleration and deceleration, though they'll have to do.

Griffin punches some lights on the console and slides forward a smaller stick beneath the big one.

The ship lurches forwards and Griffin gives a small 'Yes!' under his breath.

The craft accelerates hard and Ziggy feels herself pinned back in her seat.

Then Griffin throttles back. 'Just engaging hover,' he says.

She feels another shudder through the body of the craft and she sees that they are stationary, miles above a black landscape. Griffin dips the nose and she sees the tree beneath them.

'OK,' says Griffin, 'let's see if there's a ceiling.'

He raises the nose again and engages the rear thrusters, which hum mightily from behind the cargo bay.

Ziggy looks up through the mantis-eye windows. A grey sky is above them. Then they are travelling through cloud, continuing to rise, or so it feels from the push of the motors.

They have been travelling five or so minutes when a huge thud shakes the Eagle. Griffin throttles back, hovers the craft.

'We hit something,' he says.

She looks up. There is only the grey of the sky.

'Could be a force field,' says Melnyk.

'Or just the ceiling,' says Griffin.

'I have an idea,' says Kovacs.

She closes her eyes and concentrates.

'What the fuck is she doing?' says Griffin. 'Taking a nap?'

No one answers him.

Ten minutes go by, twenty. Kovacs still sits with her eyes closed.

'Fuck me!' says Griffin. 'If we can't keep going up, I say we go forward. We'll try to get out of these ashlands, maybe find the forest again, get our suits. If we can, we'll get a way out or—'

'Look!' says Kovacs.

She is pointing up at the cockpit windows.

Above them a piece of the sky slides away like a hatch, revealing a massive field of stars beyond.

'Jesus!' says Griffin.

He quickly has the Eagle pointing up and fires the rockets to propel it through the doors Kovacs has summoned.

Ziggy looks down through the glass of the cockpit beneath her feet. The Moon's surface glares up at her, white and harsh even through the reflective glass. There is the lander, beneath her, a Soviet one not so far away.

'Do you think we can get home on this?' says Ziggy.

'No idea,' says Griffin, 'but let's try. Let's hope we've got enough grunt to escape the Moon's gravity.'

'You know which way to go?' says Ziggy.

'Aim at the big blue ball!' says Griffin.

The rockets shudder again and Ziggy is pressed back in her seat once more.

It's a short burn before Griffin shuts off the engines and the spaceship is silent.

'Fuel looks good,' says Griffin. 'Speed picking up. Estimate time to Earth about three days. Fuck me, I think we might just get home. Melnyk, you keep an eye on this. I'm going to see if they've got a Coke back in the bay.'

He gets out of his seat and takes a couple of springy steps towards the door. He still hasn't let go of his gun.

'What do you think?' says Kovacs.

'I think we're clearly still in a gravity field,' says Ziggy. 'Did you see the way Griffin walked down there?'

'Yes. So this isn't space.'

'Clearly not.'

Griffin comes back.

'They have indeed got a Coke,' he says, waving a tin of the drink, 'Things truly are looking up.'

'Griffin,' says Ziggy. 'You're still under the effects of gravity.'

'No!' says Griffin. 'Oh shit, no. That's just the push from the rockets. I must have overdone the power when I turned the hover engines on. We're being pushed up, that's all.'

'Not as far as I can see,' says Melnyk. 'Engines not firing. You turned them off. All engines dead.'

Griffin begins to shake. 'What the fuck have you done?' he says.

No one knows who he is talking to, so no one replies.

He points at Ziggy. 'This is you,' he says. 'I'm sure it's you. I know I've seen you before.'

'I'm your buddy, Griffin. We came on the same ship.'

'You were in the camp,' says Griffin. 'I've seen you. You were the worst. That was the idea, wasn't it? You build up

our hopes with a female interrogator, get us to think you're softer. Then you hit us with all the stuff you've got! Bam!'

'I'm Second Lieutenant Zigsa Da Luca, a NASA employee,' says Ziggy.

'Put the gun down, Griffin,' says Kovacs.

'Fuck that,' says Griffin. 'I did that once before. Never again. I know you people. I'd rather die.'

He rushes up to the control panel.

'We're going home,' he says. 'We're going home.'

The panel blurs, loses focus. The can of Coke in his hand seems to fade in and out of existence, appearing translucent, ghostly, and then disappearing. The whole ship blurs, the walls fading to gossamer. Outside the stars shine, the blue orb of the Earth sparkles.

'We're going to be thrown out into space!' says Melnyk.

'Not going to be a problem for you!' says Griffin. He shoulders his gun and aims at Melnyk.

Ziggy breathes deeply. An image has come to her from her childhood. A boy at her school had a space rifle, a toy with a big clear plastic bubble on the back. When you pulled the trigger, it showered sparks throughout the plastic bubble and made a sort of whirring noise.

She sees that now, turns it around in her mind, hears the whirr of the flint wheel inside the mechanism, sees the sparks flash, recalls the pressed blue tin of the gun, the shooting star design on the side, the orange plastic of the grip. And then, *bing!*

'Shit!' says Griffin.

The M16 has changed in his hands. It's now that space gun, a funny concertina shape before the barrel. Griffin reflexively squeezes the trigger. There's a whirr and a shower of sparks from inside the clear bubble.

Melnyk laughs. 'That's some trick!' he says.

'You see,' says Kovacs. 'We are magicians. Here, if we choose to be. This is an amazing place. If we can learn to manipulate things, we could be as gods here. Perhaps elsewhere, too!'

'I told you. I'd rather just find a way home,' says Ziggy.

'Put this back to being a weapon!' says Griffin.

'No,' says Ziggy.

A white light in her mind, like a flashlight in the face in the pitch dark. Griffin is on her, throwing her down, his hands at her throat. She tries to get her fingers into his face to fight him off, but he is terribly strong. Lights flash at the periphery of her vision; her consciousness dips as Griffin's grip compresses her neck.

Melnyk charges Griffin, knocks him down, but Griffin rolls away. Melnyk tries to jump on top of him, but Griffin is on his feet and lands a hefty kick to Melnyk's head. The cosmonaut is stunned, on all fours, blood pouring from his mouth.

Griffin looks down at his gun. It is an M16.

'Hey, look, I put it back!' he says. He steps towards Ziggy and cries out, 'What!' A hole has opened up at his feet and he falls in a slow-motion tumble, dropping the gun as his arms flail in a vain attempt to grab something to prevent his fall.

Ziggy rushes to where Griffin was standing. A deep pit has opened up and Griffin is lying at the bottom, a bamboo spike sticking red out of his leg. The gun is nowhere to be seen. Three other spikes appear to have missed him.

The pit is deep, twelve feet at least. It should be just empty space beneath the floor of the spaceship, but the pit looks as if it's cut into earth.

'Shit, we have to get him out!' says Ziggy.

'Are you joking?' says Kovacs. 'He tried to strangle you.'

'My mother told me you meet violence with compassion,' says Ziggy.

'And then did she tell you to die? Is that the rest of what she said?'

'He's a crew member. This place is having very strange effects. He is not responsible for that. We will rescue him,' says Ziggy.

'Not my crew,' says Kovacs. 'He's in the best place for him.'

'Leave the imperialist aggressor in the hole!' says Melnyk.

'No,' says Ziggy. 'I'm going to get him out.'

The spaceship phases between being solid and almost spectral, the stars visible through its walls.

'He put himself in there!' says Kovacs. 'This is his way of solving a contradiction. In his rage he wants to kill you, but you're American and on his team. So, as he's just about to blast you to pieces, his subconscious steps in and opens up a Viet Cong trap for him. That's his verdict on himself, right there!'

'I don't accept his verdict,' says Ziggy. 'Now help me get him out!'

'How?' says Melnyk.

'Never mind, how, why?' says Kovacs. 'He will endanger the rest of us.'

'Yeah, but if we leave him here, it'll endanger him,' says Ziggy. 'He's an American serviceman, so am I. So I help him. Personal feelings don't come into it.'

But they do. Giving up on Griffin just doesn't seem like an option. She's not leaving a second person to die and, just because she loved her sister and pretty much can't stand

Griffin, that doesn't make it some sort of cosmic yin-yang thing where that balances out if she saves him. You either believe in the power of compassion and forgiveness or you don't and, if you do, you stick to that, even if it feels like the hardest thing in the world.

The ship flickers and fades. In the pit, Griffin has found the M16 beneath him and is trying to get it out. Ziggy steps back from the edge, so he can't see her.

The ship judders, groans. The walls are invisible now; only the scaffolding at the rear and the flight deck remain, along with Griffin's pit.

'I think this conversation may be immaterial in a minute,' says Melnyk.

'Let me try,' says Ziggy.

Ziggy sits, breathes, concentrating only on her breath. She summons the image of the *dakini* knife into her mind. The ship shakes. The can of Coke rolls into her. She cuts it with the image of the knife. It disappears in a blink.

The ship loses form, drifts away. She is sitting opposite Kovacs on a plane of metal suspended in space. Above her, the stars are vast. Griffin is below her, though there is no pit now. He is just in a different space, separate in a kind of dreamlike understanding of separation – compartmentalised, away. His leg is bloody. He is separate in space but also in pain and, here, in this odd state of being, pain feels like a dimension you could measure and plot. Melnyk is frantic, punching away at something invisible. There is nothing for him to punch at and Ziggy finds his actions oddly funny.

'Where are we?' says Kovacs. Her voice is in Ziggy's head. Ziggy is sure she hasn't spoken.

'I will see,' says Ziggy. The *dakini* knife hovers above her head. Its presence feels more familiar; she has a sense now of how to use it. It's not meant for her companions, even for Kovacs.

She feels its sharp edge in her mind, sees it twinkling in the starlight. Then she allows it to fall, swift and true, on herself.

Chapter 13

They are in a white space, falling – Melnyk, Griffin, Kovacs and Ziggy.

At least she thinks they are falling: they are weightless, tumbling together, head over heels.

And then a heavy impact, a bone-jarring thump, and the space cracks, throws them out, sprawling into a sea of mist that hangs at the level of her knees when Ziggy gets to her feet.

Griffin tumbles out, still clutching his bloody leg. Kovacs seems stunned, or still meditative; Melnyk sits, blinking.

They have been encased in, and then thrown out of, what appears to be a huge, pale blue egg. It is largely still intact with only a hole in its side, through which they've fallen.

Ziggy looks around her and realises she is completely surrounded by astronauts. Hundreds upon hundreds of suited space people stand in deep rows, stretching out in concentric circles all around the egg. The egg is not the centre of the circle, however, but sits nearer the circumference. Inside this ring of spacemen is another smaller ring of astronauts, in rows twenty deep, all facing in to the circle's centre point.

The spacesuits of the figures in the outer circle are standard NASA issue. Those in the inner circle are clearly cosmonauts, their suits khaki, not white, and with the distinctive self-righting ring around the middle.

None of the figures moves or try to communicate in any way. They simply stand and gaze forward.

Griffin spills out, limping, trying to shoulder his gun.

'You can't shoot everyone, Griffin,' says Ziggy. 'Put down your gun.'

Griffin's leg gives way under him and he sits on the ground, gun across his lap. She has the strong sense that he wants to cry; there is a desperation about him, a feeling like he might be on the point of collapse. His posture, cross-legged, head slumped, is that of a miserable child.

The feelings of empathy, telepathy, the hallucinatory shiver that has been shaking her mind for much of the time in the ship, are very strong here. It seems as if it could shake her apart. Painfully vivid images come into her head: unions, couplings; two atoms becoming one, sparking light, light that is the beginning, causing other atoms to fuse, to twist and turn in long chains, spawning longer chains, cells that divide. She sees them as she's seen them in a microscope, grouped, in outlines like a patchwork of fields or a cracked river bed. The images are so strong, almost blinding: these cells, wriggling, dividing, replicating until . . . what? A different kind of light comes. This is an inner light, and it shines on nothing but the self.

She sees images of awakening, morning, of herself before the bathroom mirror.

'What is this place?' says Melnyk.

Kovacs coughs.

'So who's responsible for these guys?' she says.

255

It's as if the astronauts are triggered by her voice. They begin to step to their side, the great outer circle turning clockwise, the great inner circle anticlockwise.

'Busby Berkeley!' says Melnyk.

'How do you know about that stuff?' says Kovacs.

'The group dynamic at show in those films, the synchronised dancing, points to a future where the collective will be the star of films, rather than any individual, and therefore shows the seed of a communistic conscience,' says Melnyk.

Ziggy has gone over to tend to Griffin. He has a raw puncture wound in his calf, though whatever caused it seems to have disappeared along with the Eagle.

'You threw a trap at me, you fucking witch,' says Griffin.

'I did no such thing, Griffin.'

'You did. I've seen what you can do. You called that squirrel woman out, you probably caused all of this. You knew about this place from your studies. You've conjured all this up.'

'Glad to see you remember who I am now. Let me see your leg. Griffin, you've gone from calling me completely incompetent to granting me godlike powers combined with amazing foresight and planning. You really want to make up your mind.'

'You put me in that trap. A fucking punji stick trap. I went a year in the jungle without stepping in one of those and you got me with one.'

'Griffin, think about it. The first I ever heard of a punji stick trap was when you just mentioned it. You know a lot more about them than I do. If anyone summoned that trap, it was you.'

Griffin groans, turns away. His pain is like a struck gong in a temple, a water splash in a cave; it echoes, resonates

through her. It's so intense, the sensation, like nothing she's ever felt before. She isn't feeling the physical agony of a wounded leg but she's feeling all of Griffin's anger, fear, confusion. She steadies herself, reminds herself to concentrate on the task at hand.

'Let me have a look at your leg and then we'll decide what to do. Drink some water.'

'I'm out of water.'

Again, his fear, his anger sweeps over her.

'Have some of mine.' She leans in to him, allows him to suck at her drinking tube.

He grabs at her arm. 'If you can manipulate reality, why not manipulate us up a med kit?' he says.

'I'll try,' she says. 'Kovacs. I'm going to try to conjure up something to help fix Griffin's leg.'

'OK,' says Kovacs. 'But first, he needs to give me his gun.'

'Not happening,' says Griffin.

'You are a danger to us, Griffin. We need to reduce that danger as much as we can. Your influence here has cost me at least four of my team. You are showing signs of psychosis. For the good of the team, you need to surrender that weapon.'

'While I've got a gun, you've got a problem taking my gun,' he says.

'The perennial American point of view,' says Kovacs. 'However, while you've got a gun, you have a problem. I think that's what landed you in the pit.'

'How so?' He looks pale, and grimaces with pain.

'In some cultures, the interface between the subconscious and the conscious is managed by a ritual item. A cross, a prayer bead, a relic, a crystal ball, or even a church or

mosque. Those things are used to shape an experience, to quote the estimable psychologist Dr Leary, to provide a "set", a background and flavour for the experience to come. I think that gun is an interface between your subconscious and conscious. I think your attention to it is sparking some of the things we have seen here.'

'I saw gooks before I had the gun,' says Griffin.

'Yes, but not so many and not quite so fixed. If I'm right, the zombie spacemen appeared with different faces depending on who was looking at them,' says Kovacs.

'Yes.'

'Since you've had the gun, we haven't been in a skirmish, we've been in a war.'

'You're not taking my gun.'

'It's a focus for your trauma,' says Kovacs. 'If you continue to have it, we will continue to be attacked. As soon as we went into a stressful situation, your version of reality asserted itself. Bang! Back to the jungle. I think it couldn't hurt to give that to me, or to Da Luca. I'm assuming mission command and I'm ordering you to pass it over.'

'Who made you the fucking leader?' says Griffin.

'You,' says Kovacs. 'With your leaky subconscious and unresolved issues. You lack the perspective on your problems that would enable you to lead.'

'I got the gun,' says Griffin. 'That makes me a leader.'

'An absolute illustration of what I was saying,' says Kovacs. 'American thinking in a nutshell again.'

'You don't like Americans, do you?' says Griffin.

'I haven't met them all, so I don't know,' says Kovacs. 'What I would say is that there is a tendency in all humanity to mistake a partial viewpoint for a complete one. It's one

thing to make that mistake, it's another to be smug about it, which seems to be the American position.'

Griffin points the weapon at Kovacs. Kovacs stares at him.

'Shoot me and you fuck yourself,' she says. 'Or should I say, fuck yourself more, fuck yourself again. You know, Griffin, I don't think you were cut out for the life you chose. There's something inside you that you're ashamed of, isn't there? More than whatever happened in Vietnam, something fundamental.'

Griffin's hands are shaking.

'Demanding father?' she says. 'Never thought you were quite up to it? Then you went away to the army to show him, even got into the air force, a top pilot. But you were an imposter, not the real deal and, somewhere in the jungles, Charlie showed you that.'

Griffin can't speak; he's dripping saliva from his mouth, trying to swallow back pain.

'Now I know I'm no sort of psychoanalyst,' says Kovacs, 'but I'm going to help you here. It's OK. You were up to it. The Viet Cong would get to anybody. Anybody at all. Bring me your heroes, your Achilles and your Lancelot, Trotsky or Stalin. Any of them would break if they'd been through what you have.'

Griffin lowers the gun, slumps forward, grasps his leg.

'I will never let this go,' he says, his knuckles white on the gun.

A wave of anger emanates from Kovacs. 'I could make the ground swallow you now,' she says.

'Like you did with Toog?' says Griffin.

Kovacs actually sways slightly, as if suddenly dizzy, or maybe just in an effort to control her anger. 'No. But if you want to go like that, I could arrange it. Give me the gun!'

'Come and take it,' says Griffin.

It's as if the words of the argument between Griffin and Kovacs have almost solid form, like rocks they are tossing between each other, rocks that land with an enormous rancorous clang on a metal surface, the feeling is so intense to Ziggy.

'Please stop,' she says. 'This is hurting me. I can feel it. It's physically hurting me.'

Griffin and Kovacs do not stop. Words like machine-gun fire, shaking her with their violence.

'Stop,' she says. 'Stop!'

She screams so loud that Griffin and Kovacs pause their argument.

'Stop,' she says. 'The situation is what it is. We have enough to concern us here without starting fights we don't need to.'

Kovacs snorts.

'As you wish,' she says. 'But you will regret it.'

'Add it to the list. We need to see if we can work some influence on this place. Kovacs, if you think you can make the ground swallow people, you can work with me to see if we can summon up a medical kit.'

'You try,' says Kovacs. 'I'm not very inclined to help him.'

Ziggy tries to concentrate on calling forth a medical kit for Griffin. She sees pressure pads, bandages, antibiotic spray, painkillers, but none of these things have any emotional charge for her and she cannot get them to manifest properly in her mind, let alone persuade the structure to produce them.

She feels very strange. The word 'persuade' occurred to her, but that's what it felt like when she found Galina for Antonov, like she was persuading the ship to call the woman

into existence. Griffin had said she had called things up, but that wasn't quite right.

It felt like a negotiation with the structure, an offering. She was saying: 'Here is Antonov's desire. Isn't it a rich and worthy thing? Shouldn't it be rewarded?' If she was calling anything, it was the attention of the structure to Antonov, putting him forward for consideration. She can't do the same with a medical kit. There are no deeper roots to Griffin's need for the kit, or none she can work with.

'This isn't my kind of suffering,' she says to herself, and wonders what she means by that. Maybe that she has never experienced great physical pain, only emotional pain, longing, grief, the expression of love denied.

She feels dizzy. Each thought is a radioactive atom splitting in two, sparking a chain of other emotions that will not be denied. Pain, loss, grief, Maria's loss, love, jealousy, insecurity, all tumble through her in cascades of agony. She has to step back from herself, breathe, let her identity, her ego, fade, as she has been taught to do in meditation.

There is another noise: a sound like a deep temple bell resonating around them.

Another sound, the same, and a third.

It's coming from within the turning circle of astronauts.

She feels impelled to go towards it, to explore what it is.

'Wait here,' she says to Griffin.

Ziggy goes towards the inner circle. Kovacs and Melnyk follow her. All the wheeling cosmonauts of the inner circle are facing inwards, turning in perfect step.

She tries to see what is making the noise. Beyond the circle of cosmonauts, she can see only mist. The bell, or whatever it is, sounds again and the mist clears slightly. In

the distance, there is some great dark shape, some enormous monolith that appears in a glimpse and then is gone again.

The bell sounds a final time and light flickers far above her, within the ring of cosmonauts. It illuminates a huge mountain, two faces of its upper slopes visible from where she is. One flashes gold in the light, the other blue. The mountain is like nothing she's seen on Earth. It's shaped more like an hourglass, tapering in the middle but expanding in shining slopes up to an unimaginable height.

She recognises the structure immediately – it's Mount Meru, the mythical mountain that sits at the centre of the world, though here it seems transposed to the Moon.

Kovacs is beside her.

'What do you see?' she says.

'The seat of heaven,' says Ziggy.

'No,' says Kovacs. 'Or not necessarily. I saw something else. I'll see if I can make it come back.'

'No, I . . .'

Too late. Kovacs closes her eyes. The mountain is lost in the mist for an instant before a row of lights spark up. Where the mountain was is now a huge yellow building in a baroque style, rows of columns along its front, horizontal lines marking each level beneath tall windows. Lights shine along the top of its roof and, to one side, a clock reads midnight.

'The Lubyanka,' says Kovacs. 'Headquarters of the KGB. Guardian of the revolution.'

'It's not as beautiful as Mount Meru,' says Ziggy.

'It will be easier to enter and have better facilities,' says Kovacs. 'There is a hospital there, if you want to get your cowboy friend to it.'

'Are you sure?'

'That is the chief interrogation centre of the KGB. There was need for excellent medical facilities there. No one can tell you anything if they're dead. It contains a prison which required a doctor service, too.'

'Is that your sacred object?' says Ziggy.

'I have no sacred objects,' says Kovacs. 'The sacred as a domain, or rather the practices that attend it, have been useful to me. They are tricks of understanding and insight, that is all. The revolution is reality, ongoing, forever. It will set humanity free.'

'You need a prison to do that?'

'You can't make an omelette without breaking eggs,' says Kovacs.

'You can't make an omelette just breaking eggs. You kind of need to do some cooking, too,' says Ziggy.

'I wouldn't expect an American to understand,' says Kovacs.

'Probably wise,' says Ziggy. 'How are we to be sure it has hospital facilities?'

'The Eagle was well equipped, why not here?'

'I'm not sure about that place,' says Melnyk, coming up behind them. 'It's a bad spot for a conversation about film.'

'It's here under my influence,' says Kovacs. 'You won't need to answer for your viewing habits.'

'Are you sure?'

'No. But I'm reasonably confident.'

'Come on, then,' says Ziggy. 'If there are medical facilities there, let's get Griffin to them.'

They go back to Griffin, help him stand. Still he grasps the gun. Melnyk gets the other side of Griffin and supports him. He is light in the low *g*.

They move towards the circle of cosmonauts, towards the Lubyanka.

'This place frightens me,' says Melnyk.

'Don't worry, comrade,' says Kovacs. 'You are with me. Your loyalty to the revolution has been exemplary. And, in case you haven't noticed, there is nowhere else to go.'

'It's unlikely to be actually full of commissars,' says Ziggy.

'And what if it is?'

'Well . . . You're a hero, you have nothing to fear.'

'So was Gagarin. Look what they did to him!'

'That was an accident,' says Kovacs.

'Absolutely,' says Melnyk.

At the circle of cosmonauts, it appears there is no way through. The spacemen are packed shoulder-to-shoulder, still turning, stepping slowly around.

'Comrades, let us through,' says Kovacs. Nothing happens.

'We won't get through like this if they don't move,' says Ziggy, meaning with Griffin between them.

'Hey, assholes! Let us through!' shouts Melnyk.

The circle stops turning.

Ziggy glances at her companions. 'Try to get through?' she says.

'Yes,' says Kovacs. 'Melnyk, you go first, you seem to be able to communicate with them.'

Melnyk, Griffin and Ziggy make their way through the circle. The cosmonauts are impassive as they sidle past them, just staring into nothing.

Kovacs follows close behind.

'Do you know what the place you saw was?' says Kovacs.

'It was like something from Tibetan mythology, but not,' says Ziggy. 'It's sort of a heaven but the idea doesn't translate exactly. It's supposed to be the centre of the world.'

'But this is the Moon.'

'I don't think anyone told it that,' says Ziggy.

They shoulder through the cosmonauts, who stand in a rank about twenty deep. Those spacesuits! Ziggy can hear the fans whirr on the life support systems, a hum like a strange summer, a field of electric crickets. Not that she's ever been in a field of crickets, electric or otherwise.

The Lubyanka stands about 200 yards away, at the centre of the circle. Will there really be treatment for Griffin here? She has to trust that there will be.

As she breaks past the final astronaut a wave of feeling sweeps over her, that sensation of her head being a radio tuned in to ten channels at once. She feels fear, apprehension, excitement, weariness, coming into her mind on a tide of images. She feels a longing and sees Melnyk in his apartment with his wife and some children; she sees flashes of sunlight, hears cruel laughter, feels Griffin's panic, she sees an image of the Lubyanka laid over the Lubyanka, like a long exposure shot from a camera that's been moved halfway through, but it slips and in its place is a portcullis gate in a yellow wall. It is a place of dread. There are words above the gateway – 'Maison Centrale' – then that image slips and the Lubyanka is back.

She knows what is happening here. Kovacs is maintaining her interpretation of whatever it is that is anchoring the manifestation of the building they are going to; Griffin's fear and pain is coming up with something else. La Maison Centrale was the Hanoi Hilton – a notorious torture centre of the Vietnam War.

They keep on, Griffin's weight light on her shoulder. It's difficult to keep a good gait, though. Still Ziggy and Griffin bounce along in the low *g*, their heads describing waves of clashing amplitude and length. They manage somehow.

Kovacs says nothing, keeps staring ahead, her eyes fixed on the facade of the building.

'Where are you taking me?' says Griffin.

'To where you can get some treatment, we hope,' says Ziggy.

Griffin looks at her oddly.

'If it's back to the camp, kill me here.' She feels the pain in his foot almost as if it were her own.

'We're not going back to a camp, Griffin.'

'Speak English,' he says. 'I can't tell you anything, I'm just a pilot. I get my orders in the morning, do a mission and come back. It's nothing personal. You're just co-ordinates on a map to me.'

She feels the confusion inside him.

'Griffin,' she says. 'It's Ziggy. This is the Moon.'

'Believe me, please. I have nothing to tell you beyond what you've got from me already. There's no use in torturing me any more.'

'Griffin!' she says.

Ziggy hears voices in her head now, shifting in pitch and volume, spoken up close and then as if far away, momentarily clear and then indistinct, as if caught in a breeze.

Griffin's is loudest among them. 'Help me, help me. God will have vengeance upon you for what you've done. Stay strong, boys, stay strong. I can't be strong. I will be strong. Forgive me.'

She sees into his mind: wide vistas of jungle rolling under the wings of his plane, a flash, a judder, panic as he tugs

at useless controls, the thump of an ejector seat, the rush of wind; she feels the swing of the chute dropping not into a jungle but into yawning jaws that loom through Griffin's mind.

The feelings here are so strong, almost overwhelming.

Melnyk, on the other side of Griffin, looks odd, his clothing blurring, refocusing. He's wearing a dress all of a sudden, blue with a pattern of flowers – she recognises it as one her aunt wore. His clothes blur again and he has a duffel coat on, like her old PhD supervisor used to wear – it's even got the tiny Stars and Stripes pin he wore on the breast; it blurs again and it's back to his undersuit.

They make it to the big doors of the building. Kovacs turns the handle and opens the door on to a long hallway, tiled with shiny wood on the floor, bare white walls and a baroque seventeenth-century statue of a man halfway along.

'Come on,' says Kovacs. Ziggy gets vague feelings from her, but nothing like the torrent of emotions and images that is pouring from Melnyk and Griffin.

They go within to an ornate elevator with a wrought-iron gate.

Kovacs presses the button to call it.

'The hospital's on the top floor,' she says. 'We need to go to the top anyway.'

'Why?' says Ziggy.

Kovacs smiles. 'This is Mount Meru,' she says. 'And turning it in to a building may be the quickest way to the top.'

'We've come to get Griffin's leg fixed,' says Ziggy.

'That too,' says Kovacs. 'But I think you and I might be able to do a lot more than that.'

'Like what?'

'Wait,' says Kovacs.

The elevator arrives and she pulls back the gate. They get inside and Kovacs presses the button for the top floor. The elevator car jerks on its cable and shoots upwards. It's hard to concentrate on the floor indicators. There seem to be about four of them, and then twenty, and then maybe four times that, and then the whole panel is twinkling in countless little lights.

'If they come for us,' says Griffin, 'I'm saving the last bullet for myself.'

His eyes are wild and he is pale with the pain.

'Nobody's coming for us, Griffin. Not to hurt us, anyway,' says Ziggy.

The lift continues rising, the little lights on the control panel winking away as each new floor is indicated.

It's a long time – maybe twenty minutes – before it comes to a rest. Kovacs opens the grille and they get out into another corridor very like the one they've left on the lower floor.

This one, however, has several doors coming off it. Kovacs walks along them until she comes to the one at the end.

'Exactly what I wanted,' she says, and goes in.

Ziggy and Melnyk support Griffin, limping along to follow her.

They find themselves in a good-sized library, the walls lined with bound volumes that are clearly all of a set, like you might find in a legal practice or historic house.

In the centre of the room is a large pale oak table with chairs all around it, similar to the arrangement you might find in a boardroom. They lower Griffin into one. He puts the gun on the table, resting his hands on it.

Ziggy slumps into a chair, too, as do the others. They are tired.

'This isn't the hospital,' says Ziggy.

'No, but it's something that may be more useful. I have been thinking a lot about the nature of this place. It opens our consciousness, it responds to our subconscious, it even answers to conscious direction, right up to the creation of whole simulacra, as we saw when you very remarkably called the woman into existence.'

'Not exactly,' says Ziggy. 'I just let Antonov's thoughts take form. It wasn't like I was doing much at all.'

'Yes,' says Kovacs. 'And so it's always been with readings in the Twilight Language. Trying is failing, you must have found that.'

Ziggy shrugs. It's more a question, she thinks, of letting your desire for an answer sit, to be able to walk around it in your mind, examine it, laugh at it, even. It was similar when she pulled Antonov's wife into existence. She sat with the intention, looking at it as something outside of herself, an object that she could almost hold in her hands.

'Well,' says Kovacs, 'you and I have worked on the sort of problems we're facing now for many years. We know the answers can't be found by the traditional route of academic enquiry. This relies on intuition, meditation, making connections that occur to you in the middle of the night and wake you from dreams.'

'Yes,' says Ziggy.

'Here, though, we are not limited to the power of one mind. This place, the Thunderbolt Vehicle, is the vehicle that leads to enlightenment, and it can have more than one passenger. Together, I think we might fathom its purpose and its workings.'

'How about me?' says Melnyk.

Something strange is happening to him. It's like he's falling into his essential lines and colours, like a Picasso painting. It's not that the actual Melnyk isn't visible, it's just that there is the suggestion of this othered, fractured Melnyk that seems to overlie him, almost more important than the physical reality of the man she sees.

Melnyk exists in shattered stained glass, each shard an image of a creeping witch or a galloping horse, a longboat riding on a sea of fire, a rocket riding on a sea of fire, a dog offering a paw for a treat, a woman face down on the snow, blood at her mouth, blood at her ear.

'You don't count,' says Kovacs. 'When I have a problem that requires your input, I'll ask for it.'

Ziggy's sister Maria sits at the table. She is wearing a ceremonial dress that is heavy with beads, all her mother's coral and gold, and she is wearing the white dress she wore to the confirmation their grandmother insisted upon, and she is wearing that crazy crêpe and cape dress thing she wore to the prom, the one that made her dad call her Batgirl, and she is wearing her graduation robes, and she is wearing the funeral shroud that she never wore. All these costumes are there simultaneously, vying for existence in Ziggy's mind.

'This is an important moment,' says Maria. 'This is everything.'

'We need to get Griffin's foot fixed,' says Ziggy.

'Who is that?' says Kovacs.

'What do you mean?' says Ziggy.

'There's someone else here. I can sense there's another presence in the room.'

'I think it's my sister,' says Ziggy.

'She seems very real,' says Kovacs. 'It's like she's just there, if only I could get my head turned to look at her.'

Ziggy knows what she means. It's that dream sense where there is something or someone just out of your full awareness, though you cannot control your attention sufficiently to see them.

'Why is she here?' says Kovacs. 'I don't sense good intent.'

Ziggy looks over to her sister, who is green and white and blue Tara, who is the lady born of tears.

'There's no one there,' says Melnyk.

'Tell her nothing,' says Griffin, 'she could be a spy. Look for a gaberdine mac. Simon and Garfunkel warned me about those.'

'Can you see her, Griffin?'

'Yes,' says Griffin. 'The women can be the worst. They try to outdo men for cruelty. The women are the worst.'

Once more he puts his hands on the gun.

'What does your sister want? Is it your sister? I am sure I have encountered a similar thing before, in my investigations,' says Kovacs.

'What do you mean, encountered?'

'When I meditate and dream. She's there, watching.'

'That doesn't seem like bad intent.'

'It does in our countries,' says Melnyk. 'Watching shows very bad intent.'

'I just wonder what she's doing here,' says Kovacs.

'She's my sister. She's always with me.'

Kovacs snorts. 'Maybe. Or maybe she's another of these chimeras, of a rather different sort. This place responds to our psychic make-up. There may be some form in here that's generating this particular phenomenon.'

Ziggy looks over to Maria. Phenomenon is a good word, tracing back to the Greek for 'shining'. She does seem to shine, with a golden light.

'The question is,' says Kovacs, 'why is it manifesting strongly for you and not for us? We can all see the gun there. We all saw the dog and we saw the chimeras of astronauts and friends. Why can't I see her?'

The building shakes and shifts. They are in a dirty cell lit by a single bulb, blood on the walls. Where the table was, there is a wooden crate with a lock on it. The chairs of the library remain.

Griffin starts. 'You don't put me in there!' he says, pointing to the crate.

Kovacs closes her eyes, puts her hands on her knees. The room shifts and blurs again and they are back in the library.

'We need to get to work,' she says. 'Griffin's subconscious is manifesting here. That could prevent us doing what we need to do. We can't work in a torture camp.'

'What sort of work?'

'We're going to find out about the nature of this place,' says Kovacs. 'And how we can get out.'

'She doesn't want to get out,' says Maria in Ziggy's thoughts.

'Then what does she want?' says Ziggy.

'Up,' says Maria and fades to nothing.

Chapter 14

Kovacs' plan is to use the increasingly powerful psychic enhancements of the Thunderbolt Vehicle for what she believes they are designed to do – offer enlightenment. She and Ziggy will concentrate their mediation on the question of what this place is for. The telepathy and empathetic enhancement they've experienced so far should mean they make more progress than either could alone.

'We know the answers, I am sure,' says Kovacs. 'But they are locked inside. With each other's help we will get to where we need to go.'

Kovacs has conjured the library setting as an aid to study, to set the right associations before they begin their work.

'What if Griffin takes over while we're otherwise engaged?' says Ziggy. 'We really should get him some treatment.'

'If this works, he'll have whatever he wants. We'll understand the controls of the Thunderbolt Vehicle. Anything is possible then. Melnyk, you need to be our backstop,' says Kovacs.

'How so?'

'Like you did with the woods. Keep us in this room. Or

a library, something like it. What are your strongest associations with a library?'

'At university,' he says. 'The library there.'

'So read a book, here,' she says. 'What was your subject?'

'Aeronautical engineering.'

Kovacs takes out a book from the shelf. It's a large leather-bound volume, inlaid in gold, that resembles a law book.

'OK, relax, think of the key text you used. Any particular problem, maybe something you were proud of solving?'

'I solved them all,' says Melnyk, matter of factly. 'But I've contributed to a few textbooks, I can recall those.'

'Good. Think about it and open the book.'

Melnyk pauses momentarily and then opens the book.

'Nothing,' he says. The book has blank pages. Then: 'Whoa!'

The nose of an aircraft rises from the pages – a MiG fighter, the image surrounded by lines, graphs and figures. It turns above the book, its movement accompanied by whirling dials that float at its side and seemingly track its orientation.

'Shoot that down,' says Griffin, staring at the gun. 'Shoot that shit down.' His tone is blank, his eyes vacant.

'Is he going to be OK?' says Melnyk.

'Just try to make sure your reality dominates his,' says Kovacs. 'Try to put yourself back in school, keep concentrating on that book. Now, Ziggy, come.'

Kovacs comes to sit next to Ziggy, pulling her chair around to face her. She takes Ziggy's hands in hers.

'I'm going to open my mind,' she says.

Ziggy looks into her eyes and it's as if she has fallen off a cliff. A lurch in her belly, a drop as if from the edge of sleep, a sensation of total weightlessness and a bright cold light.

'Here you are.' She hears Kovacs' voice in her mind, and she is standing with her on the steps of a great temple she recognises immediately as the Ziggurat of Ur. It's where she was working with Maria, in Iraq, alongside the restoration project.

It's vast, intersecting staircases rising up in red brick. This is not Saddam's reconstruction, she instinctively knows, but the temple as it was, as she – nor anyone alive – has ever seen it. A bloated Moon rises behind the structure, taking up half the sky. This is the temple of Saen, of Naanna, the Moon God, he who rides the winged bull and is father of the Sun.

'You have been here?' says Ziggy.

'In body and in mind. In the Twilight, I have found my way back to this time.'

Ziggy is enraptured. She walks up the first staircase, marvelling at the gritty brick that sparkles in the half-light.

Kovacs follows her. They climb the side of the building, looking up to the big Moon. Ziggy has the sensation that it is watching them.

'I have been here, too,' says Ziggy. She means more than when she visited with Maria. There is a sense she has travelled here like this before, in a dream.

'What did you find here?' says Kovacs.

'My king, something has been created that no one has created before,' says Ziggy, but they are not her words she is speaking. She looks down at her arms. They are circled in bracelets of lapis lazuli that glint in the moonlight. She wears a dress of woollen tufts in red and green down to her ankles, and a heavy black wig sits on her head.

'You are the first poet,' says Kovacs.

'Because of you, the threshold of tears is opened, and people walk along the path of the house of great lamentations,' says Ziggy. Again, the words come unbidden.

'Because of you, the light is seen over the western marshes. Because of you the light is seen,' says Kovacs. 'You fly on the wings of a bee and your foot rests on the lion's back.'

They climb still until they pass through a great gate. Here there are another three levels of ziggurat, culminating in a structure that appears like a huge sandcastle, complete with crenellations.

She and Kovacs walk on, up smaller staircases. She has no sense of being tired, though she feels her full weight here, as if she is back on Earth.

Underneath the sandcastle-like structure is a huge arch, with a small doorway cut into it. The women go up a winding staircase to find themselves at the very top of the temple.

'You made the Earth shine,' says Kovacs.

'We behold and are beholden,' says Ziggy. 'And, in that beholding is all. The light looks at itself and is shared.' It feels strange to say these words. They don't come from any conscious thought; it's as if she is reciting them but she has no script to follow. It's like the words were already there in this place and she is just the vehicle that speaks them.

Kovacs looks at her strangely. Kovacs is dressed differently now, also in a long skirt full of tufts, but much plainer and duller, and the bracelets that encircle her arms are of a dull gold colour, not adorned with jewels.

'Those robes are mine,' she says.

'You can take them,' says Ziggy. The words come to her as they might in a dream. 'I just want to go home.'

'There is no home now,' says Kovacs, 'only this.' She holds out her arm to gesture to the Moon.

'Have it,' says Ziggy. 'I want to go home.'

'This is my home,' says Kovacs.

Another lurch, like cresting a wave, and they tumble, the Moon streaking upwards as the temple falls.

She is in a town, somewhere in middle Europe, it appears from the architecture – all daub and wattle, houses leaning in as if trying to peer over your shoulder. A bell strikes five. In a pale sky the full Moon balances on the pinnacle of a clock tower. A cat in boots strolls past and Ziggy spends a second marvelling at it.

Kovacs is nowhere to be seen. Ziggy goes into a house. It's dark and dusty inside, wood-panelled walls and a single candle illuminating a woman at a spinning wheel.

She runs wool fibres through her fingers, but what emerges at the other side isn't a thread but a golden stream of light.

'What is this?' says Ziggy.

'This is the Thunderbolt Vehicle,' says the woman, tapping the spinning wheel. 'This is what it does.'

'What does it do?'

'It is a thing of becoming. It changes one thing to another. Look, fibre without form or point. And yet what emerges lightens the world with purpose and usefulness. The garment I will make will keep me warm many a winter. If you want to know more you should follow the cat.'

Ziggy goes out of the house again, into the street. She walks up towards the clock tower where the cat went.

There it is, leaning against a pillar, examining its paws.

'I should follow you,' says Ziggy.

'That is a wise choice,' says the cat.

'What will I learn?'

'What's the difference between a normal cat and I?'

'Shouldn't you say, "Between a normal cat and me"?' It feels foolish but irresistible to correct a speaking cat on its grammar.

'I know what I mean,' says the cat. 'What is the difference between a normal cat and I?'

'Normal cats don't walk upright in boots.'

'More important than that,' says the cat. 'That's just detail.'

'You can talk?'

'Detail,' says the cat, a long feline 'e' in the word. 'We are talking about the most essential things here. What makes I me. I am giving you a clue!'

It wipes its paws over its face and flicks out a pink tongue to clean them.

'I don't know.'

'But you do know I!' says the cat. 'You can't say "I" unless you know this and there's no "me" unless you do.'

'You know you're a cat,' says Ziggy. The words seem to come from nowhere, unpreceded by knowledge or insight.

'Correct!' says the cat. 'The mouser stalking on the fence doesn't know that he isn't the entire world. He's just existing without knowledge of his own existence, or catness. He has no ability to evolve morals or qualms about what he does, no more than a tree can develop a point of view. He is simply the universe. He is not the universe looking at itself, as you and I are.'

'He knows he's not a mouse,' says Ziggy.

'He has an oppositional sense of himself, perhaps, and perhaps not. But he has no true sense of self. If he saw himself in a mirror, he would hiss, whereas I preen.'

'Are there not degrees of these things?' says Ziggy. 'Can you be more conscious, in the same way you can be cleverer or stronger?'

'Now you are getting somewhere!' says the cat.

'Where am I getting?'

'Enlightenment!' says the cat. 'Wide mind. sky-going mind! Dakini mind!'

He waves his paw and she is spinning, violently lurching up, down, left and right, strapped in to the passenger seat of a fighter aircraft.

Griffin's voice comes over the intercom, urgent.

'Two MiGs on our tail. I can't shake 'em in this thing.'

The jet climbs through blinding sunlight, pinning her to her seat, the roar of its engines loud in her ears.

A judder, a shake. 'Lost the stick,' says Griffin. 'Hit the eject!'

Ziggy has a choice here: fight Griffin's creation or accept it and bail. No certainty the first will work in time. She reaches up and pulls the eject lever. There's an almighty bang and a spine-crunching kick as she's fired out of the plane. Wind slams her face, despite the shield that's dropped in front of her eyes when ejected. Another bang, and the parachute has deployed and she sees she's far above a huge mountain, the same one she saw when she first was dropped in front of the ring of astronauts – Mount Meru, five snow-capped peaks above the gold and crystal faces that are turned towards her, glinting in the weak sun.

She sees Griffin descending below her – or at least the bulge of his parachute canopy – and there, distantly, the two MiGs make big turns through the cold blue sky. She knows instinctively that it's Melnyk and Kovacs inside them, caught in Griffin's dream-reality and knows, with the same

certainty, that they are coming to finish the job. God knows who they think was in the US fighter.

'It's us, it's us!' She tries to project the thought as hard as she can. Almost instantly, she gets a reply. 'Not coming for you, Ziggy. Griffin's too much of a danger to allow to continue. He's done this himself. I should have finished him a long time ago.'

Both jets cut vapour trails in arcs as they turn.

Ziggy concentrates, then remembers not to concentrate. She lets her mind drift, allowing the answer she needs to arrive, not asking, nor expecting, just waiting in certainty, as you might wait for dawn to arrive.

The jets are so fast, once they are turned. She sees a bloom of gunfire from their cannons and then she has it. Or rather Melnyk does. She has entered his mind, gone to a dark house in an old city where an ancient lady told him tales of witches, vampires, deep woods. She hears the old woman's voice playing in his head, down deep in the dark forests of his mind. 'Find your way beyond thrice-nine lands, in the thrice-ten kingdom. So Baba Yaga bids you.'

The MiGs are gone and both Melnyk and Kovacs are tipped out onto flying carpets. She sees them beneath her, spiralling down onto the slopes of the mountain.

Her seat keeps dropping, and the land spreads out before her. This will be OK, she feels, this will be fine. It's her creation, or whatever, her subconscious that has brought this to being. There will be peace there, she thinks. Meru is Heaven, the highest plane of existence that is in contact with the Earth.

Something flickers on the mountaintop, like a fire but not a fire, more like a flash of gold: an electrical discharge. It burns for a few seconds and then is gone.

The chute keeps descending and she wonders where she will land. She can see Griffin's canopy below her and doesn't know if she wants to land near to him or apart.

In an instant, she gets her answer. The mountain scene blurs, loses focus, and she sees she is not dropping onto a mountain at all but onto a scrubby hillside where a shattered village burns, sending plumes of smoke into the grey sky. It's suddenly much hotter and she knows she has fallen into Griffin's nightmare again. That village down there looks exactly like the Vietnamese villages she's seen on the news and in documentaries.

She closes her eyes, tries to recall the five-peaked mountain. The scene blurs again, the mountain re-emerges, but then it's gone. Griffin's nightmare returns, smoke drifting into her eyes as the canopy bumps into the ground. It falls onto its back, leaving her looking up.

There are Vietnamese faces above her, full of mistrust, and of rage.

She's unclipped from her seat and dragged to her feet. She feels a jab in the back, so hard she thinks it might have broken a rib, and she sinks to her knees.

Someone asks a question in heavily accented English. 'Red?'

'Red,' says Griffin's voice. 'Son of a bitch shot me down. Get 'em into interrogation now. Interrogate now. Ask. Little box. Put her in the box. Box!'

A rain of blows comes down on her, fists, sticks. She blacks out momentarily and when she comes round she is being dragged through the village. Some huts here are burned but some are intact straw-roofed things. It's a strange mix: the place looks like it's been hit by a firestorm, but one that

only hit three out of four huts. Griffin's memory might be incomplete or unreliable. All thoughts of that are driven out of her when she sees where she's going. There's a slatted box about the size of a tea chest in front of one of the huts.

'Get her in there!' shouts Griffin. 'In, in!'

She's shoved towards the box and tries to fight, but there are too many people around her, kicking, punching, scratching. She's bodily lifted and shoved down into the box, which is sealed with a short bar of wood.

The box is tiny: her knees are up by her face, her head is bent down and already she is painfully uncomfortable.

'Now let's hunt for the other Reds,' says Griffin. 'I saw the planes come down!'

'Griffin!' she calls.

Griffin comes up close to the box, puts his face near to hers.

'I've been watching you for years, Da Luca,' he says. 'And I know what you are – you're a gook spy. I just got all the confirmation I needed when you called in your friends in the MiGs.'

'I saved you!'

'Sure you did. Sure. You speak Russian, you look like a gook, no one knows how you got on the programme. Well, I tell you this, lady, you're going to tell me everything you know if you ever want letting out of your little hutch here.'

Ziggy cries out, in pain and frustration.

'Oh, don't be getting all "poor me" on us,' says Griffin. 'You ain't been in there five minutes yet. I'll see you tomorrow. Now you think about what you want to confess.'

He stomps unevenly off, followed by five or six villagers, who bang the crate as they go.

Ziggy tries to clear her mind, to get a grip of this. She thinks of the mountain, its five peaks glistening, its beautiful slopes of gold, crystal, lapis lazuli and ruby.

She can't do it, can't clear her mind to let the vision grow inside her and come to life around her, she can't make her reality dominant.

The pain is excruciating. A nail has been left sticking into the interior of the box and it is agony in her back. Cramp shoots through her neck and shoulders, her legs, too. She tries to kick at the box, testing its strength. It is solid, unbreakable.

She is being crushed, condensed. She calls out to God, to the goddess Tara, to her sister, but, if they hear, they don't reply. She is on her own in this box, struggling even to breathe.

The day is hot, mosquitos bite her, the pain is so intense she retches. No one comes. No one is coming. She reaches out to Kovacs. 'Are you there?' she says.

If Kovacs does reply, Ziggy is too consumed by the agony to hear her.

Her muscles convulse and shake, aching for movement and release. A boy comes up to the box, peers in, laughs and walks away.

Dusk falls, with smells of cooking and the calls of children. She is terribly thirsty now. She no longer has a body; she is just an ache trapped in a box, a screaming want for anything that is not the box.

She passes out, jolts awake. Her scalp is rubbed raw from contact with the box's lid. She is ten, twenty, one hundred agonies all competing for attention.

Then Kovacs is in her mind.

'I told you to kill him while you had the chance.'

'Where are you?'

'Hiding. They are looking for us.'

'Where is Griffin?'

'I don't know. I can't find him. If we find him, we can kill him.'

'I can't kill anyone.'

'Yes you can. You can join with me. We can go into his mind. There's so much in there. We can make him kill himself.'

'I won't do that.'

'It will release you from this hell.'

'And put me into another one.'

'He hates you.'

'I can't control that. I can control my response.'

'See what you say tomorrow. If you're alive.'

Kovacs disappears – it's as if an iron shutter has come down over her thoughts.

Ziggy tries to wriggle in the box, to get some sort of blood flow going. It's impossible. Her head feels as if someone has driven a hot spike into it and her knuckles are raw, salt sweat turning them to fire.

Chapter 15

Time condenses, congeals, loses shape and definition. She imagines herself in the box as a child might imagine its address: the box, the Thunderbolt Vehicle, the Moon, the solar system, the galaxy, the universe, the multiverse; light and sound beyond that. Each pulling back of her focus seems to her itself a box, as if she were a Russian doll, the last little bean in the centre of enclosing shells.

'Where is Griffin?'

There is a voice in her head. It's her own voice, or her sister's, she can't tell.

'I don't know.'

'Here is Griffin.'

She is outside now, though she senses it is not a real liberation, just a hallucination caused by her confinement. She is curled into a little ball on black and burning cinders, fire rising in flares all around her, as if from a volcano's side. Griffin stands above her, leaning on a crutch, his foot bandaged. He is many things – Captain Hook, a wounded vet begging at a subway station; he is Griffin and he is the Devil.

'Like to confess?' he says. 'Tell me what you've done, Red. How have you sold our country down the river?'

'I left her behind,' she says. 'I left my sister behind.'

'That's a sin,' he says.

'It's a stain on my soul,' says Ziggy.

Griffin smiles. 'Then you should be where you are.'

'I am where I deserve to be.'

'I put you there.'

'I was always here.'

Ziggy feels the frames of reference extending above her, the orb of the solar system, the vast galaxy, universe and beyond, but then she falls within, through the constellations of herself, the planets and the moons of her atomic structure. She tumbles, trailing images of her father, her mother, Andy at the beach goofing at the water's edge, a paintbox she had as a child, its colours bright, almost seeming to hum in their intensity, the colours of a Polaroid summer day, a New York winter, the golden light of a bookshop, cosy in the snow, her mother's little garden shining green in the morning, a sparrow on the little bird house, its white throat bright in the sun. Energies spit and crackle within her; she is born of them, things that can neither be said to be here nor there but who move in their own odd ways of time and no-time, creating time.

She sees now how these points of energy were set jumbling and dancing generations and generations before by a visitor, something that came from the Moon to speak a word. 'Behold!' The visitor was itself an energy that saw the world, delighted in it and wanted to share that delight. Behold. Behold. Behold. The word shakes through her, its sound deep and resonant.

There is a woman beside her. That's all she knows about the presence: it is female. Maybe not a woman. Something vaster, deeper, more energetic. No, a woman. The echo of a woman.

It is not Kovacs. Kovacs is there, though. Ziggy cannot move; she is paralysed in her foetal position on the hot cinders. Griffin's crutch isn't a crutch. It is a gun. It is a pitchfork. It is a gun. And it is a crutch – all these things at once.

He aims it at her head.

'Kill him or he will kill you,' says Kovacs. 'Come with me!'

She seizes Ziggy's hand and they are in Griffin's mind.

Ziggy still cannot move, she is still hunched as if in the crate, though she manages to force her head to look up. Kovacs stands above her. They are in a dingy room with cracking plaster walls, a faint blue tinge to the light that comes from a single bulb.

'I'm always here,' says Griffin's voice. Griffin is suspended by a rope that pulls his hands behind his back to a meat hook sunk into the ceiling.

In front of him is a man in a floppy jungle hat, green fatigues and flip-flops. Ziggy recognises this as the uniform of the Viet Cong.

'I'm always here, too,' says the man. 'Although I think Mr Griffin is lying.'

'I'm always here,' says Griffin. 'Never left.'

'Yes you did,' says the man. 'You left when you got the chance.'

Ziggy feels a lurch of compassion, of understanding. Griffin is like her. He left someone behind, whether alive or dead, it doesn't matter.

'Everyone has their breaking point,' says Griffin. 'Everyone. I didn't ask for the swap, it was offered to me.'

'Nor did you refuse it,' says the man.

'I stayed in these bonds for life!' says Griffin. 'What more do you want?'

'He'll never be free,' says Kovacs. 'Never. Ziggy, what should our man in green do to Griffin?'

Ziggy floats on the edge of consciousness. She wishes she could stand up, stretch, move. She can't bring herself to speak.

'Get rid of Griffin, you are trapped in a manifestation of his mind. You need to get rid of him.'

'Why not you?'

'I've tried. I can't do it on my own. Tell our Vietnamese friend what he needs to do.'

'If you kill me, I'd be happy,' says Griffin. 'I should die here. I left so many friends here.'

'You'd be doing him a favour,' says Kovacs.

Ziggy can't stand the pain any longer. Griffin must die. Everyone must die. If not now, later.

There is a box within a box here, she thinks, something else contained within this room that needs exploring.

'Kovacs,' she says.

'Yes.'

'Face me.'

Kovacs comes to her, squats down and looks into her eyes. Their minds lock, a feeling much deeper than the telepathy she has experienced so far. This is like an alchemical process: the melting of two metals to form an alloy much stronger than either metal by itself.

She feels Kovacs taking that feeling, shaping it. An alloy

to make a weapon – a shining dagger to plunge into Griffin, to set them free of the monstrosities inside his head.

'Can this kill him?' says Ziggy.

A long knife is in Kovacs' hand, not the *dakini* knife, but a more conventional blade. It shines in the weak blue light. 'Yes.'

And then Ziggy sees it: what Kovacs did to Lenov and Shirokov, to root them to the spot as the helicopter swept down on them, to make them stand still for an easy kill. She sees Kovacs stepping into the minds of the cosmonauts, pulling out the monsters of childhood, the lurkers in the dark beneath the bed, the irrational and rational fears of the adult men, an alcoholic uncle who seemed to lead Lenov like the Pied Piper towards madness and death, a party commissar who came for Shirokov's father, school bullies, a day Lenov was lost in the snow as a child and nearly died. She has amplified these horrors, set them looming from the shadows of the mind to rise up and make these men stand as if struck by a Gorgon before the cannons of a helicopter gunship.

And she has tried to work such tricks with Griffin, but he was made of tougher stuff. His mind was full of scar tissue, impervious to further attack. He died in this blue room already; there are no greater fears in his subconscious than those that stalk his waking mind. Is that the explanation? Not quite, she senses. There was some other reason Griffin was kept alive.

'Together we can get him,' says Kovacs. 'Look what he's done, look what he's doing to you. You can't move.'

She is deep in Kovacs' mind. She is still in the cramped position, head forced down, but somehow she is able to see. She is in a garden below mountains, big purple flowers raised

on teetering stems all around her. Kovacs is a child – that is to say she does not look like a child but has the dream sense of a child about her. She is sitting on a chair, under which run two poles to make a palanquin. Four children balance the poles on their shoulders, one to each corner, and carry her along. On Kovacs' head is a crown of golden paper and she directs the way with a candlestick she uses as a sceptre.

'Is this all there is?' says Ziggy.

It's not all there is. The palanquin is taken down to a stream – a small river, really – that runs through the bottom of the garden.

'You cannot force me to speak,' says Kovacs. 'I didn't invite you here for that.'

'I can force you to speak. Speak!'

'Of what?'

'Show me your nightmares. I need to know you.'

'All my nightmares are just beautiful dreams,' says Kovacs.

'Then show me your dreams.'

'I had a sister once,' says Kovacs. 'Just like you.'

'What happened to her?'

'I will not show you.'

'You will show me.'

Kovacs gets down from the palanquin and the other children retire, backing away like courtiers dismissed.

Kovacs walks down to the river. There is a little girl there, maybe three years old. She wears a white dress splattered with mud and sits at the water's edge.

Kovacs picks her up and hugs her. Then she hurls the child into the river. The child cries out but only momentarily; she goes under and is pulled away by the current, her white dress rising like a jellyfish before plunging into the depths.

Ziggy feels a rush of cold glee go through Kovacs, an exultation as sharp as it is fleeting. In a second, it is gone.

Kovacs turns to Ziggy.

'I still have her teddy bear at home,' says Kovacs. 'I stroke it whenever I want to feel like that again. Which is often. You are making me tell you this. I don't want to tell you this. It's not why I invited you in here. There's really nothing to see. If we kill Griffin then you can stand up again. We'll be free to discover the truth about this place without dodging his nightmares.'

Ziggy really is in intense pain. It needs to end and it needs to end now.

She loses consciousness momentarily and then is back in the blue room, Griffin on the ropes, the Viet Cong torturer standing next to him.

'Let me help you,' says Kovacs.

She bends to Ziggy. There is a scraping sound, wood on wood, and Kovacs pulls Ziggy from the crate. The pain of this unfurling is huge, as if her limbs are cracked like chicken bones in order for her to stretch out. She cannot stand, can hardly even stretch out. She still feels the compression on her head and her back, the push on her knees.

'Am I really out?'

'You are out. But as soon as Griffin finds us, you'll be back in again.'

'Griffin is there.'

'Yes and no. He's sleeping. Come on, join with me. We can make all this go away.'

Ziggy can't tell how long it is – it feels like an age before she can stand. Eventually Kovacs helps her to her feet. She presses the knife they forged together into Ziggy's hand.

'Give it to the guard,' she says.

'Why not you?'

'He won't take it from me.'

'Why not?'

'You occupy a special place in Griffin's psychological make-up. You're the right racial type,' she says.

'Is that it?' Ziggy senses it's not true.

'Yes.'

'You've been in here before,' says Ziggy. 'What have you learned, Kovacs?'

Kovacs says nothing.

'I took you from the crate he put you in. Do it.'

Ziggy steps towards the guard and looks closely at him. He looks familiar.

Then she realises where she's seen him before.

'This is you, isn't it, Kovacs? You opened the door to this place in Griffin's mind and took him back in.'

The face of the guard is Kovacs' face, though Kovacs is standing just behind Ziggy.

'What does this mean?' says Ziggy.

'He's a danger. He needs eliminating. Do it.'

Ziggy looks down at her hand. The knife is there. She goes to pass the knife to the guard but pauses. Something about the way the blade is shaped is odd. She has the feeling she is holding it wrong. She adjusts her grip and the knife transforms in her hand. There it is: the curve of the *dakini* knife, its grip nestling in her palm.

'Where did you get that?' says Kovacs. 'Give it to me!'

'Griffin,' says Ziggy.

'Go on, gook, do your worst,' says Griffin.

'Griffin. It's OK,' she says. 'You did what anyone would do.'

'Are you going to forgive me?' says Griffin, his voice crackling with contempt.

'There's nothing to forgive,' says Ziggy. 'Be free.'

She steps forward and uses the *dakini* knife to slice at Griffin's bonds. They rupture, snap back under their tension and Griffin falls into her arms. His weight is not great in the weak *g* but still her legs buckle and cramp as she lowers him to the ground.

When she looks up, they are in the library. Griffin lies back in a chair, eyes open but staring at the ceiling. Melnyk is still looking at his book of aeroplane drawings.

'You are a killer,' says Ziggy to Kovacs.

Kovacs smiles. 'You have brought us nearer to where we need to be. You are the great helper,' she says. 'Let's look at the insight you have earned.'

She goes to a shelf and takes out a heavy bound volume. She lays it on the table. Ziggy comes alongside her to stand at her shoulder. The writing is in every language, it seems, simultaneously. She sees Greek letters, Roman, Chinese, Japanese, Arabic and Sanskrit, and she makes sense of them all.

'The nature and purpose of the Thunderbolt Vehicle,' it says at the top of the page.

A chrysalis turns on the page, pale and grey, the colour of moon rock. It darkens, stained glass colours emerging within it as from within a fog, the skin rupturing and a shining butterfly emerging to take wing.

A world turns on the page. It's Earth, it would appear, blue with wispy white clouds, but when the focus deepens she sees the continents are unfamiliar. The butterfly flies down to the planet and its wings stretch around the globe

in rainbow colours. It bursts, dropping seeds of light, seeds of itself. One strikes an ape that looks at its reflection in a pool, stretches a paw to touch the image and then withdraws it, tapping its chest.

The planet changes; continents shift until she can see the Americas appear, Europe, Africa. Images she has seen in the Thunderbolt Vehicle flicker across the globe – a man lifts a long shape into the air. It's almost identical to the basic form of Griffin's gun, but it's a spear and now a bow and now a musket and rifle. She understands now that it is not a tool or a weapon but an obstacle. It is something to overcome on a path to enlightenment. A grey ship like the ones they saw in the harbour sails and it's a raft of reeds, a Greek trireme, a Roman galley, a Viking longboat, a pilgrim's ship. The ship wants to be a vessel of exploration and understanding, but something dark, something unintended, or maybe even a strange and necessary force of the universe, drives it across the oceans.

Dark wheels turn as smoke drifts across the planet, moving shadows like the ones they saw beneath them on the invisible floor.

'This is a recording device,' says Kovacs. 'This ship has recorded human history.'

'Or a blueprint,' says Ziggy. 'Perhaps it's set the direction and form of human history, but it's done more than that.'

'The chrysalis,' says Kovacs.

'That butterfly,' says Ziggy. 'It carried seeds of light.'

It's then she sees it, in the intuitive certainty she knows from her experience with the Twilight Language. This ship, this vehicle, carries the seed of consciousness with it. It's the means by which the universe comes to look at itself. The

page turns and on it she sees a dancing woman in a fiery headdress and knows this is the *dakini*, the butterfly, the pilot of the Thunderbolt Vehicle – she who transforms the poisons of the mind into pure light, she who is energy and fire and who sparks the lights of consciousness.

'This is a consciousness generating machine,' says Kovacs. 'That's what the whole structure is for. It grows and spreads the seeds of light. It's had that effect on Earth at a distance of 38,000 kilometres. No wonder it's been having such a strong effect on us. It's worked on our unconsciousness, and our expectations. That's where the attackers came from.'

The library is gone and they stand on top of the five-peaked mountain. Above it is a great dome, covered by rock, but Ziggy senses the stars that pepper the sky above that crust.

On the mountainside is a great granite throne, images of dancing women carved around its frame.

She touches the throne. 'Transform yourself,' says a voice. 'You are the *dakini* in human form. Return to light and travel forever. Forever reborn. Forever seeding the light of yourself through billions of consciousnesses until it grows powerful enough for you to return here and travel again.'

Kovacs is at her side. She touches the throne, too.

'Immortal, omnipotent, travelling the stars with the power of a god. What a weapon I would be. A goddess, all the Earth to bend the knee to me,' she says.

'You are a killer,' says Ziggy. 'No one should take this throne, least of all you.'

But a horrible certainty sits inside her, solid as a lump in the throat. Someone must. This is not communicated in words but in the odd feeling of the Twilight Language. It feels like a law of nature, as unnegotiable as time. Ziggy

looks to her feet. Her spacesuit is there, Griffin's and the cosmonauts', too. On the other peak of the mountain sit the lunar landers. Above them there are three streaks in the sky. There is the outline of a hatch between her and the landers, just hanging in the mountain air. The message is clear. Ascend the throne and the others can go.

Ziggy thinks of Andy, her parents, her life on Earth. It is transient, nothing to cling to. The dakini has the three bodies of Buddhahood – the woman, the deity and the fundamental, the illusion-free spirit. She shivers, recalling Antonov's words. 'You are a god.' She created the squirrel woman, has done feats that would be seen as wonders on Earth. Now the next step awaits.

Kovacs steps towards the throne.

'No,' says Ziggy. She touches Kovacs' arm and steps into her mind, willing her, 'Stop!'

She sees Kovacs at a typewriter, a thick manuscript beside her. The title of the manuscript is 'Ascent to the Superhuman: Explorations in the Twilight Language based on the Moon Mandala of the Temple of Gelug and the six dharmas of Nāropā.'

She sees Kovacs meditating, taking out liquid from a vial and dropping it onto her tongue. The liquid is a rainbow and fills her body with rainbow light.

'It's for me,' says Kovacs. 'The throne is for me. You are a *dakini* of the mandala. You are here to help. It's not for you to complete the journey. I saw you in my visions. I saw this destiny but did not know until now how to read it. You are there.'

Kovacs' body flickers as if lit from within by a rainbow. She extends her hand and Ziggy sees an I Ching hexagram,

five straight lines above, a broken line and a final straight line below. 'Your sign,' she says. 'Hexagram 13, Concording People. You have helped me understand this place and to attain this mountain. Now your use is at an end.'

She moves her hand again and another set of six straight lines hovers in front of her.

'This is my hexagram. God.'

'You can't ascend to Buddhahood with selfish aims. That is a contradiction,' says Ziggy.

'You have followed one yoga, I another. I have beaten the drum of skulls, cut the bone from the thigh of a corpse and used it as a trumpet. I have made myself worthy of taking on the knife of the *dakini* by going beyond even that into the yoga of the Kāpālika. There are many paths to enlightenment. All opposites are illusory. There is no good and bad. See what I have done at midnight to sharpen my sight. I have made a corpse my altar, I have smeared myself with the cremation ash of lovers, I have made the charnel ground my home, made a crown of bones and walked the path of Sati, who fired her chakras with anger. I am the *dakini* in her form as the Very Wrathful Mother!'

In Kovacs' mind, Ziggy sees a dark wood with the body of a young man lying naked beneath the trees. His eyes sprout candles and flowers adorn his chest. With horror, Ziggy realises Kovacs has killed him, and maybe others, too. She watches in timeless time while Kovacs builds a bonfire, puts the young man on it and watches him burn, his ribcage flaring like a fire basket, a grey smoke rising into a steel sky. When the fire dies down, Kovacs smears her naked body with the ash and sits meditating beneath the crescent Moon.

This is a form of yoga Ziggy has heard of – if you can call it a yoga – that is a union with the divine. It was practised in ancient India, where yogis made drinking vessels of skulls and lived like rats among the dead, using shock to pierce the veil of illusion.

'You have walked without understanding,' says Ziggy. 'Those practices are dangerous and should not be trifled with.'

'I have trifled with nothing. My insights and studies led me here – no, I was called here. This Vehicle has sparked consciousness, jealousy, wars. It has been the blueprint of wars, determining their weapons, their sparking and creative animosities. This is perfect, for it is the will of the universe, of Lord Shiva, of God, for he is perfect and responsible for everything, so everything is perfect. War, famine, greed and hate are all perfect and sent from God.'

'No!'

'Yes.'

Ziggy sees now why Kovacs was trying to make her kill Griffin. Such an action, while being no bar to Kovacs' chosen path to enlightenment, would have been fatal to Ziggy's practice. But why bother trying to deflect her from taking the *dakini* throne? Ziggy doesn't want it. A sick realisation sweeps over her. That is precisely what qualifies her to take it, perhaps even impels her.

'You will have to kill me first!' says Ziggy.

'I know. We have a connection, you and me. I couldn't have negotiated the ship without you. I have touched your mind, felt your compassion and been moved by it. Now I must destroy it. Otherwise, who knows, the ship might choose you for godhead.'

'Hello, Ziggy.'

In front of her is someone so like her it could be her. Maria, her sister.

She is holding a gun.

'You left me, Ziggy,' she says.

'I didn't know it would end like that.'

'You left me.'

Kovacs stands next to her. 'You know what to do, Maria. It's what she wants really.'

Ziggy reels. Kovacs' words hit her like blows. It is what she wants. She has never recovered from what happened to Maria and would gladly have taken her place. But Kovacs has opened a door to something within her. The guilt is overwhelming; Ziggy deserves to die.

'Shoot me,' she says.

Maria looks at the gun. 'I've been inside you all along, Zig,' she says.

'Do as she says and shoot her,' says Kovacs.

Maria turns to Kovacs. 'Let me show you something,' she says.

They are back in the garden beneath the mountain, among the teetering purple flowers by the river.

'Why are we here?' says Kovacs.

'Because you need something,' says Maria.

'What is that?'

Maria smiles. 'You have prepared very well. Your body is ready to be a vehicle of enlightenment, your helper has led the way, but you cannot take the final step. You are a woman alone. You can unite with nothing.'

'I have achieved great things,' says Kovacs.

'But you don't have what you need to take the next step.'

'What do I need?'

'All the rites of the skull people, who walk with the skull-topped trident and carry the skull begging bowl, can't avail you.'

'Why not?'

'You have no compassion to break down, no boundaries to smash, so you may pick up their pieces and build a path to Heaven.'

Ziggy feels a wave of distress from Kovacs. Her sister's words are true.

'I will help you,' says Maria. She picks one of the tall-stemmed flowers. It becomes a lotus in her hand, a delicate shade of lilac. 'Here. The gift of compassion,' she says.

Ziggy imagines good feelings, empathy, warmth and understanding pouring into the bloom of that flower. It feels like a force flowing from her, lighting the flower to radiance.

Kovacs takes the flower. 'This is mine?' she says. 'It's a wonderful bloom.'

'You see its beauty?' says Maria.

'It is entrancing.'

'Then cast it away, and with it all illusion.'

Kovacs walks down to the river and Ziggy follows her.

'This is your gift of compassion,' she says, holding the lotus. 'Here I discard it and look cold-minded on the universe. I am the spirit of destruction, purging and renewing. I will exorcise the bad spirits of the world, remove its empires and let humanity live as it once did before the fall into knowledge, as beasts beneath the stars. History ends with me, and the dreamtime restarts once the world has burned.'

'I am the spirit of creation,' Ziggy hears herself say. 'I will fly through the universe, seeding consciousness where I go, a spark, not a fire, a creator of beauty and the eyes to see it.'

'You will not oppose me,' says Kovacs. 'You are the enabler who has become the impediment. You will be removed.'

'I will not oppose you,' says Ziggy.

Kovacs bends and sets the flower on the water.

'I am free,' she says, pushing it away, but tiny hands reach out to grip her arm.

'No!' says Kovacs. It is Kovacs' murdered sister, who pulls her into the water.

Kovacs goes in thrashing, but the child has a terrible grip on her arm, pulling her down into the river, where she disappears from sight.

'She's gone,' says Maria.

'Yes,' says Ziggy, staring into the waters. She feels sorry for Kovacs: to live life without feelings of connection or love must be a terrible thing.

'What now?' says Maria.

'I love you,' says Ziggy.

'And I you.'

The two women embrace, and Ziggy finds herself streaming with tears.

'I will take a flower and go!' says Maria.

She shoves Ziggy hard in the chest, levels the gun at her. There is a great cry from the river. Kovacs has stood up in the water, her hair covered in weeds like a witch from a story.

'You don't run from yourself so easily!' she shouts. 'Feel what you have done!'

A tidal wave of guilt comes crashing down on Ziggy. She is the one to blame – she is the betrayer, the abandoner; if she had been there, she could have defended her sister, or bought her time to escape.

Ziggy kneels. 'Shoot me!' she says to Maria.

Maria levels the gun and there is the explosion of two shots in rapid sequence. Then two more, and one more.

Kovacs cries out, falls back into the river, a burst of blood at her chest.

Griffin is on the bank with the gun smoking in his hand.

'She was right,' he says. 'She should have got the gun off me.'

A sensation of lightness comes over Ziggy, the lifting of a weight from her mind. Kovacs is dead, she feels it, sucked back into the cycle of rebirth.

Maria drops her pistol to her side, and then lowers it to the floor. It is absorbed quickly, vanishing to nothing. Then she goes, too, sinking into the ground. Ziggy puts out her hands on instinct as if to hold her, but she's gone in an instant.

Griffin comes to her, puts his arm on her shoulder.

'Thank you,' says Ziggy to Griffin. It seems wrong to thank someone for killing, but this death feels like a liberation, not just for Ziggy but for Kovacs, too.

'Thank you,' says Griffin. 'I . . .' He doesn't have the words to say what he is feeling, but Ziggy senses very strongly that the blue room is no longer inside him. He isn't there any more, on those ropes.

'Who was the other woman?' says Griffin.

'I'd guess it was her sister,' says Melnyk, 'given the resemblance.'

'Where the fuck were you?' says Griffin.

'I got stuck on my flying carpet. It wouldn't come down. But more pressing, you've killed my mission commander, I think.'

'That a problem for you, Melnyk?' says Griffin.

Melnyk goes to Kovacs' body.

'No,' he says. 'I think she was in my head. I think it was her who was pulling out Baba Yaga. Funny she got done by a rusalka. I wonder if that was me.'

'What the fuck is a rusalka?' says Griffin.

'A water spirit. The spirit of a drowned child, it lives in rivers. Frightened the life out of me as a kid.'

'I think it was all of us,' says Ziggy. 'She could keep that thing at bay as long as she remained amoral. Once she had accepted the gift of compassion, it got her. I don't think we need to hand out medals for achievement over this.'

'Maybe she dug out your Viet Cong, Griffin,' says Melnyk.

'I didn't need any help with that,' says Griffin.

'Why did she do it?' says Melnyk.

'Nuts,' says Griffin.

It's as good an explanation as any, thinks Ziggy, and there will be enough time for lectures on Buddhist and Hindu theology if they ever get back to Earth. Before the transformation into the *dakini*, the woman needs to become a deity – shaping worlds, creating beauty or maybe even monsters. Did Kovacs know that before she came here? Or was she moving on instinct, creating her own proving ground as she went, trials by which to ascend the godhead. She aimed to become Buddha but only got as far as Mara, who challenged him beneath the Bodhi tree.

Melnyk sits on the stone throne.

'What is this thing?' he says.

'Commander's chair,' says Ziggy. 'You want to convert yourself to energy and take this ship through space and time to seed consciousness on other worlds, Melnyk?'

'What's the pay like?' says Melnyk. 'Sounds OK to me.'

'It's a female only deal,' says Ziggy.

'You know that?'

'Yes, I know it.'

That seems obvious, a certainty, like a law of physics.

'Then why don't you sit in it and command us back to Earth?' says Griffin.

'I think that, if I do, my priorities will change so much that I won't want to go there. And, if I take this vessel out into the stars, in a journey of centuries, or longer, I think you might get bored.'

The words strike a chord within her. Is this ship more than just a seed, a cosmic blueprint for development? Is it designed for comfort, too, to keep the *dakini* occupied in dreams, visions and stories in a journey that could last thousands or even millions of years?

She looks at the throne. Does she want to be immortal? In no way. She wants to go back to Andy, visit her mom and dad, watch the Knicks, see the sun go down over the Hudson and eat pastrami with her fingers straight out of the fridge.

She has curiosity to sit on it, just to see, but she senses that any transformation would be irreversible.

'Let's suit up and get to the hatch,' says Griffin. 'Melnyk, can we get a lift home with your guys, do you think? Can you clear that for us?'

'Is your guy not there?'

'You killed him, remember?'

'We really didn't. It must have been the influence of the ship.'

'Why didn't it affect other lunar missions, then?'

'It had never been breached before,' says Ziggy. 'I tell you, this thing is still largely dormant, I can feel it. If you're here

when it fires up its consciousness generators properly, you're going on a trip you're not coming back from, I'd say.'

'Are these real?' says Melnyk, picking up his suit. He sniffs the interior. 'Smells real,' he says. 'It's like an old sock.'

'I think they are,' says Ziggy. She picks up her own suit. It still bears the damage to the cooling system, the marks of the shark's teeth. Next to it is Toog's suit.

'Do we take the O_2?' she says.

'Toog ain't here and I think our chances of finding him, even if he is alive, are slim,' says Griffin. 'Take it.'

'You go,' says Ziggy. 'I will look for Toog. He's here somewhere, I can feel it.'

Ziggy unclips the oxygen cylinder, and passes it to Griffin.

'You will come with us, that's an order,' says Griffin.

'I won't,' says Ziggy. She thinks of Andy, of her mom. But Toog has family, too. He must be found if she can.

'I'll come when a relief mission's been sent here,' says Ziggy.

'Then you're an idiot. Help me get my suit on at least.'

The astronauts help each other and Melnyk into their suits, pressure up.

'You're not shitting us, Melnyk, you really didn't fire on our ship?'

'No way,' says Melnyk. 'Our orbiters should all be there.'

'Why did we suffer hallucinations?' says Griffin.

'A defence mechanism?' says Melnyk.

'I don't know,' says Ziggy. 'The intelligence at work here doesn't think like us. I really don't know.'

They walk across the mountainside to the hatch. It bears the gateway symbol of the other strange doorways they've encountered.

'I understand now,' says Ziggy. 'These membrane doors are an alternative to air locks. You shove through them, and they instantly seal behind you. It would allow any part of the ship to be pressurised or depressurised, according to what you wanted.'

'Why was the outer door a conventional hatch, then?' says Griffin.

'That led to the only part of the ship that didn't have an atmosphere,' says Ziggy. 'But the true answer is that, again, I've got no idea. Maybe it wanted to be found, this was the time.'

She shudders at the implications of that. All human history developing to a point where it could produce a consciousness capable of ascending to the ship's throne, setting out into the darkness and seeding a world with consciousness for it to grow and bloom to a point where it was ready to seed again. She is that seed but unfortunately, she has other plans. Godhood is not on her schedule for today.

'Ready to go?' says Griffin.

'Yeah.'

She pushes at the hatch. Nothing happens. She closes her eyes, wills it to open. Nothing.

'Problem?' says Griffin.

'This isn't working,' says Ziggy.

Chapter 16

Griffin pushes the hatch. Nothing. Melnyk tries. Same result.

'So now what?' says Griffin.

'Maybe we should look for another hatch,' says Melnyk.

'I don't think so,' says Ziggy. 'There's nothing to say they will open. We need to work on this one.'

'If it's a hatch at all,' says Griffin. 'It could just look like a hatch.'

'It's a hatch,' says Ziggy.

'How do you know?'

'Feels like one,' says Ziggy.

Griffin nods. 'Good enough for me,' he says. 'Look. You think that seat up there is the captain's chair?'

'Yes.'

'Then we should sit in it, try to work the ship.'

'I think that will come at a cost,' says Ziggy.

'What cost?'

'Buddhahood,' she says. 'And while I really should want to attain that, I was kinda thinking of finding Toog, getting home, watching some TV instead.'

'I'll try,' says Griffin.

'It won't work,' says Ziggy.

'Why not?'

'Like I said, this is a girls only deal. And besides, Griffin, we may have worked through some of your issues but, and don't take this the wrong way, I think you're a little far off enlightenment just yet.'

'You could be right,' says Griffin.

'I'll try,' says Melnyk.

'Not sure I want this place turned into a witch's hut or fairytale castle,' says Griffin.

They walk back to the throne. By now she is used to the gravity of the Moon and her gait is nearer to the way she walks on Earth, though the steps are still a little longer, the lift a little higher.

Melnyk doesn't wait; he just plonks himself down on the throne.

Nothing happens. 'I guess we should be grateful we've not been attacked by flying monkeys,' says Griffin.

'Or helicopters,' says Melnyk.

He gets out of the seat. 'It doesn't do anything. Do you want to try, Da Luca?'

Ziggy doesn't know what to say. She is convinced that the chair will do something to her. If it does what she suspects it will do and transforms her into a *dakini*, then her old life will be over. Once she is a *dakini*, she won't care about that. But she isn't a *dakini* and she does care. She feels like a child looking at an adult and comprehending that, when she becomes one, she will no longer want to play with toys, watch cartoons, play in a treehouse, and she's scared of that transformation. The adult will look at a child and struggle to recall how a doll or a game could occupy her for hours.

So it will be if she goes beyond what she has done here – stepped up the ladder of enlightenment.

Could she open the hatch if she sat in that chair? If so, then she owes it to the others to let them out and to the landers. Maybe she could even find Toog and bring him to them.

'Whaddya think, Da Luca?' says Griffin.

'We can't be here forever,' she says. Although she suspects maybe that she will be here forever. That is what she saw in her confrontation with Kovacs. But is it true?

'You can always get off it if it gets too hard,' says Griffin.

Ziggy stands with the back of her knees to the seat, summoning up the courage to sit. Will she lose all human contact: Andy, her mom and dad, friends?

She sits, breathes. Nothing happens. It's simply a seat.

'Anything?' says Griffin.

'Nothing at all,' says Ziggy. She puts her arms on the throne's rests.

'Dead piece of stone,' says Griffin.

'Try to think about opening the hatch,' says Melnyk.

She senses that won't work, so instead simply meditates on the image of the gateway. She concentrates on her breath, keeping the image of the gate in her mind.

'You can't take me with you.' It's her sister's voice, close at her ear.

'You're always with me, you always were.'

'It's time to say goodbye.'

'I don't want to leave you.'

'I will leave you.'

A shudder shakes the ground. The throne is not there. Instead, there is a seething lattice of energy underneath her.

The framing her experience comes over again as it sweeps in from the universe, through galaxies and the solar system to herself sitting above this sparkling, turbulent energy field. It falls within, where cells twitch and pulse, atoms buzz, smaller particles blink into life and out again, are there and simultaneously absent.

'We were born to go,' says Maria. Ziggy can't see her sister, but her voice sounds very close.

A noise is growing, like the firing of jet engines, a rumble that makes the whole mountainside tremble.

'Open the hatch!' shouts Griffin.

Ziggy tries to understand what's happening. The chair is light. Everything is light. The ship around her is just a web of fizzing energy, light frozen almost to a standstill but not quite, a golden net. She is trapped light, her hands a network of glowing lines, her body the same.

There is a deep bang, a great shaking.

'Open the hatch!' shouts Griffin. 'The hatch, the hatch, Da Luca, the hatch!'

The gateway symbol appears in her mind in flowing gold. She can allow it to be itself if she wants; it longs to express its nature if only she will let it.

'Be,' she says to it.

'Look!' shouts Melnyk. 'Look! The hatch is glowing. We can try again.'

'Da Luca, can you come with us?'

She is a creature of jewels or of the essence of jewels, of the light of sapphires free of its medium, free of crystal or stone.

Griffin tries to pull her away from the throne, but he can't reach her. An invisible force throws him back.

A keening noise sounds on the mountain now, a wind shriek.

'Come on!' shouts Melnyk! 'Griffin, we have to leave her. I think this ship is about to move! Come on!'

Griffin tries again to get to her, but he can't.

'Go,' she says. 'Leave.'

She can feel her mind transforming. The world is a very different place to her now. She can feel the relationship between things or, rather, that there are no things, that the universe is just a field and its phenomena are bumps or knots within that field. She is such a knot, a knot of light, waiting to be untied.

The Earth is such a knot, its continents and seas, too. There is no difference between her and them, only that she can perceive them. That perceiving seems like the most precious thing in the world, or that it could be if she just gave herself to it, let go and became a sky-goer, a watcher, a bringer of sight.

Andy is walking to his class at the University of Florida, bright sunlight shining on him, shining through him. He shines back, a beautiful man, the energy from which he is made glittering from him.

Her dad is walking the dog. He sparkles, it sparkles.

Her mom is meditating in front of the bedroom window, the dappled light of a tree stroking her body, which responds with its own light. Her mother is an atomic ocean, a nebula, a spirit.

'Go?' she asks her.

Her mother just smiles. She doesn't know Ziggy is watching her, but Ziggy senses she is always watching Ziggy, holding her in her heart. In the nexus of energy that is her

mother is the nexus of energy that is also Ziggy and that is also Maria.

'Go.' It's another voice. Maria.

'Who will hold the door?' says Ziggy. 'Who will find Toog?'

'I will,' says Maria.

Ziggy stands up, but something is left behind her. Her sister falls out of the bright grid of energy that is Ziggy and takes form as herself on the throne.

'You carried me with you,' says her sister.

Ziggy turns to see her, made of light.

She looks down at her own body.

It is solidifying, falling from jewel-sparkle to grimy space-suit cloth.

'Maria, I love you,' she says.

'And I you.'

The ground shakes again.

'Go!' says Maria.

Ziggy raises her hand to touch her sister, but her sister is changing. She wears a crown of ruby fire, her arms are adorned in dazzling emeralds, her body is like the sun, shining.

'Goodbye, Mare,' says Ziggy.

'Goodbye, Zig.'

Ziggy runs for the hatch. Griffin and Melnyk are pushing frantically at the glowing golden symbol.

The ship – and now it's very clear it is a ship – tilts, wobbles.

'Hold hands,' says Ziggy. Griffin grabs her hand, Melnyk grabs Griffin's.

Ziggy steps towards the door with the intention, the certainty, she will make the other side.

She is out, on a steep lunar hillside, the Earth a bright blue ball in the black sky, but Griffin can't come through. The hill shakes and a great fall of rocks descends not fifty yards from where she is standing.

She tugs at Griffin's arm. It emerges from the hatch as if through a curtain. She can feel the vibrations of the shaking Thunderbolt Vehicle through it.

'Come on, Griffin,' she says. 'We can't lose you now.'

'Leave us,' says Griffin, through the radio. 'We'll find a way out.'

'No. You're coming with me. Just step into the door with the certainty you'll come through. Come on, Griffin, you owe me a beer for all the shit you've put me through.'

She pulls on his arm and suddenly he is through, Melnyk sprawling behind him.

'Run,' she says.

They bound for the Lunar Lander, the dust of the ground seeming to boil beneath their feet as the Thunderbolt Vehicle shakes free of the Moon.

It's three hundred yards to the US lander, 1000 or so to the Soviet landers.

Griffin makes the door first, slowing himself to carefully get into the lander. Ziggy glances back. The Thunderbolt Vehicle is rising like a flying city. She has no idea what sort of propulsion it uses but, if it's anything like a rocket, they will be burned if it fires.

'Melnyk, where are you going?' she says.

'To my lander.'

'No time for that. Get in here!'

She climbs the ladder and gets in, Melnyk coming up behind her.

Griffin turns to acknowledge the Ukrainian and simply says 'Strap in'.

Melnyk seals the door latches.

'No time to pressurise, let's just get out of here,' says Griffin. 'Danny, Danny, wake up, tell me you're alive and on our side of the Moon. *Salvador, Salvador,* where are you?'

'*Salvador* here!' Danny's voice is on the radio, full of delight. 'Where have you been, Griff? And what in the name of God is that thing?'

'Just getting a radar lock and we're coming up to greet you, tell you all about it then.'

'Emergency?'

'Roger. Please descend to lift-off altitude.'

'Descending. Take a few minutes, Griff.'

'Yeah, well, get there quick, Danny.'

'Doing it.'

Ziggy looks out of the porthole. The Thunderbolt Vehicle is rising, throwing off its shroud of dust and rock like a whale breaching water. Its body crackles with light, a tight web of electric pulses shooting across its surface. It's huge, and though she can't yet see its entirety, appears to be the shape of a huge ellipse, an almond, a seed.

'Hello, Littrow. Houston on the line. Met any little green men?'

'Plenty,' says Griffin. 'Requesting permission for emergency evac.'

'Trouble?'

'Roger. Emergency evac requested.'

'Granted.'

Ziggy makes sure her straps are secured, no time to get her overshoes off to bond on to the floor Velcro.

'Going to pre-ignition checks,' says Houston.

'No time for that. Fuel tanks pressurising.'

The lunar dust races towards them in a great wave and the structure of the lander shakes.

'If that thing fires rockets, we are toast,' says Griffin.

'It might not have rockets,' says Melnyk.

Another violent shaking and it feels as if the whole lander has been thrown sideways, causing the astronauts to be thrown into each other.

'Number two tank not firing,' says Griffin.

'Go again,' says Houston.

'Going again. Ah, got it. Proceeding SYS A ASC Feed 2-Open. Ascent feeds are open and shut-offs are closed.'

Another rattling jolt hits the lander.

'That picked us up!' says Melnyk.

'cross-feed on,' says Griffin. 'Master arm on, nine, eight, seven, six, five, Abort Stage, Engine Arm, Ascent, Proceed.'

Another tsunami of dust races towards them, throwing the lander upwards, though Griffin hasn't finished his countdown yet. Her body lurches against the straps.

'Four, three, two, one. Fire.'

The body of the lander shakes again; she feels weight through her feet as they shoot free of the surface of the Moon. Below them, clouds of insulation billow as the landing gear breaks free and drops to the Moon. My God, that was never designed to fire in mid-air like that, and she thanks Jesus and thirty other gods that it didn't cause them to crash.

She looks out of the window to see the Thunderbolt Vehicle hovering above the Moon's surface. It doesn't look like something made of matter, but of energy: lightning, blue fire.

It shimmers, almost seems to dematerialise, and then a field of crackling electricity sweeps the surface of the Moon, and the ship is gone.

'Bye, Maria,' she says.

Melnyk puts his arm on her shoulder. 'How does it feel to know you'll never be able to discuss that with anyone?'

'I'm not sure discussing it would help,' she says. 'There's only you, me and Griffin who will ever really understand what went on in there. What are you going to tell your people?'

'Nothing. I'm defecting. I don't want to end up with an accident, like Gagarin.'

'They'd do that to you?'

'I don't know, I don't want to give them the chance. Maybe you should defect the other way. This isn't the sort of stuff governments like their people to know. They like to appear in control.'

'They've got nothing to fear from me,' says Ziggy.

'Make sure they know that,' says Melnyk.

She nods. 'Pressurising cabin, at last,' says Griffin. 'Won't be long before we dock with *Salvador* and we can all have a coffee.'

'You have coffee on your command module?'

'It's piss,' says Griffin.

'Literally,' says Ziggy. 'Recycled.'

'Tastes as good as it smells,' says Griffin. 'Which is awful. Better get a message to your guys to tell them not to bother waiting,' he says. 'But first, we can take off our helmets.'

Ziggy helps him, turning the bowl until it clicks. Then he helps her.

'Thanks,' he says.

'Thank you,' she says.

Griffin looks at her and she realises it's the first time he's ever done that without some sort of malice in his eyes.

'Yeah, best get on with docking,' he says.

'Yeah,' she says. 'Sounds like a good motto for life.'

'You can't hug in a spacesuit anyway,' he says.

'You can try,' she says.

They put their arms around each other.

'Let's get home,' she says.

Chapter 17

There is a searchlight Moon over the Keys as Ziggy sits with Andy at the water's edge, a couple of cool beers between them.

'So, Australia,' he says.

'Yeah. We've kinda been through this.'

'Kinda, but kinda not. What was that like?'

'Interesting, yeah.'

'Yeah, I guessed it would be. Anything at all you can tell me?'

'They had kangaroos.'

'Right. So where's mine?'

He sips on his beer, then laughs.

'It's really that top secret?'

'Some of it, yeah. For no good reason, really. It's not like we were doing anything amazing.'

'Not amazing. OK, that's useful information. I can report that to my Soviet paymasters. Nothing amazing happened in Australia. With that, we will make you capitalists pay.'

'Andy, really, you know I can't say anything.'

She wants to say something. All the sensations of space travel replay in her mind. On the beach the echo of the

juddering impact of the Command Module hitting the atmosphere shudders through her bones. In the nights she has been back on Earth, strange dreams come to her. She is still in the ship, transformed into a thing of energy and light, shooting through the cosmos as a ray.

'You've seemed different since you've been back.'

'In a good way or a bad way?'

'In a way. You're more, I don't know. You look at me like a cat sometimes.'

'Like I'm a cat or you're a cat? I mean, I love cats so that would be a good way for me to look at you.'

'Like you're a cat.'

'OK, Andy.' She is serious. 'I have to say this to you. I need to level with you.'

'Yeah?'

She holds his gaze. He seems nervous and an echo of the sensitivity she had on the Thunderbolt Vehicle comes back to her. His love for her seems very fragile, beautiful but breakable. She must hold it very carefully.

'What is it?' he says.

'I'd really like some fish,' she says. They both fall about laughing.

'Are we OK?' he says.

'Yeah, we're OK. I thought of you all the time when I was away. All the time. It just made me realise what we have together. I have some news anyway.'

'Oh yeah?'

'Yeah. I'm quitting the astronaut programme. I'm never gonna get to space and it's time for something new.'

'Wow. That's a biggie. What new?'

'I don't know. Humbucker's pulled some strings and there's

talk I could get tenure at Columbia in teaching translation of ancient writing.'

'That's what the cat look's for!' he says. 'You want me to pack up the settled life I have here, leave this wonderful beach behind, transfer myself to an NYC university and go live in some poky apartment in the Bronx.'

'Yeah.'

'Great. It's too hot here and there's nothing to do. When do we go?'

She thinks of Humbucker on the naval destroyer after splashdown, talking through the wall of the quarantine chamber.

Her mind at that point was still coming down off the effects of being in the Thunderbolt Vehicle, and she could sense his incredulity, his amazement, at what she had to report. The sensations were nothing like as strong as she'd had on the Moon, but there was a strange kind of synaesthesia lingering, where powerful images came from her memories to sit over the present reality, and she couldn't help picturing him as a wide-eyed cartoon jackrabbit, nervously fingering its collar as the debrief continued.

'This gun,' he said. 'You didn't bring it back?'

'No. It got left on ship. We had to make a pretty hasty exit,' she said.

She explained what she thought had happened. Kovacs had clearly identified the ship as an effective vehicle to godhead, or at least changing into whatever alien species the *dakini* were.

Unfortunately, because of her chosen path on the left hand of yoga, certain manifestations were unavailable to her and she needed Ziggy to trigger them. Ziggy's long years

of meditation and family traditions had prepared her to be able to make the throne of the *dakini* manifest. Kovacs needed Ziggy to get her to Mount Meru. She also needed her to disqualify herself from ascending to become a *dakini* – Ziggy doesn't bother explaining to Humbucker that, by one definition, she already was a *dakini*. So, Ziggy guesses, Kovacs had tried to get her to kill Griffin, abandon compassion and disqualify herself from taking the seat. This would not have been a problem for Kovacs because her path did not involve the use of compassion – or so she thought. In fact, the practices she favoured used compassion as a sort of fuel to burn away to reach higher levels of consciousness, with a yoga of disgust and shock. Though that yoga was very different from anything Ziggy had ever practised, it might have been a viable path to enlightenment and the throne of the Thunderbolt Vehicle. However, Kovacs could never have ascended the throne because, as a psychopath, she had no compassion to burn.

The rest, she skirted around, putting every death, every inconvenience or obstacle, at Kovacs' door. She suspects Kovacs was testing herself anyway, by pulling things from Griffin's mind into violent reality. She wonders, though, why she kept Melnyk alive when she killed the others. Of course. She needed someone to fly the lander if it all went wrong.

And Toog? Gone. Humbucker will tell his family he died a hero. The alternative – that he's travelling the universe in an energy lattice – would be too much for them to take in.

Humbucker listened, nodding, taking notes. The word 'squirrel' caused him to underline three times.

'We saw the ship move,' he said. 'Which means the Soviets and the Chinese did, at the very least, too. Most of Europe

and India, too, according to the chatter the Secret Service is picking up. Probably a lot of the observatories in the Andes, too.'

'So what are the implications of that?'

'A lot of governments have a lot of covering up to do,' he said. 'This kind of thing has the potential to cause panic. We're putting it about that we were running tests on a secret moonbase up there. It won't convince all of them, but it might convince some. It's a simple explanation, anyway, unlike the one you've just given. You know you're in for a major debrief when you get out of quarantine?'

'I guessed,' she said.

Even through the door, she could sense Humbucker's fear, his uncertainty about her ability to keep silent. More so, even Melnyk's.

'You have no need to worry about us,' she told him.

'We'll be testing that over the coming weeks,' he said.

And they did. Endless interviews, mental tests, informal conversations that she was sure were being recorded. She must have given them what they wanted because, six weeks after they splashed down, she was back in her Beetle, driving up to the University of Florida to meet Andy.

She holds Andy's hand, looks up at the Moon, out to the stars beyond.

'Goodbye, Maria,' she says.

'What?' says Andy.

'Nothing,' she says, and puts her arm around him.

Ends

Credits

M.D. Lachlan and Gollancz would like to thank everyone at Orion who worked on the publication of *Celestial*.

Agent
Judith Murray

Editor
Brendan Durkin
Áine Feeney

Copy-editor
Donna Bond

Proofreader
Steve O'Gorman

Editorial Management
Jane Hughes
Charlie Panayiotou
Tamara Morriss

Audio
Paul Stark
Jake Alderson
Georgina Cutler

Contracts
Anne Goddard
Humayra Ahmed

Design
Nick Shah
Tómas Almeida
Joanna Ridley
Helen Ewing

Finance
Nick Gibson
Jasdip Nandra

Ibukun Ademefun
Sue Baker

Operations
Sharon Willis

Inventory
Jo Jacobs
Dan Stevens

Rights
Susan Howe
Krystyna Kujawinska
Jessica Purdue
Ayesha Kinley
Louise Henderson

Production
Paul Hussey
Fiona McIntosh

Publicity
Jenna Petts

Sales
Jen Wilson
Victoria Laws
Esther Waters
Frances Doyle
Ben Goddard
Jack Hallam
Anna Egelstaff